# HIDDEN

I'd been standing there for maybe five minutes when a soft noise caught my attention. Different movements make different sounds — the steady tread of someone walking, the scrape of shifting feet, the patter of someone in a hurry — and with practice you can learn to filter them, picking out the ones that don't fit in. It's nothing to do with magic, just simple awareness, a primal skill that anyone can learn but which most people in the modern age have forgotten. But anyone who lives as a predator or as prey learns it fast.

The sound I'd heard was the sound of someone trying to stay quiet and hidden, and I stepped quietly into the cover of the doorway, one hand moving to the hilt of the knife beneath my coat.

# By Benedict Jacka

# BENEDICT JACKA

# HIDDEN

www.orbitbooks.net

ORBIT

First published in Great Britain in 2014 by Orbit

5 7 9 10 8 6 4

A CIP catalogue record for this book
is available from the British Library.

ISBN 978-0-356-50231-1

Typeset in Garamond 3 by Palimpsest Book Production Limited,
Falkirk, Stirlingshire
Printed and bound by CPI Group (UK) Ltd, Croydon, CR0 4YY

Papers used by Orbit are from well-managed forests
and other responsible sources.

MIX
Paper from
responsible sources
FSC® C104740

Orbit
An imprint of
Little, Brown Book Group
Carmelite House
50 Victoria Embankment
London EC4Y 0DZ

An Hachette UK Company
www.hachette.co.uk

www.orbitbooks.net

Russell Square is one of the odder areas of London. Squeezed between Euston Road to the north and Holborn to the south, it doesn't have enough shops to be commercial and it doesn't have enough houses to be residential. Instead it has a mix of universities and hotels, rich tourists and poor students rubbing shoulders in the busy streets. It's supposed to be 'literary' — associations from the old Bloomsbury group — though given that you'd have to be a millionaire to own property there nowadays I doubt you'll find many artists living in the place.

What Russell Square does have a lot of is education: English language schools for the ex-pats, colleges for the students and the British Museum for everyone. It was one of the colleges I'd come for, a long hulking brown-and-beige cinderblock called the Institute of Education, and as I approached I reflexively scanned ahead, searching for danger. I didn't find anything and I didn't expect to, but for some reason I found myself hesitating as I drew level with the front doors. For a moment I thought about turning away, then shook my head in annoyance and headed inside.

My name's Alex Verus and I'm a probability mage, aka a diviner. I train an apprentice, do contract work for other mages and run a magic shop in Camden when I'm not otherwise occupied with personal problems or with people trying to hurt me, the second of which happens more often than I'd like. I'm good friends with a handful of mages and one giant spider, and less good friends with the magical government of Britain, otherwise known as the Light Council. The Council don't like me for two reasons: first, they think I was originally taught by a particularly nasty Dark mage named Richard Drakh and did various unpleasant things while serving as his apprentice; and second, they suspect me of being responsible for the deaths of two Light mages on separate occasions a couple of years ago. Unfortunately, it just so happens that both of those suspicions are true.

That wasn't the reason I was here today, though.

Like most British universities, the security at the Institute of Education is non-existent, and I walked past the reception desk and descended into a big square concrete well with big square concrete pillars and big square ugly paintings. A sign at the bottom said LOGAN HALL, but instead of going straight in I veered left. The entry area narrowed into a corridor with few doors or windows. To my right I could hear a voice echoing, but I kept working my way around the edge of the hall, climbing occasional small flights of steps. Only when I'd circled to the back of the hall did I look through one of the doors.

The hall was a huge auditorium, faded red seats in semicircular rows slanting down to a raised wooden stage. There were hundreds of people seated within, but the one I was interested in was the man on the stage. He was standing on the podium delivering a lecture, and behind him was a projection screen which read 'European Integration In Historical Perspective'. It was his voice I'd heard from outside.

I hadn't opened the door but there were wired-glass windows set into the wood that gave a good view inside, and I stood quietly, watching the man. He looked to be in his mid-fifties, with a stooped posture and hair that had gone nearly but not quite all the way to silvery-white. At a glance the two of us wouldn't have looked much alike, but there was something in his features of my own, aged and tempered. He hadn't seen me – the corridor was darker than the brightly lit hall and I knew the lights inside would reflect off the window glass. I could have opened the door to step inside, but I stayed where I was.

I'd been standing there for maybe five minutes when a soft noise caught my attention. Different movements make different sounds – the steady tread of someone walking, the scrape of shifting feet, the patter of someone in a hurry – and with practice you can learn to filter them, picking out the ones that don't fit in. It's nothing to do with magic, just simple awareness, a primal skill that anyone can learn but which most people in the modern age have forgotten. But anyone who lives as a predator or as prey learns it fast.

The sound I'd heard was the sound of someone trying to stay quiet and hidden, and I stepped quietly into the cover of the doorway, one hand moving to the hilt of the knife beneath my coat. The doorway blocked line of sight, hiding me from anyone behind or ahead. It blocked my view too . . . but I don't need a view to see.

The corridor was empty and ordinary, pale walls and faded blue carpet. But to my sight, it was a branching spread of possible futures, lines of light forking and multiplying in the darkness. In each possible future, I took a different action, moved a different way, and in every one of them my future self changed to match it: thousands of futures, branching into millions and billions. I picked out two of the delicate strands of light and focused on them, letting them strengthen and grow. In one, I stepped out of hiding and turned left; in the other, I moved right. My future selves walked away from me and as they did I watched, guiding the possible futures to keep myself walking down the corridor, seeing what my future eyes would see. The right-hand self found nothing. The left-hand self heard a scuffle of movement. The left-hand branches multiplied, dividing, and I guided my future self down the path where he chased after the sound. More futures branched out, and as they did I recognised a familiar element, a signature. I moved closer to look—

—and suddenly I knew who was following me. The instant that I did, the future wavered and faded into nothingness: now that I knew who it was, I had no reason to walk down there to find out. Physically carrying out all the possible actions I'd just run through would have taken the best part of a minute, but divination works at the speed of thought and the only limit on what you can do is how clearly and quickly you can focus. From beginning to end the whole thing had taken less than a second.

From down the corridor I heard another stealthy movement. I'd kept quite still as I'd used my magic, and my pursuer had no way to know that I was there. Cautious footsteps advanced up the corridor. I waited, letting them approach, then stepped out into view, the fingers of my right hand flicking forwards.

The girl who'd been following me jumped back. She was wearing jeans and a light green top and as soon as she saw me she started moving, but the metal disc I'd thrown bounced off her stomach before she could get out of the way. She began to drop into a stance, her right hand going to the small of her back.

'No use going for a weapon,' I told her. 'You're dead.'

With a sigh Luna dropped her arm and straightened. 'How long did you know I was there?'

Luna is half English and half Italian, with fair skin, wavy light brown hair and a lot more confidence than she used to have. She's an adept rather than a mage, the bearer of an ancient family curse which protects her at the expense of killing anyone who gets too close, and she's been my apprentice for around two years. Nowadays her control's developed to the point where being around her is almost safe, as long as you don't touch her.

'If you're going to make a habit of shadowing mages,' I said, 'you'll have to get better at dodging.'

'Yes, oh master,' Luna said resignedly, bending to pick up the thing I'd thrown at her. It had been a one pound coin, and as her fingers touched it I saw the silver-grey mist of her curse engulf it. As she did, she shot a quick glance at the door behind me, trying to see what was inside.

I rolled my eyes inwardly. 'Come on – upstairs,' I said, starting back towards the stairwell. The voice of the lecturer continued behind me, but I didn't look back.

'I thought I told you to mind the shop,' I told Luna.

The inner courtyard of the Institute of Education was stone with scattered trees. A faculty building which looked like a giant concrete staircase loomed over us, and high in the sky above the thin grey cylinder of the BT Tower loomed over the faculty building. The sky beyond was grey; it was an overcast day. Students walked and cycled past in ones and twos, and a cool wind gusted across the stone.

'It's not like the world's going to end if it's not open for a few hours,' Luna said. '*You* close it up all the time.'

'I close it up. Operative word: "I".'

'I'm supposed to be your apprentice,' Luna complained. 'It's not like you're paying me to be shop assistant.'

Luna used to work for me part-time finding and buying magic items, but when I took her on as an apprentice I started paying her a stipend; mage training takes as much time as a full-time job and I wanted her focused on her lessons. 'Actually, your apprentice duties are whatever I say they are,' I said. 'So in fact, right now, shop assistant is *exactly* what I'm paying you to be. Besides, you need the practice.'

'Shadowing you seems like practice.'

I gave Luna a look.

Luna put her hands up. 'Okay, okay. Look, I'm *bored*. Nothing's happening at class, there aren't any tournaments so no one wants to practise and I hardly ever see Anne and Vari these days. Even Sonder's stopped showing up. And you haven't exactly been Mr Sociable.'

I didn't answer. I don't know what my expression was like but Luna drew back slightly. 'Well, you haven't,' she said defensively.

We walked a little way in silence. A pair of girls came towards us, talking, and we split to let them pass between us. 'What were you doing there?' Luna asked.

'Looking for someone.'

'Is it something to do with Richard?'

'No.'

'I was just wondering—'

'It's nothing to do with Richard.'

'Okay.'

'I was thinking of talking to the guy giving that lecture.'

'Okay.'

I gave Luna a sharp look. She had a carefully neutral look which made me suspicious. 'So who was he?' Luna asked after a pause.

'Who was who?'

'The lecture guy.'

I very nearly told Luna to get lost. It wasn't a nice way to treat her but I've got a knee-jerk reaction to talking about anything really personal. My instinct with anything like this is to keep it to myself.

Up until last summer, my life had been going pretty well. I'd taken in a pair of young mages named Anne and Variam, and between them, Luna and a Light mage named Sonder, I'd had something close to a real social life for the first time in ten years. I'd started to believe that I might have finally gotten away from my past.

I was wrong. In August, a group of adepts calling themselves the Nightstalkers showed up, looking for revenge for one of the uglier things I'd done while I'd been Richard's apprentice. They couldn't find Richard but they found me all right, and would have killed me if my friends hadn't come to help. In the aftermath, I'd told Luna, Sonder, Anne and Variam why the Nightstalkers were after me and what I'd done for them to hate me so much.

Luna had taken it surprisingly well. She'd read between the lines and figured out most of the story before I'd even told it to her, and had decided that her loyalties lay with me. Variam, prickly but fiercely honourable, had chosen the same way. But Anne and Sonder had been less sure, and while they were still making up their minds, I'd led the Nightstalkers, young and inexperienced and painfully idealistic, into a trap in which nearly all of them had been killed. I hadn't had much choice, but that didn't make me feel any better about it.

Both Anne and Sonder cut off contact with me when they found out. I'd had a short and painful conversation with Anne in which she'd made it clear that she thought what I'd done was unforgivable, and from the brief attempts I'd made since then to talk to Sonder, I was pretty sure he felt the same way. A part of me agreed with them.

Keeping my past a secret hadn't done me any favours that time. In fact, it had probably made things worse.

'He's my father,' I told Luna.

'Really?'

'What's with that tone of voice? I do have parents.'

'Uh . . . you never talk about them.'

'Yeah, there's a reason for that. After they split up I didn't see my dad for a long time, and when I did it was after my time with Richard.' I hadn't been in good shape back then. I'd spent most of the previous year as a prisoner in Richard's mansion, getting periodic visits from one of Richard's other apprentices. 'I told him bits of the story, skipped over the magic parts, but I did tell him what I did to Tobruk.' Namely, that I'd killed the evil little bastard.

'Okay.'

'My dad's a pacifist,' I said. 'He doesn't believe in violence.'

'Seriously?'

'Why is that so hard to believe?'

'Well, you're, um . . .'

I gave Luna a narrow look. 'What?'

'. . . I'm not finishing that sentence. So the conversation didn't go well?'

'My dad's a political science professor who thinks violence is a sign of barbarism. I told him to his face that I'd committed premeditated murder and didn't regret it.' With hindsight that had been a spectacularly bad idea, but I hadn't been in much of a condition to think it through. 'How do you think the conversation went?'

'Badly?'

We'd made our way off the university campus and back out onto the London streets, heading north towards Euston Road. 'Do you talk to him much?' Luna asked.

'Last time was a couple of years ago.'

'Does he know that you're . . . ?'

'A mage? No. He thinks I got involved with criminals and that Richard was some sort of mob boss. I suppose if I worked at it I might be able to convince him that Richard was a Dark mage, but I don't think that'd be much of an improvement.' And if I told him what I'd done to those adepts last year . . .

'How about if I went and talked to him?' Luna suggested.

'No.'

'I could—'

'*No.* This is one area I do not want you messing around in.' I looked at her. 'Clear?'

I saw Luna's eyebrows go up and she shot me a quick glance. 'Clear,' she said after a moment.

We walked in silence for a few minutes. I waited to see if Luna would push her luck, but she stayed quiet. We worked our way through the London back streets, the traffic a steady noise in the background. 'So,' I said at last. 'How about you tell me why you're really here?'

'What?'

'You're working up to asking me for something.'

Luna made a face. 'Yes, it's that obvious,' I said. 'Let's hear it.'

'If it's a bad time—'

'Luna . . .'

'Okay, okay,' Luna said. 'Have you heard anything from Anne? As in lately.'

I looked at her curiously. 'No.'

'You sent her that message.'

'And I got a very polite non-answer.' It had been my third try. Give Anne credit: she does at least answer her mail. 'Would have thought you'd be in closer touch than me.'

Luna sounded like she was choosing her words carefully. 'Do you think you could invite her to move back in?'

I looked at Luna in surprise, about to ask if she was serious. The look on her face told me she was. 'I know things didn't end all that well,' Luna continued hurriedly, 'but it was nine months ago. She might have cooled off, right?'

'Why are you asking about this now?'

'Well, it'd be safer, wouldn't it? I mean, that was why you invited them to stay.'

Back when I'd first met Anne and Variam, they'd been staying with a rakshasa named Jagadev. Rakshasas are powerful tiger-like shapeshifters from the Indian subcontinent – mages don't trust them and vice versa, both with good reason. Jagadev had kicked them out shortly afterwards, leaving them as apprentices without a master, which in magical society is a lot like skinny-dipping in a shark tank. Anne and Variam's only real protection had been their membership in the Light apprentice programme, a kind of magical university. Trouble is, you're not allowed into the programme unless you're a Light or independent apprentice in good standing, which Anne and Vari weren't. To fix that I'd invited them to move in with me, effectively taking Jagadev's place as their sponsor, until last summer when they'd both moved out. In Vari's case, he'd become a Light apprentice for real, signing up with a Light Keeper. Anne hadn't.

'Back then they didn't have anywhere else to go,' I said. 'It's different now. Vari's got a master, and Anne's got that place down in Honor Oak.'

'But she doesn't have anyone sponsoring her.'

'Yeah.' We crossed the street, heading north. 'But at least she's still in the apprentice programme.'

Luna hesitated.

I looked at Luna. 'What?'

'So, about that . . .'

'Please don't tell me she left.'

'Uh . . . technically, no,' Luna said. 'It was more like got expelled.'

'You've got to be kidding me. When?'

'The announcement was yesterday.'

'Why now?' I said. 'She and Vari joined up, what, two years ago? Did some teacher get vindictive or something?'

'No,' Luna said. 'They're saying she attacked another student.'

I stared at Luna. '*Anne* attacked another student?'

'Yeah,' Luna said. 'You remember Natasha?'

'Oh,' I said. 'Okay . . .' Natasha was a Light apprentice I'd met the year before last. She'd thrown a tantrum over Luna knocking her out of a tournament, to the point of shooting her in the back with a spell which might have killed Luna if Anne hadn't been there to heal her. I hadn't been able to do anything to Natasha officially – her master was too well-connected and she'd got away with only a slap on the wrist – but I'd met Natasha's master afterwards and explained very clearly what would happen to her apprentice if she did anything like that again. Apparently the lesson had stuck because Natasha's master had kept her away from Luna ever since. If Anne had gone after Natasha, odds were Natasha had done something to deserve it.

But still . . . 'Are you sure it was Anne who started it?' I asked. 'Natasha didn't attack her first?'

'I don't think she got the chance. She went straight down and started screaming. They had to sedate her to shut her up and she hasn't been back since.'

I gave Luna a slightly disbelieving look, but she didn't look like she was exaggerating. She didn't look particularly upset either, but there was a tinge of worry there as well – no matter how good her reasons for disliking Natasha, she knew this was serious.

'Has the expulsion gone through, or is it hanging?'

'They fast-tracked it. Natasha's master isn't pushing her own charges yet, though.'

'She couldn't, not easily. Would bring up too many awkward questions about why her apprentice wasn't expelled for doing the same thing to you in Fountain Reach.' I thought for a second, then shook my head. 'Won't help with the expulsion, though. That'll be from the programme directors.'

'So?' Luna said. 'What do you think?'

'Having Anne move back in? It won't fly. Might have helped if we'd done it a month ago, but it won't be enough to get her reinstated.'

'Oh, screw getting reinstated – most of those classes are a waste of time anyway. I'm worried about *her*. Being on your own as an apprentice is a really bad idea, right? Isn't that what you keep telling me?'

'Preaching to the choir.'

'She could end up as a slave to a Dark mage or worse. Right?'

Which was exactly what had happened to Anne a few years ago. It was something we had in common. 'It's possible, yes.'

'So?'

'What do you mean, "so"?' I looked at Luna. 'Yes, you're right. Being a mage or an adept on your own at Anne's age *is* a really bad idea, *especially* when the apprentice grapevine makes sure everyone knows about it. So why are you telling all this to *me*? You should be talking to her.'

'I did.'

'And?'

Luna didn't look happy. 'Let me guess,' I said. 'She said no, so now you're coming to me?'

'Well . . . yeah. Could you ask her?'

The flipside of Luna's new self-confidence is that it's made her a lot less shy about asking for what she wants. 'She's made it pretty clear that she doesn't want to talk to me, and even if she did I don't think moving back is high on her to-do list.'

'It doesn't hurt to ask.'

'Is that your new motto for dealing with mages, or something?'

Luna came to a halt in the middle of the pavement, forcing me to stop and turn to her. 'Look, I'm worried. She's my best friend, even if I hardly see her nowadays. I know you two don't get on any more and I haven't said anything, but . . . can't you give it a try? It's not as though you lose anything if she says no, right?'

Traffic went by in the street, and pedestrians changed their course to avoid us. Luna gave me a pleading look and all of a sudden my objections felt a lot weaker. I still didn't want to do it, but it wasn't as though Luna was really asking for much . . . and she wasn't wrong about the danger Anne might be in. 'All right,' I said.

'Tonight?'

'Fine. Tonight.'

I parted company from Luna and headed south. With her out of sight it only took a couple of minutes for my thoughts to skip away from her and Anne and go back to circling the uncomfortable subject of my father.

It was probably just as well that Luna had shown up. Without her to give me a push, I might have ended up skulking outside that hall for hours. I'd been telling Luna the truth – my father had been utterly horrified at what I'd done to Tobruk (and to several others, for that matter). The bit I *hadn't* told her was that even though I couldn't see any remotely realistic way in which I could ever change my father's mind, I'd kept on trying anyway. I'd seen my father maybe a dozen times over the past ten years, and every time the meeting had ended up devolving into the same bitter argument. He couldn't see how violence was ever the right choice, and I couldn't see how that attitude could ever make sense – we always said the same things and reacted the same way, as though we were acting out the script for a play we both knew by heart, with tiny variations which ultimately didn't make any difference.

Even now, as I walked through the London streets, I found myself running through the arguments with my father for the thousandth time, debating the points and imagining the counter-arguments he'd make so that I could respond to them.

On a rational level I knew it didn't make sense. The fights with my father never achieved anything – all they did was make me strung out and depressed – yet somehow I kept having them. It was as though I needed to prove something to him; make him admit that I was right and he was wrong. It'd never happen, and I *knew* it would never happen, but still I carried on doing it. About the only thing that could pull my mind away from it was work.

Luckily, I had a meeting scheduled for exactly that.

I met Talisid in the Holborn restaurant we usually use for our discussions, an Italian place close enough to the station to be convenient and spacious enough to be private. Talisid greeted me, courteous as always, a middle-aged man an inch or two under average height, with a balding head and greying hair. At first glance he looks so bland that he could be part of the furniture, but a closer look might suggest a little more. I've known him for two years and I trust him more than anyone else on the Council, which isn't saying much. We ordered and got down to business.

'We've heard back from the Americans,' Talisid said once we'd finished with chit-chat. 'They're offering to drop the issue in exchange for more information on Richard.'

'I already told them I don't *have* any more information on Richard. Am I going to have to have this conversation with every country's Keepers?'

'Just the two, so far,' Talisid murmured.

The leader of the pack of adepts who'd come after me last year had been an American citizen named Will. After what had happened to him, the American Council had started making noises, and since Talisid owed me a couple of favours I'd asked him for help. For the last few months Talisid had been acting as my go-between, as well as adviser on the kind of points of law you really don't want to ask about in public. The really screwed-up part is that under *mage* law, what I'd done to Will and the Nightstalkers had been perfectly legal. There's a reason adepts don't like the Council much.

I twirled my butter-knife absently. 'How bad an idea would it be to tell them to get lost?'

'They're not going to try to extradite you, if that's what you're wondering,' Talisid said. 'But if you're ever planning to set foot in North America, it might be a better idea to clean this up now rather than later.'

'Fine,' I said with a sigh. 'Tell them – again – that I've no idea where Richard is or what he's been up to, but I could fill in their files about the rest of those adepts. Maybe they'll trade for that.'

'It's possible. There might be a more direct approach.'

I eyed Talisid. 'Such as?'

'The American Council are as interested in the reports concerning Richard as we are,' Talisid said. 'If you could confirm or deny them . . .'

I sighed. 'Not this again.'

'You *are* uniquely qualified to investigate the issue.'

'Investigate what? A bunch of rumours?'

'Those same rumours have persisted for almost a year,' Talisid said. 'In my experience that tends to indicate an active source. Besides—'

'Is there any actual *proof*?'

'No,' Talisid said after a very slight pause.

'I'm not keen on poking around asking questions on the Dark side of the fence just so the Council can feel better about themselves. I'm not exactly popular there, in case you've forgotten.'

'I would have thought it concerns you rather directly as well.'

'Richard's gone,' I said. It came out more harshly than I'd intended. I'd had a dream last year in which Richard had definitely *not* been gone, and it had shaken me more than I was willing to admit. But months had passed and nothing had happened, and eventually I'd been able to make myself believe that it really had only been a dream. The only reason I hadn't managed to put it out of my mind completely was that everyone else kept bringing it up.

Talisid opened his mouth and I raised my hand to cut him off. 'You've asked me to do this, what, three times now? The answer's still no.'

Talisid paused again, studying me, and I felt the futures swirl. 'As you wish,' he said at last.

Food arrived and occupied us for some minutes. 'Have you been following the political developments?' Talisid asked.

'Which ones?'

'The movement to include Dark mages on the Council has picked up again. The main one pushing for it appears to be your old friend Morden.'

'He's not my friend, and no, I hadn't heard. Doesn't this come up every few years?'

'This time may be different – the unity bloc has been gaining influence. I was wondering if you'd heard anything.'

'That kind of stuff's above my pay grade.'

'Would you be interested in changing that?'

I shot Talisid a look. 'What's that supposed to mean?'

'The faction I represent has reasons to be concerned with the current state of affairs. A better-developed intelligence network would be useful.'

'And you want me to do what – play James Bond?' I said in amusement. 'I think most of the agents in those stories had a really short life expectancy.'

'It's a little less dramatic than that,' Talisid said with a slight smile. 'It's information we need, not commando raids. We simply never know as much as we'd like to. It's more for the future than right now – there's nothing that needs immediate attention. Just something to think about.'

'Hm.' I started to lift my water glass, then stopped. 'Wait a second. Is this what you've been planning all along?'

'How do you mean?'

I stared at Talisid, glass in hand, as things suddenly fell into place. 'This is what you've been working up to, isn't it? I always wondered why someone as high up as you would be keeping up a relationship with an ex-Dark diviner. You've been hoping I'll sign on with you. Have you been testing me all this time? Was that what all those jobs were about?'

Talisid raised a hand. 'Slow down.'

'Bit late for that.' I was running over my past encounters with Talisid, making connections. 'So which is it?'

'While your conclusion is . . . not exactly *in*correct, you have things slightly out of order.' Talisid didn't look particularly surprised, and I realised that he must have been anticipating the way the conversation was going to go. 'I originally approached you because your position and abilities were favourably placed to help us. On the basis of that performance I approached you again, and so on. I didn't involve you in past events in order to make you this offer. I'm making you this offer because of your performance in past events.'

'And what exactly *is* the offer?'

'Verus, sometimes a cigar is just a cigar. I said that we needed information, and that was what I meant.' Talisid watched me mildly. 'You aren't under any obligation to undertake tasks that you don't want to. Isn't that exactly the basis on which we've worked before?'

*The difference is that I'd be an employee instead of a freelancer.* But I didn't say that out loud because, as usual, Talisid was being reasonable. I *had* worked for him enough times by now, and he *had* dealt honestly with me each time. Looked at that way, it wasn't really that big a step.

Except . . . it would mean joining the Council. 'I appreciate the offer,' I said with an effort. 'But I don't think I'd make a very good Light mage.'

'Why?'

*Because I used to be a Dark mage and half the Council hate me for it. Because the Council left me to die when I needed them most and I hate them for it. Because I think the Council are treacherous weasels. And because I don't think I've got any right to call myself a servant of light, even if most of the Council don't deserve that title either . . .*

'Verus?' Talisid said when I stared past him without answering.

'Let's just say I don't think we'd get on,' I said at last.

'I'm aware of your past history.' Talisid's voice was gentle, and I looked at him in surprise. The sympathy in his eyes might be fake, but if it was, it was a convincing fake. 'But what's done is done. I think you could have a future with the Council. I won't press you, but the offer is open. When you have the time, think it over.' Talisid paid the bill and walked out towards the exit, leaving me sitting at the table staring after him.

I took the tube from Holborn, changing at Liverpool Street and again at Whitechapel to take the London Overground south over the river. It was a long journey, and it gave me plenty of time to think.

Talisid's offer had come as more of a shock than it really should have. I'd been working for him for two years on and off, and if I'd been paying attention I would have noticed the way things had been heading a while ago. Probably the reason I hadn't picked up on it was that it had simply never occurred to me that anyone on the Council would actually want me on their side.

The more I thought about it, the more tempting it sounded. Talisid wouldn't be able to snap his fingers and put me into the Council's inner circle, but he could do a lot towards getting me accepted. And being a Light mage, even a probationary one, would make my life easier in a hundred little ways. I'd have a stronger legal footing in case of any disputes, which would make it that much less likely that anyone would challenge me in the first place, and it would *really* help with Luna's education. I'd be able to get her into restricted classes in the apprentice programme, maybe even find her a Light chance mage as a specialist instructor.

But . . . there were reasons to hesitate too. There's a reason I fell out with the Council: I don't agree with half their policies and I don't trust them to keep to the other half. I also have a small but significant number of enemies on the Council, including a nasty piece of work named Levistus, and getting closer to them wouldn't do any favours to my life expectancy. Most of all, though, I wasn't sure how well the Light mages of the Council would like me. Going from Dark to independent is one thing; going from Dark to Light is something else. Talisid might be able to get me in the door but he wouldn't be able to hide the fact that I was the ex-apprentice of a particularly notorious Dark mage with a worryingly high body count of my own. Now there are altogether too many Light mages who couldn't care less about body counts, but the fact that a couple of the deaths attributed to my name were Light mages would probably make even them think twice. And ironically enough, the Light mages whose good opinion I'd most value and whose respect I'd most want to earn would be exactly the ones *least* likely to trust me.

Maybe staying outside the fold as an independent was better.

But was that wisdom talking, or fear?

Anne lives in Honor Oak, a mostly forgotten part of south London with an abundance of hills. Price-wise it's not as expensive as the inner city, but nothing in London is exactly cheap and I was pretty sure the only reason Anne could afford to live there was because Sonder had set her up in Council-owned property. (The Council is not known for its spontaneous generosity but it owns a lot of buildings it doesn't use, and given the amount of stuff it's responsible for, a lot gets by under its radar.) Anne's place is near the top of a hill, by the side of a gateway leading down into a wooded area. It was after working hours, but as I looked ahead I was surprised to see a small crowd.

Anne's flat was on the first floor of a converted building, and there was a line of people outside her door. As I studied them from a distance I realised that they were queued up (more or less) and waiting to go inside. Now that I thought about it, I remembered Luna had told me something about Anne running a clinic out of her flat. Luna had made it sound small-scale though. By my count there were a good fifteen people there.

There wasn't any danger, but it did pose a problem. Anne had never explicitly told me to stay away but I knew her current feelings towards me were ambivalent at best. Getting her to talk to me was not going to be easy, and having a crowd waiting outside would more or less guarantee a response of not-now-I'm-busy. No obvious solution presented itself so I found a nearby spot to observe from.

The people outside Anne's flat were a mixed bag: male and female, white and Asian, short and tall. The youngest was a babe in arms while the oldest looked to be fifty or so. Most were working class, a smaller fraction were middle class, and there were two or three who I was pretty sure were addicts. The different members of the queue were very obviously uncomfortable with each other, and there was the sort of low-grade tension in the air that you get in job centres and NHS waiting rooms. From within the flat I could just make out Anne's soft voice, along with the sound of the man she was talking to.

I sat on the landing above Anne's flat and waited. Twenty minutes passed, then forty. Every now and then Anne would finish with one person and admit a new one, or a new arrival would show up at the back of the queue. The queue seemed to be getting longer rather than shorter, which didn't bode well for the 'wait for her to finish' plan. I toyed with a few ideas to speed things up: the plan involving a smoke bomb and the fire alarm was tempting, but I had the feeling Anne wouldn't appreciate it. In the absence of anything else to do, I fell back on my short-range eavesdropping to see what Anne was up to: it's not as reliable as other methods of magical surveillance, but it's virtually impossible to detect. (Yes, it's spying. I'm a diviner; it's what I do.)

Just as Luna had said, Anne was running a clinic, and she was getting a *really* big variety of patients. Some were what you'd expect, like the woman with flu or the man with backache. Some were odd, like the guy claiming he'd been bitten by his cat. And some were depressing, like the girl who'd cut her wrists and now was afraid someone would see it. Anne asked gently why she'd done it. After some probing, the girl revealed it was because her boyfriend had been threatening her. Anne asked if she'd considered leaving. The girl said she couldn't; she loved him. The conversation more or less hit a dead end from there.

Watching Anne's technique for treatment was interesting. She hardly used any active magic at all: she'd just do a quick check-over, then recommend a remedy. She'd make a show of doing a physical examination, but I was pretty sure what she was really relying on was her lifesight. It's one of the signature abilities of life mages, letting them 'see' someone's physiology and the workings of their body just by looking at them, and it makes diagnosis *really* easy, not to mention being great for spotting people. Lifesight's probably the weakest spell Anne knows, but in magic, as with many other things, the most powerful techniques aren't necessarily the most useful. In theory Anne could just cure anybody who walked in, healing their wounds and rebuilding their bodies, but doing so would exhaust her quickly – healing spells consume a lot of physical energy, as well as being really hard to pass off as coincidence. By using her abilities to diagnose people and then recommending a non-magical treatment, she could help them a lot more efficiently and without any risk of being revealed as a mage. It was a smart way to handle it.

As I kept watching, though, I started to notice something odd in how the patients reacted to Anne. Anne didn't seem to be charging money, she was attentive and polite to everyone who came through the door and she was faster and more accurate than any doctor. Her patients ought to have been grateful, and some were . . . but a surprising number weren't. Many had a kind of entitled attitude: they didn't seem to acknowledge anything that Anne was doing for them; they just treated it as their due. Others would argue when they didn't get the diagnosis they wanted. Strangest of all, though, were the ones who seemed weirdly uncomfortable in Anne's presence. They'd ask for her help but with reluctance, as though even being near her made them uneasy. And it wasn't just one or two; it was something like every third person through the door.

After I'd been watching for somewhere over an hour, I heard a commotion. A new guy had arrived at the end of the line; apparently he hadn't been pleased by the length of the queue because he'd started shoving his way to the front. The people already in the queue – some of whom had been waiting for over an hour – objected. The shouting and swearing grew steadily louder until the new arrival barged into Anne's flat. I listened to the raised voices for a few seconds before rising to my feet and slipping downstairs past the crowd, homing in on the noise.

The room inside Anne's flat was sparsely furnished, obviously meant for public access rather than her own use, but there were touches of her personality all the same: green upholstered chairs; potted plants by the window. Two doors led inwards, both closed. The crowd had spilled a few feet inside, but were hanging around the door, apparently unwilling to get any closer.

The reason for their reluctance was standing in the middle of the room, shouting at Anne. He was a big guy, powerfully built with a scarred and shaven head. There was a spider's web tattooed on the side of his neck, and ACAB was spelt out across the knuckles of his right fist in blue India ink. His speech was a little hard to decipher but he seemed to want something, and Anne was standing right in front of him.

Anne is tall and slim, with black hair and reddish-brown eyes. She's got a quiet way of speaking and moving which tends to make her blend into the background, although it wasn't working very well this time. Some people seem to find her looks off-putting, though I've never really understood why.

Anne is one of the few people I know who could make a legitimate claim to having had a worse childhood than either Luna or me – about five years ago, while she was still in school, she was kidnapped by a Dark mage named Sagash who wanted to mould her into his apprentice. With Variam's help she managed to get away, but it took most of a year and Anne's never told either Luna or me exactly what happened in those nine months. She gave me a quick glance with no sign of surprise as I walked in: she'd seen me coming. 'Hi,' I said.

'—can I?' the man was demanding in a loud voice. 'I'm what this government's made me, aren't I? My dad sent me to reform when I was a kid, and they treated me like a criminal. Well, now they've got what they—'

'Need a hand?' I asked.

Anne held a hand up and turned halfway between Tattoo Guy and me, speaking with her soft voice. 'Not a good time.'

'I'd go through the public and the police like they were nothing. They wouldn't know what hit them. They're vermin; they're nothing to me. They wouldn't know what—'

'Do you mind?' I asked the man.

Tattoo Guy glared at me. 'Who the fuck are you?'

'Friend of a friend. Sorry, do I know you?'

I watched as the guy's brain switched gears. It was a slow process, and I saw the possible futures branch out before me.

He could bluster; he could back down; he could kick off a fight. I was kind of hoping he'd choose the last one. Tattoo Guy was big and nasty, but my standards of 'nasty' are seriously skewed compared to normal people, and as far as serious threats went he didn't even make it onto my radar. I'd had a stressful day and the prospect of taking it out on someone was more attractive than it should have been.

'*Alex!*' Anne said.

I gave her a sideways glance. 'What's up?'

'Please don't.'

'Don't what?'

'You *know* what.' Anne looked slightly frustrated. 'I appreciate the help, but I'm fine.'

Tattoo Guy had been looking between us in confusion; now his expression changed to something uglier and I felt the futures shift. With me, Anne and the crowd in the door all watching him, he would have to be seriously stupid to start something, but stupid and aggressive people are in absolutely no danger of extinction and Tattoo Guy was proving a fine example of the breed. 'Hey! I'm fucking talking to you!'

'I'm sorry,' Anne told him. 'I don't keep any drugs here. If you sit down I can—'

'Shut the fuck up!' Tattoo Guy took a step forward, leaning over Anne. He didn't have much of a height advantage to lean with but his bulk made up for it. 'Don't bullshit me. They all lied and I fucking made them pay for it, yeah?' He started to take another step forward and as he did he reached out for Anne. 'I—'

As the man's hand reached out my fingers twitched. I wanted to step in and I could see the sequence of moves with crystal clarity: I'd block his arm, he'd grab me, I'd shrug him off, he'd have all the excuse he needed to swing at me and I'd have all the excuse *I* needed to drop him. He might be strong but I was quicker and better trained and could predict his every move. There was only one way it could end . . .

. . . and Anne had just specifically told me *not* to do that. Anne knows what I can do, and that was why she'd said 'don't'. She wasn't in any danger – up close she's far more deadly than me. If I stepped in, I wouldn't be doing it for her sake; I'd be acting out of pride, trying to prove something.

I held my ground. The man grabbed Anne, thick fingers going all the way around her upper arm. 'I'm not fucking telling you again.'

Anne held the man's gaze and all of a sudden she looked subtly different. Most people flinch when they're grabbed, but Anne didn't. She stared up at the man without reacting; it didn't even look as though she was breathing. 'I don't have what you're looking for,' she said clearly. 'Let me go, please.'

I saw the man hesitate. Somewhere in his toxin-fogged brain, the message was probably trying to get through that Anne wasn't acting very victim-like. But if someone's dumb enough to start a fight in front of a crowd, then it usually takes clearly overwhelming force to make them back down, and Anne doesn't *look* dangerous. He reached for her neck.

Something flickered in Anne's eyes.

Divination magic can look forward in time, but not back. When someone's making a choice then if you're quick you can get a glimpse of what they're choosing between. For a fraction of a second, as Anne raised her hand, I saw a spread of possibilities open up, fleeting images jumping out from the branches: a subtle spell, stillness and quiet, a slumping body, someone screaming their lungs out, more talking – wait, back up, what was that last—?

—and gone. Anne's fingers touched the man's wrist and green light glowed, there and gone in an instant. The spell was complex, one I hadn't seen before.

The man staggered and stopped. The aggression went out of his eyes and all of a sudden he just looked confused.

'Please sit down,' Anne said. Her voice was still polite, and the man obeyed, collapsing into one of the chairs as though his limbs were very heavy. Anne turned to me. 'I'm a little busy.'

I looked back at Anne — what had I seen for a second there? — then shook it off. Maybe I'd imagined it. 'Is this your way of asking me to come back some other day?'

'Yes.' Anne looked at me steadily. 'I'm sorry. This isn't a good time.'

I paused, then nodded. I left through the crowd, pushing my way past. Behind me, I heard Anne start to shoo them out.

Beside the building which held Anne's flat was what looked from the outside like allotments or a small park, sealed off behind an iron fence and a locked gate. It wasn't signposted but my phone labelled it as the Garthorne Road Nature Reserve.

Inside, the reserve was much bigger than it looked from the street, spreading out to either side and forming a long strip of land behind the houses that hid it. A railway cutting ran through the centre, forming a fenced-off valley with forested slopes. I got in over the fence, did a quick scout, then sat at a wooden bench and waited.

Time passed. The sun set and the sky faded from blue to indigo to black, lit from below by the orange glow of the London skyline. I've always been drawn to places like this, hidden away behind streets and buildings – I like nature, but I'm an urban person at heart and it's deep in the city where I feel most comfortable. The nature reserve was very nearly pitch-dark, the street lights blocked off by trees and houses, and the wind rustled in the leaves in a steady rise and fall. From time to time, a train would pass along the railway line, rattle and bang and roar, leaving an eerie quiet in its wake. As I sat still and silent, rustles of movement began to filter through the undergrowth, the reserve's nocturnal inhabitants growing accustomed to my presence. I saw the quick scuttling movements of rodents, and a hedgehog bustled past only a few feet away. The wind was beginning to blow away the clouds, and stars gleamed down from patches of clear sky.

It was nearly ten o'clock when I heard the sound of someone moving from the direction of the entrance to the reserve, footsteps on grass coming downhill towards me. I could tell the exact moment when I came within Anne's lifesight because she stopped. I saw the possibilities branch – would she keep coming or would she back off? – but just as I knew that she'd seen me, she knew that I'd seen her. The future in which she left winked out, she kept coming and a moment later I saw a slim shadow against the trees. 'Hey,' I said.

'I thought you were going,' Anne said. I couldn't see her face in the darkness.

'I didn't say where.'

I heard Anne sigh. 'I'm going to have to phrase what I say more carefully, aren't I?' She paused. 'How did you know I'd come here?'

I shrugged. 'This place suits you.'

Anne had come to a halt beside an old clay oven. I'd

expected her to keep her distance but she started forward, slipping around the edge of the woodpile before sitting on the bench opposite me, curling her feet up to sit cross-legged. We sat for a little while in silence.

'It's nice here,' I said eventually. I meant it. Despite the railway line and the streets all around, the reserve felt peaceful.

'It's not mine.'

'You come here often, don't you?'

'When I can,' Anne said. From across the bench I could just make out her features, dim in the starlight.

There was a pause. 'So,' I said. 'How's the clinic going?'

'It's okay.' Anne sounded tired.

'Are you still working at that supermarket?'

'Yes.' Anne looked up at me. 'I don't think you came to ask about my job.'

'I heard you left the apprentice programme.'

'Is that what they're saying?'

'Not exactly.' I paused, but Anne didn't fill in the gap. Oh well, tiptoeing around wasn't working anyway. 'They're saying that you got expelled because you attacked Natasha.'

Anne was silent.

'Is it true?' I asked.

'Does it matter?'

'*Yes*, it matters. Don't you at least want to give me your side of the story?'

Anne sounded weary. 'Why bother?'

I wasn't sure what to say to that. 'Did Natasha attack you? Or set you up or something?'

'No,' Anne said with a sigh. 'She just . . . acted like Natasha.'

'So . . . what *did* you do?'

'Do you really want to know?' Anne looked up at me, meeting my gaze in the darkness. 'I triggered all her pain receptors and looped them so that they'd keep firing for a couple of hours.'

I stared. I couldn't picture Anne doing something like that. Okay, come to think of it I *had* seen her do something *exactly* like that, worse in fact, but . . .

'It doesn't do any permanent damage,' Anne said when I didn't answer. She sounded defensive.

'What did she do?'

'Nothing,' Anne said in frustration. 'Nothing *different*. She said something about what I must have done to stay in the programme. It wasn't the worst thing she's said, it's probably not even in the top ten, and Natasha isn't even the worst of them. There wasn't anything special about it. It was just . . . one last straw. That was all.'

'What were all the other straws?' I said quietly.

Anne let out a long breath. 'Do you know how long I've been in the programme?'

'No.' The first time I'd met Anne had been at Luna's apprenticeship ceremony, almost two years ago. 'Two years?'

'Three and a bit.' Anne looked at me. 'Do you know how many days I went to classes and someone *didn't* remind me that the Light mages didn't want me there?'

I shook my head.

'None of them,' Anne said. 'They don't like me. Because I used to be with Sagash. Because I was staying with Jagadev. Because I'm a life mage. Because I was arrested for murder and some of them think I should have been found guilty. If it's not one reason it's another, and I'm tired of it. You know the first thing I felt when I found out that I was expelled? It was a relief. Because I wouldn't have to keep seeing them every day. Back when I joined the apprentice programme, I thought I was going to be part of the Light mages, that I'd get accepted someday. Then when I had to deal with girls like Tash and Christine I thought they'd get over it, it wouldn't last, but . . . it never stops. I'm so sick of the way things work in the classes, with the Light mages. I'm tired of the other apprentices whispering behind my back, of how whenever we do pair work the teachers take my partner aside where they think I can't hear and ask if they're okay with being paired with me. I'm tired of being shut out, the looks, the jokes. I'm just tired.' Anne fell silent.

'That's been going on all this time?' I said quietly. I'd known that Anne and Variam weren't popular but I'd never known it was this bad.

'I didn't want to talk about it,' Anne said wearily. 'And it's not that bad, not any one day. It just . . . it adds up. Most of the Light mages, the teachers, they're not horrible. But I'm not one of them. And they never let you forget it.'

I was silent for a moment. 'I know what you mean.'

Anne wasn't telling me anything I hadn't found out myself. The Light mages of the Council are close, an extended family – even when they fight amongst themselves, they still basically understand one another. To them, Dark mages are the *other*, their ancient enemy, and if you're associated with a Dark mage then you're always on the outside, never fully trusted. It's part of the reason I've always felt a kinship with Anne and Vari – I know what it's like to be shut out. 'Do you need any help?'

'I don't want to go back to the apprentice programme.'

'You don't have to.' I chose my words carefully; I was getting onto dangerous ground now. 'You could move back in at my shop.'

Anne was silent. 'I know you're settled here,' I said, 'but it's not the safest place long-term. Your flat doesn't have any wards, and with what happened . . . well, people are going to be sniffing around.'

Anne didn't look at me. 'Did someone tell you to ask me that?' she said at last.

I didn't want to bring up Luna's name. 'Ah . . .'

'It was Luna, wasn't it? Was this whole thing her idea?' Anne shook her head. 'I asked her not to do this.'

Anne can be scarily good at reading people. 'She's worried about you.'

'I'm fine.'

'You don't look fine.'

'I'm not a wilting flower.' There was an edge in Anne's voice. 'I can take care of myself.'

'That's what everyone thinks until they find out they can't.'

Anne turned to look at me. 'Is that what you're here for? To tell me that?'

'I'm telling you that you're painting a bull's-eye on your back,' I said. 'You and Vari aren't exactly short of enemies. What do you think they'll do if they find out that you're not under anyone's protection?'

'When I was living with you last summer, I had a bomb go off over my head,' Anne said. 'You aren't exactly the safest person to be around either.'

'You know what I mean!'

'No, I don't. What do you want?'

'I'm trying to stop you from doing—' *something really stupid,* '—something that might get you killed. Okay, you don't want to stay in the apprentice programme. But if you're not doing that, then you're going to have to do something else. Can we at least sit down and go through the options?'

Anne looked back at me for a few seconds before answering. 'No.'

'*Why not?*'

'Because I'm tired of spending my life being told what to do,' Anne said. 'Sagash, Jagadev, the Light teachers. You.'

'Okay, what?' I said. I was starting to get angry now. 'All the time you and Vari were staying with me, I barely asked anything from *either* of you.'

'No,' Anne said. 'You killed five adepts instead.'

What felt like cold water spread through me, and my anger flickered and died. 'I know you didn't do it yourself,' Anne said. 'But you were the one who set it up.' She looked at me. 'I thought I could trust you.'

'Then what do you think I should have done?'

'I don't know,' Anne said simply. 'All I know is that the longer I spend with mages, the more I get shaped into what they want me to be. And I don't want to become the kind of person who could do what you did.'

I didn't meet Anne's eyes. 'Sometimes there aren't any good choices,' I said at last, my voice quiet in the darkness. 'Some things you do because everything else is worse.'

'And then it's easier the next time,' Anne said. There was something distant in her voice and I looked up sharply, but in the darkness I couldn't make out her features. It lasted only a second, then she looked aside and her voice was back to normal. 'Maybe there's nothing better. But at least you can make up for it afterwards.'

'And is that what this is? Your clinic?'

'Maybe,' Anne said. 'Yes. If you spend your time using

your magic to help people, then maybe if you do it long enough it'll make you into a better person. Won't it?'

'I . . . guess.' Something about the way Anne was saying that made me uneasy. I felt as though something was missing. 'I guess you could make a living out of it if you wanted to.'

'The way those other life mages do? Sell healing to rich people?' Anne shook her head. 'I just want to be left alone.'

'And does that include me?'

Anne didn't answer.

'Do you want me to go away?' I asked. 'Is that it?'

Anne was quiet for a moment. 'Yes,' she said at last.

Silence fell. I waited a long time but Anne didn't speak again. 'Fine,' I said, and rose. I began to walk past Anne up the slope, then paused and turned. 'But let me tell you something I've learned the hard way. You think you can take care of yourself? Well, you're probably right. But if you have enough enemies then it doesn't *matter* how good you are at taking care of yourself. One apprentice on their own isn't a hero; they're a target. If you can beat another mage then someone who wants to hurt you won't send one mage, they'll send three. If you can beat three, they'll send ten. Maybe if you follow other mages then you do have to pay a price for it, but they're not just doing it for themselves. The only kind of safety that lasts involves other people.'

Anne didn't meet my eyes, and this time I didn't have anything more to say. I walked away.

I rode the Overground back north, the train rolling through the darkness. Other people crowded the seats, the couples talking and the singles bent over their phones, but I didn't pay them any attention. When I reached Camden Road I stayed on the train, getting off at Hampstead Heath station instead. The heath was empty and black and I walked into the darkness of the park, hearing the sounds of voices fade away behind me until I was alone in the night.

Hampstead Heath is the home of a magical creature named Arachne. She's probably the closest friend and ally that I have, and I often come out here when I'm worried or unhappy about something. Arachne's very old and very wise, and talking to her usually helps me decide what to do.

But while Arachne might be my friend, she doesn't just sit in her lair all day waiting for me to drop by. From time to time she disappears, often for several days in a row, and as I looked ahead I saw that this was one of those times. I've never figured out where Arachne goes on these trips. Given her appearance, I'm pretty sure it's not a case of going out for a walk. I suspect it's got something to do with the tunnels under her lair and what's in them, but she's never brought up the subject and I haven't asked.

The dark and empty heath was well-suited to path-walking, and it didn't take me long to figure out that Arachne wasn't home. I should have checked in advance, but between Talisid, Anne and my father, I'd had a distracting sort of day. I kept going anyway – Arachne might not be at her home but it's deserted enough to work pretty well as a meeting place, and looking ahead I saw that while Arachne might not be available, someone else was.

I reached the ravine with the oak tree that hid the entrance to Arachne's lair, then took out my phone. The touch screen was bright in the darkness, and I tapped a name and put the phone to my ear. 'Hey,' I said into the receiver when I got an answer. 'You up for a chat? I wanted to talk something over . . . Not that long . . .

At Arachne's . . . Yeah . . . Okay. See you in a bit.' I hung up, leant against the tree, and waited.

For five minutes nothing happened. Then in the air in front of me an orange-red flame kindled and grew, lighting the ravine and the grass in a fiery glow. The light spread, forming a vertical oval six feet high, before its centre darkened to form a window into somewhere far away. I had a brief glimpse of a room, clothes scattered across the floor, then someone was stepping through in front of me. As soon as both his feet were on the ground, the gateway winked shut behind him. An orb of firelight hovered at his side, casting his dark skin in a reddish glow.

'Hey, Vari,' I said with a smile. 'Good to see you.'

Variam is small and wiry, quick to move and to speak. He used to go to the same school as Anne, and they both got caught up in some kind of nasty magic-related business involving one of their teachers that I don't know the details of. Then Anne got kidnapped by Sagash, Variam went to rescue Anne, and the two of them stuck together from that point on, for self-protection as much as anything else. Despite their shared history, they're less close than you'd think: they might have spent a lot of their lives together, but the more I've got to know Anne and Variam, the more I've come to realise just how different they are.

The major break came last year. At the same time that Anne left to live on her own, Vari got apprenticed to a Council Keeper. He took to it pretty well, after the initial rough patches, but the two of them don't do everything together the way they once did. 'So what's so important?' Variam asked. 'I've got an op tomorrow morning.'

'It's about Anne.'

Variam made a face.

'This is about her getting kicked from the programme, isn't it?' Variam said.

We were in a café near the heath, a little off Highgate Road, seated on plastic chairs at a two-person table where wisps of steam rose from two untouched cups of tea. A waitress was half-asleep at the counter and weak lights struggled against the darkness outside. 'I found out from Luna,' I said. 'I went by Anne's flat this evening.'

'And it didn't go so well, right?'

'I'm worried about her,' I said. 'You guys have got almost as many enemies as I do. Right now you're protected; she's not. Any chance she'd listen to you?'

'Tried it,' Variam said with a grimace. 'Didn't work.'

'When?'

'Last month after the Legion first picks. There was a Council sponsorship going so I tried to get her to apply. She said no.'

I tilted my head. Variam didn't look happy and I had the feeling there was more to the story. 'That was it?'

'We had a bit of a fight,' Variam said reluctantly. 'Haven't talked since.'

'Hard to imagine you two having a fight.'

Variam snorted. 'You never saw us at Jagadev's.'

'I always thought Anne followed your advice.'

'When she wants to,' Variam said. 'When she doesn't, it's like talking to a bloody rock. She doesn't even argue, she just sits there and says no.'

Which, come to think of it, had been how most of my disagreements with her had gone. I drummed my fingers on the table. 'Are there any Light types she'd trust? I thought she got on with some of the apprentices.'

'Only the younger ones, and that was before that whole murder charge thing at Fountain Reach.'

'How can they take that seriously?' I was getting frustrated with this – it should be such a simple problem. 'They have to know Anne wouldn't do something like that.'

Variam raised his eyebrows. 'Uh, no they don't.'

'Oh, come on. Why do the Lights and independents have such a problem with Anne, anyway?'

'You mean apart from the obvious?'

'You guys have been in the programme for years. They should be used to it by now.'

'Well, yeah, but . . .' Variam frowned. 'You *know* what their issue is with Anne, right?'

'Honestly?' I said. 'No. Yeah, I know there's the whole ex-Dark thing, but it always seemed like a pretty lousy reason. You only have to spend a few minutes around Anne to figure out she's not like that.'

Variam stared at me, then shook his head. 'You really are strange, you know that?'

'What?'

'Half the time you act like you know everything, then you say stuff like this.'

'I don't know everything, I've told you that enough times by now. What are you getting at?'

'The Light mages don't like Anne,' Variam said, 'because she comes across as incredibly creepy.'

I blinked. Whatever I'd been expecting Variam to say, it hadn't been that. 'What?'

'Creepy. As in weird and disturbing. The Light apprentices think she's creepy, the non-Light apprentices think she's creepy, even the teachers think she's creepy. Literally everyone sees it except you. Dunno why.'

'She's not creepy.'

'She acts like she can see under everyone's skin, she doesn't blink or sleep or breathe except when she wants to and she's got this way of looking at people like she's thinking how difficult it'd be to stop their heart.'

'Well . . . I guess.' I didn't really see what Variam was getting at. 'But she's a life mage.'

'Okay, first,' Variam said, 'life mages creep people out already. Second, the way Anne comes across, she looks like she might have done the heart-stopping thing a few times already.'

'No, she doesn't.'

'Argh.' Variam covered his eyes. 'I don't even know how to explain this. I mean, it's *good*, we haven't exactly got many friends, I'm not complaining or anything. I just don't get how you're the one mage who can't see how this would freak anyone out.'

'Well, it's not like she's going to do anything to hurt us.'

Variam was silent. I frowned. 'What?'

'Nothing.'

I shook my head. 'So how are we going to get Anne somewhere safer?'

'We can't,' Variam said. 'She said no and she meant it, so unless you're planning to knock her out and carry her off somewhere, you might as well give up.'

I thought about it for a second.

Variam scowled at me. 'I was *kidding*.'

'Yeah,' I said, abandoning the plan. I could probably pull it off, but Anne would kill me when she woke up. Well, she wouldn't *kill* me, but it wouldn't exactly improve our relationship and . . .

. . . and that was quite possibly the most stupid plan I'd ever come up with in my entire life. Why was I even *thinking* about this? If I'd got to the point where I was considering something this crazy, it was time to give up.

'Look, this isn't anything new,' Variam said seriously. 'I've got a couple of new ideas to bounce off her tomorrow, and if she doesn't answer I'll keep calling till she does. It's not like this is our first fight.' He paused. 'But thanks for trying. Back when things were bad, you and Luna were about the only people who cared enough to help. I haven't forgotten that.'

'Yeah,' I said. 'Okay. I'll leave it to you.'

The teas had grown cold on the table and we left them there when we got up to leave. Variam returned to Arachne's lair to gate back to Scotland, and I caught a bus home.

I had another nightmare that night.

It started as they always did, with me being chased. I kept moving, trying to put enough turnings between me and my pursuer, but every time I stopped I could hear him coming closer. Finally I stopped running and waited around a corner to ambush him. He came around into my reach and I caught him, forcing him to the ground and breaking his neck.

There were more people in the next room. All were sitting and they didn't seem to have noticed me. I went to the first and tried to wrestle him down, but it was taking too long so I had to go back and get a knife and start stabbing him instead. I kept it up until he stopped moving and went on to the next. He took longer, and the one after that took longer still. I kept stabbing his torso but there was so much resistance that the blade was hardly going in and the wounds weren't bleeding. The man I was stabbing didn't fight back, and no one else in the room seemed to even notice.

The next one was a woman, and as I moved in she looked up at me. My arms were sticky and my movements were tired and slow. Something made me stop and turn around, and as I did I saw bodies lying behind me. Some of them were still moving and with a thrill of horror I realised there weren't just two or three; there were dozens. I turned back to the woman, trying to say something to justify myself, but the words died on my lips. She didn't scream or run or try to defend herself; she just sat there looking at me. The knife was still in my hands and I could see the target area at her neck. I stepped forward, and as I did I realised that this was a dream, *had* to be a dream, and I tried desperately to wake up and escape. I caught the woman's hair with my left hand, forcing her head back and exposing her throat, while the knife came across to—

—I came awake, breathing hard. I felt sick and wanted to throw up and I clawed open the window next to my bed. Cold air rushed in and I knelt up on the bed, leaning out into the night, taking deep breaths in and out. Gradually the nausea faded and I reached for my bedside table, fumbling for my phone. I needed to call Anne. I knocked my clock off the table, along with my keys, two different one-shots and a scattering of coins before my fingers found my phone and activated it, casting a faint blueish light over my bedroom. The clock on the screen said 02:49.

I'd opened my contacts list and scrolled down to 'W' for Anne Walker before my thoughts caught up with what I was doing. What was I going to say? 'Hi, I had a bad dream and I wanted to—' . . . what? Why *did* I want to call her? Now that I thought about it, I couldn't remember why.

I stared down at the 'Call' button and just out of habit looked to see what would happen if I pressed it. Anne wasn't going to pick up, which quite frankly was exactly what you'd expect.

I put the phone down and leant back out of the window, breathing in the fresh air. The dream had shaken me, partly for what it had been but more for the memories it had pulled up. Last year I'd had a nightmare in which I'd been seeing through Rachel's eyes. Nightmares aren't anything new for me but this one had been vivid and horrible, and what I'd seen had been enough to terrify me. I'd seen Richard return, step back through a gate and into our world.

I hadn't slept well for a month. Every night there'd been the fear hovering at the back of my mind that it had been real, that it was going to start all over again. But as week after week went by and nothing happened, the fear began to recede, and slowly I was able to convince myself that it had just been a dream. If only the damn rumours would stop.

The sky had grown overcast again and the orange glow of the London street lights reflected off the bottom of the clouds. I stayed there for a good twenty minutes, looking out over the Camden night and listening to the distant traffic and the rumble of trains. When the nausea was gone and I felt calm again, I closed the window and pulled the covers up. It took me a long time to get back to sleep.

## 3

When I woke up the next morning it was raining. It wasn't a passing shower but a steady drumbeat of water, the kind of rain that settles in, puts its feet up and makes it clear that it's not going to leave. Water poured from the gutters above and spattered on the street, and cars rolled slowly through the sheets of falling raindrops, their wipers flicking back and forth. The clouds were heavy and grey with a look of permanency to them, and I was probably going to have to leave the lights on all day.

I opened the shop but business was slow: the inhabitants of London didn't seem in the mood for shopping and I couldn't really blame them. The day wore on and morning turned into afternoon but neither the weather nor the attendance improved, and when Luna finally dropped by I gave up and closed early to do inventory.

'Okay,' Luna said. 'The next one's a teacup.'

'What colour?'

'Cream.'

'You mean white?'

'Not all of us have 16-colour vision, you know. It's got a picture of a sailing boat on the side.'

'Got it,' I said, tapping the notebook. 'It's a water magic focus.'

My shop's called the Arcana Emporium, and if you live in London and want a magic item then it's the place to go. Most of the items I sell aren't actually magical, but then most of my customers don't know the difference. I do have a collection of genuine magical items in the roped-off area in the right corner, but I try to avoid selling them to anyone who doesn't know what they're doing because quite frankly it's dangerous and someone could get hurt. The downside to this is that the magic item shelves get kind of crowded. When the stacks get high enough to start causing landslides, I go through the piles and try to match the items with the notes I scrawled when I got them. This time I'd pulled in Luna to help, partly so she could get some practice at identification and partly because if you've got a boring job you might as well have some company.

'What does it do?' Luna asked.

'When you pour any liquid inside it changes the flavour over the next five minutes.'

'Sounds pretty useful.'

'Yeah, except the guy who made it had really specific tastes. His favourite seasoning was chilli sauce, so if you put anything in there then after a few minutes that's what it tastes of. Chilli-sauce-flavoured tea, chilli-sauce-flavoured beer, chilli-sauce-flavoured milk, chilli-sauce-flavoured apple juice—'

'I get it,' Luna said with a shudder. 'Storage?'

'Storage. Unless I find someone who *really* likes chilli sauce.'

Luna craned her neck down. 'The next one's a book. It doesn't have a label.'

'Colour?'

'Teal.'

'Why can't you just say "blue" or "green" like a normal person?' I flipped through the notebook. 'What's inside?'

'Hang on . . .' There was a rustling sound. 'Okay, what's next?'

'What about the book?'

'What book?'

'The one which is apparently teal, whatever that means. What's inside?'

'Uh . . .' Luna paused. 'What were we doing?'

'Looking at the book.'

'What book?'

I looked up in exasperation. 'Will you stop being a smart-arse?'

'Look, it kind of helps if you tell me what you want.'

I started to answer, then frowned. 'Hang on a second. Take a look at that book on the shelf.'

'That one?'

'Yeah, that one. Open it and tell me what you see.'

Luna picked up the cloth-bound book, the silver mist of her curse folding around it, and this time I watched closely. She opened the book, glanced briefly at the first page, then her eyes unfocused and she closed it and replaced it on the shelf before turning to me. 'Hm? What?'

'What was in that book?'

'What book?' Luna stopped and frowned. 'Wait – didn't I just say that?'

Empirical testing confirmed what I suspected: the book had some kind of mind or enchantment effect, causing anyone who opened it to replace the book and forget about it. The pages seemed blank, but it was hard to concentrate long enough to be sure. 'Huh,' I said eventually. 'I wonder what's powering it?'

'Am I some sort of guinea pig here?' Luna asked

sceptically. 'Is that why I'm the one picking these things up and you're over there going through the records?'

'Risk builds character.'

'Last month you said people trying to kill you builds character.'

'So think what a wonderful person you're growing up to be. Anyway, you need the practice.'

Luna muttered something under her breath which I didn't try too hard to hear and reached for the next thing along. 'Okay, next one's . . . a little figure of a cat.'

'Can you tell what it is?'

'Kind of . . . It feels like it's something for talking. Communicating? Does it let you talk to cats?'

'Not bad,' I said. That had been right on target. 'It's a summoning focus. Toss it over and I'll show you.'

Luna slid the figurine across the desk and I picked it up. It was made of alabaster, and I traced a finger across the smooth surface to the cat's chest and tapped it. 'See this point? When you channel your magic there, it sends out a call to the nearest feline within range of about the right size and draws it to you.'

'So it summons a housecat?'

'As long as there's one around.'

'That sounds cool. So what, you can get it to spy on people and stuff?'

'No, it acts like a normal cat. It checks to see if you've brought it anything to eat, and if not it buggers off.'

Luna gave me a look. 'You know, I think I'm starting to see why no one uses these things.'

'It works on dogs as well, if that helps.'

'I'll pass. So . . . ?'

'So?'

'How'd the meeting with Anne go?'

'I asked if she wanted my help; she said no.' I stuck the figurine into my pocket. 'Several times. By the way, you might have mentioned that Anne specifically asked you *not* to bring me in on this.'

'If I'd told you that you wouldn't have gone.'

I glared at Luna.

'Okay, okay, I'm sorry.' I've developed a fine ear for Luna's apologies over the last couple of years and this was one of her I'm-not-sorry-but-I'll-pretend-to-be varieties. 'So what did you do?'

'I left.'

Luna paused. 'That was it?'

'For the purposes of what you're talking about, yes. And because I know you're going to ask: yes, we talked about other things and no, none of it made her even the slightest bit inclined to come back. What were you expecting me to do, anyway?'

Luna scratched her hair. 'I don't know. I just thought you might be able to talk her into it.'

'You have a really inflated opinion of what I can do.'

'I've seen you talk to Dark mages who want to kill you, and you get them doing what you want inside five minutes.'

'Okay,' I said. 'There's a bit of a difference there. Tricking people who want to hurt or manipulate me? Something I'm good at. Getting people to like and trust me? Something I'm bad at. Even if I could, I'm running out of motivation to do it.'

Luna frowned. 'Why?'

'Because Anne's made it *beyond* clear that she's not interested and it's getting to the point where carrying on is starting to feel like harassing her.'

'So what should we do?'

'Nothing. I'm not Anne's master. She's an adult and it's her decision.'

'It's a *stupid* decision,' Luna said angrily. 'I don't care if it's up to her – she's my best friend. I don't want something to happen just because you two had a fight!'

I sighed. 'Look, I know this hasn't turned out well, but sometimes relationships just end. Maybe you'll get back in contact someday and maybe you won't, but forcing it doesn't help.'

Luna looked back at me, her face stubborn and set. 'I'm calling her again,' she told me, and walked out the back door. There was a bang and I heard her feet racing up the stairs. I rolled my eyes and went back to the inventory.

Luna stayed in her room for the rest of the day – strictly speaking it's not 'her' room, but it's the only spare bedroom and now that Anne and Variam don't live here any more she's the only one who uses it. I was less than halfway through the items by the time the sun had set, and was just debating whether to put in a couple more hours or leave it to another day when Luna reappeared in the doorway. 'Can you get through to Anne?' she asked.

'I have no idea.'

'Check.'

I wanted to tell Luna to go away but something in her voice made me glance at her, and the look in her eyes changed my mind. I took out my phone and studied it. 'She's not going to answer.'

'She hasn't been picking up all day.'

'So maybe she left her phone off.'

'She *never* leaves her phone off and if she does she always calls back. Even if she doesn't want to talk she leaves a message.'

I opened my mouth but Luna cut me off. 'Look, I've talked to Anne more than you have. The only times I've ever seen her do something like this is when something's wrong. I want to go and check up on her.'

I looked at the pile of un-inventoried items. 'Can it wait?'

'No,' Luna said. 'I'm worried and I'm going to her flat. Coming?'

'Why should I come?'

'Because I think something's happened to her,' Luna said. 'And if I'm right then it'll be dangerous. You're my master so you're supposed to protect me, and the only way you can do that is if you come too.'

'How about I just order you not to go?'

'I only have to follow your orders when I'm acting as your apprentice. You can't order me not to visit my friends.'

'You just said it might be dangerous and that you'd need my help.'

'So you agree it's dangerous?'

'No! There's no reason to believe it's dangerous!'

'Well, in that case, you shouldn't mind me going, should you? You know, to the place you just agreed might be dangerous. And if I do just decide to go, you can't actually stop me. So you can let me go off on my own to something you're supposed to be protecting me from, or you can come too.' Luna looked at me expectantly. 'Up to you.'

I stared at her.

'You are the most annoying apprentice I've ever met,' I told Luna fifteen minutes later.

We were in a taxi heading south, the rain drumming on the roof as the wipers swept back and forth across the windscreen. Other cars swooshed past, their lights turning them into luminous ghosts though the curtain of water. The taxi driver, a heavyset man with close-cropped black hair, had taken one look as we got in and wisely elected to keep his mouth shut.

'You can shout at me afterwards,' Luna said. She was in the back seat and looking out at the rain.

'Why did I get stuck with you? Everyone else gets apprentices who do as they're told.'

'Right, like you did?'

We would have kept arguing, but the presence of the taxi driver put a lid on how much we could say and the argument tailed off into silence, which was probably for the best. Luna kept staring out the window as we crossed London.

The weather hadn't improved by the time we reached Honor Oak. I paid the driver and watched the taxi disappear into the rain. 'So now what?' Luna asked. She'd brought along a big golf umbrella and was quite dry. The umbrella was more than big enough to share, except that her curse meant that I couldn't get close enough and had to stand out in the rain getting wet instead, which seemed highly unfair.

'Wait out here and watch the door,' I said shortly. The weather wasn't improving my mood. 'I'll check her flat and then we'll go.' I headed for the building without waiting for an answer.

Once I was inside, I shook water out of my hair and started upstairs. I hadn't path-walked to see what would happen when I knocked on the door — it's a hassle to do it while your movements are under the control of a driver and quite frankly it hadn't been worth the effort. I tried it now and found to my absolute lack of surprise that Anne wasn't going to answer.

I wanted to walk away, but I knew Luna would just do something even more annoying if I didn't do a proper check. I climbed the stairs to Anne's flat. There weren't any would-be patients this time. I knelt on the concrete landing, put my ear to the wooden door, took out my phone and called Anne's number, then let out my breath and listened.

After a moment, I heard the faint sounds of Anne's ringtone through the wood. Apparently she hadn't changed it since last year. It rang, then went to voicemail. I redialled and got the same result. Looking through the futures I could tell she wasn't going to answer.

I looked to see what would happen if I just kicked the door down. Nothing. She definitely wasn't in.

So why had she left her phone?

It probably didn't mean anything, but it was enough to make me stick around. I glanced around to make sure no one was watching, then took out my picks and got to work on the door. It wasn't a particularly good lock and after only a few minutes it clicked open. I stepped though and shut the door behind me. Anne *really* needed better security in this place.

The flat was pitch-black and I stood for a minute in the darkness, letting my eyes adjust. There was no sound in the present and no movement in the future. I took out a torch and clicked it on; the entry corridor was bare and so was the room I'd been in before. I moved deeper into the flat. The bathroom was neat and clean and empty, bottles stacked by the shower and on the glass shelf above the sink. In the kitchen, dishes and cooking pans for a meal for one had been washed and were sitting in the rack by the sink. Flashing my light over them, I saw that they were dry.

Still nothing definite. If Anne suddenly showed up (which, so far, I had no reason to believe wouldn't happen) then I'd have serious trouble explaining what I was doing here. All the same something felt off – I couldn't put my finger on exactly what it was, but something was making me feel uneasy and I've learned to listen to those instincts. The only room I hadn't checked was the bedroom, and the door was ajar. I slipped the sleeve of my coat down over my hand so that it covered my fingers, then pushed it open.

Anne's bedroom was small, sized for only one person, with a window that would have given a view over the nature reserve if the curtains hadn't been drawn. It smelt of some fragrance I couldn't place but which made me think of flowers. Again, most of the room was neat and tidy – closed cupboard, clean desk, clothes folded on a chair – except for two things. The first thing was that the bed wasn't made. The bedclothes had been pulled off and were lying in a trampled heap half on and half off the floor.

The second thing was that the bedside table had been knocked over.

I crouched beside it, careful not to touch anything. The contents of the table had been scattered across the carpet and the wooden planks. In the middle of the mess was Anne's phone: it had been charging and the power lead was still plugged in, tethering it to the wall socket. There'd been a glass on the table and it had shattered when it had hit the floor, leaving a spray of shards all the way to the wall. They glinted in the light of my torch; as I studied them I saw that several had been crushed, as though from footsteps. Spread between the broken glass were the remaining contents of the table: a bedside lamp, small plastic jars of face cream, cotton buds, a set of keys, a hairbrush, nail polish, hand lotion . . . a wallet. Looking into the futures in which I opened it, I saw money and a bank card.

If Anne was going out, why would she leave her phone *and* her keys *and* her wallet?

I wasn't just uneasy now – I was worried. I quickly checked the rest of the room. The window was closed and locked from the inside and didn't show any signs of tampering. I'd already seen that the front door had been locked and unforced. As far as I can see, there weren't any other ways in.

What had happened here?

I saw that my phone was going to ring; it was Luna. I took it out and answered before it could sound. 'I'm inside.'

'Someone just went into the building,' Luna said. Her voice was sharp and tense. 'I couldn't get a good look, but I think it was a woman. Too big to be Anne.'

'Okay. Stay where you are and text if anyone follows.' I set my phone to silent and dropped it into my pocket, already scanning ahead to see if the person Luna had spotted was coming here.

They were, and they were close; less than thirty seconds out. The bedroom was the worst place for me to be: too small, only one exit, and if the new visitor was here for the same reason I was then it would be the place they'd search most closely. I switched off my torch and moved back to the entry room, relying on my diviner's senses to navigate. I could hear footsteps approaching the door. They'd be opening it with a key . . . How did they have a key? The room didn't have many hiding places, so I stepped behind the door. Even if they switched the light on I'd be out of sight.

The key turned in the lock and the door swung open. Skimming through the futures I could see violence – were they going to detect me? What did I need to do to stay hidden? Heavy footfalls approached. Every future held confrontation or combat, there didn't seem to be any way of avoiding – they knew I was there. In fact, they knew *exactly* where I was and they were coming for me.

So much for the subtle approach.

The footsteps entered the room, passing me by on the other side of the open door. They checked and turned, and I knew my mystery guest was about to yank the door open and pull me out. *Screw that.* I kicked the door into them as they reached for it and followed it out with a double-handed shove.

I caught her (it was definitely a her) by surprise, but she was big and tough and I didn't push her back far. It was still pitch-black and I tried to slip past, picking out the futures in which I found the gap, but she moved to block me and that future winked out. She tried a grab; I ducked and heard her arm swoosh over my head as I hit her in the gut, left and right. I'd used an open-palm strike and it was just as well: her body felt like rock and if I'd punched I probably would have broken my knuckles. She aimed a knee at my head which would have knocked me out if it had connected; I half-blocked it and while I was still staggering from that she grabbed me and did her level best to slam me into the floor.

The two of us struggled in the darkness, twisting and stumbling. The woman was strong, *really* strong, and I could feel magic radiating from her limbs and body. I knew I wasn't going to win a wrestling match, and I abruptly stopped resisting and went with the throw, rolling backwards on the carpet, bristles digging into my neck and skin as I came over and back to my feet. The movement had reversed the hold and now I had her arm twisted around, but even with the leverage I couldn't force her down and she slammed me into the door, sending pain stabbing through my back. I stomped on the side of her knee, making her stagger, then yanked an item from my belt and stabbed her with it.

The focus was a thin sliver of metal, and if there had been any light it would have looked silver. Its tip was blunt but as it struck it discharged the energy stored inside it, sending it flashing out and though her body. The magic radiating from her suddenly vanished.

Knocking out the woman's defensive spells accomplished what hitting her hadn't. She swore and let go, jumping back out of range. I took one step towards the doorway, then paused. In my mage's sight I could see the brownish glow of earth magic as the woman recast her spells, rebuilding her defences. The pattern was familiar . . . 'Caldera?'

Caldera had been about to advance again, but now she stopped. 'Who are you?'

'Who am *I*? What the hell are you doing?'

'This is private property,' Caldera said sharply. 'Identify yourself.'

'I'm not talking to you in the dark. Switch the damn light on.'

There was a suspicious silence, then Caldera moved to the wall and light flooded the room with a click. We stood and blinked at each other for a moment. 'Verus?' Caldera said in disbelief.

'What are you doing here?'

'What are *you* doing here?'

'I asked first.'

'This isn't a bloody playground,' Caldera said in annoyance. 'You're on Council property.'

Caldera is thirty or so, with a round face and red cheeks. She's half a foot shorter than me and a lot wider, with a body that's heavy with fat and muscle, and she's a Council Keeper of the Order of the Star, which in magical terms is something like a cross between political investigator and military police. Caldera's on the 'military police' end of the scale, but I've worked with her a few times over the past year. I wouldn't say we're friends, but she's always kept her word and I'd trust her more than any other Keeper I can think of. Whether she felt the same way about me was another question, although given the circumstances it looked as though I might be about to find out.

'I don't know about the Council property part,' I said, 'but I do know that a friend of mine lives here.' Stretching the truth twice in one sentence, but Caldera probably didn't know that . . . 'You have any idea where she's gone?'

'When did you last see her?'

*Just last night; we were having an argument alone in the woods right before she disappeared . . .* Yeah, that was going to get a great reaction. 'Why are you asking?' I said, then raised my hands. 'Okay, okay, look. There's a mage living here by the name of Anne Walker, as I'm guessing you already know or you wouldn't be here. My apprentice has been trying to call her all day and she hasn't been picking up, so I headed over to see if she was all right.'

'Then what was the idea of picking a fight with me?'

'You started it.'

'You're a suspect at a potential crime scene,' Caldera said. I noticed she said *you're* instead of *you were*. 'You make a habit of attacking Keepers on official business?'

'For all I knew, *you* were a subject at a potential crime scene. And if you're acting in your capacity as a Keeper, maybe you should announce that first. Seriously, this is, what, the second time you've had a go at throwing me around? Were you disappointed you didn't get a good enough fight the first try?'

Caldera made an exasperated noise. 'I don't have time to argue with you. Let me do my job, all right?'

'There's something I'd better show you first,' I said, becoming serious. 'If you're here for the same reason I am, you're going to want to take a look at this.'

Once in Anne's bedroom, Caldera made a beeline for the overturned table and crouched next to it, frowning. 'Did you touch anything?'

'No.'

Caldera twisted her neck to stare at me. 'You sure?'

'This is how it looked when I got here.'

Caldera grunted and turned back to the scattered debris. I stayed quiet and didn't bug her. 'I'm going to make a call,' she said at last, rising to her feet. 'You stay here. If you do a runner I'll arrest you. Clear?'

'The threats don't help, you know,' I said mildly. 'Yes, you're clear.'

Caldera went out into the entry corridor and I promptly

started looking into the futures to eavesdrop. A brisk contest of stealth and perception took place between hypothetical future me and hypothetical future Caldera, which ended with me able to pick out odd words of her half of the conversation. She was telling someone to come here and to hurry. I took the opportunity to send Luna a message updating her on what was going on.

'Right,' Caldera said once she'd finished, dropping her phone into her pocket as she re-entered the bedroom. 'When did you last see Miss Walker? And don't dodge the question this time.'

Apparently my earlier evasion hadn't been all that subtle. I'd had time to think about how to answer and had decided to go with the truth – it's easier to remember and you don't have to worry so much about being caught out. 'Last night,' I began, and gave Caldera a short account of the evening, accurate as far as it went but with the more personal details edited out.

'. . . and that was the last time I saw her,' I finished.

'Has anybody else you know had any contact with her since then?'

'No. I told you, we haven't heard anything else.'

Caldera grunted and I knew she'd be checking up on that later. 'Okay, I've answered your questions,' I said. 'Now why are *you* here?'

'This is Council property.'

'That's not an answer.'

'Sorry. Classified.'

I studied Caldera and folded my arms.

Caldera glanced around. 'You need to clear the area. There'll be someone—'

'Keepers from the Order of the Star don't get sent on

property inspections,' I said. 'You'd only be here if there was something involving the Concord of the Council.' I looked at Caldera thoughtfully. 'I'm guessing something triggered a flag. Maybe a report . . . or some kind of alarm? Otherwise you wouldn't have assumed I was a suspect.'

Caldera looked back at me without expression. 'But your remit is the Concord,' I said. 'Anne's not a recognised mage or an apprentice of one. You shouldn't have any reason to be here . . . unless someone from the Council specifically asked you to . . .' I started scanning through the futures. Who was Caldera waiting for?

'You can go now,' Caldera said.

The future I was looking for came into focus and I snapped my fingers. 'Sonder.' I pointed at Caldera. 'He's the reason you're here. And you're waiting for him to show up so he can look back to see what happened.' I paused. 'So do you still need me to go? I'm pretty sure I already know anything I'd learn from seeing Sonder show up, but if it's important . . .'

Caldera sighed. 'Goddamn it. Do you have any idea how annoying you are?'

That was more or less what I'd said to Luna. Maybe I *was* teaching her bad habits. 'Look, I'm sorry about the fight. If I'd known it was you—'

'You know what?' Caldera said. 'I'm going to do what I ought to do more often. I'm making you someone else's problem.'

We stood in silence for a little while. My chest and hands still ached a little from the scuffle. 'So, you practise judo?' I asked. 'That felt like a hip throw.'

'Just the techniques,' Caldera said. 'I don't have a belt.' She eyed me. 'What was that thing you hit me with?'

'Dispelling focus.'

'You get into fights with mages that often?'

'It's meant more for constructs. Just out of curiosity, how much of that strength of yours is muscle and how much is magic?'

'Drop by the gym some day and find out.'

I grinned at her. 'Is that a challenge?'

Caldera's phone rang and she moved off again to answer it. I took the opportunity to send Luna another message, telling her where to run into Sonder. He was only a few minutes out, and it didn't take long before I heard his voice and Luna's echoing up the stairs.

Sonder is a Light mage with messy hair and glasses, twenty-two years old but still with a teenager's awkwardness. He's actually younger than Luna, Anne and Variam, but he's a journeyman mage while they're still apprentices, despite the fact that all three could probably take him in a fight. (In theory your rank in the Light Council is a reflection of your skill as a mage, but in practice good connections count for a lot more than ability, which I suppose isn't very different from most jobs.)

Sonder and I used to get on pretty well, at least until last year. Anne wasn't the only mage who'd had a problem with what I'd done to the Nightstalkers; Sonder really isn't comfortable with violence and his finding out how I'd dealt with the adepts last summer had pretty much killed our friendship. I'd made a few attempts to get back in touch with him and we'd met once or twice, but there had been a distance in his manner which hadn't been there before. I wasn't expecting this conversation to go well.

Sonder entered Anne's flat and stopped as he saw me. 'Why are *you* here?'

I sighed. When you're dealing with people who aren't going to be happy to see you, being able to see the future isn't as much fun as you'd think. 'Is everyone going to say that?'

Sonder turned to Caldera. 'What's he doing here?'

Caldera finished her call and started typing into her phone instead, giving Sonder a shrug. 'He says same reason as you.'

Luna stuck her head in around the door. 'Something wrong?'

Sonder turned distractedly from her to Caldera. 'Can't you get rid of him?'

'It's your investigation,' Caldera told Sonder without looking up.

I blinked. *Sonder's* investigation?

'I don't think you should be here,' Sonder told me.

'Not this again,' I said. 'Look, I've just spent half an hour telling the story to Caldera. Are you here because of Anne or not?'

'Yes, but—'

'Then you need to check the bedroom. I think something's happened to her and whatever it is, it's a lot more important than arguing with me. If you look back and there's nothing to see then great, you can interrogate me afterwards. But if something *has* happened then we're wasting time we probably don't have.'

'Sonder?' Luna said. 'What's the problem?'

Sonder hesitated. It was obvious he didn't want me around, but he was rational enough to realise that what I was saying made sense. And there was another factor, which had been behind my reason to send Luna after him: Sonder's had a not-very-subtle crush on Luna for years, and he had to be aware that starting a fight with me in front of her wouldn't end well.

'All right,' Sonder said at last with poor grace. He started past me.

'The bedroom's—' I began as Sonder passed.

'I know where it is.'

I watched Sonder go then turned to Caldera, who'd been observing the whole thing with undisguised amusement. 'Why is it that whenever I actually try to help someone I never get any credit for it?'

'Now you know what every day of my job's like,' Caldera said. 'Quit whining; you've got it easy.'

'What's the problem?' Luna asked.

'Don't ask. Did Sonder tell you why he was here?'

'Yeah, he said there was an alarm triggered last night.' Luna looked worried. 'Some kind of passive sensor. Where's Anne?'

'Sonder'll know what happened soon enough.' I knew that if I walked into the bedroom right now I'd see him staring into space, lost in the trance of his timesight. I looked at Caldera. 'How did you get involved?'

'How do you think?'

'Look, it's not that I'm not grateful for having you around,' I said. 'But given that Anne isn't covered by the Concord, why *are* you here?'

Caldera paused for a moment. 'Why are *you* here?'

'Because I'm worried about Anne,' I said. 'Luna thinks something might have happened and I think she's right.' Not to mention that I was looking into the future to see what Sonder was going to tell us, and the signs were looking worse and worse.

'That's the only reason?' Caldera said. 'No vigilantes

chasing you this time? You doing this just to save your own neck?'

'No.'

Caldera studied me for a long moment and I looked back at her, holding her gaze. 'My boss said the same thing you did,' she said at last. 'That it wasn't a Concord matter.'

'And?'

'And Sonder pointed out that the last person known to have attacked Miss Walker was someone who very definitely *does* come under our jurisdiction. A mage named Crystal who's a wanted fugitive.'

'Ah,' I said. Crystal is a mind magic user and an ex-Light mage who came to the Council's attention a year and a half ago when she made use of her abilities and position to kidnap several Light apprentices, all of whom ended up murdered in a particularly horrific way. The Council might not care much about non-Light apprentices but that is very definitely *not* the case when it comes to their *own* apprentices, and they'd gone after Crystal in a fury. She'd managed to evade capture so far, but she was still on the Council's most-wanted list and even the off-chance of finding her would be enough to get the Keeper orders *very* interested. 'And if investigating that should happen to mean helping Anne . . . ?'

'Well, that's just the way it goes, isn't it?'

I gave Caldera a half-smile, but it faded quickly. Sonder might have just made that argument to enlist Caldera's help, but the more I thought about it, the more plausible it sounded. The last in the series of apprentices that Crystal had kidnapped back then had been Anne, and Crystal hadn't picked her at random – she'd been researching a method of magical immortality, and she'd come to believe that by taking Anne's life she could extend her own. We'd stopped Crystal before she could complete her ritual . . . but nothing was stopping her from trying again.

Over the last hour my priorities had shifted. Step by step, the evidence for what had happened to Anne had gotten worse and worse, and my earlier worries about coming across as pushy seemed very childish now. If it really *had* been Crystal, we might already be too late.

Luna looked bleak, and I knew she was thinking the same thing. Caldera seemed less anxious, but in an unpleasant sort of way this was probably something she was used to. The Order of the Star are the ones among the Keepers who deal with crimes involving Dark mages: kidnap and murder are old hat as far as they're concerned. No one broke the silence, and I was left alone with my thoughts, waiting for Sonder to return.

When Sonder came back, the news was bad enough that he didn't put up even a token protest about me listening in.

Time magic falls into two branches: direct manipulation of the flow of time, such as accelerating or slowing the timestream, and perception of past events. Sonder's competent at the first, but it's timesight he's really good at. By using his magic he can look back into the past of his current location, perceiving what happened at an earlier point in time. He can only see what his ordinary senses would, but it's still an incredibly powerful tool for investigation. The more recent the event, the easier it is to view, which meant that for Sonder, seeing what had happened last night was very, very simple.

Anne had been kidnapped. Her attackers had gated into the living room, walked into her bedroom as she slept, and hit her with a bolt of lightning before she'd even woken up. There had been two of them, both mages, and Sonder hadn't been able to identify either. Caldera questioned Sonder meticulously for descriptions, but as they'd both worn ski masks there was little Sonder had been able to see. Both were male, one light-skinned and one dark, but beyond that all he could give were vague guesses as to height and weight. Anne had apparently been knocked out by the second lightning blast, and while one of them went back to recast the gateway the other had heaved her up with a view to dragging her through.

But that was where things had gone wrong.

I hadn't known everything that Sonder was going to say – conversations are hard to predict, and while you can get a general impression if you concentrate it's usually easier just to wait for them to tell it to you – but I'd known the news was bad. As he kept talking, though, something made me look up. Sonder *was* acting as though the news was bad, but there was more. 'It was here,' Sonder said, pointing to a spot in the middle of the room. 'That one had just opened a gate and he was about to carry Anne through.'

'Then what happened?' Caldera asked.

'There was a green flash and this guy just dropped. He was—'

'Which guy?' Caldera said.

'The one carrying Anne.'

'I thought she wasn't awake?'

'That was what I thought too,' Sonder said excitedly. 'Anyway, he goes down just here and she falls on top of him, but the gate's still up. I think he must have been using a focus with a safety buffer, because I don't think he could have kept concentration with—'

'Forget about the focus,' Caldera said. 'What happened next?'

'Anne gets up here and the other guy comes out of the bedroom.' Sonder pointed back towards the door. 'I think the one on the ground was half-stunned but he hit Anne with another spell, death magic I think – it hurt her but it didn't stop her. The other one aimed another lightning bolt, but she jumped back through the gateway . . .' Sonder shifted position, squinting as if trying to see something.

'And then?' Caldera prompted.

Sonder stared at her. 'It closed.'

'What closed? The gate?'

Sonder nodded uncertainly. 'The cut-off must have triggered.'

'So she ended up on the other side of the gate, and the two of them were left back here?'

'Where did the gate go?' Luna asked.

'Hang on a second,' Sonder said, frowning. He shifted position, peering from side to side, while I made myself stay still. I wanted to tell him to hurry up, but I knew that would just make things worse.

'The gate's black,' Sonder said at last.

'So what, somewhere dark?' Caldera said.

'No, if it were just dark I'd be able to see reflected light from the room. I think it's masked.'

'No signature?'

'No.'

Caldera frowned, thinking. 'So these two were left behind? What did they do?'

According to Sonder they'd started arguing. It had taken them a couple of minutes to finish blaming each other and follow her, reopening the same gate and disappearing through. Caldera started cross-questioning Sonder, picking through their conversation for clues, but my thoughts were elsewhere.

It was still bad news, but at least whoever Anne's attackers were, they weren't having it all their own way. They'd underestimated her, and she'd managed to turn the tables on them and get away though the gate . . . but where? If the gate had been masked then Sonder wouldn't be able to see where it led, no matter how long he tried. That meant the only clue we had was the people who'd created it. Where would two hostile mages want to take a kidnapped and unconscious life apprentice?

I didn't know, but I didn't think it was going to be anywhere pleasant.

Sonder and Caldera were winding down, and Sonder belatedly seemed to realise that I was there. 'We need to find her,' he told me. The tone of his voice made it clear that the 'we' wasn't meant to be inclusive.

'Us as well,' I said.

Sonder hesitated. I knew he was about to object, but that future faded out as he reconsidered. He looked at Caldera.

'I'm not crazy about it,' Caldera said. 'But we're not exactly overstaffed.'

'All right,' Sonder said reluctantly. He braced himself and turned to me. 'But I'm in charge, not you. You have to follow my orders.'

I kept my face carefully straight. 'Okay.'

Sonder gave me a suspicious look, then Caldera told him she was going to start gathering the materials for a tracer spell and he got distracted. I arranged with Caldera to meet tomorrow, and left with Luna before Sonder could change his mind.

'Who were they?' Luna said once we were out of the flat. 'Why would they want to go after Anne?'

'Until we get something more concrete, there's no point guessing. Have you talked to Vari?'

'Yeah, I just got a text. He hasn't heard from her.'

I grimaced, even though it had been what I was expecting. 'She left her phone back there,' Luna said. 'Maybe that's why she hasn't called?'

'It's been nearly a full day,' I said. 'She should have been able to figure out a way to get in touch . . .' I shook my head. 'I want you to find Vari. Tell him everything and make sure he's there tomorrow. We're going to need all the help we can get and he knows Anne better than anyone.'

Luna nodded. 'What are you going to do?'

'Dig up whatever I can find. We need to move fast.'

By the time I got back to my flat, it was late. I spent an hour or two calling around and checking my contacts. None of them had seen Anne, which wasn't surprising – as far as they were concerned, she was just another apprentice. I put the word out that I was in the market for news on Anne's whereabouts and got a few promises to look into it, but I didn't hold out much hope. If any of them found her, it'd be pure luck.

The ugly thing was that what had just happened to Anne wasn't all that unusual. Young people in the magical world go missing a lot, and the reasons are rarely good. If you have a master, you're relatively safe – you have rights under the Concord, and (more importantly) there's someone who'll care if you go missing and who's powerful enough to do something about it. But if you're an adept or a novice mage on your own, then you're in very real danger. The disappearance rate of unattached adepts and mages in the teenage bracket is worryingly high, and while some of those disappearances are benign (abandoning their magic, choosing to stay away from the magical community, signing up as apprentice to a secretive mage), most aren't. It used to be that young and inexperienced mages were the favourite prey of non-human magical predators. Nowadays that particular spot on the food chain has been taken over by *human* magical predators, and being the same species doesn't make them any less cruel.

Luna had asked why a mage would go after Anne; there were a lot of answers to that question and none were good. Some mages like taking slaves; Dark mages in particular. The more able and powerful the slave, the more prestige they bring, and young and attractive ones are favoured. There are mages like Crystal who prefer human subjects for their experiments, and since those experiments generally involve magic, magic-using subjects are correspondingly valuable. Some mages target others for Harvesting, turning their victims into fuel sources. And then there are other reasons, running the gamut from the brutal and logical to the totally incomprehensible. In the end, all the reasons come down to the same thing: because they want to, and because they can.

Enslavement, imprisonment, experimentation, death . . . it wasn't a happy picture. For all I knew Anne's fate was being decided right now, and I couldn't think of a single thing to do about it. Divination is great for finding people, but only if you know where to look: trying to find a specific person by walking down random futures has about the same chance of working as trying to get someone's phone number by dialling random digits. Without something to go on there wasn't much I could do.

The only plan I could think of that had a chance of working was to use Elsewhere, the half-real place between dreams and thoughts that I've used before. If you know someone well enough, you can touch their dreams through Elsewhere; talk to them across worlds. It's a dangerous place and I've tried to avoid it in the past year – too many narrow escapes – but right now it was the best chance I had. I undressed, switched off the lights and lay in bed staring up at the ceiling, searching through the futures to see if a visit to Elsewhere would find Anne.

It didn't work. I lay awake in bed for a long time, searching back and forth through the hours of the night, but every time I came up dry. Either Anne wasn't asleep, or there was some other reason I couldn't reach her. At last exhaustion caught up with me and I fell into restless dreams where I was lost in an endless maze of corridors, trying to reach someone whom I could hear calling but who never seemed to come any closer. There was somebody following me but I couldn't see who it was, and every time I turned on them their footsteps would fade into silence and I was left alone.

# 4

It was early next morning.

Sonder's flat is in St John's Wood, a London borough just north-west of the city centre. It's famous for the Lord's cricket ground and for being one of the most expensive places to live in all of Britain, if not Europe. I used to come by often, but it had been nearly a year since my last visit.

The interior of the flat was a mess: it didn't look as though Sonder had tidied up since the last time I'd been here. Dust-covered computer equipment competed for shelf space with stacks of books: the books tended to win the argument, leaving cables and electronics to be pushed with old piles of paper into the corners. A new and well-cared-for PC sat on the desk, along with piles of notes and empty glasses. Caldera, Variam, Luna and I were spaced around the room on whatever seating arrangements we could get, while Sonder was in front of the desk balancing a white-board on a stand. He'd brought a set of markers and was testing them on the board to see if they worked.

'What's with the board?' Variam said. He'd come down to London instantly upon Luna's call and she'd caught him up on what had happened.

'Maybe it's Lupus,' Luna suggested with a grin.

'Nah,' Variam said. 'It's never Lupus.'

Sonder shot a slightly harassed look at them. 'What?'

'Now is not the time,' Caldera said, and Luna and Variam's grins vanished. There was an uncomfortable silence for a moment, then Caldera gave Sonder a go-ahead nod.

'Right,' Sonder said nervously, fiddling with a board marker. 'Um. Okay. We need to find out where Anne is and what's happened to her, and get her back.'

'Then why are we sitting here?' Variam said.

'We need to figure out what to do,' Sonder said. 'We don't know who's behind this, so—'

'Yes we do. His name's Sagash.'

'That hasn't been proved. Crystal has a more recent record of—'

'Sagash kidnapped Anne once already,' Variam snapped. 'How much more proof do you need?'

'We can't just go—'

'Variam,' Caldera said. 'Do you have evidence that Sagash was behind the attack?'

'All we have to do is go to his shadow realm and—'

'Do you have *evidence* that Sagash was behind the attack?'

Variam glowered.

'I don't know what your master's been teaching you,' Caldera said, 'but Keepers do not get to kick a mage's door down and go in shooting just because they *might* have done something.'

'I've seen Keepers do a lot more than that.'

'With evidence,' Caldera said. 'So far we have nothing linking the two suspects to Sagash. Unless there's something you're keeping from us?'

Variam was silent. Caldera nodded again to Sonder. 'Go on.'

'Okay,' Sonder said, sounding slightly annoyed. 'So, um . . . First we have the two mages who carried out the attack.' He wrote ATTACKERS in the top right of the whiteboard in blue marker and drew a circle around the word.

'We don't have very much information on them, but I've put what we do know on these handouts. So, uh, take one before you go and see if you can find any leads.'

*Handouts*, I thought. *Right.*

Sonder had written SUSPECTS in the top left, underlined it and written CRYSTAL underneath. 'So while we're doing that, I think we should start looking at who might be behind this. We've agreed that the most likely—'

'Point of order,' I said, raising a finger. 'How do we know someone's behind this, rather than those two attackers acting on their own?'

'I don't think that's helpful,' Sonder said with a frown.

'Okay,' I said. 'Why do *you* think that someone's behind this?'

'Ah . . .' Sonder looked at Caldera.

'Typically in these kinds of cases the victim has had prior contact with the perpetrator,' Caldera said. 'When we check the history, about eighty per cent of the time we find an escalating series of incidents. The abduction's just the final step. In Anne's case, she's been targeted for similar attacks on two previous occasions.'

'Sagash and Crystal,' I said. 'So you think this was aimed at Anne specifically?'

'So far I'd say this has features in common with a targeted attack. Random abductions by strangers are very rare. The way it was carried out combined with the fact that our tracers haven't been working would suggest advance planning.'

'Do you think—?'

'Excuse me?' Sonder said. He was giving me an annoyed look. 'Could you let me finish, please?'

Luna raised her eyebrows. I sat back in my chair.

'Thank you,' Sonder said. 'As I was saying, I think Crystal should be our primary suspect. She did something like this to Anne once already and she's got a clear motivation for trying again.'

'It wasn't Crystal who snatched Anne in Fountain Reach,' Variam said with a frown. 'It was Vitus.'

'She was still involved.'

'Ah, question?' Luna said, raising a hand. 'Isn't Crystal wanted for murder?'

'Yes, that's the point.'

'So the Council hasn't found her, or they would have tried and executed her already, right?'

'Yes . . .'

'So if *they* can't find her, how are *we* going to find her?' Luna asked. 'And if we can't find her, what's the point of making her a suspect?'

'It's just the most logical possibility,' Sonder said. He was looking harassed again.

'Last time Crystal used a shroud,' Variam said. 'Why not this time?'

'She can't move as freely now. There's no reason to—'

'Let's move on,' Caldera said.

'Right,' Sonder said. 'The next possibility is the rakshasa Jagadev.'

Luna and Variam shared a surprised look as Sonder wrote JAGADEV on the board. 'Didn't he sponsor you and Anne?' Luna asked Variam.

'He fell out with her afterwards,' Sonder said. His eyes flicked to me. 'There were . . . issues.'

'Yeah, but he still helped us,' Variam said with a frown. 'I'm not saying I like the guy but . . .'

I stayed silent. Variam and Anne didn't know why

Jagadev had banished them, but I did. In fact, I was the one who had made it happen. And Sonder (as far as I knew) was the only other person who knew the secret, given that it was his research that had uncovered it.

But Sonder stayed quiet. 'There are reasons to be suspicious of Jagadev,' Caldera said when Sonder didn't speak. 'I can't give you most of the details because you're not cleared for them. No, not even you, Variam. Let's just say that the Order of the Star has abundant evidence that Jagadev is mixed up in some very shady stuff.'

'Is he being investigated?' Luna asked.

'Jagadev is very careful never to be directly implicated in anything,' Caldera said. 'He works through proxies and cat's-paws. He's suspected of being connected to half the high-profile magical crimes in the country, but we don't have any proof. And he's got influence on the Council. Investigations which target him have a bad habit of getting their resources pulled.'

'He sounds almost as impossible a target as Crystal,' I said.

Caldera shook her head. 'Jagadev's not untouchable. Someday he'll slip up. We just need to be patient.'

'What about Sagash?' Variam said.

'The *final* suspect is Sagash,' Sonder said, writing the last name on the board. 'So far there's been no evidence of any connection between him and Anne—'

'You mean since we shot our way out of his shadow realm?'

'Maybe you ought to tell them the story,' Luna said, intervening before the conversation could get derailed further.

I looked at Variam, as did Sonder and Caldera. 'Fine,' Variam said, obviously reluctant. 'Back when Anne and I were in school we had a teacher who was a sensitive who wanted to be a mage. She got her hands on a focus somehow and started Harvesting kids.'

'Is this in Keeper records?' Caldera asked.

'No,' Variam said shortly. 'People died and so did she – we didn't know at the time; we just thought she'd gone somewhere else. A few years passed and then Sagash showed up. Turned out the teacher had been his ex and he was pissed. He snatched Anne right out of school and took her to his shadow realm, this huge castle in the middle of the sea. Anne was supposed to be his apprentice as payment for the whole thing – she didn't want to but he didn't give her much choice. I went looking for them, I found them, there was a big fight and we got out. That's it.'

'Who is Sagash, anyway?' Luna asked. 'You and Anne talk about him sometimes but . . .'

'Dark death mage,' Caldera said. 'We don't know much about him, but what we do know matches with Variam's experience. He's supposed to be secretive to the point of paranoia – hardly ever leaves his personal shadow realm. Apart from Variam, I don't know of any Light mage who's been inside. We've had a few reports, mostly from independents who visited at some time or another, but it's all out of date. Sagash generally stays off our radar, and he's powerful enough that people leave him alone.'

'Where's the shadow realm linked to?' I said.

'Never managed to find out,' Variam said.

'Excuse me?' Sonder said. 'I think we're getting off topic.' He tapped the board with the marker pen. 'Our focus ought to be Crystal.'

'Screw Crystal,' Variam said.

'She's the most likely suspect!'

'Do we have anything linking these guys to her?' Luna asked. 'Because if not, I'm kind of with Vari.'

Sonder was looking frustrated again. 'We don't have any evidence that they were linked to Sagash either.'

'Right now I don't think it matters,' I said. Sonder, Variam and Luna turned to me and I glanced between them. 'We don't have any clue as to Crystal's location and we don't have any evidence for Sagash's involvement. We can't effectively go after either of them.'

'Which brings us to what we *should* be doing,' Caldera said. 'Sonder and I are going to work the forensic end of this. We're waiting on lab analysis of the samples we took from the flat, and Sonder's going to scan other periods to see if we can pick anything up. Honestly, none of you can be much help with that. You can't help Sonder, and you're not cleared for Keeper facilities. Except you, Variam, but it'd be probationary and I think there's something more useful you could be doing.'

Variam looked alert. 'The fact that Anne disappeared so soon after her removal from the apprentice programme probably isn't a coincidence,' Caldera said. 'It's likely that the information spread from there to the people behind the attack. If we work on that assumption, then we may be able to find the ones behind it.' Caldera glanced at Luna and Variam. 'Luna, if you're willing to do it, I think you'd be best placed to investigate this angle. You're the only one active in the London apprentice programme, and the other apprentices will be more willing to talk to you. Before you agree, bear in mind that this might be dangerous. You're not Keeper personnel, so I can't ask you to do this without your consent and that of your master.'

Luna looked at me. 'I'm willing if you are,' I said.

Luna nodded. 'I'll do it.'

'Variam, I want you to start checking up on Anne's friends and acquaintances,' Caldera said. 'Concentrate on anyone she's been in contact with recently, and if you find any leads report them to me immediately. You will NOT approach Sagash or anyone connected to Sagash, and that's an order. Your master seconded you to me for this, and you'll do what I say or you're off the case. Clear?'

Variam didn't look happy. 'I get it.'

'You get it, or you're going to do it?'

'No going near Sagash. I got it.'

'Verus,' Caldera said. 'I'm going to need your help for tonight. There's an audience scheduled to take place at the Tiger's Palace. It'll be the largest concentration of Dark mages this month in all of the British Isles.'

'Sounds lovely. How's that going to help?'

'It's Jagadev's club and Sagash is supposed to be on the guest list. That's two out of our three suspects in one place, and even if they don't have anything to do with it there's a good chance someone there will know someone who does.'

'And you're planning to go?' I asked.

'I'm going with Sonder. As I understand it you've got some past experience with the place. If you could go over the layout and anything else you know before we go in, that'd be helpful.'

'Not planning to take anyone else?'

'We don't need anyone else,' Sonder said.

I looked between Sonder and Caldera, then shrugged. 'Okay.'

'Anyone have any questions?' Caldera asked, looking around. No one answered and after a pause she nodded.

'All right. Verus, I'll meet you at midday. You've all got your tasks. Let's get to work.'

'I thought Sonder was supposed to be smart,' Variam said once we were outside and walking down the street.

'There's a reason he's playing it this way,' I said. Luna, Variam and I were out in St John's Wood, heading towards the tube station. Sonder and Caldera had stayed behind to do something else, the details of which they hadn't elected to share.

'It's Sagash,' Variam said.

'It might be any of the three, or someone completely different,' I said. 'Sonder knows that; he's not stupid.'

'So why was he acting so sure it was Crystal?' Luna asked.

'You know which order Caldera is a member of?'

'Order of the Star,' Variam said.

'Remember what their remit is?' I asked Luna.

Luna rolled her eyes slightly, but didn't complain about me testing her. 'First and second clauses of the Concord,' she recited. 'They're supposed to keep the peace in magical society, punish anyone who ticks off the Council.'

'Second clause of the Concord only forbids hostile action against *recognised* mages and apprentices,' I said. 'Crystal broke that clause when she helped kill off those apprentices in Fountain Reach, but she *didn't* break that clause when she attacked Anne. Anne's got no legal status. If Sagash was the one behind this attack then as far as the Council's concerned he hasn't done anything wrong.'

'But the Council still want Crystal,' Luna said.

'Which means that Caldera's on our side for exactly as long as Crystal stays a suspect. If we can prove that Crystal's behind this, we'll get Caldera and a whole Keeper task force backing us up. But if we prove Sagash is behind it then there's nothing Caldera can do. Sonder has to push Crystal as the prime suspect, because as soon as she's not then he stops getting help from the Keepers.'

'I hate Light politics so much,' Variam muttered.

'Better get used to it.'

'Why are you so sure it's Sagash?' Luna asked.

'Because this was what he did before,' Variam said. 'He got a couple of idiots to kidnap Anne out of school.'

'But that was what – five years ago?'

'Four if you count from when we got out.'

'You're seriously saying he sat around for *four years* before coming back?'

'Yes,' Variam said with emphasis. 'Because that's what he did the *first* time. It was three years between the deaths at our school and when Sagash showed up. The guy holds a grudge like you wouldn't believe.'

'Say it was him,' I said. 'Why would he go after Anne now? What would he want from her?'

'Best case? He still wants her as his apprentice and he'll pick up right where he left off.' Variam's face was grim. He didn't say what the worst case was, but I could guess.

Once we reached the station Variam split off, disappearing into the underground to begin his search. Luna hung back. 'Caldera's sidelining us, isn't she?'

I gave her an appraising look. 'You noticed.'

'Well, she didn't exactly make it subtle,' Luna said. 'Ask around the apprentice programme to find who it was? What are they going to say? "Oh yeah, I was just talking about Anne to these two sinister-looking hunchbacked guys in black cloaks. Here's their address and mobile number."'

'Black cloaks aside, that probably *is* how they found out.'

'That still leaves about a thousand people who it might have been. And same goes for Vari. She's just trying to get us out of the way.'

'Not quite. If she really thought there was no chance of finding anything useful, I doubt she'd have asked you to do it. I think she's giving us peripheral jobs to keep you out of trouble.'

'You know,' Luna said, 'I'm getting really tired of mages thinking I'm useless.'

'We're not Light mages,' I said. 'And we're not Keepers. Caldera knows she could use our help, but we're always going to be on the outside. From her perspective we're amateurs. Well-meaning amateurs, but . . .'

'Sonder probably wants that too, doesn't he?' Luna said. 'He wants to keep me on a shelf somewhere nice and safe.' She gave me a challenging look. 'Are you okay with that?'

'Well.' I gave Luna a grin. 'Caldera *is* on our side, so I think we should help her out. But I don't see why we can't show a little initiative . . .'

We parted company and I headed home, picking up a few things from the shops along the way. By the time Caldera arrived a couple of hours later, I'd had the chance to make some preparations.

'. . . and beyond Jagadev's throne room are the private rooms and living quarters,' I said. Caldera and I were standing over a sketched map on the small table in my kitchen. 'That was where Anne and Vari lived while they were there.'

'Other exits?' Caldera asked.

'At least two that I know about,' I said, pointing. 'Here

and here. There's roof access too, but I don't know the way inside. According to Vari, it's a bit of a maze, so I'd get directions if you're planning to go exploring.'

'What sort of security force does Jagadev keep on hand?'

'Last that I saw, a lot. At least twenty armed guards, some of them adepts, and that's not counting wards and automated defences. I wouldn't recommend starting a fight.'

'I'll be there in my capacity as a Keeper.'

'Mm.' I was pretty sure Jagadev was too smart to challenge the Keeper orders directly, but the assembled Dark mages might be another story. 'I'm guessing you haven't been to the Tiger's Palace before?'

'Other Keepers have. We poke around so often it's practically the Order of the Star's local pub.'

'But they probably don't do it on the nights Dark mages throw a party.'

Caldera shrugged.

'Sure you don't want me along?'

'Very sure,' Caldera said definitely. 'Don't take this personally, but right now having you mixed up in this is the last thing I want. You're a trouble magnet, you're not trained for police operations, I can't rely on you to follow orders and on top of that, according to Sonder you have some kind of history with Jagadev. I'm already going to be babysitting one civilian in there; I don't need another.'

I looked at Caldera in amusement. 'Guess that answers that.'

'This is my job, not yours. If you really want to do me a favour, scout the Tiger's Palace for tonight so that I can get Sonder in and out without anything screwing up. That's one thing I *could* use help with.'

'Are you okay with Sonder having dragged you into this?'

'Sonder didn't drag me in, I volunteered,' Caldera said.

'Even if he *did* do it by convincing my boss that this was connected to the Crystal investigation when it probably isn't. But your friend needs help, and stopping this kind of thing from happening is the reason I joined the Order of the Star in the first place. Besides, Sonder's helped me out enough times that I owe him a favour.'

'That's it?' I asked. 'You don't mind?'

'Do you have any idea how many cases like this the Order of the Star gets?' Caldera asked me. 'Kidnap, manslaughter, abuse . . . Not a day goes by where someone doesn't come to us for help. I've got fifteen cases sitting on my desk back at the station right now. When I check in tomorrow it'll be sixteen. Every hour I spend helping you and Sonder, I'm ignoring someone else.'

'I'm not the one who needs help, and neither is Sonder.'

'And that's why I'm here. But your friend's not the only case out there.'

'Are you saying you'd be rather be working on those other cases?'

'What are you expecting me to say, Verus?' Caldera asked. 'That I'm pissed off with Sonder? Well, maybe I am, a little bit. But I'm still going to do what I can to get you your friend back. Just like I do for everyone else who comes to us.'

I studied Caldera curiously. 'Does it ever get to you? Seeing the same things happen over and over again?'

'Ask me that sometime when I've drunk a lot more. Come on, go through the layout once more, then I'm heading back to the lab. I'll get you an earpiece for tonight.'

I spent the afternoon trying the remainder of my contacts. I didn't find out anything about Anne but the one bit of good news was that I managed to get through to Arachne. I caught her up on the situation; we discussed plans and agreed to meet that evening. As the afternoon wore on, I spent a couple of hours in the bathroom and then went to meet Variam on the heath.

The sun was setting by the time Variam showed up, and he actually looked right past me without recognising me. 'Hey, Vari,' I said as he was about to pass by.

Variam looked at me more closely, then his eyes went wide in disbelief. 'Alex?'

'Notice anything different?'

'What the hell did you do to your hair?'

My hair's naturally jet-black, with a tendency to spike upwards. Right now it was combed back and dyed a vivid blond – the bottle had advertised something a little more natural-looking, but I'm not exactly a stylist. 'Like it?'

'This really the time?'

'Oh, you know,' I said. 'Just felt like a change. Come along to Arachne's and I'll explain once we get there.'

Variam walked into Arachne's cave just ahead of me and stopped dead. Luna was standing in the main cavern near the door and she'd obviously heard us coming. 'Hey,' she said with a grin, giving her dress a swirl. 'What do you think?'

Variam stared. Luna looked satisfied, then she saw me and her eyebrows rose. 'You went for *that* colour?'

'Like it?'

'You look like a Bond villain.'

'Now that's just mean. And I was about to say something nice about how you looked too.'

Luna's dress was dark red, darkening from vermillion at the torso to the colour of dried blood at the skirts, which had a rumpled, crushed-velvet look. Fingerless gloves ran to above her elbows, a feathery ruff rested on her bare shoulders and she'd even dyed her hair red with orange highlights to match the rest of the outfit. 'Nice wasn't exactly what I was going for.'

'Oh, there you are, Alex,' Arachne said as she emerged from behind Luna. 'What on earth have you done to your hair?'

I sighed. 'Everyone's a critic.'

'I told you your hair needed to be medium *ash*-brown with golden blond.' Arachne is a gigantic tarantula-like spider, black and hairy with fangs the size of kitchen knives, a detail neither Variam nor I paid attention to. You get used to anything given time. 'Not *bleach* blond. There's no point in doing this if you don't get the colour exactly right.'

'Colours aren't my strong point, okay?'

'Wait,' Variam said. 'You're going to the Tiger's Palace?'

'See?' I said as I headed past Luna. 'Told you he'd get it.'

'Are you nuts? Jagadev said he'd kill you if you ever showed up again!'

'Oh, I doubt he'd do that in front of fifty Dark mages.'

'That's because if they figure out you're spying on them they'll do it first!'

'Technically *all* the Dark mages are going to be there to spy on one another,' I said as I found the selection of clothes Arachne had laid out for me. 'If I didn't do it too they'd probably get suspicious.'

'Does Caldera know you're doing this?'

'Sure, kind of . . . Oh, that one looks good.'

'No, that's in Chojan's style,' Arachne said, lifting a leg to tap one of the others. 'He's going to be there. Try this one instead.'

'What do you mean, "kind of"?' Variam said, walking around. His eyes kept drifting back to Luna.

'Well, she did ask me to scout out the Tiger's Palace. I'll just be doing it a bit more proactively.'

'How long have you been planning this?'

'Since about thirty seconds after Caldera and Sonder told us about the party. I didn't tell you until now because I knew you'd be giving Caldera a report before meeting us. This way you didn't have to lie to her.'

'She's going to be pissed,' Variam said, then suddenly shook his head. 'Wait, why should I care? Gah, I hate having to think about whether the boss is happy.'

'I know, but you want to be a member, you have to pay the dues, and we *are* going to need help for this one. Whether or not Sonder's right about it being Crystal, I doubt we've got the resources to do this on our own.'

Luna and Variam shared stories on how the day had gone – they'd turned up a lot of bits and pieces but nothing solid – while Arachne continued her efforts to educate me in the basics of hair care. 'Use this after you dress,' Arachne said, handing me a small jar. 'The gel should recolour your hair close enough to the right shade to pass a fairly thorough inspection, but don't get it wet. It won't persist as well as a proper dye.'

I nodded. 'Thanks for helping out on such short notice, by the way. You been okay?'

'For the moment,' Arachne said, the clicking rustle of her mandibles a counterpoint to her voice. 'Although some of the recent political developments are . . . worrying. If you have the time, I'd appreciate hearing what you discover at this audience.'

'Sure. What are you worried about specifically?'

'Specifically?' Arachne said. 'Your ex-master.'

I felt my heart sink. 'His name has been linked to Morden's current project,' Arachne said. 'A discouragement to those thinking of standing in opposition.'

'It could be a bluff.'

'I very much doubt Morden would make a threat like that without something to back it up.'

'That doesn't mean it's him,' I said. It didn't sound as convincing as I'd like. 'He might be doing it as part of some other game.'

Arachne studied me with her eight eyes. 'What's wrong?' I asked.

'I understand Luna's been hearing rumours of Richard's return,' Arachne said. 'She's reported them to you.'

'Luna needs to learn to keep her mouth shut.'

'Hasn't that contact of yours from the Council been saying something similar? Talisid?'

I was silent.

'Have you ever heard the parable of the horse which was a mule?' Arachne said. 'You go to market and buy a horse. On your way home, if one person looks at the horse and tells you it's a mule, you should ignore him. If a second person looks at the horse and tells you it's a mule, you should go back and check. If a third person looks at the horse and tells you it's a mule, then it's a mule.'

I looked up at Arachne. 'What's your point?'

'Exactly how many people need to tell you that Richard might have returned before you start listening?'

'They're just rumours—'

'*Repeated* rumours, and I've known you to act on less. Why haven't you?'

I took a glance over towards Luna and Variam. Both

were out of earshot and distracted in any case: they'd got into one of their usual arguments and Variam was pointing out of the tunnel for emphasis. 'Say I do believe them,' I said quietly. 'What would I do about it? If he is back, if he does come after me . . . then I'm screwed. It doesn't matter how much warning I have.'

Arachne paused, tapping two of her front legs against the floor. 'I think you're mistaken,' she said at last, 'but you may be right that you should be focusing on what you're doing tonight. Do you know *why* you're doing this, by the way?'

'What do you mean?' It was an odd question, but I was relieved at the change of subject. 'I don't think there's any way of doing this that isn't dangerous.'

'True, but not necessarily to you. From what you and Luna have told me, you could just as easily leave the work and the danger to the Keepers.'

I had to think about that one for a few seconds. As soon as Sonder had confirmed my fears last night about what had happened to Anne, I'd decided to drop everything else to try to find her, but I hadn't thought about why. 'You remember what you asked me last year?' I said eventually. 'About what kind of person I want to be?'

Arachne made an affirmative gesture. 'I never used to care about anyone else,' I said. 'Not really. I mean, I'd do something nice now and again, but I always came first, you know?' I looked over at where Luna was making some point or other to Variam, using her hands for emphasis. 'I'm not sure who changed that, you or Luna, but . . . I think it was Luna. You helped me when I needed it most, but I always saw you as above me, I guess. I could never really imagine you needing me for anything, not until that.' I gestured up at the jagged gash in the rock above one of the side tunnels, a souvenir of two years back. Arachne could have repaired it but she'd chosen to leave it untouched, maybe as a remainder. 'But Luna *did* need me. So I started thinking more and more about my friends. I kind of divided the world up into them, and everyone else. If you were inside that group, you mattered.'

'And now?'

'Now . . .' I shrugged. 'Anne isn't really one of my friends any more. She made that pretty clear.' I was quiet for a moment. 'For a while I thought that if I could save her, then I could prove . . . I don't know. That what I did last year was okay? That my way of doing things was right? But it's a bad reason. Helping her just so that she'd be grateful, that she'd owe me something . . . I think even if we *do* manage to pull this off, if Anne does end up safe again, then we still won't be friends.'

'But you're still going to do it?'

'Yeah, I am.' I looked up at Arachne. 'Because after you strip away all the history and all the arguments, she's in trouble and she still needs help. We might not manage to do this. Maybe we'll fail and maybe we'll give up. But it's still worth doing.'

Arachne looked at me thoughtfully for a moment, then nodded. I had the odd feeling it was almost as if she were smiling. 'Good luck.'

'So,' Luna said. 'Not bringing the armour?'

We were in Soho near the Tiger's Palace, standing in a doorway just a couple of buildings down. I'd needed to be close to get a good angle on the reactions of the door security. Neon lights shone down from above, blotting out the stars, and the air was filled with the din of overlapping music. Groups of people were scattered across the street, laughter and yells echoing between the buildings. Occasionally a passer-by would give us a glance, but we didn't get many catcalls: it was a Saturday night in Soho and our outfits weren't even close to the weirdest ones out there.

'Sends the wrong impression,' I said. Arachne made me an imbued item last year, a suit of reactive armour: it's very good at what it does, but now wasn't the time to break it out. 'You don't want to look like you need it. Your communicator working?'

Luna tapped her ear. 'I think so. Calling Vari, can you—?'

'Hitting it doesn't help.'

Luna made a face at me. 'Vari, can you hear me? Alex is being mean again.'

'You probably deserve it,' Variam's voice said in my ear.

The transparent focus set into my ear was a synchronous communicator, one of the nicer toys that Council mages get to play with. They're lightweight, voice-activated and allow you to talk to someone without a radio signal, which is handy when some of the people you're sharing a room with can see electromagnetic waves. 'Calling Vari, Luna,' I said. 'Can you hear me?'

'Receiving,' Variam said.

'I'm right here, you know,' Luna said.

'Don't be a smart-arse. Vari, you've found a good place?'

'I'm on the lower roof overlooking the front door and the back alley entrance,' Variam said. 'You got the position?'

'Yeah. Keep us updated once we're inside. You're sure these things can't be intercepted?'

'Sure. Unless the Council aren't as good as they think

they are, but what are the chances of that?' There was a chime and the channel closed.

'So, you going to tell me who we're supposed to be?' Luna asked. She was carrying her focus weapon: Arachne had made her a red silk cover for it, attached at the focus's narrow end to a long braided rope, coiled in her hands. Disguising a whip as a whip; Arachne does have a sense of humour.

'I'm going to be a fairly reclusive Dark mage named Avis,' I said. 'He's important enough that he gets invited to these sorts of get-togethers, but he doesn't like taking sides so he always turns them down.'

'Sounds fun. How about me?'

'It looks like Avis has just taken on a new apprentice. Come up with a name for yourself, and don't use any kind of pun on "moon".'

'Like I'd want to. I'm going to be Zarine.'

'Zarine?'

'If I'm a new apprentice I wouldn't have a mage identity, right? Anyway, I always liked that name.'

'Zarine it is.'

We set off up the street. 'No ribbon this time?' I asked as we approached the Tiger's Palace.

'God no. Those things *absorb* my curse. I want to be at full strength.'

The entrance to Jagadev's club is via basement level. We skirted a laughing pack of drunken twenty-somethings and started down the stairs. 'Arachne would make you another if you asked.'

'I know, but I don't want to. Having it turned off for a few hours is great but when it's done I feel *worse*. If I'm going to fix this I want it so that *I* can do it.'

'I think you will. Some day.'

Luna gave me a quick smile. 'All right,' I said. 'Game face on. Ready?'

'Let's do it,' Luna said. I strode through the front entrance of Jagadev's lair.

The outfit Arachne had made for me was a long military-style coat with gold tracing at the lapels and wrist and a white ruff at the neck, combined with a waistcoat and narrow trousers. It made me feel like I was going to a steampunk convention, but from examining myself in the mirror I had to admit it looked good. Whoever Avis was, he had a sense of style. A dark-blue mask covered the upper half of my face, while Luna wore a narrower dark-red band at eye level. We'd put them on before making our final approach.

The bouncers on the door were a different lot from the usual: more social graces, fewer broken noses. Evidently this evening rated a higher class of doorman. 'May I take your name, please?' the one at the front asked. His manner was pleasant, but his eyes and those of the men behind him were alert and ready.

'Avis,' I said, meeting his gaze. I'd changed my posture subtly as I approached, standing a little straighter, my movements a little more deliberate. My voice was flat and calm.

The doorman nodded. 'Welcome to the Tiger's Palace.'

I walked towards the door at the other end, ignoring the doormen; Luna followed a pace behind. No one tried to stop us. The door swung shut and we were walking down a stone corridor. I'd known we were going to get this far; from now on things would get interesting. We reached the door at the end and I pushed it open, and the two of us walked out onto the main floor of Jagadev's lair.

5

The last time I'd visited the Tiger's Palace had been a year and a half ago. When I'd seen it then, it had been a dance club, hundreds of boys and girls in their teens and twenties packed into a concrete box filled with the pounding of industrial music. Now the concrete walls had been hidden by drapes of red cloth, and Indian artwork had been set up around the edge of the room. Carpets and tables were spaced across the floor and the upper balcony had been decorated as well, though no amount of decoration could hide the dominating view it gave over the lower level.

It looked luxurious, almost enough to be a real palace . . . but not quite. It might have been the absence of people – the club had been designed to hold nearly a thousand, and the fifty or so figures scattered across the main floor left it feeling vast and empty – but I didn't think it was the guests. Jagadev is the owner of the Tiger's Palace, and there's little love lost between him and mages. Maybe I was imagining it, but I thought I could feel something of his presence in the building, a kind of cold indifference. Jagadev might live amongst humans, but he doesn't like them.

We'd attracted attention the instant we walked in, and I could see half a dozen people eyeing us from across the wide expanse of the floor. 'Vari,' I said. 'We're in. Alex out.'

'Received,' Variam's voice said into my ear.

'Here's where the fun begins,' Luna murmured. Behind the mask, her eyes were bright with anticipation.

'I'll take the adult mages,' I said quietly. 'You cover the apprentices.'

'I'll start with the ones on the far wall.'

'Stay in touch.' A man moved away from a group ahead of us and looked towards me. 'Go.' Luna split off, angling past the duelling ring towards a cluster of Dark apprentices standing in the shadow of the balcony. The man took a few steps towards me, and I slowed to let him intercept my path.

The funny thing is that what I was trying to do here would never work at a Light ball. Light mages are so much more organised: you don't even get in the door without an invitation and the guest list is examined carefully. Their society is more close-knit, and even the most reclusive Light mages have colleagues. Dark society, on the other hand, isn't really a society at all. Among Dark mages, security and relationships are all handled on an individual level: if you have a problem then by default it's up to you to do something about it. While there's a loose code of conduct, the only way rules are imposed is if the one in charge is powerful enough to enforce his will on a collection of Dark mages (rare) or if the Dark mages in question are willing to submit to him (even rarer).

Secrecy and paranoia are also much bigger deals in the Dark world – Light mages aren't exactly trusting, but Dark mages take it to the extreme. I wasn't the only mage here wearing a mask, and it was a safe bet that I wasn't the only one pretending to be someone I wasn't either. The *really* paranoid mages wouldn't physically be here at all: they'd be miles away, utilising projections or simulacra. The man in front of me wasn't one of them, though, as far as I could tell – he was wearing a mask, but my best guess was that he was here in the flesh. 'Avis,' he said with a nod.

As soon as he'd made a move towards me I'd begun searching through the futures in which I spoke to him, cross-referencing against the names I'd seen from Jagadev's guest list. Futures flashed past, there and discarded in a fraction of a second, flick-flick-flick: Ansek, Chance, Chojan, Emerel, Ever, Fabius, Gorith – close but not quite, similar sound – *there*. 'Ordith,' I replied.

Ordith fell into step beside me. I didn't know anything about the man except his name and that he was a mage. He was wearing brown and silver, and radiated no magic. 'Generous of you to show up.'

The tone was slightly mocking, but Ordith's body language was cautious. 'I did not come here for you to waste my time,' I told him. 'Get to the point.'

I felt Ordith's eyebrows rise. 'Sensitive,' he murmured. 'I was just curious about your position on the new proposal.'

*What proposal?* A figure caught my eye at the foot of the stairs, slim and deadly: Onyx. If Onyx was here then so was his master, and Talisid had— I stopped and turned on Ordith. To approach me first, he must be at the bottom of the chain, not the top. 'Is that your game now?'

'What do you mean?'

I shook my head. 'Tell Morden to run his own errands.' I was trying lines of dialogue through the futures. I didn't need to get it perfect, just to avoid the puzzled reaction that indicated a misstep.

'Come on,' Ordith said. He was wearing a smile intended to take the edge off his words. 'You're hardly an active player.'

'I hope you aren't expecting anything for free.' What *was* Morden up to? I should have paid more attention to what Talisid had been telling me. 'What about Jagadev?'

'Jagadev knows not to take sides in such matters.'

I didn't really have any idea what we were talking about but one of the things my first master drilled into us was that when you're uncertain, you attack. 'I have no intention of rearranging my plans to suit Morden's convenience.'

Ordith's smile didn't change. 'Morden can be quite persuasive.'

'Don't try to threaten me. I will support whoever offers the greatest benefit – as will those I represent.'

Ordith's smile faltered a little. 'Those you—?'

'Enough,' I said curtly. I couldn't see any way I could bring Anne into this conversation, which meant I was wasting my time. 'I have other business.' I changed direction and walked away.

Without looking, I knew that Ordith was staring after me; after a moment he turned and headed towards the foot of the stairs. Maybe messing around in Dark politics wasn't the smartest thing I could possibly be doing. Oh well.

The communicator in my ear gave a quiet two-tone beep, followed by Caldera's voice. 'Testing. Verus, do you read?'

'Receiving,' I said, turning away from the bulk of the crowd.

'We're approaching the Tiger's Palace. Did you manage to scout it out?'

'Yep,' I said, turning to look back over the floor. I could see an interesting-looking group of people near the stairs. 'Got a really good view, actually.'

'Any guests I should know about?'

'Morden.' And possibly me, but no point worrying her with trivialities.

'Should have guessed.' Caldera broke off for a second, then resumed. 'Sonder and I are ten minutes out. Keep up observation and let us know the instant something happens. *Don't* go inside. Clear?'

It looked as though the one at the centre of the crowd was Morden. I started walking towards him. 'Stay where I am,' I said. 'Got it.'

'Good. Heading in now.' The communicator beeped as the connection closed.

For a diviner, going into the middle of a crowd like this is dangerous. The major limiting factor on how far divination magic can look into the future is unpredictability: the more variables in your surroundings, the shorter your viewing range. In a sealed room with no extraneous movement I can see ahead for hours, days if I push it. Here, I could see ahead for maybe a minute at best. Different futures branched and broke off ahead of me, shadowy and twisting, individual Dark mages noticing me, approaching, interacting, every possibility changing at a moment's notice. The futures in which I spoke to someone broke up almost immediately, thousands of branching choices all packed in upon each other, the unpredictable elements building upon each other and multiplying into an ever-changing blur.

If something went wrong here, I'd have very little time to react. When divination's your primary defence it's much safer to avoid these gatherings, and that's exactly what most diviners do: hide themselves away in some deserted location where they can see any potential threats a long way off. But divination magic works in close quarters too, as long as you don't mind a little risk. When you're talking face to face with someone you might be able to see ahead only a few seconds, but they're an important few seconds, and you can learn a lot more than you would staying at home.

As I approached the stairs I saw that Morden had quite

an audience going, with half a dozen Dark mages gathered around him. He also had Onyx standing right at his shoulder, which was enough to make me very sure I didn't want to stop for a chat. Ordith was hovering at the edge of the conversation, looking as though he was waiting for Morden to finish. I stayed out of earshot, but as I did I picked out the futures in which I moved closer, looking to see what I would hear if I joined their group.

'. . . be the case,' Morden was saying. He wasn't wearing a mask: the really powerful Dark mages usually don't. Dark-haired and handsome, he looked like a politician, though most politicians can't kill you from across the room without lifting a finger. 'I hope I can count on your support.'

'Your interest in this cause is hardly universal, Morden,' another mage said. 'The Light mages have little to offer us.'

'Then perhaps those who feel that way would prefer to take it up with my associate.'

A faint ripple, almost too quick to be sensed, went through the audience. Morden looked inquiringly from side to side; when no answer came he went on. 'Neither of us expects any great sacrifice. All you have to do is stand aside and let nature take its course.'

'Nature?'

'It's the direction things have been going, wouldn't you say?'

All the time Morden had been talking I'd been moving, and I was reaching the point where I was about to pass out of eavesdropping range. I could linger but I'd risk detection, and it didn't sound as though this had anything to do with Anne . . .

. . . except that Anne had once told me a long time ago

that Morden had offered her the position of his apprentice. She'd turned him down – did he still hold a grudge?

As if I didn't have enough to worry about already.

I took the stairs up to the balcony. A pair of women were speaking quietly under their breath on the landing; they fell silent and eyed me when I passed. Something caught my attention as I searched through the futures, a familiar presence. My eyes narrowed. *Her? Now isn't that interesting . . .*

A man and a woman were by the balcony railing. The man was masked, and beyond checking to see that he wasn't going to cause trouble I didn't pay him any attention. The woman was another story altogether. She was small and delicate-looking, with coppery skin and deep dark eyes. Her hair was done up in an elaborate style with lacquered sticks, and she wore a narrow black dress which showed off her figure. Right now she was laughing, one hand resting naturally on the man's arm. '—isn't it?' she was saying, her voice warm and captivating. 'If you could, that would be wonderful.'

'No problem,' the man said. He looked like he was trying to come across as casual and doing a bad job of it. 'This evening, then.'

'See you then,' the woman said. The smile stayed on her face as she watched him go.

I'd timed my approach carefully and reached the woman just as she began to turn away. As I passed I caught her arm and swept her along with me. 'Meredith,' I said into her ear. From this close I could smell her perfume, something flowery and expensive. 'Nice to see you again.'

Meredith is an enchantress, petite and beautiful and, from my fairly definite experience, entirely self-interested. As soon as she heard my voice her head jerked slightly. 'Alex?'

'I'd wondered where you'd disappeared to. Who's your new friend?'

I'd got Meredith as far as the balcony railing; she pulled away and I let her go. As I did her eyes flicked quickly down to the club floor. It was so fast it was almost impossible to see, but I'd been watching for it and I knew that the one she'd been looking towards was Morden. When I'd first met Meredith, she'd been working for a Light mage called Belthas – he was gone now but he and Morden had a lot of things in common, and Meredith wasn't the sort to be especially concerned about whether someone was Dark or Light.

'What are you doing here?' Meredith asked. She was keeping herself under control, but she was on edge, and for good reason. The last time Meredith and I had met, we'd parted on bad terms and she'd given me more than enough reason to hold a grudge.

'Funny,' I said. 'I was just about to ask you that. You like to get yourself into trouble, don't you?'

'What do you mean?'

'The name Anne Walker mean anything to you?'

Meredith shook her head; her eyes were wary but her reaction had been instant and I was fairly sure she was telling the truth. 'Hm,' I said. 'I guess your new boss works on a need-to-know basis.'

'What are you talking about?'

'Anne Walker's an apprentice from the Light programme,' I said. 'She's gone missing lately. The Keepers are concerned.'

'Well, that's nothing to do with me.'

I raised an eyebrow.

Meredith looked at me, waiting. I counted off seconds in my head as Meredith's expression began to shade into annoyance. 'Is this it?' she asked. 'There isn't—'

Right on cue, a voice spoke loudly from the far side of the club, pitched to carry across the floor. 'Announcing Keeper Caldera of the Order of the Star.'

Every conversation in the Tiger's Palace fell silent at once, as if someone had hit the mute button. Caldera was a small figure at the front door, with Sonder a step behind, and she was advancing across the floor. The doorman hadn't announced anyone else that I'd seen and I was fairly sure the special treatment hadn't been meant to do Caldera any favours. Nearly a hundred pairs of eyes watched Caldera and Sonder as they came closer.

'What's she doing here?' Meredith whispered, looking suddenly unsettled.

I smiled slightly. 'Done anything the Keepers might object to lately?'

'Don't be like that!' Meredith kept her voice low. 'Do you know why she's here?'

'Let's just say that you might want to find out exactly what Morden's connection with that girl is. Fast.'

'I don't *know*!'

I shrugged and started to turn away.

'Wait!' Meredith caught my shoulder. 'Can't you tell me?'

'I don't owe you anything.'

'Please.'

'You know what?' I said. 'I'll make you a deal. I'm interested in Anne Walker's location. Morden knows where she is. Find out, and I'll tell you why that Keeper's here and what she wants. And what you need to do to stay away from her.'

Meredith gave me an uncertain look, then hurried away. I leant on the balcony railing, watching Caldera and Sonder approach. As I did, the communicator chimed and I heard Luna's voice in my ear. 'Alex? I can't see you.'

I was turned away from the others on the balcony, but I kept my voice very quiet. 'I'm on the balcony. What's your status?'

Caldera was approaching the stairs up to the balcony at a steady pace. There was a clear path between her and the stairs and the Dark mages didn't exactly block her way . . . but they didn't move aside either. Everyone was watching the two of them, and there was a kind of lazy tension in the air, a pack of wolves studying a wolfhound. Caldera's face was stone, and almost against my will I felt a flash of admiration. The Order of the Star goes after mages who violate the Concord, and no matter how you interpret that, Dark mages are right at the top of their suspect list. Caldera was quite literally walking into a crowd of people whom she hunted for a living, and if those people decided to turn the tables and hunt *her*, she wouldn't have a hope in hell of making it out alive. But there was no fear on Caldera's face or in the way she moved, and the Dark mages stood still, letting her pass. Predators are drawn to weakness, and Caldera wasn't showing any.

Sonder was another matter. He was half a step behind Caldera, and as the two of them approached I saw eyes drift away from the heavier woman and lock onto him instead. Sonder's head was up and he was putting on a brave face, but his movements were too quick, too nervous. He looked like a new fish on the prison yard. Without Caldera, I put his life expectancy here at about twenty minutes.

'I've been talking to the apprentices,' Luna said into my ear. 'Most of them are talking about Morden and that proposal – you know, Dark mages and the Council – but

I found out something else. Sagash has apprentices, and they're here.'

'Good,' I said quietly. Beneath me, I saw Meredith appear from the direction of the stairs and move towards Morden's little crowd. Caldera and Sonder entered where she'd left, disappearing from my view.

'I think I can find them. I can go after them, or I could try Morden's—'

'Go after the apprentices. I'll deal with Morden.'

'Got it.'

From behind me I heard footsteps and I knew Caldera and Sonder were at my back. I stayed facing away, leaning on the balcony rail and tracking them in my future sight. Only after they'd passed by did I turn my head slightly to look. The two of them were moving around the semicircular balcony, heading for the room at the far end. Jagadev would be within.

I was torn. I badly wanted to talk to Sagash; I hadn't spotted him yet, but if his apprentices were here he probably was too. On the other hand, looking for him meant leaving Sonder and Caldera on their own, and I could already see two or three Dark mages drifting after them. Caldera should be able to take care of herself, but I wasn't so sure about Sonder . . .

Sonder and Caldera vanished behind a pillar and I shook my head and turned away. They were adults; they'd have to handle themselves. The only place I hadn't checked yet was the far side of the balcony, and I headed along it. Down on the club floor I could see that Meredith was talking to one of the mages around Morden. I needed to hurry.

Sagash was at the very end of the balcony, and he was alone. None of the other mages had approached him, and even from a distance I could see why. Being a Dark mage comes with a certain automatic intimidation factor – you don't get far in Dark society without being ruthless, and even the ones who *haven't* reached their current position over a pile of bodies are not to be messed with – but still, most of them practise a certain minimum level of subtlety. Fear is useful, but sometimes you just want to blend in.

Apparently Sagash was of the opinion that blending in was for wimps.

He was taller than me, and skeletally thin. The flesh of his hands and neck was withered, stretched tight over clearly visible tendons and bones, and the fingers grasping the balcony railing looked like claws. His lips were pulled slightly back over his mouth, showing his teeth in an endless mirthless grin, and his skin was yellowed and pale. A black cap covered his skull, and dark robes hung from his bony shoulders. He looked like a cross between a famine survivor and an animated skeleton, but his thin limbs gave no impression of weakness: there was a kind of unnatural immobility about him, coiled and ready for action. I'm not going to say he was the *most* terrifying-looking human being I've ever seen, but I'd have trouble coming up with a better candidate at short notice.

I swallowed quietly. *Well, you're always telling Luna not to judge by appearances, right?*

Sagash turned to face me as I approached, and it was just as well I'd had advance warning or I would have flinched. Up close his face looked even worse: the flesh was stretched over the skull, and pinpoints of yellow light glowed from sunken eye sockets. 'Sagash,' I said. I managed to keep my voice steady, but it was a near thing. 'I'm glad I caught you.' *Let's not get into the question of who's caught whom . . .*

Sagash stared at me. I'd thought of a dozen lies and half-truths, but as I looked into his eyes I abandoned them all. There was something inhuman about Sagash and my instincts told me that the tricks which had worked on Meredith and Ordith wouldn't work on him. 'I wonder if you might be able to help me,' I said. 'I'm interested in the whereabouts of an apprentice called Anne Walker.'

Sagash studied me for a moment before speaking. His voice had a grating, rasping sound, like a piece of sandpaper working on a particularly stubborn lump of wood. 'You are misinformed.'

'I was under the impression she used to be your apprentice?'

'No longer.' Sagash still hadn't asked my name. I suspected he didn't care.

'But I assume you keep tabs on her.'

'I neither know her present status, nor care.'

'Ah, my mistake,' I said. 'My apologies. You don't make any claim on her, then?'

Sagash's yellow-pinpoint eyes focused on me and I had to force myself to hold my ground. 'Your activities are not my concern,' he rasped. 'The girl's life is of no interest to me. Do with her as you wish.' He turned to face me, one bony hand hanging at his side: he held no weapon, but the threat was clear. 'You have your answer. Leave.'

I looked – very quickly – at the consequences of staying, then bowed slightly and withdrew. Sagash watched me go, then turned back to overlook the club floor. As I turned away, there was a chime in my ear and I heard Luna's voice again. 'Found them.'

'The apprentices?' I said very quietly. There were people close enough to overhear.

'They're in the far corner. Listen, I'm going to try something. Back in a sec.'

'Wait, what are you—?' The communicator cut off, and I swore under my breath. What did she mean, 'try something'?

Looking into the futures, I could sense something happening around the entrance to Jagadev's throne room, and I changed direction to head towards it. As I did I ran over what Sagash had told me. Now that it was too late, I wished I'd questioned Anne more thoroughly about her time with him: it would have made it a lot easier to figure out whether Sagash was lying. My divination magic hadn't been much use – if someone isn't going to tell you something, then looking into the futures of questioning them won't help. He might be lying . . . but why? If it really had been Sagash who'd been behind Anne's disappearance, he hadn't broken any laws. What did he have to gain from hiding it?

The far right end of the balcony terminated in a wide doorway. Some of Jagadev's men had been stationed outside but I couldn't see any trace of Jagadev himself; he must be in the rooms beyond. I couldn't see Caldera but I could see Sonder: he'd been approached by a girl in her twenties and was talking to her. 'Caldera,' I murmured, letting a pillar conceal me. 'Where are you?'

There was a pause before Caldera answered, and when she did her voice was muffled. 'Not a good time.'

'Let me guess,' I said. 'Jagadev let you in to see him but he's keeping you waiting, and he made Sonder wait outside?'

'Yeah.'

'Know if you'll be done soon? It's just that Sonder—'

'Look, whatever this is, take care of it on your own, all right? Kind of busy here.'

'No problem,' I said. 'Alex out.' I walked out from behind the pillar and towards where Sonder was standing.

After you've spent a while in certain types of environments, you get a nose for trouble. I didn't know the girl Sonder was talking to, and I didn't know the boy hanging back in the shadows, but I recognised the way they were standing and that was all I needed to be sure about what was going to happen. In the time I'd been talking to Caldera, Sonder had been drawn a few steps away from the entrance to Jagadev's throne room and he looked on the point of following the girl. 'Please?' she was saying. 'There's no one else I can ask.'

'How far is he?' Sonder asked. He was hesitating but I knew he was close to being convinced.

'Just in the next room,' the girl said. She was petite and wiry, with a birdlike way of moving, and she looked very appealing as she gazed up at Sonder. 'Isn't there anything you can do? I don't have much, but if there's anything I can offer you, I—'

'Leave,' I told the girl, doing my best imitation of Avis.

The girl turned, taken aback. 'I don't— What do you mean?'

'This is not something you want to involve yourself in,' I said, making my voice harsh. 'Take your partner and get lost.'

The girl looked back at me for a second, then her face changed and she straightened. All of a sudden she looked a lot less vulnerable. She gave me a disgusted glance and walked away without a word. In my peripheral vision, I saw the boy slip something back into his pocket and disappear from view.

Sonder had watched the whole thing in confusion; now

as I turned back to him he drew back suspiciously. 'Who are you?'

I shook my head and switched to my normal voice. 'Sonder, if fooling you is this easy, you *really* shouldn't be hanging out at Dark audiences.'

Sonder stared. '*Alex?*'

I took a step away. 'Come on. Those two might decide to come back, and if they do they'll bring company.'

Sonder didn't follow. 'What are you doing here? We didn't invite you!'

'"Why, thank you, Alex",' I said to the open air. '"You're welcome, Sonder."'

'I didn't need your help!'

'Another three minutes,' I told Sonder, 'and you would have been challenged to a duel. Traditional, not azimuth.'

'For *what?*'

'Making a move on someone's girlfriend, breaking a social taboo, stealing something that just would have happened to turn up in your pocket . . . whatever they decided to set you up for. Are you coming or not?'

'No!' Sonder glared at me. 'You're not in charge and we've got work to do.'

I let out a breath. I hadn't really expected Sonder to be happy to see me, but this was starting to wear on my nerves and I'd already seen that Meredith was looking for me. 'Suit yourself.' I turned and walked away. Sonder didn't follow.

Meredith found me less than two minutes later, and from the way she was looking at me I knew this conversation was going to go less smoothly than the last one. 'Morden says he doesn't know anything about that girl,' she said without preamble.

'Really.'

'I think he's telling the truth,' Meredith said. Her eyes were narrowed as she watched me. 'You were lying to me. You weren't trying to help at all.'

'Lying and pretending to care about someone? What kind of terrible person would do that?' I leant closer towards Meredith and dropped the pretence, letting her see the coldness in my eyes. 'You set me up to be killed. Did you think I forgot?'

Meredith backed away; she looked afraid, but there was anger underneath it. Without saying a word she spun and marched away. She'd lost her usual grace and her movements were spiky and quick.

I watched her go. Meredith doesn't have much combat magic, but it's a big mistake to think that that means she can't be dangerous. It was probably a good time to start thinking about leaving. There was a chime and Luna spoke into my ear. 'Well, that didn't work.'

I started towards the balcony. 'What didn't?'

'I found Sagash's apprentices. Two of them, anyway.'

I leant over the balcony and scanned the crowd below. 'Two guys by the long table on the far right?'

'That's them.'

The two mages I was looking at were too far away for me to get a good view, but it looked as though one was blond-haired and white, and the other West Indian or African. Both wore masks, and they were talking quietly, standing close together at an angle where they could watch each other's backs. 'Huh,' I said. 'You know, they look awfully like those descriptions Sonder gave us.'

'Yep.'

'You were talking to them, right? Did you get anything?'

'Kind of. I challenged the blond one to a duel.'

'You did *what*?'

'Relax – he turned me down. Anyway, it was only a first-blood thing.'

'"First blood" means something a bit different here. What were you thinking?'

'Well, Sonder got a look at the magic those two were using, right? I figured if he said yes, Sonder could watch and we could check to see if it was really them.'

'That . . .' I paused. '. . . Could work, actually.'

'I know, right? Anyway, I tried calling him a coward, but that didn't draw him out either so—'

'*What?*' A passing mage gave me a curious look and I glared at him, then hurriedly turned away.

'I said he turned me down; calm down already. It's kind of a pity, I've never had a match against a Dark apprentice.'

'You're out of your mind. Never mind. I'll come down and we can—'

I was facing out over the main club floor, directly above Morden's group, and at this point I caught sight of Meredith. She was talking to Onyx, and as I watched she pointed up to the balcony in the direction of the spot we'd last been talking. Onyx turned his head towards me and I ducked back out of sight. 'Uh-oh.'

'Uh-oh, what?'

'Change of plan,' I said. Going down to floor level would mean passing Onyx and walking out into the open, neither of which struck me as a good idea just now. 'Get Sonder.'

'What for?'

'I'm guessing you asked those apprentices a bunch of leading questions? Odds are as soon as you were out of earshot they started trying to figure out how much you knew. If you can get Sonder there—'

'—then he can look back to see what they said! Let's do it.'

Looking into the future, I knew that Onyx was heading in my direction. I moved towards the wall and behind the cover of a pillar. 'Sonder,' I said. 'You there?'

'What?' Sonder said after a pause. He sounded harassed, as though he'd been in the middle of another conversation.

'Got a job for you. Mind helping Luna out with something?'

'Luna— She's *here*?'

'Bingo,' Luna said over the link. 'Meet me at the foot of the stairs, okay?'

'What were you thinking, bringing her here?' Sonder said. 'You're her master – you're supposed to look after her!'

From the other side of the pillar, I heard quick footsteps as Onyx strode past. Onyx is Morden's Chosen, slim and deadly; he's an extremely powerful and specialised battle mage and he hates my guts. The one bright side (from my point of view) is that he's *so* specialised a battle mage that he's very bad at anything that doesn't directly involve hurting or killing things, meaning that while he's very dangerous in a fight, he's remarkably bad at spotting anyone hiding from him. 'Excuse me?' Luna said in annoyance. 'I'm older than you are.'

'You're still only an apprentice. You shouldn't be here!'

'Since when did you get to—?'

Another chime sounded in my ear. 'Hold please,' I said as I emerged from behind the pillar and headed in the opposite direction from Onyx. I switched circuits. 'Hello?'

Sonder and Luna's voices cut out and Caldera's voice

sounded in my ear. She sounded pissed. 'Verus, what are you playing at?'

'You know, this isn't a great time,' I said, taking a glance around. I couldn't see Meredith but I knew Onyx was coming back for another pass. 'Can I call you back?'

'I told you not to go inside!'

'Technically I was inside already.'

'You bloody well knew what I meant!'

'Well, here's the thing. As you made clear to Variam earlier today, you Keepers have a strict chain of command, and I'm not in it.'

Caldera started swearing. Onyx was heading back towards me and I slipped into a side-room. 'I am going to kill you,' Caldera said once she was coherent again.

'You might have to get in line,' I said. The communicator chimed again. 'Hold please.'

'No! Where are—?'

I switched channels. 'Receiving,' I said, then stepped back into the shadows behind a wall hanging.

'Alex?' Variam said into my ear. 'Think we might have a problem.'

Onyx appeared in my view through the doorway. He looked as pissed off as Caldera had sounded. He turned his head from side to side, searching, then whirled and headed back the way he'd come. 'Someone's just arrived at the front,' Variam said. 'His get-up looks really similar to what you're wearing. Like, *really* similar.'

'Oh, come *on*,' I muttered. '*Now?*'

'You made sure the real Avis wasn't coming tonight, right?'

'I did! Everyone told me he never shows up to these things!'

'Yeah, well, unless he's got an identical twin you might want to qualify that, because someone who looks exactly like him just walked in the front door.'

'Okay.' I started walking towards the stairs, trying not to make it too obvious that I was hurrying. 'I think it's time to leave.'

'I'll get to the evac point. Call when you're a minute out.'

I switched channels again and came in the middle of Sonder and Luna arguing. '—risky,' Sonder was saying. 'What if they see?'

'You said they can't tell if you're using timesight.'

'They might notice that I'm—'

'Luna, start closing,' I said. 'Five minutes, then we're leaving, back entrance.'

'Got it. By the way, we just ducked Onyx. Seemed like he was looking for someone. Know who it might be?'

'Very funny.' Looking ahead, I saw that Caldera was just about to come around the corner ahead of me. 'Oh, great.'

'They're still standing where they were,' Sonder objected. 'How are we going to—?'

'Do I have to think of everything?' Luna said. 'Alex, I'll meet you at the door in five.'

'Got it. Alex out.'

Caldera came striding around the corner and fixed me with a look of death. Obviously Sonder had told her what I was wearing. 'You!'

'Keeper,' I said formally. 'Is there something I can help you with?'

Caldera had been about to start swearing at me again, but my tone brought her up short. Looking from side to side, she saw that two Dark mages were within earshot and both were watching with undisguised interest. 'Mage,' she said through clenched teeth. 'Would you mind if we spoke privately?'

'I'm afraid I was just leaving,' I said. 'How was your meeting with Lord Jagadev?'

'Screw Jagadev!'

In the futures in which I went to the balcony edge and looked over, I could see Onyx talking to Meredith. He looked even angrier if anything, and she didn't look happy either. He made a cutting motion with his hand; Meredith pointed again in the direction of the balcony. Onyx turned and stormed off towards the stairs. 'I doubt you're his type.'

Caldera took a deep breath, obviously getting herself under control. The futures shifted and I glanced ahead: yet another person I didn't want to talk to was heading my way. 'I recommend you locate your assistant,' I said. 'I think he might need assistance himself.'

'What? What have you done now?'

From behind Caldera someone cleared his throat. Caldera turned to see Morden standing behind her. 'Keeper,' Morden said. 'If it's not too much trouble, would it be possible for me to speak with Avis?'

Morden put just the tiniest accent on *Avis*, enough to let me know that he knew who I was, not quite enough to make it obvious to Caldera. Caldera knew I wasn't Avis, but she didn't know that *Morden* knew I wasn't Avis . . . This was getting confusing. Caldera gave me a last warning glance, which I returned blandly. 'We are going to talk later,' Caldera said to Morden. 'Don't go anywhere.'

Morden bowed slightly. 'I look forward to it.'

Caldera walked off around the left-hand curve of the balcony. She was heading in Sagash's direction, and I had to fight off the impulse to eavesdrop. Watching those two bounce off each other would be interesting, as long as I was at a safe distance. 'Can I assume you're here to support my proposal?' Morden asked.

Was that why the real Avis was breaking his usual habits and showing up? I *really* should have done more digging on what Morden was up to. 'Not in a million years,' I said. I didn't bother disguising my voice: trying to play those kinds of games with someone like Morden is a waste of time. 'What do you want?'

'I believe that's my line.'

Onyx had come up to the balcony again. Luckily this time he'd turned the wrong way, but he'd be back. 'I'm a little short on time,' I said. 'Could we hurry this up?'

'You know, Verus, you should learn to be more polite,' Morden said with a smile. 'Someone might take offence.'

I looked at Morden. His smile didn't waver, and I felt a brief chill. Morden doesn't look dangerous but he's *very* powerful, and if he decided to make a serious attempt to get rid of me I don't think my life would be worth much. He wouldn't even have to do anything himself; all he'd have to do would be to point Onyx in my direction. He hadn't − yet − but I started mentally planning out escape routes, and this time I kept my mouth shut.

'Better,' Morden said when I didn't answer. 'I understand you have an interest in Anne?'

'As do you, last I heard. Do you happen to know where she is?'

'What are you offering?'

'I'm not going to work for you.'

'Really? I'd hoped you'd reconsidered.'

I took a breath. 'Morden,' I said. 'Exactly how many

times does that sociopathic Chosen of yours have to try to kill me before you register that it might be a problem?'

'I'd really hoped the two of you could work out your differences,' Morden said. 'Ah, well. Someone else has a prior claim.'

'You don't know where Anne is either, do you?'

Morden shook his head. 'Your fishing attempts are actively painful to watch. Enough games. I do not know Anne Walker's location, but fortunately for you I have my own interests in her well-being. By this time tomorrow, I will know where she is and why, and I will take my own measures. Go home, Verus. You and your Keeper friend. I will take care of this from here.'

I stared at Morden, trying to work out if he was telling the truth.

A flicker of movement from the direction of the entrance caught my eye, and as I looked towards the front entrance a nasty feeling went through my gut. There was someone crossing the floor wearing a mask and an outfit very similar to mine, and from his body language he looked extremely unhappy about something. If he'd just had to get past a group of Jagadev's guards, all of whom had been under the impression that they'd let him in already, I could understand why. A strange two-tone bell sounded, echoing through the club, and people looked up.

'Avis seems a little upset,' Morden said as I stood there, hesitating. 'Tell me, is there anyone at this audience whom you *haven't* managed to aggravate?'

'The ones I haven't met?' Several of Jagadev's men were moving in a purposeful way towards the front entrance. That chime had sounded a lot like an alarm . . . almost as if Avis had had to fight his way in . . . in which case they'd be looking for someone dressed exactly like . . . 'Got to go,' I told Morden. 'Later.'

'Have you made your choice yet?'

I'd moved past Morden, but that made me pause. 'What?'

Morden was watching me, his head tilted slightly. 'He won't wait for ever, you know.'

Something about the words made my hair stand on end. I backed away, not taking my eyes off Morden, and the Dark mage watched me go. I put a pillar between us and started walking fast.

As I headed for the stairs, I switched back to Luna and Sonder's circuit. '—trying,' Sonder was saying.

'Can you hurry this up?' Luna said. 'Running out of time here.'

'I . . .' Sonder paused again. It sounded like he was using one of his spells, but his voice didn't have the usual sureness it does when he's seeing into the past. 'I'm not sure.'

'You're not sure, *what*?'

'Time's up,' I broke in, broadcasting only to Luna. 'Luna, we're going.'

'Fine,' Luna said. 'I'm thirty seconds out.'

'Good, I'll— Shit. Wait a sec.' Avis was heading straight for the stairs. I cut the connection and tried to figure out if I could get past him. No good: the stairway wasn't wide enough. I moved past, heading for the nearest corner—

—and Onyx was right on the other side. I scanned left and right for ways to avoid him and realised with a sinking heart that he was standing still. If he'd been moving in any direction I could have dodged him, but I couldn't sneak past on an open balcony. Below, I knew that Avis was just about to start up the stairs. I had maybe twenty seconds to get out of sight.

I looked around, thinking fast. There was a doorway set into the wall but the room beyond was a dead end. If I went back the way I came I'd run straight into Morden, and eventually Sagash and Caldera. I could hide, but that meant giving up any control over whether I'd be found. I looked into the futures in which I got spotted by Onyx and Avis. Both were about ready to kill me on sight.

*Kill on sight* . . . I stopped. *Wait a minute* . . .

Ten seconds. I moved to the corner, snatched up a wooden statuette from the table, waited two seconds for Onyx to turn his head the other way, then stepped around the corner and threw. Two other Dark mages whipped their heads around as the statuette described a neat ballistic arc before hitting Onyx in the back of the head.

Onyx staggered but recovered almost instantly, whirling around as a transparent bubble of force flashed into existence around him. He stared at me, then down at the statuette, then back up at me again. I think the sheer ridiculousness of it threw him for a second: *no one* does that kind of thing to a Dark mage. I figured he needed some extra motivation, so I gave him the finger just to make my feelings clear.

That did the trick. Onyx's eyes lit up with fury, and as his hands came up I jumped back around the corner and darted into the room. Just as I got inside, Avis appeared at the top of the stairs, turning in my direction. I held dead still as Avis stalked by outside, passed my hiding place and turned the corner to where Onyx was waiting.

There was a moment's silence, then the flat *wham* of a force spell and Avis went flying straight out over the club floor. He clipped the railing on his way over, but his shield was already up and it only sent him tumbling. Avis didn't fall but kept going horizontally, doing two full backflips before steadying himself to hover in mid-air, grey light gathering at his hands, storm winds whipping at his hair and clothes. He threw out an arm and something translucent flashed out just in time to meet Onyx's second strike.

I was already running, using the brief moment of distraction to make it to the stairwell. I raced down the stairs three at a time, sending Dark mages jumping out of the way. A thunderclap shook the room as I made it to the ground floor; Luna was waiting by a side-door behind one of the tables, looking up at the battle with wide eyes. 'We're leaving!' I told her as I came to a halt, dumping the contents of a small pouch into my right hand. It sparkled briefly before I closed my fist around it.

Luna nodded, not taking her eyes off the scene at my back. Behind and above, Avis was still duelling with Onyx, the air mage a blur of motion as he wove through Onyx's shots; he hadn't yet noticed me and I wasn't planning on giving him the chance. I pushed the door open.

The route Variam had told me about led through the kitchens and out one of the side-doors. It would have been nice if it had been unguarded, but unfortunately Jagadev's the thorough type and there was a security man standing inside the anteroom. He didn't carry a visible weapon but I could see a bulge inside his jacket. 'I'm sorry, sir,' he said to the two of us. 'These are the kitchens.'

'That's all right,' I said. I'd slowed before opening the door and now I walked forward in a self-assured sort of way, obviously dismissing the guard. 'I know where I'm going.' He wasn't going for his gun; he couldn't have been given my description yet. Good.

'I'm sorry, sir,' the guard said again, moving to block my

path. I didn't change course, and he held out an arm to bar my way as I walked into him. 'I'm afraid you'll have to—'

The guard's arm blocked his view of what I was doing, and he had only an instant to react before I threw the handful of glitterdust right in his face. Sparkling flecks clung to his eyes, blinding him; he staggered back, hands coming up instinctively. The movement left his lower body open so I kicked him in the groin, then when he doubled over I hit him on the back of his head. He went down hard and I kept going; the whole fight had taken less than two seconds. Luna gave the guy an interested glance and followed.

We passed through the door and into a wide kitchen full of men and women in aprons. Steam and the scent of food filled the air, and between the din of cooking and the chatter of voices it was hard to hear. Someone shouted something as we reached the other side, but I didn't turn to look and in only a second we were into the corridor beyond. The route Variam had given us was good, and although I'd been searching ahead to map our way it hadn't been necessary. The corridor ended in a flight of stairs, and at the top was a fire door. I pushed it open and stepped out into the cool spring night.

We were in a Soho alley, the sounds of the city all around. Lights glowed from the street at the far end, a narrow window onto a brighter world. Music echoed down the alley, interrupted by a shriek. It sounded like excitement rather than pain . . . probably. 'Vari,' I said as I trotted down the steps and turned right. 'Two of us coming in cold.'

'Gating,' Variam said. From the end of the alley I felt a flicker of magic.

For his gate location Variam had chosen a hulking dark building at the end of the alley. The door was ajar rather than burnt to ashes: apparently even Variam's capable of being subtle sometimes. 'Taxi,' Luna called out as we walked in.

'You wish,' Variam said. The room was big and dark with metal racks along the walls and ceiling, and he was standing in a corner, the fiery glow of his magic lighting the gloomy interior. 'We good to go?'

'All clear,' I said, shutting the door behind us. I'd been checking for any signs of pursuit, and while it was going to come, it was still a few minutes out. By the time they traced us here there'd be nothing but an empty room.

'Calling Sonder,' I heard Luna say into her communicator. 'Sonder, everything okay?'

'What?' Sonder said. He sounded distracted. 'No, it's fine.'

'Tell Caldera we're out, okay? Oh, and have fun at the party.'

Variam's gate bloomed and took shape in the air in front of him, a fiery ring leading into a place of trees and grass. I stepped through and let it take me away.

## 6

We gated through a couple of staging points, then returned to my shop. I'd already told Luna to stay the night, and Variam ended up staying as well: given the amount of trouble I'd stirred up, I had the feeling that it might be a good idea to take a few extra precautions for a while.

I tried raising Sonder on the communicator, but couldn't reach him. Synchronous communicators are supposed to have an unlimited range but the smaller ones don't work that way in practice; apparently there are some engineering problems that haven't been worked out. From looking into the futures in which I called them, I could tell Sonder and Caldera were at least still able to answer their phones. I couldn't really think of anything I could do that wouldn't risk making matters worse, and in any case I had the feeling it might be a good idea to give Caldera a bit of time to cool off, so I left Sonder a message asking to meet tomorrow. I checked the building defences, spent a while looking into the future for attacks, then once I was reasonably sure no one was going to try to assassinate us during the night I left Luna and Variam to argue over who was going to get dinner and went to bed.

Even then, I didn't sleep. I could feel Elsewhere hanging somewhere between waking and dreams, and again I probed the futures in which I travelled there, searching for Anne. Again I couldn't see any trace of her . . . but then I couldn't see much trace of anything else either. My magic is unreliable when it comes to Elsewhere. I've always been much better at physical divination than mental: it's easy for me to see what'll happen to my body; less so my mind. I'm not sure whether it's because my talents lean that way or because mental divination is just more difficult. Whatever the reason, the pathways in which I visited Elsewhere felt like shifting sand, and I only felt blurred impressions before they closed off again.

I could just go to Elsewhere anyway. I could see what I'd find, try to find a way into Anne's dreams . . . but I had the feeling that was a bad idea. My instincts were telling me that something very nasty could be waiting inside, and over the years I've learned to listen to those feelings. Elsewhere is not a safe place, and I've pushed my luck there enough times. I didn't want to risk it again.

I was still worrying over it when exhaustion caught up with me and I fell asleep.

I woke early and lay in bed for a few minutes looking out of my window at the sunrise, watching the light creep across the chimneys. When I was fully awake I headed for the bathroom and spent a while re-dying my hair. I'd never realised just how much work colouring is. When my hair was somewhere close to its natural shade I emerged into the kitchen.

Luna was sitting at the table, going through messages on her phone. 'Morning,' she said without looking up. 'Sonder says he wants us to meet at his flat in an hour.'

'Good.' I put the kettle on and started making toast. I wasn't hungry – I don't eat much when I'm worried – but fuel is fuel.

'Anything from Elsewhere?'

I shook my head, leaning against the counter. 'I can't see if she's there, and I'm afraid to go poking around without a path to follow.' There aren't many people I would have admitted the last part to, but I've come to trust Luna over the past two years. She's one of the few people I've been to Elsewhere with, and she knows exactly how scary it can be.

'Why can't you find her?' Luna said. 'You found me.'

'Just because it works with one person doesn't mean it'll work with another.'

'Then why not her?'

I took the toast out from under the grill and began spreading butter on it. 'Maybe she isn't asleep when I'm trying to do it,' I said at last. 'Anne can stay awake for days if she has to. Or maybe she *is* asleep and I just can't reach her. Because I don't know her well enough, because she doesn't trust me enough, because there isn't enough of a connection for us to find each other . . .'

I took the food to the table and sat down. Luna was silent and I knew she'd figured out the third possible reason, the one I hadn't said out loud. You have to be alive to sleep. I finished my breakfast in silence, and Luna didn't speak again. Eventually Variam appeared and we headed to Sonder's flat.

The meeting went a lot less smoothly than the last one.

Things kicked off with both Sonder and Caldera chewing me out. I'd expected it and pursued my normal strategy for dealing with angry people in a position of authority: avoid a confrontation, don't commit to anything and wait. Caldera gave up after only a few half-hearted threats. I think underneath the posturing she was a bit embarrassed that I'd had to help Sonder out. More surprising was that

Sonder actually seemed *more* angry about the whole thing than Caldera was.

'We told you not to come!' Sonder said for the third time. He was standing in front of his whiteboard, glaring at me.

'Strictly speaking, you said you didn't *need* us,' I said, leaning back against the wall. I didn't bring up how he'd needed bailing out within ten minutes of getting through the front door.

'You knew what I meant!'

'Well, I didn't exactly. I mean, you did make it clear that you weren't expecting to need any extra help, but we never discussed what we were going to do if extra information came up that changed the situation.'

'There wasn't any extra information!'

'Sonder,' Caldera said from where she was sitting. 'Let's move on.'

'Yeah,' Luna said. To begin with she'd found it hilarious that Sonder and Caldera were reprimanding me, but the joke had obviously gotten old. 'What about those apprentices? What did they say?'

The mention of Sagash's apprentices was enough to get Sonder's attention. 'They . . .' Sonder hesitated. 'It wasn't any good.'

'Did they do it or not?'

'I don't think so.'

'How do you know?'

'Well, they didn't talk about Anne.'

'They recognised her name,' Luna said.

'Okay, they knew who she *was*, but I don't think they knew anything else.'

'What else did they say?' I asked.

'Nothing,' Sonder said. 'Something about a third apprentice – some other girl. It wasn't Anne.'

'That was it?' I asked. 'That was all you could see in the whole conversation?'

'There wasn't anything else,' Sonder said in annoyance. 'Anyway, you were distracting me.'

I held back my retort, feeling frustrated. Normally when it comes to timesight, Sonder'll tell you everything you could possibly want to know – the hard part is getting him to shut up. He'd picked a hell of a time to start being uninformative.

'What about Sagash?' Variam asked Caldera. 'You spoke to him, right?'

'Sagash claims he hasn't had any contact with Anne since she left his apprenticeship,' Caldera said.

'Is he lying?'

'I'm not a mind mage,' Caldera said. 'I was asking in my capacity as a Keeper. If Sagash *did* have Anne, he could have just told me. There's nothing more I could do without a Council order.'

'Maybe there was something else he was covering up,' Luna said.

'He's a Dark mage: of course there's something he's covering up. But there's no evidence that it's what we're looking for.'

'Jagadev?' I asked.

'Stonewalled.'

'What about Crystal?' Sonder said.

'I got the latest report from the Crystal team this morning,' Caldera said. 'I'll read it more thoroughly later, but the short version is there aren't any leads connecting her to Anne.'

'Can't we just give up on Crystal already?' Variam said.

I had to hold back a sigh. The whole reason I'd explained where Sonder was coming from to Vari yesterday was so that he *wouldn't* push Sonder about Crystal. Vari's a good guy to have at your back in a fight, but he's not a great listener.

'Crystal was responsible for the deaths of four Light apprentices over several months without anyone suspecting her,' Sonder said. 'We wouldn't expect to see any evidence that it was her, not easily.'

'Let's go back to Sagash's apprentices,' I said, looking at Caldera. 'Luna found out a bit about them, but I guess you've got their files?'

'We're not Big Brother,' Caldera said. 'We don't have files on every mage in the country.'

I looked at her with eyebrows raised.

'I know a little bit of *common knowledge* about them,' Caldera said with a scowl. 'Sagash has three apprentices – Darren Smith, Yun Ji-yeong and Sam Taylor. First two are living family, third is an elementalist. The two boys have been his apprentices for at least one year, the girl at least six months, but those are lowball estimates.'

Luna stirred. 'Wait. Elemental and living?' She looked at Sonder. 'Wasn't that what you saw when Anne was kidnapped?'

'Not exactly . . .'

'You said lightning and death magic.' Luna looked around. 'Doesn't that fit?'

'We don't know that. They could—'

'They're both guys,' Luna interrupted, and started ticking off points on her fingers. 'They're the right height and weight and skin colour. Their magic types match.

They've got a connection to Sagash. Isn't this making kind of a pattern here?'

'They said it wasn't them.'

'And there's no way they could possibly be lying?'

'But they . . .'

The argument went on. Variam and Luna were convinced that it had to be Sagash and his apprentices, while Sonder held out stubbornly. At last Caldera spoke up. 'Enough. This isn't getting us anywhere.'

*And this is where she tells us what to do again*, I thought.

'Sagash's apprentices should be the focus of the investigation,' Caldera said, then raised a hand when Sonder started to object. 'I know it's not conclusive but so far they're the closest match to our suspects and we don't have any other active leads.' She looked around. 'Variam, you're with me – we're going to try and track them down. Sonder, I'll send you the Crystal report. Maybe you can get something out of it that I missed. Luna, Alex, you're on standby. Once we find those apprentices I'll call you in.' She gave me a look. 'Ordering you to stay out of trouble doesn't seem to work very well so I'm going to keep you where I can keep an eye on you instead. Do you think you can manage not to start any wars with Dark mages while I'm gone?'

'I'll do my best,' I said with a straight face.

The meeting broke up, Caldera and Variam heading out. Luna and I were following when Sonder broke in. 'Luna? Can I speak to you privately, please?'

Luna gave him a curious look. 'Okay . . .'

Sonder gave me a pointed look. I shrugged. 'I'll wait for you outside.'

I went out of Sonder's flat and down to the first-floor

landing. It was carpeted and well heated, and I looked out the window to see a carefully cultivated area of grass and bushes. The buildings were a doughnut-block design with a small park at the centre where some children were playing, supervised by an equal number of adults. The buildings muffled the noise from the streets outside and it all looked very peaceful. I've always felt that Sonder's flat suits him pretty well – well off and sheltered. I could have eavesdropped on him and Luna easily enough but didn't.

After five minutes or so I started to hear raised voices. The volume rose, then cut off and there were rapid footsteps. Sonder's door opened and Luna appeared; she shut it with a bang and walked quickly down the stairs. The silvery mist of her curse was lashing and twisting around her, reaching out to twice its normal length. I leant back into the wall and she pulled the tendrils in as she passed, then let them expand again as soon as she was out of range of me. 'Didn't go well?' I said.

Luna gave me a look from the landing below and kept going. I started to follow her down, keeping a careful distance. Luna's become much better at controlling her curse but there's no point tempting fate. 'What was that about?'

'You don't want to know.'

'Seriously?' Luna didn't answer, and I shook my head. 'Maybe not, but it sounds like I'd better.'

'He wanted me to leave you and be a Council apprentice instead.'

I stopped. 'He did *what*?'

Luna had reached the front door; I was halfway up the last flight of stairs. 'Told you you wouldn't like it,' Luna said.

'What did you say?'

'I told him to get lost, what do you think?'

I stared at Luna. 'Okay, screw this,' I said after a few seconds. I turned and started back up the stairs.

'Alex . . .' Luna said warningly.

'We're just going to talk,' I called over my shoulder as I disappeared from her view.

When I reached Sonder's flat, I didn't use the bell but banged on the door with my fist. I kept banging until Sonder yelled, 'All right, all right!' and opened it. As soon as he did, I pushed past into his living room.

Sonder followed, looking peevish. 'Would you mind—?'

'Okay, Sonder,' I said, turning on him. 'I am officially out of patience. Not wanting me around I can put up with. Your whining last night – that was just annoying. But this? This is over the line.'

'What?'

'You know *exactly* what!'

'It's not your business what Luna does,' Sonder said.

I took a deep breath, trying to control my temper. Sonder was still young; he couldn't be expected to know how insulting it was to headhunt another mage's apprentice . . . actually, screw that, he'd grown up as a Light apprentice and he had to know *exactly* how insulting it was. 'If you have a problem with Luna being my apprentice, you bring it to me,' I said. 'You do not go behind my back. Clear?'

'Well, what if the problem *is* you?'

'And what exactly do you mean by that?'

'Maybe if you actually cared about her you wouldn't be teaching her at all,' Sonder said. 'You'd be finding someone else.'

'Not that it's any of your business,' I said, 'but finding chance mage teachers isn't easy. Especially not with Luna's curse.'

'I don't mean that! I don't want you teaching her to be the same kind of person *you* are!'

My anger vanished and I looked at Sonder. He was glaring at me: he'd obviously been working himself up to this. 'Okay,' I said, holding quite still. 'Now we're getting to it. What exactly is your problem with me?'

'What do you think?'

'I think I can guess, but why don't you tell me?'

'Remember back when we went after Belthas?' Sonder said. 'Two years ago with that Dark mage, Cinder? Up on the mountain, we were trying to find a way in to Belthas past his security men.'

I paused. 'Okay.'

'Then before that. When we went to that factory and that man followed us there?'

This wasn't how I'd expected the conversation to go — I'd been expecting a repeat of the argument with Anne. 'Yeah . . .'

'And before *that*. When Griff tried to get the fateweaver. Remember that?'

'Are you going somewhere with—?'

'I'm not finished. Those three men who tried to kill Anne while we were investigating those disappearances running up to the White Stone? Remember them?'

'*Yes*, I remember them. What are you getting at?'

'Why don't you tell me what they've all got in common?'

'I don't know. What have they got in common?'

'*They're all dead.*'

Sonder was glaring at me. 'What's your point?' I said.

'You know last year, when I found out you'd killed all those adepts?' Sonder said. 'It really shook me up. I couldn't believe you'd do something like that. And then I started going back and thinking about it, and you know what hit me? *It wasn't anything new.* Every time you've got into something like this, every time someone goes after you, they end up dead. You killed those adepts because *that's what you do.*'

'Okay, wait a second.' I was starting to get angry again. 'Pretty much every single one of those guys you just listed was trying to kill me at the time. What exactly do you think I should have done?'

'That's what you said back on the mountain. You said it was self-defence, that there was no other way. You made it sound really convincing but that's always your line, isn't it? It's never your fault.'

'I don't care whose fault it is,' I said tightly. 'It's about surviving.'

'Well, you know what?' Sonder said. 'There are lots of Light mages around in Britain who've survived pretty well. And you know what they haven't done? They haven't killed anyone. Most people don't; that's why we have laws against murder! It's just *you* who can't seem to go a whole year without killing someone. Maybe it's not about surviving or self-defence, or because there's no other way. Maybe it's you.'

I rocked back slightly, feeling a stab of fear. 'I see,' I said once I'd got myself just barely under control. 'And you've felt this way for how long?'

'It's not just me,' Sonder said. 'People in the Council are talking about you. The longer Luna stays with you, the harder it'll be for her to find anyone else. If you really want to help her, you should find her another teacher.'

I looked back at Sonder and counted silently to ten, forcing myself back to calm. 'Thank you for your honesty,' I said at last, my voice cold. 'Allow me to retort. I'm quite sure you're right – your friends on the Council don't kill, not personally. They have people to do that for them. But the orders they pass down cause more deaths than I ever will. I would also note that you didn't seem terribly bothered about my methods when it was *your* life on the line. Remember that little episode with Griff? If I hadn't dealt with him and Onyx, exactly what do you think your chances would have been of getting out of that bubble alive?'

'You didn't have to kill him! You could have found some other way!'

'It's easy to say there's another way when you're not the one who has to find it.' Sonder started to answer and I spoke over him, my voice hard. 'Shut up, Sonder. You had your say; now it's my turn. I'd also like to point out that while you might not like the way I do things, the times in the past that you or Anne or Luna *have* been in trouble I've done a pretty good job of helping you. So you might want to ask yourself what's more important to you: helping Anne, or your issues with me?'

Sonder stared at me. I turned to leave.

'Anne thinks the same thing, you know,' Sonder said just as I was turning the handle. I didn't answer, and I banged the door behind me exactly as Luna had.

I went home, but I had trouble concentrating. Sonder's words kept going around my head; I was angry at how unfair he was being, and afraid that he might be right. It was distracting me from trying to find Anne . . . not that there was much I could do in the first place, and *that* wasn't making me feel any better either.

Novices and adepts think a diviner can find out anything, and I usually let them believe it – a slightly exaggerated reputation never hurts – but it just doesn't work that way. Most 'finding' uses of divination come down to a very long string of if/then conditions. You come up with an avenue of investigation, then you test it. If you don't have anywhere to start, then divination just amounts to wild guessing, with about the same odds of success . . . and that was a problem because time was running out. I used to know an independent mage who specialised in missing persons cases, and he told me about something he called the seventy-two-hour rule: if you don't find someone within seventy-two hours, then odds are you won't find them at all. Anne had been missing for nearly sixty.

I needed to do something, but I wasn't sure what. Until Caldera got back in touch, there wasn't much I *could* do to help with the search.

Every few minutes, I found my thoughts drifting back to Sonder, coming up with more things to say: justifications; arguments. Then I found it blending into my feelings about Anne, imagining that I was arguing with her instead. I wanted to talk to one of them or both of them: try to explain; work something out. But Anne wasn't there and Sonder wouldn't listen, and I knew it was a stupid thing to do anyway. Anne and Sonder weren't the problem, not really. The problem was . . .

My heart sank as I realised where the train of thought was heading. *Yeah. That's who I actually need to talk to, isn't it?*

I looked into the future to see whether Caldera was going

to call soon, half hoping for an excuse to stay home. She wasn't and I set out.

For the second time in four days, I was back at the Institute of Education.

I was in the basement atrium, standing against one of the pillars. The lecture had just ended and students were streaming out, shouting and talking and checking their phones. None of them paid any attention to me. I searched their faces as they went past, boys and girls all with their school bags and middle-class clothes. They looked so *young*, and there was something dismaying about the thought. I was only ten years older than they were, less for the mature students, but it felt as though I had nothing in common with them at all.

Watching the sea of students – children – pulled my thoughts away, associations from point to point. Crowds of teenagers, faces, classrooms. It reminded me of childhood, and they weren't good memories. Things were never really good at home when I was young, even before the divorce, and they were worse at school. I'd been an introverted kid, intelligent and sensitive and socially clumsy. Bad combination if you go to a British state school. I once read an article which made the argument that modern Western schools have a good deal in common with modern prisons, and I've always thought it was pretty accurate. With both schools and prisons, the ones running the system have a very simple set of priorities for their inmates: they want them to stay on the premises, they want them to stay healthy and watered and fed, and they want them not to be gratuitously violent in a way that'll draw public attention. Beyond that, they don't really care. There are plenty of teachers who do their best to help, but they're swimming upstream and most of the time the kids end up creating their own society. It's ruthless and cruel, and it is not fun to be at the bottom of it.

When my magic started developing, it only made things worse. Universal magic is the hardest of all the families for humans to use – it's too abstract, too alien. When you're a novice diviner, your power comes in flashes: sometimes you just catch a glimpse of possibilities and sometimes you see *all* of them, every future at once, crashing into your mind like an ocean trying to fill a water bowl. It didn't send me crazy, not quite, but I wasn't exactly stable either and the fact that I had no idea what was happening to me didn't help. Maybe if I'd had someone to talk to I might have tried to explain it, but there wasn't anyone left by then, not really. My dad had lost custody, I didn't get on with my mother and my near-psychotic episodes had cut off the few friendships I'd had.

So I learned to control my power. I learned to focus my mind; block out the futures I didn't want to see; *direct* my perception instead of taking in everything. I learned to select futures; search out along those not-quite-visible strands of possibility; shut them off when it was too much and I needed time to recover. And I did it alone, because I had to. And it worked.

It didn't make me any happier. My crude ability to see the future didn't make me any friends – the opposite, if anything. I had knowledge, but there wasn't anything I could *do* with it. I was left just as isolated, hating the people who'd ostracised me. Until one cold autumn day when Richard had stepped onto the schoolyard where I was standing, promising me everything I'd secretly wanted if I'd follow him and call him master. And I'd said yes.

Movement from inside the hall broke me out of my reverie. Nearly all of the students had disappeared up the stairs; only a few stragglers were left, one or two of them giving me curious glances now that I was the only person standing still in the atrium. A buzz of conversation from inside grew louder, then tailed off. A man appeared at the doors, white-haired, lecture notes tucked under one arm. He spotted me two steps into the room and came to a stop.

'Hey, Dad,' I said.

The inner courtyard of the Institute of Education was cold. It had been a long winter – we'd had flurries of snow as recently as a couple of weeks ago, even though it was April. My father and I sat on one of the benches, the cold of the wood creeping through my clothes. Students passed by in ones and twos, coats closed against the chill wind.

'I didn't know you'd moved here,' I said.

'Here?' My father looked at me, confused.

'The institute.'

'What? Oh, no – I'm still at UCL.'

I found myself watching my father out of the corner of my eye. His hair seemed a little thinner and the lines on his face deeper since the last time I'd seen him, his posture a little more stooped. Did he look older, or was I just noticing it now? His voice sounded frail, and watching him gave me a strange feeling. For mages, age isn't a sign of weakness, it's the opposite – white hair is a sign that they've lived long enough to be dangerous. My father didn't look dangerous. He looked apologetic.

'Teaching?' I said.

'Yes, the usual courses. This is just a part of the spring schedule. Eight lectures.'

'Cool.'

We sat in silence. A few more students walked by.

'So, congratulations on making professor,' I said.

'Thank you. I mean, it's not confirmed yet, but . . .'

'Yeah.'

Another pause.

'How are things working out with the shop?' my father asked.

'Oh, fine. Business as usual.' I paused. 'I'm taking a few days off because a friend of mine got partially abducted by some people who probably want to hurt or kill her, so we're trying to track her down before they do.'

My father twisted around to look at me. I looked back.

'Are you . . . Could you say that again?'

'Friend abducted; trying to find her.'

'Isn't that a job for the police?'

'We're working with a . . .' I tried to think of how to describe Caldera in non-magical terms. 'With a branch of the police. Not sure how long we'll have their support though.'

'How do you mean?'

'They might pull their people off the case.' Of which the odds were two in three and climbing, assuming we were weighing the suspects equally. 'If they do, we'll have to finish things on our own.'

My father was silent for a little while. 'You're planning to take matters into your own hands.'

I didn't answer.

'Will there be trouble?'

'Possibly.' *Probably.*

'I'd thought . . .' My father paused. 'The last time, you said you were trying to put this sort of thing behind you.'

'Yeah, well, it turns out trying to put the past behind you doesn't work too well when the past doesn't cooperate.'

'I'm . . . I have to say, I'm not comfortable with you doing this.' My father clasped his hands, elbows resting on knees. 'It sounds too close to what you were doing with that man you were involved with, Richard.'

I felt a flare of anger. How do parents always know how to get under your skin? 'It's nothing to do with Richard,' I said levelly. 'I'm trying to help someone.'

'You ought to leave it to the authorities.'

'The authorities are overworked, their freedom of action is limited and they don't care very much about this person in the first place.'

'I know these situations are frustrating but breaking the law just makes things worse, even if you *are* trying to help. These rules are in place for a reason. There's no guarantee that trying to interfere will make things any better, and even if you do, you're setting a bad precedent.'

'How can you believe this with what you teach?' I asked. I pointed down through the flagstones, towards the lecture hall. 'European history is one very long study in conflict, violence and rule-breaking.'

'Haven't we advanced beyond that? There's no excuse for resolving our disagreements with violence any more.'

'What exactly do you think the police and military do?'

'Look,' my father said. 'We've had this discussion before. I'm just worried that you're working up to something.'

'Mostly just what I told you,' I said. 'Well, plus last year a bunch of teenagers tried to assassinate me so I killed them all, but that's not important right now.'

My father frowned. 'You're not serious.'

I sighed. 'I was kidding.' *No, I wasn't.*

'I think that joke's in rather poor taste.'

I looked at my father with a hopeless feeling. What was I doing here? I couldn't talk to him about my life; what I'd done to survive. Out of morbid curiosity, I looked to see what his reaction would be if I *did* tell him the truth about last year, and almost immediately wished I hadn't. Shock, disbelief, horror. It'd leave him devastated.

'Sorry,' I said. Another awkward silence.

'I . . . know things haven't always been easy for you,' my father said. 'I've always regretted not being there when you were younger. And I know we've had our disagreements. Is there, well . . . anything you'd like to tell me?'

I looked back at him. *Anything I'd like to tell you . . . How about that everything you taught me was wrong? Your pacifism didn't help when I was getting bullied for years on end. Didn't help when my mother divorced you and got custody. If you hadn't been so weak, maybe I wouldn't have jumped at the first offer that let me think I could be strong . . .*

'No,' I said. 'I'm fine.'

'All right.'

My phone vibrated. Looking into the future in which I checked it, I saw that it was Caldera. News. 'I'd better go,' I said, standing.

My father rose with me. 'Ah. You know, you're welcome to visit for dinner sometime.'

*A whole evening of this?* The thought made me flinch. 'Yeah,' I said. 'I'll be in touch.'

'Well, goodbye.' My father paused. 'Be careful.'

'I will.' At least that was close to true.

My father walked back to the institute, and I watched

him go. To my eyes, he looked thin and frail. As he reached the doors I shook my head and turned away, heading north with long strides, taking out my phone and dialling a number.

Caldera answered on the second ring. 'Alex?'

'It's me.'

'We've got an address for one of Sagash's apprentices.' Caldera's voice was curt. 'Meet there as soon as possible. Be ready for trouble.'

'I'll be there in forty minutes.'

Caldera hung up and I dropped my phone back into my pocket. I was still pissed off, and I knew why. It had been my father's implication that I was going back to how I'd been with Richard. It was too close to what Sonder had said, and the unfairness of it made me angry. It was so black and white, their world. Either you were a sheep or you were a wolf. You didn't use violence or you were a thug. Nothing in between.

Well, screw them both. I wasn't going to be like my father, but I wasn't going to be like Richard either. I was going to help Anne no matter what they thought.

'Are they going to stand there all day or what?' Variam asked.

We were on a council estate in Tufnell Park. My divination magic had found us an empty flat with a good view, and we were inside the cramped upper bedroom, looking out of the window. The interior of the flat was dusty and cold, with old magazines scattered across the floor; whoever lived here hadn't been home for a long time. Through the window, we could see a courtyard of pebble-set concrete, with more flats rising opposite. Caldera and Sonder were on the upper walkway fifty feet across, heads bent over the door of flat number 229. According to Caldera, that flat was the residence of one Darren Smith, Sagash's apprentice. The sky was overcast and grey, and wind whined past outside.

'Maybe they're knocking on the door and saying they have a warrant,' I said.

'Then shouldn't we be over there?'

'Caldera wants us around for backup,' I said. *And to keep an eye on us.* 'Sonder doesn't want us around at all. I guess this is the compromise.'

Opposite, the door opened and Caldera walked inside. Sonder started to follow but Caldera made a gesture and Sonder hung back. 'Four of us for one Dark apprentice who isn't even there,' Variam muttered. 'This is such a waste of time.' He gave me a look. 'Why are you wearing that armour anyway?'

'Not everyone gets to have your fancy elemental shields, you know.' The armour I was wearing was an imbued item Arachne had made for me: a close-woven mesh with re-inforcing plates. It's black and grey and not particularly bulky, but it's still not the best thing to wear for blending into a crowd, which was why I'd covered it with a great-coat. I could feel its presence, protective and watchful, but it matched my movements so well that it was easy to forget it was there. 'And if there was one thing I learned last year, it was that it's a lot better to have armour and not need it than to need it and not have it.'

Variam fell silent and I went back to looking into the future, searching for the tell-tale signs of combat. I'd already confirmed that no one was in the flat, but a common trick mages use is to set up silent alarms in places they want protected. The intruder breaks in and has just enough time to relax before a prepared and pissed-off mage gates in on top of them.

If something like that did happen, then Caldera and Sonder's chances would be a lot better if they had advance warning, which from this distance was a lot harder for me to give. Yet despite that, Sonder still didn't want me around, which bothered me more than I liked to admit.

Minutes passed. Sonder had followed Caldera into the flat and shut the door behind them. With no direct physical or visual link I couldn't easily path-walk to their location, so I switched my focus to the futures of the communication channel, trusting Caldera to stay in touch. If anything happened she should be able to send me a message.

Probably.

It wasn't a good sign that I was saying 'probably' about something like that.

'Did you turn up anything?' I asked Variam.

'If I had, you think I'd be here?'

We sat in silence a little while longer. 'Why do you care so much about protecting Anne?' I said at last.

Variam shot me a look. 'This really the time?'

'Maybe not, but I've asked you that question a few times now and you always find some reason not to answer.'

Variam didn't reply. 'You said something last year which stuck in my head,' I said. 'You said taking care of Anne was your job. I know the two of you grew up together. But the way you act towards her . . .' I looked at Variam. 'Has it got something to do with Sagash? Is that why you're so convinced it's him? I know you don't want to talk about it but if there's any way it could help . . . now might be the time.'

Variam stood for a minute in silence. I didn't disturb him, watching the futures flicking back and forth: I knew he was making his decision. Slowly the futures firmed and settled. 'If I tell you this, you can't tell anyone else,' Variam said at last. 'Not Luna, not Arachne, definitely not Anne. No one.' He stared at me. 'You got it?'

I nodded.

'Swear.'

'I won't tell anyone else without your permission. You have my word.'

'When Anne got taken by Sagash that first time, I went looking for her,' Variam said. 'You know how hard it is to find someone when you don't have anywhere to start?'

'Yeah.'

'I didn't know anything. Didn't know where to look, didn't know what to ask. Took months before I even figured out how the Light and Dark thing worked. I tried adepts, independents, the Council. They didn't know; they didn't care.' Variam looked up through the window towards the light behind the clouds. 'Then one day I heard something. About a creature that could answer any question you asked it. The Fire Dragon.'

I looked at Variam sharply.

'You know what it's like, meeting a dragon?' Variam was still staring out at the sky. 'It was . . . light. Blackness. Flame. I . . . saw a movie about astronomy once, back in school. There were pictures of the sun, solar flares. You saw them and they looked like little flickers of fire, except each one was bigger than the planet. That was what it felt like. Like you were trying to see something on a scale you just didn't *work* on. I don't know where we were or how long it lasted, but when I was done I was just back again.'

'What did it tell you?' I asked quietly.

'It didn't talk. It was more like . . . visions. I saw what I'd come to ask, and I saw the answers. Other things, too . . .' Variam trailed off for a second, then shook his head. 'It doesn't matter. But some of it was about Anne, and that bit I *did* understand. I saw Sagash, and I knew she was with him. And I knew if I didn't get her away, then something would happen to her.'

'Something?'

'Sagash wasn't going to kill her. She was going to be turned into something. She'd stop being who she was and become something else. It felt like she was . . . falling into darkness. She'd still be there, but I got the feeling it might be better if she wasn't.' Variam looked at me. 'You get what it means? That would happen if she stayed with Sagash. It didn't say *which time*. As long as he's still out there . . .'

'Does Anne know?'

Variam shook his head again. 'I thought about telling her but . . . I never knew how it was going to happen, you know? I mean, back when I met you and Luna, I thought maybe *you'd* be the ones who'd pull her back to Sagash.'

I snorted.

'Yeah, you can laugh, but it might have been. How're you supposed to stop something when you don't know how it'll happen? I even thought about going after Sagash, but it's dumb. Just because he won't kill Anne doesn't mean he won't kill me.'

'Did you think about asking her?'

'No,' Variam said. 'Because that vision I got? I was never sure whether it was something that *happened* to her or something she *decided*.'

Variam fell silent again, and this time he didn't go on. The vision Variam was talking about sounded vague, but I didn't think that was his fault. I met a dragon once too – or at least I think I did – and trying to remember it gives me the same weird disjointed feeling, like you're trying to visualise something that doesn't work in human terms. There are stories of mages going searching for dragons as Variam had, looking for secrets or wisdom or prophecy. Sometimes they can be found, sometimes not, but I've never heard of them being wrong. If Variam had received that vision, it was worrying.

But I couldn't see anything useful to do about it, and if we couldn't find Anne then it didn't matter anyway. I went back to searching the futures and saw a strengthening branch of forks heading our way. 'They're coming out,' I said.

Opposite us, the door to Darren's flat opened and Sonder and Caldera emerged, locking it behind them. They headed our way along the walkway, disappearing from sight. I walked into the hall of 'our' flat and opened the door to let them in, shivering briefly in the gust of cold air. 'Anything?' I asked once we were all inside.

'Ask him,' Caldera said with a nod to Sonder. Her manner had been different since we'd met at the flats, though I couldn't put my finger on exactly how.

Variam looked at Sonder. 'So?'

'It's his flat, but there's nothing about Anne,' Sonder said.

'Then what was the point of coming here?'

'He still uses it. There might be—'

'What's going on?' I murmured to Caldera.

'Shh,' Caldera said. She was watching Sonder.

I frowned. For some reason Caldera wasn't taking command, as though she was waiting for something.

'Then we should be going there,' Variam was saying.

'It's not Sagash, all right?' Sonder said in annoyance.

'Sonder,' I said slowly. 'If it's not Sagash, and you're *sure* it's not Sagash, what are we doing here? I thought you were sure it was Crystal.'

'It *is* Crystal!'

'Then why are we searching this flat?' Something wasn't adding up. 'What's Crystal got to do with Sagash's apprentices?'

'She's still the most likely one to be behind this,' Sonder argued. 'You know how good she was at using people; maybe *she* was the one who got them to do it. It would fit with everything—'

'Fuck Crystal,' Variam said. 'I don't think you care about finding Anne at all.'

'Well, I haven't seen *you* doing—'

The argument started up again, along predictable lines. Usually this was the point at which Caldera would step in, but glancing at her I saw she was still just watching. She still seemed to be waiting—

I stopped as my brain caught up with something I'd heard. 'Wait,' I said to Sonder. 'What did you just say?'

Sonder broke off arguing with Variam. 'What?'

'About Crystal being behind it.'

'I said that if it *was* Sagash's apprentices, maybe it was Crystal who got them to do it in the first place.'

'No,' I said slowly. 'You said "maybe she was the one who got them to do it".'

'Yeah, if it really *was* them,' Sonder said. He looked annoyed. 'I don't think it was; I'm just saying that even if that was true, it still *might* have been her.'

I stared at Sonder. 'You didn't say "if".'

Variam was looking at me curiously. 'Yes, I did,' Sonder said.

'Why did you come here in the first place?' I asked Sonder. 'You're supposed to be in charge, not Caldera. If you were really so sure that Sagash's apprentices had nothing to do with this, you shouldn't have been wasting time using your timesight on that flat.'

'Well—' Sonder hesitated. 'I didn't think so. You did.'

I looked at Sonder for a long moment, flicking through futures. Divination isn't much use in normal conversations – too many ways for things to go. But if you know the right questions to ask . . .

'It *was* them, wasn't it?' I said. 'The ones who took Anne were Sagash's two apprentices, Darren and Sam. You've known since last night. When you listened to their conversations after they'd met Luna, you found out that they were the ones who did it. You've been keeping it from us.'

Variam had been looking at me; now he turned to stare at Sonder. There was a silent question in his eyes.

Lying well takes practice. An amateur can pull off a lie as long as no one's looking for it, but as soon as they get cross-questioned they go to pieces. A professional, on the other hand, can manage interrogation just fine – they submerge themselves in the lie so well that they actually believe it themselves. There are subtle signs which you can look for, but a good liar never makes it obvious.

Sonder wasn't a good liar.

Variam's face darkened. Orange-red light sprang up at his hands, licking outwards. 'You cowardly little—' he began, his voice soft as he took a step towards Sonder. Sonder flinched back.

Then Caldera was there, putting her arm between Variam

and Sonder. 'Variam,' she said, and the note of command was back in her voice. 'Stand down.' Her eyes stayed locked on Sonder. 'Explain.'

'Uh . . .' Sonder began. He looked as though he'd rather be absolutely anywhere else.

'So that's the truth,' I said quietly.

'I was going to tell you!'

'Shut up, Verus,' Caldera said. 'Explain.'

'Look, I wasn't sure,' Sonder began. 'I mean, they said some things last night, but it could have meant anything . . .'

I shook my head in disgust. *I should have seen this coming.* The biggest problem with the information magic of a universal mage is that no one else can perceive it. Council trials which rely on timesight will use multiple time mages, all of whom give testimony independently. But Sonder had never lied about it before, and it just hadn't occurred to me that he might start now.

'You want her to stay with Sagash?' Variam said. His voice was soft, but fiery light was still flickering at his hands and I wouldn't have liked to be Sonder if Caldera wasn't there. 'That what it is?'

'It's not that!' Sonder looked angry. I didn't think he understood just how close Variam was to snapping. 'You can't do anything about it anyway!'

Variam took a slow breath in, then out. He looked as though he was fighting to keep himself under control, and barely succeeding. 'Why?' Caldera said.

'Because she's in Sagash's shadow realm!'

Variam went still. 'So that was where that gate led,' I said quietly. 'And that's why you haven't been telling us. Because a Keeper investigation can't go there without some kind of link to Crystal.'

'There *is* one,' Sonder insisted. He looked between us. 'I know there is.'

No one answered. 'Variam, wait in the hall,' Caldera said. 'We're going back to the station.'

Variam left without a word. I noticed that Caldera's eyes followed him: Sonder might have missed how close that had been but Caldera hadn't. 'Look, this can still work,' Sonder began.

Caldera waited for Variam to disappear, then shook her head at Sonder. 'Come off it.' She started to turn away. 'My report's due.'

'Wait! You could tell them—'

Caldera shot Sonder a withering look, and Sonder stopped. 'Really?' Caldera said. '*Really?* You think I'll tell a lie *that* stupid? You found out Anne's with Sagash. That's the truth and that's what I'll report. I'll ask to follow up too, I owe you that much. But I already know what they're going to say.' She paused. 'You really fucked this up, Sonder.' Caldera walked out into the hall. I heard her footsteps merge with Variam's and a second later the front door opened and closed.

Sonder and I were left alone in the flat and I studied him, thinking. Now that I knew what he'd really seen, everything was fitting together. 'Well,' I said at last. 'That could have gone better.'

Sonder glared at me through his glasses but didn't answer. 'She knew you were hiding something,' I said. 'I guess you don't get to be a Keeper without being pretty good at knowing when you're being lied to.'

'Oh, shut up.'

I shrugged. 'At least now we know where she is.'

'Yeah, that's great! We know she's in some impenetrable fortress we can't find! That's really helpful, isn't it?'

'Variam got her out once already.'

'And then what? Sagash hasn't done anything *wrong*! If we go after him *we'll* be the ones breaking the Concord!'

'Gosh.' I raised my eyebrows. 'Breaking the Concord. Couldn't have that.'

Sonder glared at me. 'You're enjoying this, aren't you? You think this proves you were right.'

'Do you really think I'm that petty?' I shook my head. 'This isn't about you.'

Sonder let out a breath and sagged. 'It doesn't matter,' he said, and all of a sudden he just sounded tired. 'None of it.' He walked out.

I watched him go, then turned to look thoughtfully back out of the window.

'So what do we do now?' Variam said over the phone.

It was some time later – long enough for Variam's temper to have cooled, though there was still an edge to his voice. 'That's what we're going to decide,' I said. 'You free to talk?'

'Yeah, Caldera's in with the captain.'

'I can't believe Sonder would pull something like this,' Luna said over the phone line. She sounded almost as pissed off as Variam. Between this and what had happened in the morning, I was pretty sure whatever slim hopes Sonder might have had in Luna's direction were going to have to be taken out the back and shot.

I was still in the flat, Variam was at the Keeper station in Marylebone and Luna was in Islington where she'd been unsuccessfully chasing leads. 'We're still better off than we were this morning,' I said. 'At least now we know where to go.'

'Yeah, except we're also down from five to three,' Luna said. 'We've lost Caldera, right?'

'She told me to take off and report back to Scotland for tomorrow,' Variam said.

'I think that's a yes,' I said. 'Okay, Vari, you're the only one who's been into Sagash's shadow realm. Let's hear about it.'

'Giant freaky castle,' Variam said. 'Looks like it's on an island just off the coastline . . . not really, though, I don't think the boundary goes that far. It's *really* big. Anne tried hiding there a few times, managed to stay out of sight for a while. Problem was the shadows. They're some kind of construct; Sagash mass-produces the things. They're not that tough, but no matter how many you burn there's always more.'

'How do you get in?' I asked.

'That's the tricky part. The whole castle's warded with a gate lock – the only place you can gate in and out is from the front courtyard, and even then you need an access key.'

'Don't suppose you've got one?'

'Yep.'

'What?' Luna said. 'Why didn't you tell us?'

'Does it still work?' I asked.

'Nope.'

'I'm guessing you've tried.'

'Yesterday.'

'Wasn't that right after Caldera told you *not* to try to contact Sagash?' Luna asked, briefly diverted.

'Screw Caldera.'

'So after you and Anne did your prison-break, Sagash changed the locks,' I said. 'Okay, our first problem is how to get in.'

'Sonder said Sagash's apprentices were using a focus,'

Luna said. 'Sagash must have given them copies of the new access keys.'

'So we find them,' Variam said.

'Agreed,' I said. 'But when we do, we're not going to start a fight.'

'Why the hell not?'

'Because the first thing I'm going to do is ask if we can buy or trade Anne back.'

'*What?*'

'What's the alternative – storm the castle? Okay, we could probably get in. But launching a frontal assault on Sagash plus his apprentices plus an army of constructs plus whatever the hell else he's got up his sleeve is not my idea of a good plan.'

'We did it before!'

'Somehow I doubt you managed it by marching up to the front door and blasting your way in.'

'Anne's not a thing!'

'To Dark mages that's exactly what she is: a commodity. Look, shut up a second and listen. I don't honestly expect this to work, but as long as there's *any* chance it's worth trying. I know it's not very heroic, but it's practical.'

'What's the backup plan?' Luna asked.

'We steal an access key and sneak in, but I don't like that plan for a whole lot of reasons. Number one is that if Sagash *is* the one behind this, then he's got to be expecting Vari to try some sort of rescue attempt, because that's what he did last time. If I were Sagash, I'd put enough security in that shadow realm to turn it into a death-trap.'

'That doesn't do us much good if we can't get an access key in the first place.'

'So, backup backup plan. Luna, I want you to go find

Arachne. I don't know much about gate wards but she does, and if there's a way into this fortress of Sagash's, there's a good chance she'll know some way to find it. Vari, if you can still do it safely, see what else you can find about Sagash's apprentices, especially the other two. See if you can get anything that'd let us track them down, or find out where they might have hidden something like an access key. They can't live in a shadow realm twenty-four-seven.'

'Got it,' Variam said.

'What about you?' Luna asked.

'I'm going to keep staking out the flat. Let's see if Mr Darren Smith makes a visit.'

I stayed in that flat for half the day. From time to time Variam or Luna would call to give me an update, and we'd share information. I left Sonder a message but didn't get a reply.

I searched the futures for any trace of Sagash's apprentices, but found nothing. There was little to do but look out of the window and watch the movement on the estate. As the hours slipped by and afternoon wore into evening, the place grew more active. A trickle of school-age kids began to filter in, passing through the corridors and heading for the football courts. Women and men climbed the stairs carrying their shopping; they disappeared inside their flats and windows lit up. A group of teenagers took up places down in the courtyard, leaning against the pillars and smoking and eyeing passers-by. One flat door on the second floor opened and a big German shepherd was let out; he trotted confidently down the row of flats to the stairs and disappeared down into the lower levels.

It was twilight when a ripple in the futures ahead caught

my attention. Someone was going to open the door to Darren's flat. I backtracked to see who it was, and . . . *Well hello, guy-I-saw-last-night. Fancy meeting you here.* I slipped out into the cold evening air and started down the walkway.

I'd had lots of time to think while I'd been waiting, and the best plans I could come up with were still 'negotiate' and 'steal the key'. I'd wavered between the two but in the end I'd decided to go with 'negotiate'. The 'steal' plan would more or less require me to use my mist cloak, an imbued item I keep stored back at my flat which is very good at hiding me. In fact, it's *so* good at hiding me that the last time I used it I nearly turned into a wraith, and I did not want to use it again if I could help it. The most likely place for Darren to be keeping the access key was on his person, and I couldn't see any way of taking it off him without getting into a fight, which I didn't want to do for a variety of reasons, not least that it'd mean attacking the apprentice of a recognised mage. That would mean *I'd* be the one breaking the Concord, which could quite possibly lead to the Keepers of Caldera's order going after *me*. No matter how bad our odds might be of getting to Anne, that would make them worse. My best chance was that Darren would be willing to cut a deal. I turned into the stairwell, waited forty seconds, then came out, turning towards Darren's flat.

Darren was on the walkway about to reach his flat, and he spotted me instantly. He was fit and tough-looking, with dark skin and curly black hair cut close to his skull. He didn't move but watched as I approached, his eyes hard and alert. I kept my motions smooth and my hands visible, and didn't make any sudden movements. The kids in the courtyard below were still in view; this wasn't the place for a fight . . . unless someone got jumpy.

We came to a halt outside Darren's flat, facing each other on the concrete walkway. A cold wind blew through the railings, and voices echoed up from the corridors below. 'Darren Smith?' I asked.

'Fuck off,' Darren said. His hands were slightly apart from his sides, and he was watching me like a hawk.

'I'd like to discuss some business with you. It involves you and your colleague Sam Taylor.'

'Never heard of him.'

'It's about a girl you've had some dealings with recently,' I said. 'By the name of Anne Walker.' I paused. 'Or if you'd prefer not to talk to me, I could take it up with Sagash.' *Fingers crossed . . .*

Darren stared at me. I felt the futures shift and flicker, and knew he was deciding what to do. One future grew and eclipsed the others, becoming real; Darren turned half away from me, still watching me in his peripheral vision, and unlocked the door to his flat. 'Inside,' he said curtly and went in. I followed.

The flat was the same design as the one I'd been using: five rooms with narrow windows looking down onto the inner flats of the council estate. I shut the door behind me without being asked and followed Darren into the living room. He'd switched the lights on as he'd come in, suggesting his magical senses weren't good enough for him to consider darkness an advantage. Once inside the living room he stripped off his coat and tossed it onto the sofa before turning to face me. Up close he looked tough, with flat eyes. Not that experienced, maybe, but you don't need to be experienced to be dangerous. 'Who are you supposed to be?'

'Nobody important,' I said. 'I'm representing someone who's interested in the welfare of Anne Walker. I

understand you may be able to help my client with that.'
Presenting yourself as an agent rather than a principal has
its drawbacks, but it does help discourage your opponent
from being too trigger-happy.

'Don't know who you're talking about.'

'Of course you don't,' I said. 'Let's put this another way.
I think you were at the audience last night?'

Darren didn't answer. 'I'm sure you saw what happened,'
I went on. 'Miss Walker's disappearance has caused . . .
disruption. We'd be interested in resolving this with as
little fuss as possible.'

'Yeah? So who's this guy?'

'Some individuals who value their privacy,' I said. 'They
also want Miss Walker back – alive and in good condition.
That's not negotiable.'

I felt Darren tense slightly, and the futures of violence
loomed larger. 'On the other hand,' I said, 'they aren't
unreasonable. They'd be willing to compensate you for her
safe return.'

Darren looked at me for a long moment, and I felt the
futures shift and swirl. 'You a mage?'

Divination spells can't generally be detected by
magesight. My armour's a different story, but the greatcoat
I was wearing was long enough to cover it, and there was
a good chance that Darren wouldn't be able to see any
magical auras when he looked at me. 'Does it matter?'

'How come you're talking to me?'

'Because you're the one who did the job,' I said. 'Look,
I don't see any need for your name to come into this, as
long as we can work this out. Why should someone like
Anne Walker matter to you anyway? You can have any
other girl. Just not this one.'

Darren studied me. 'Sounds like you haven't told anyone else.'

*Uh-oh.* I kept still. 'Don't get stupid.'

'Oh, you think I'm stupid? Yeah, I guess you do, *Verus*.' Darren tilted his head. 'You think I didn't know?'

Shit, shit, shit. The futures were still branching, but now all of them looked bad. 'Who I am doesn't matter.' I kept my voice calm. 'You—'

'I think it matters,' Darren said, and my heart sank as I saw the way he was standing. 'I think it matters a *lot*. See, the way I heard it, you're a rogue. Council doesn't like you, Dark mages don't like you . . . You know what I think? I don't think there's a bunch of mages behind you. You're all on your own.' He took a step forward, squaring his stance.

I held quite still, flicking through the possible futures. Violence, violence, excessive violence, really excessive violence . . . *New plan.*

'You're supposed to be pretty good, right?' Darren cocked his head. I felt magic beginning to build, and black light flickered at his hands. 'Let's see how you do against the real thing.'

I held still a moment longer, then my composure broke. 'Okay, okay!' My voice cracked, became high and wavering. 'It wasn't my idea!'

Darren stared at me. I drew back, raising my hands. 'I didn't want to do this! I don't even know her; it's nothing to do with me. Just let me go, okay? I'll do anything you want!'

'That was it?' Darren said, staring. 'That's the best you got?'

'It's not me. I didn't want to get involved; they made me. I just wanted—'

'Shut up,' Darren said. He raised his voice. 'I said SHUT UP! Jesus, this is pathetic.'

'No, you're going to kill me, I know you are – oh God, please don't. I'll do anything.' I dropped to one knee, my hands out, pleading. 'Please, I'll do anything you say, just don't kill me; it's not my fault—'

'Will you shut the fuck *up* already?'

'Please don't kill me, please, I'm begging you—'

'This is just fucking embarrassing.' Darren looked at me in disgust. 'I thought you were supposed to be tough.'

I kept begging and pleading. 'What a waste of time,' Darren muttered. He'd dropped his spell, and now he walked forward to give me a kick. 'Get—'

Interesting bit of trivia: most men will instinctively shield their groin against a kick, but not against a punch. A rising leg registers as a threat but a dropping hand doesn't. Another bit of trivia: you can lunge really hard from one knee.

My fist slammed into Darren's crotch with my weight behind it and he doubled over, his eyes bugging out. I surged to my feet and caught Darren's kicking leg on the way up, lifting it up and over his head. He tumbled over; he was clearly in agony but a black shield flickered into life around him just as my heel came down.

Against a veteran Dark mage, none of this would have worked. They wouldn't have let their guard down so easily in the first place, and their shield would have been strong enough to hold off the blows. Too bad for Darren that he wasn't a veteran. I stomped on Darren while he was still down and nauseated, slamming my foot down onto him again and again in short, brutal, rib-breaking kicks. The shield took the worst of the impact and the death energy stung my ankles but it wasn't enough to hold them off, and the rain of blows thudding into his body kept Darren stunned and off-balance, unable to counterattack. A kick landed in his kidney and he convulsed, his shield winking out. I yanked a slim silver needle from one pocket and stabbed it into his thigh. Green light flickered and I saw the spell flash through Darren's body. He jerked, then his eyes rolled up and he went limp.

I straightened, heart racing. Check surroundings; check the futures . . . no threats, everything was clear. I looked down at Darren and saw that he was out cold. 'Well, shit,' I said to no one in particular.

The focus I'd just used was a nerve scrambler: it disrupted signals to a living brain. Enough to keep someone out for a few minutes but no more – I had to move fast. I rolled Darren onto his back; there was blood on his face from where one of my kicks had cut his forehead, but I ignored it and started going through his pockets, tossing out the contents. Money, keys, wallet, phone . . .

'Well, hello there,' I murmured. The object was a fluted rod eight inches long, ringed at either end, and it radiated magic. I know a gate stone when I see one. I looked through the futures in which I activated it and . . . yes, this was it.

Now what was I going to do about its owner?

I looked down at Darren, flicking quickly through possibilities. Keeping him restrained was not an option. My scrambler was discharged, and I didn't have anything else that'd keep him unconscious. Anne would have been able to do it easily . . . why do you always need a mage's abilities when they're not there?

(For the record, no, at no point did I consider just

killing him, and I suppose some of you are wondering why. Point one: killing the apprentice of a recognised mage would violate the Concord and would give Sagash full grounds to demand that the Keepers arrest me. Point two: it would escalate things and cut off any possibility of negotiation with Sagash, which was still a viable way of resolving this even if it was getting less likely by the minute. Point three: what the hell is wrong with you? You seriously think I want to be responsible for *more* dead kids? Jesus.)

I could take the focus and find the others, but as soon as Darren woke up he'd miss it and raise the alarm. They'd put a guard on the shadow realm's entrance . . . assuming they hadn't done that already . . .

. . . Why not take a look and see?

I quickly looked through the futures in which I tried the gate stone – some failed unpredictably, making the path unstable, but by piecing them together I managed to get a vague impression of what was waiting for me. I ignored details, looking for encounters or danger, and couldn't sense either. No security – that was strange. That couldn't last.

On the other hand, the front door was open *now* . . .

*When in doubt, attack.* I grabbed Darren's phone and pocketed it, then started channelling my magic into the rod, using it as a focus. As I did I pulled out my own phone and speed-dialled Luna's number. It went to voice-mail and I dialled again. This time she picked up.

'Hey, Alex—' Luna began.

I lost my grip on the gate spell and it fizzled out. 'Listen closely,' I said as I recast it. 'I found Darren; we fought; he lost. He's unconscious and waking up in three minutes.

I'm going to use his focus to get into Sagash's shadow realm. I'll be out of contact once I do.'

'You— Wait! Can't I—'

'No time.' A black shape wavered, starting to form in mid-air, then the spell fizzled again and it winked out. 'Damn it! Not *now*!'

'What?'

'Nothing.' Darren was starting to stir and I was out of time. I tried the focus yet again and this time I put everything I had into it. 'Keep working on finding a way to break into that shadow realm. Watch your back, stop Vari from starting any wars and do what you can to keep Sonder and Caldera onside. We're going to need help before this is over.'

'Goddamn it,' Luna said, and I heard her sigh. 'Fine, understood. Just for the record, you are not allowed to complain about me doing dangerous stuff ever again.'

The gate spell caught and a black oval appeared in mid-air, a dark contrast to the drab living room. No light came through the warded gate, but the still air rippled and a breeze touched my face, carrying with it the smell of the sea and ancient stone. 'Gate's open,' I said. 'Going through. Good luck.'

'You're the one who needs it. Be careful.'

I stepped through the gate and into Sagash's shadow realm.

## 7

I came down into a sea breeze and dazzling sunlight. The gate closed behind me and I was alone.

I was standing on a stone platform on the edge of a massive cliff. The cliff stretched away to my left and right; as my eyes adjusted I saw that it went on as far as I could see. Behind was forest and greenery and the sun was shining down out of a cloudy sky, filling the air with haze. At the foot of the cliff and stretching away into the distance was an endless ocean, and the rush of waves on rock was a steady sound in the background.

Directly ahead was an enormous castle. It was built upon a rocky island offshore, several hundred feet from the cliff, and a long narrow bridge stretched from my feet to some sort of courtyard directly ahead. The castle was made out of yellow-grey stone, and it was *huge*. Square towers and buttresses reached up into the clouded sky, arched windows peeking down from layered walls, with a darker, tower-like building beyond the first few layers of ramparts.

I was still holding my phone in one hand; the signal indicator was spinning uselessly and I switched it off. As I did, I searched ahead, looking for danger, and came up blank. As far as I could tell I was alone out here. Of course, given how big it was, it was going to be pretty hard to tell the difference between 'alone' and 'nobody in range' . . .

I shook my head and focused. Back in London, Darren would be waking up right now. He'd notice I'd stolen his gate stone and it wouldn't take him long to figure out what I'd done with it. There wouldn't be any easy way for him to report to Sagash (and given the typical attitude Dark masters have towards failure, he probably wouldn't want to) so his most likely next move would be to contact one of the other apprentices. I'd taken his phone specifically to slow that down but he'd manage it sooner or later, and once he did I could expect him to show up here with reinforcements. I needed to find Anne before then.

I started walking forwards across the bridge. It was a full fifteen feet wide, which was good because there was no railing, just a sheer drop. The cliff face was vertical, and I glanced down after a few steps to confirm that there was absolutely nothing below me except a long, long fall of hundreds of feet to the water. Sea breezes tugged at me, whipping my hair and pushing me from side to side. I had a macabre impulse to look into the future in which I jumped off the edge, down and down to those little wavelets below, but shook it off.

I couldn't help feeling relieved when I made it across. The courtyard beyond was vast, more than a hundred feet deep with ledged walls reaching a good forty feet above my head. A straight stone path ran to a huge door which led deeper into the castle, and grass grew on either side. I'd been scanning for danger as I'd been crossing but I hadn't found anything – either nobody had noticed me, or I really *was* alone. Something caught my peripheral vision; I looked right to see what it was and jumped.

Standing in the shadow of the outer wall, just a few feet away from where the bridge met the courtyard, was a fuzzy mass of darkness which looked like a humanoid sculpted out of shadow and black smoke. Its only features were a pair of faintly glowing white eyes through which it watched me silently. It wasn't moving, and as far as I could tell it wasn't going to.

I looked at the thing, puzzled. It was a construct, and as soon as I'd seen the thing my hand had gone to the pocket where I kept my focus, but as I studied the futures I saw that the thing wasn't going to attack. Unless I bothered it, it was just going to stand there. Variam had said something about shadow constructs used as a security force, but this one didn't seem to be doing very much in the way of security . . .

. . . unless it wasn't there to keep me out but to keep someone else *in*. Experimentally, I looked into the futures in which I walked back out over the bridge. No response. Constructs aren't alive and can't take initiative; they only do what they've been specifically ordered to do. If the construct had been told to watch for one particular person then it wouldn't react to anything else.

I was tempted to keep experimenting, but it didn't relate to my primary goal of finding Anne and the clock was ticking. I walked away from the bridge and deeper into the castle. The shadow watched me go, white eyes tracking me silently.

The first courtyard led into a bigger courtyard with multiple levels, patches of grass crossed by walkways. Now that I was out of the wind, I was getting hot: the castle wasn't tropical but it was much warmer than the cold London spring. I stripped off my greatcoat and slung it over one arm, looking from side to side around the high courtyard walls. There were several ways out and no obvious correct direction; given enough time I could map the place blind, but I was on a clock. I searched the short-term futures and saw that one of the back staircases led up to a high tower.

The interior of the tower was the same yellow stone and it felt dark and gloomy compared to the bright sun outside. There was something eerie about the castle, something that was hard to pin down, like a feeling of being watched. I climbed the spiral staircase which lined the inside of the tower wall, going up and up until at last sunlight broke through the gap in the ceiling above me and I came up into the light again. I shielded my eyes as I did, looking around over the tower parapet, and for a moment thought that I'd become disorientated. When I realised what I was seeing, my eyes went wide.

It had been my fault, honestly. Variam had said the castle was huge but I hadn't really listened – after all, most castles are pretty damn big by normal standards. But this place wasn't big, it was *gigantic*. From my position on top of the tower, I could see dozens of buildings and other towers rising out of the haze, clustered together and built on top of one another. Sun-drenched courtyards separated the buildings, and sheer drops plunged from vertical walls down into lower levels. The tower I'd just climbed had to be close to a hundred feet, and it wasn't even the tallest. The ocean was to my left and right, and behind the castle too; the island kept going away from the mainland, but not for ever. I'd never heard of a shadow realm so big. Most are little pocket realities, no bigger than a football pitch; this place could have swallowed up every other shadow realm I'd ever seen with room to spare.

Towards the centre of the castle, rising up above the lower halls and towers, was a square keep. It was darker than the construction around it, a dull matte-black instead of the sandstone shades of the other buildings. The design felt different too. It wasn't exactly the architecture: it just didn't quite fit with the castle around it. The rest of the shadow realm was a single unit but the keep jarred somehow — didn't blend in.

I looked for magical signatures, and found them. Wards covered the castle — scratch that: they covered the whole shadow realm. They were so omnipresent that they were hard to see, huge background currents like a haze in the air. I couldn't pick them all out but I could identify some. Most recognisable was the gate ward that Vari had warned me about. It didn't look as though point-to-point transport *within* the shadow realm was impeded, but gating directly out was going to be impossible. There were also shroud effects, subtle and layered, though I wasn't sure what they were meant to guard against. They weren't blocking my divination, at least. Maybe they were designed to stop longer-range spells.

Two places stood out in my mage's sight. The first was the platform back on the mainland, on the other side of the bridge. A space magic effect was bound around the standing stones, allowing passage in and out. The second was the dark stone keep. Wards were laced over it, tight and dangerous-looking. It was hard to be sure at this distance, but they seemed to have a different style than the universal effects over the shadow realm — they were more focused and aggressive.

I understood now what Vari had meant when he'd said that Anne had hidden here, all those years ago. With its size and the shrouds, this place could hide an army. Anne had managed to stay concealed here once; maybe she'd managed it again.

Time to think. Anne had arrived here three days ago, almost certainly to the same platform which I'd just come down on. Where would she have gone?

She could have run directly away from the castle. Turning to look, I could see the narrow bridge running to the cliff face, and the platform at the top. Beyond was grass and light woodland, green and inviting. Or she could have done what I'd done: crossed the bridge and disappeared into the castle. Instinctively that felt like the *worst* direction, but if you want to lose pursuers, you go where they're not expecting.

And then there was a third possibility – Anne's pursuers might have caught her. In which case (assuming she was still alive) she'd be in whichever part of the castle that they used as a prison. I had a nasty feeling it would be that keep.

Three possibilities, three directions, and I didn't have time to search them all. Which to choose?

I spent a precious minute thinking. What swung my decision in the end was that shadow I'd seen in the court-yard. It hadn't been on general guard duty or it wouldn't have let me in, but its presence there made perfect sense if it was meant to stop Anne from getting out, which suggested that someone thought Anne was still inside. Until I found something better, I'd assume Anne was hiding somewhere in the castle.

The bad news was that anything that could hide her from her pursuers would also hide her from me. If I was hiding, and she was hiding, how was I going to find her?

Well, there are mundane ways to track people, but it's complicated and quite frankly finding stuff the normal way takes too damn long. Divination it was.

I moved to the edge of the tower parapet. The breeze ruffled my hair, though it wasn't as strong as the wind should be in a tower so high. I looked into the future to see what would happen if I stood there and screamed 'ANNE!' at the top of my voice.

No response from Anne, which wasn't surprising. No response from anyone else, which was more surprising – the wind and the sea must be making it hard to hear. I looked to see what would happen if I kept screaming. Nothing . . . nothing . . . *ah*. Futures of shadows closing in on my position . . . they could fly? Didn't know that. And . . . a person? It looked like a girl . . . Could it be Anne? It felt similar to her . . . maybe . . . At this distance I couldn't be sure. I needed a closer look.

I gave the castle a last glance, fixing its layout in my mind, then went jogging down the stairs of the tower. When I reached the bottom, I picked a direction towards where I'd seen the figure in my vision and started working my way deeper into the castle. The layout of the place was winding and confusing – instead of straight corridors, I had to take side routes to get anywhere. Luckily, finding paths is something my magic is very good at, and I made good time.

I stopped inside a huge, cathedral-like hall. Narrow windows cast slivers of light through the gloom, and rafters criss-crossed the roof above. The floor had a gaping chasm in the middle, but a railed walkway ran around the walls and a catwalk crossed the cathedral lengthways. Movement in the future caught my attention and I stopped to look. Movement, a presence . . . There was a girl heading this way, and it wasn't Anne.

I had more than enough time to avoid her, but I needed

information. There were doorways along the wall leading into side-rooms. I checked to make sure I'd have a way out in case things went wrong, then slipped into one of the rooms and waited. Footsteps broke the silence, quiet but growing louder, until someone emerged at the cathedral's north end.

I stayed out of sight behind the wall, watching her through the futures in which I leaned out. She was slim, with short black hair and South East Asian features; her clothes were grey, and a pair of short-swords were sheathed at her belt. Assuming Sagash didn't have more than one armed Korean girl hanging around his shadow realm (which didn't seem too likely unless he had a very specific fetish), then this was the third apprentice Caldera had told us about, Yun Ji-yeong. Right now her arms were folded and she was standing at the cathedral's north entrance. *I wonder what you're waiting for . . . oh. That.* Sagash's other two apprentices were on their way, and they were in a hurry.

Three Dark apprentices at once were more than I could handle. I did not want to be found here, but I did want to eavesdrop. I checked again to make sure I wouldn't be spotted, then hunkered down and waited.

Darren and the other apprentice from the ball appeared at the south end of the cathedral two minutes later. They stopped as soon as they saw Ji-yeong; I couldn't make out what they were saying but their body language wasn't friendly. After a pause they started across the central walkway.

'What are you doing?' Ji-yeong said as they approached.

Neither of the two boys answered. Ji-yeong stepped out onto the walkway, blocking their path. 'Hey.'

'What?' Darren said. He was wearing the same clothes

as when I'd knocked him out, and was moving stiffly, obviously hurt. He didn't look ready to quit though.

'Where have you been?'

'Out.'

'Who were you fighting?'

'None of your business.'

Ji-yeong looked him up and down. 'You lost, didn't you?'

Darren's eyes narrowed. The other boy – Sam Taylor, if Caldera's info was right – put an arm across to hold Darren back. I couldn't get a good look at him, but he looked smaller and slighter than Darren, and he had a faint Manchester accent. 'We're a bit busy. Can this wait?'

'Busy with what?'

Neither boy answered. 'You said busy,' Ji-yeong said. Her speech was slightly accented, more formal than Sam's or Darren's. 'Busy with what?'

'None of your fucking business,' Darren told her.

Ji-yeong looked at Sam, ignoring Darren. 'You're looking for something?'

Darren started to answer, and again Sam held him back. 'Trying to get the fox,' Sam said. 'It was in the castle again.'

'The fox?'

'Yeah.'

Ji-yeong cocked her head. 'That was why you sent all those shadows to the main gate half an hour ago?'

*Uh-oh.* Getting out of here might be a little harder than getting in.

Sam and Darren didn't answer. 'Sending all eight of your shadows to guard the gate,' Ji-yeong said. 'You must really want that fox. It's funny. Didn't you have that one guarding the gate already?'

'You going to get out of the way?' Sam was giving Ji-yeong a hard look. There was no trace of friendliness in his voice any more.

'Okay,' Ji-yeong said, smiling suddenly. 'Maybe I'll go talk to Sagash.'

Both Darren and Sam stopped. 'About what?' Sam said.

Ji-yeong shrugged. 'Nothing.'

Darren took a threatening step forward. 'What are you telling him?'

'What's the problem?' Ji-yeong said. 'You've got nothing to hide, right?' The smile didn't leave her face, but suddenly her right hand was resting on the hilt of one of her swords.

'Okay, okay.' Sam stepped between them, arms out. 'Look, let's talk about this. Ji—' His voice lowered and I lost the rest of the sentence.

*Damn, just when it was getting interesting.* The trouble with divination-as-eavesdropping is that it's got a very limited range. I wanted to sneak closer but I couldn't risk it: living magic is very good at detecting people, and with three different mages the chances were too good that one would spot me. Instead I looked through the futures in which I approached, trying to pick through the ones in which I was noticed to the ones in which I caught a few words.

'—listening to her?' Ji-yeong was saying.

Sam answered, but he was turned away from me and I couldn't hear what he was saying. 'No, she isn't,' Ji-yeong said.

'So what?' Darren said. He still sounded angry.

'So she's using you?'

Sam answered again, and Ji-yeong said something I couldn't quite catch; Darren had moved in front of her.

*Will you get out of the way?* I adjusted the futures I was watching, cycling through angles.

'—taking the blame,' Ji-yeong was saying.

'So get off your arse and help,' Darren said.

'Look, let's go back to the keep,' Sam said. 'We can—' He moved forward and again I lost the thread of the conversation. This time Ji-yeong let him pass and Sam headed for the northern exit, still talking. Darren and Ji-yeong followed, eyeing each other like a pair of wary dogs. The three of them disappeared through the archway and were gone.

I straightened up from where I'd been crouched, frowning as I tried to put the subtext of that conversation together. Secrets, Sagash, a fox . . . Apparently Darren and Sam had been hiding what they were doing from Ji-yeong. Maybe the House of Sagash wasn't as united as it looked.

One very definite impression I was picking up from watching Sagash's apprentices was that they were a step below Anne in terms of power. They might be ruthless, but they weren't as skilled or experienced, and I suspected Sagash's isolation might be a reason for that. He wasn't as connected as Morden, and he hadn't found apprentices as dangerous as Onyx. Maybe that was why he'd resorted to kidnapping the first time round . . . though this lot seemed to be here willingly.

I didn't want to run into the three apprentices accidentally so I trailed them at a distance, using divination to track their passing while staying well outside their detection range. After only a few minutes they crossed a drawbridge over a lower courtyard and disappeared into a set of halls. Looming over the halls was the dark shape of the keep, and it didn't take long to confirm that that was where they were going. Sagash was probably there.

A bigger worry was whether *Anne* was there. But I hadn't heard anything about her being captured, and until I did I'd stick with the plan. I turned around and started working my way towards the castle's edge. The high buildings of the castle made it hard to see the sun, but assigning that direction as west put the cliff to the south. The keep was south-central, relatively close to the exit. If I were Anne, I would have tried to put myself as far from the keep as I could. I began heading east, hoping to curve around the keep towards the north.

As I walked, I looked into the futures of what would happen if I yelled for Anne. I cycled through a variety of calls, eventually settling on 'Hey, Anne, it's Alex – could you come out please?' To begin with I saw futures of movement from the direction of the keep, but as I put more distance and stone walls between Sagash's apprentices and me, the chance of detection decreased until I could shout as loudly as I wanted.

While I walked, the back of my mind was turning over what I'd overheard. Ji-yeong had mentioned telling Sagash, and it had been a threat. What if Sagash didn't know anything about the attack on Anne at all?

If that was true, then not only would it explain why Sagash had denied knowing about it, it would also fit with how crude the attack had been. Darren and Sam had caught Anne totally by surprise, yet they'd still botched the job and let her get away. Not the kind of performance you'd expect from a Dark master mage, but exactly the kind of performance you'd expect from a pair of ruthless but inexperienced apprentices.

But if they weren't doing it on Sagash's orders, why had they targeted Anne? From what Variam had said, it didn't sound as though Anne had even met these three, much less given them a reason to go after her. And if they'd just been looking for a victim, why pick her? Had they chosen her at random? That felt like too much of a coincidence.

I was still missing something.

I wound my way through halls and across courtyards, up and down staircases, futures spreading through possible paths before me like spider-webs. The castle had a strange brooding feel to it, hushed and watchful. It didn't feel threatening, not exactly – it was more secretive, as though you could live in this place for years without ever really understanding it. I could hear the sea from over the walls and the wind around the towers, but after a while it just became background noise and the castle felt silent. Sagash's apprentices were long gone and the only living things I could see were the white birds which soared over the castle towers and perched on the rooftops.

As I travelled, I passed all kinds of strange constructions. A crane occupied one tower, a chain trailing from its tip down and down to a circle of grass far below. Other sets of rooms were filled with weird ancient machinery made out of black iron. There was even a railway running along the outside of the castle's north-east wall, with a horrifying drop to the rocks far below. I path-walked along the railway line and it curved around the castle's north-east corner before ending as inexplicably as it had started. Sagash hadn't built this place, of that I was sure. His life and Anne's were just one more story out of hundreds stretching back in time.

I'd been at it for more than two hours now and it was getting dark. The sun had disappeared below the western walls, and the sky was turning a dusky purple. I'd come to a section of high walls and narrow walkways; endless drops stretched down into darkness and the golden light of sunset cast long shadows on the walls. The wind had dropped with the coming dusk and the castle felt empty and lonely, as though I was the only person left alive in a silent world. In the still air, my voice carried further, and for the thousandth time I sent my future selves path-walking in different directions, calling for Anne. There was no response, but just as I was about to cut the spell I sensed something from the route through the lower archway. *Someone there . . .* I tried again, focusing on it this time, then started walking, matching my future self's path. As I drew closer to the archway, I could hear a strange creaking sound.

The archway led into a small grassy area, enclosed on three sides. Grey-tinted walls rose up to the left and right, but up ahead the ground dropped away to a beautiful view of the ocean. The sun was setting beneath the clouds, its light reflecting off the waves in a long rippling beam. I was right on the edge of the cliff, and looking out at the sea it was as if the water stretched out to infinity.

In the centre of the grassy space was a windmill. It was made of stone and wood, with eight long canvas sails, and they were turning very slowly in the gentle breeze. The rotating sails made the rhythmic *creak . . . creak . . . creak . . .* that I'd heard before, mixing with the sound of waves on the rocks far below. Next to the windmill was a pool ringed with rushes, and white birds were perched beside it, dipping their beaks into the fresh water.

I walked towards the windmill, my footsteps quiet on the grass. The birds took flight as I approached, circling up into the warm air. I halted a little way from the windmill, looking up at the stone windows. 'Anne?' I called quietly. My voice cracked, and I had to swallow and try again. 'Anne, it's Alex. I'm down here.'

There was a moment's pause, then a face appeared in one of the open windows. It was Anne, and at the sight of her something tense inside me relaxed at last as a warm feeling of relief went through my body. It had been worth it.

Anne's face was in shadow and I couldn't read her expression as she stared down at me. 'Alex?'

'Mind if I come in?' I said. 'You look like you've got fewer patients this time.'

Anne stood for a second, then disappeared. I heard running footsteps, then the door swung open and Anne stepped out into the evening light. She was staring, and I knew she was using her lifesight, checking to see whether it was really me. 'It is you,' she said. 'I didn't believe— How did . . . ?'

All the time I'd been searching for Anne I'd only looked for her presence, the sound of her voice, because that was the quickest way to identify her through the futures. I hadn't bothered to check for what she'd *looked* like. Now that I thought about it, I should have been expecting it. She'd been attacked while she was sleeping, after all.

Anne was wearing a long T-shirt and a pair of boxer shorts. The T-shirt had once been bright pink but had faded with age, and there were holes along the seams. On the front was a picture of the Disney cast of *Winnie the Pooh*, all sharing a hug and waving, with 'Sweet Dreams' written underneath the picture in cutesy lettering, decorated with yellow stars. I stared at it for a second, then I burst out laughing.

Anne looked at me in confusion, then she figured it out

and her expression changed to exasperation. She folded her arms, covering up the 'Sweet Dreams' and shifting her bare feet on the stone steps. I kept laughing and she spoke loudly enough for me to hear over it. 'Are you finished?'

I shook my head. Somehow it felt like the most hilarious thing I'd ever seen. I think it was relief more than anything else – I'd been so wound up that now I just couldn't stop laughing. 'That—' I managed. 'That T-shirt.'

'*What* about my T-shirt?'

I looked at Anne. She didn't look particularly embarrassed about being caught in her sleepwear – she just looked annoyed, and the expression on her face made me double over and crack up again.

'Could you please stop doing that?' Anne said over my laughter.

'I'm sorry,' I said, wiping my eyes. 'It's just— It looks like a nightie for a little girl.'

'I was *asleep*. What did you think I'd be wearing?'

'Honestly? Never thought about it.' I still had the urge to keep laughing.

'Look, I'm sorry if it doesn't look nice, but I didn't know I was going to be kidnapped when I was choosing what to wear to bed. It's not like—'

I closed the distance to Anne in two quick strides and put my arms around her. Pressed against me, she felt light and underweight, as though she'd been starved. 'Alex?' Anne said in surprise.

'I'm glad you're okay,' I said quietly.

I'd expected Anne to pull away but she didn't move. We stood there for a little while, the sails of the windmill gliding steadily by over our heads as the rays of the setting sun fell all around. From above the birds looked down curiously, watching from their perches upon the high walls.

'So what happened?' I asked Anne a little while later.

The interior of the windmill was roomy, with high ceilings and ancient iron machinery. Square windows looked out onto the ocean, and the beams of the setting sun painted gold light onto the stone walls. Anne was curled up like a mouse in a nest of old sacks she'd made for herself. I'd given her my greatcoat; she was tall enough that it fit even if it was a little baggy. There wasn't anything I could do about her bare feet, but she'd tucked them into her sack-bed for now. I'd finished telling Anne the shortened version of my side of the story, and now I wanted to hear hers.

'I don't remember much of it,' Anne said in her soft voice. 'After I finished talking to you that night I went home, made dinner, washed up and went to bed. Then the next thing I knew my head was spinning, all my nerves were screaming and I was being hit with lightning.'

'You played dead?'

'It was all I could think to do. I didn't know what was going on, but he wasn't trying to kill me. So I stopped moving and waited for him to get close.'

'He thought you were knocked out?'

'I nearly was,' Anne admitted. 'But . . . I can take a lot more than most people think I can. I've been shot and stabbed and a lot worse, and it *hurts* but I can fix it. Once I had the chance to brace myself, that electric spell wasn't too bad.'

I raised my eyebrows at that. I've never been hit by a really powerful electric shock so I don't know what it feels like, but I had to wonder what kind of things Anne was comparing it to if a full-power lightning spell 'wasn't too bad'. 'So you stunned him and jumped through the gate?'

'I didn't mean to. I wanted to get out the door, but when I saw it was locked I knew I wouldn't be able to get it open in time.' Anne was briefly silent. 'I knew where I was the instant I stepped through, but by then it was too late. I just ran for the bridge.'

'Why not the woods?'

'Because I tried that the first time I ran away. It doesn't work: there isn't enough forest before you hit the boundary. I went into the castle instead, then those Dark mages came through behind me.'

'They're Sagash's apprentices.'

Anne nodded. 'I thought they were. The first place they checked was the forest. It gave me enough time to get into the castle and I lost them in the courtyards.'

'You did a pretty good job,' I said. 'I don't think many mages would have lasted this long here.'

Anne didn't smile. 'It's not my first time.'

'Well,' I said, 'you're the expert. What's the best way out?'

'The main gate. But I don't have a key.'

I held up the fluted rod I'd taken from Darren. 'You mean one of these?'

'That's it.'

'One slight problem,' I said. 'Darren and Sam stuck a squad of eight of those shadows on top of the platform.' I'd taken a few minutes to confirm it after breaking away from the three apprentices, and Ji-yeong had been telling the truth. 'Don't suppose you know a way to deal with those things?'

Anne shook her head; she looked weary. 'They're not

alive; my magic can't touch them. It was why I could never get away. There are too many and they don't get tired or give up.'

Anne's head was down. 'Well, it might not be that bad,' I said, trying to sound cheerful. 'From what I overheard, I think Sagash only lets his apprentices play with four of them each. If they've got their shadows there, they haven't got them out here looking for us.'

Anne didn't answer. 'Any other ways out?' I asked.

'Maybe.' Anne shook her head. 'Yeah. I don't know exactly . . . Somewhere.' Her eyes drifted closed for half a second then she pulled herself awake again. 'What was that?'

I frowned. 'Are you okay?'

'. . . Little tired.'

'Have you slept since you got here?'

'They've been looking for me,' Anne said. 'They searched here the first night. If I'm asleep . . .' She trailed off.

'You've been awake for *three days*?'

'I can go longer than this if I have to.' Anne sounded defensive.

'That doesn't mean it's a good idea.' I looked at Anne, and this time I noticed the little signs I'd missed: her eyes were slightly dulled, her movements not as quick or as sure. She must have been running on adrenalin since she'd heard me, and now it had worn off. I made a quick decision. 'Get some sleep and I'll keep watch. I can use the time to scout ahead.'

Anne put up a token protest but it didn't last long. She curled up in the nest of sacks like a dormouse, and when I next looked she was fast asleep.

I leant back against the wall with a sigh. *Well, that's step one. Now we just need to get out.* I looked through the futures in which I sat still, watching to see if anyone would come. Apart from the futures in which Anne woke, nothing disturbed us. For now at least, we were alone.

I looked over at Anne and saw that she was shivering slightly. I walked quietly across the floor and tucked my coat more closely around her. She settled into it with a sighing sound and her shivering slowed. I looked down at her and had to smile. Asleep, Anne looked very young and delicate. It was good to know she was safe.

Though her surviving shouldn't really have been a surprise. I once saw Anne shot with a full clip of bullets, and by the next day she was walking around as though nothing had happened. I've also seen her rip the life out of another mage in the blink of an eye. She might look delicate, but she isn't.

How much of that came from what had happened to her here?

I shook my head and straightened, then walked to the stairs and climbed up to the next floor. The staircase led into an upper level with windows open in all four directions, giving a view down onto the grass and the pool and out to sea. The sun had set and the sky was a tapestry of red cloud fading into dusky purple to the east. I sat on the stone floor, resting my back against the wall with a sigh. My armour isn't really designed for lying around in, but it's a lot better than anything made out of metal or Kevlar and I was comfortable enough. I closed my eyes and started searching for a way out.

Just as the conditions at the Tiger's Palace had been terrible for path-walking, the conditions in the castle were nearly perfect. Path-walking requires a long chain of highly predictable links, and as soon as one link becomes unstable, everything beyond it collapses. If you're within a busy environment like a city, then normally the only way to do any kind of long-distance path-walking is to limit it to your own home or some other controlled environment where you don't have to worry about passers-by destroying your intricate probabilistic house of cards. But here, path-walking was easy. The castle wasn't deserted but it was pretty close, and the only uncertainty came from the ocean winds and the foraging birds. There was still just enough light for my future self to see by, and I sent him running south, working his way back towards the entryway as the sky darkened above him. I couldn't see any trace of Sagash's apprentices, but the castle was so big that wasn't really a surprise. There were a lot of places they could be, and I didn't try to find them; instead I explored my way south, running up against dead ends and memorising them as I did, building up a mental map of the castle so that with each wrong turning I could find the path a little faster next time.

Just as I expected, reaching the bridge and crossing the cliff to the platform caused the painstakingly held thread of my future to break apart into the chaos of combat. There were a bunch of shadow constructs on the door, and this time they weren't going to let me past. Constructs aren't sapient, which means it's theoretically possible to predict how a fight with one will go, but it didn't really matter in this case: the shadows were individually weak but there were too many of them. The focus in my pocket would take out one, but not the other seven.

I tried to work around the fight but the combination of distance, darkness and cumulative uncertainty was making it hard to see. It didn't help that I was pretty tired myself. It had been a long day.

I opened my eyes and looked up out of the window. I'd lost track of time while I'd been path-walking, and the last traces of sunlight had faded from the sky. In their place a moon had risen, shining through the eastern window and turning the dark tower of the windmill into a strange place of black shadow and knife-edged moonlight. The sails still swung past outside, the rhythmic creaking blending with the rush of the waves on the rocks far below. The moonlight on the clouds gave it a misty halo, rings of light spreading out through the sky, and I sat there for a while, gazing up at it. I've always loved looking at the moon, and I wondered idly what I was really seeing. Was it our moon, its light transported, or another one? Did the shadow realm have its own sun and moon and stars, or did it borrow them from our world?

*Who knows.* Whatever that moon was, I was glad it was there.

Movement in the futures caught my attention, and as I glanced at them I saw that Anne was awake. I was within the radius of her lifesight so I didn't need to tell her where I'd gone. After a minute I heard quiet footsteps on stone and a shadow appeared at the staircase. 'Alex?' Anne said softly.

'Trouble sleeping?' I asked.

Anne nodded. She had my coat wrapped around her. 'Come over here,' I said. 'You look cold.'

'I'm not,' Anne said. She sat down against the stone wall opposite, shivering slightly.

I looked at Anne for a second, then got up. I'm not much good at knowing what to do when someone's upset or unhappy, but every now and then my divination gives me a hint. I sat down next to Anne and put my arm around her. 'What's wrong? Did you get hurt?'

Anne shook her head. I could still feel her shivering against me. 'You're sure you're not cold?' I asked. Anne wasn't exactly heavily dressed, but the stones of the castle were still warm.

'It's not that.'

'Did something wake you up?'

'No,' Anne said. 'I mean, I was asleep . . . I was afraid they were coming. I wanted to sleep; I had to make myself wake up. Then when I did it was like they were there – I couldn't see them, but they could have been . . .' Anne's shoulders hunched and she fell silent.

*Oh. Right.* Anne had just spent three days without rest or sleep, alone and on the run with Dark mages trying to abduct her or worse. On top of that, she'd been dragged back to the same shadow realm that had been the site of probably the most horrible experiences of her life. Anne always seems so self-possessed but she's actually younger than Luna, and what she'd just gone through would have sent most people into a nervous breakdown. 'It's okay,' I said, trying to sound reassuring. 'You're safe.'

'We're not safe.' Anne's voice was slightly muffled, and she didn't look up at me. 'They're still after us. And now you're going to get hurt too.'

'Okay, I'm not saying it's *impossible* that things'll turn out that way, but let's look on the bright side. You're here; I'm here: we're both alive and safe, and you get to have a good night's sleep for once. Why not enjoy it?'

Anne was silent. 'Come on,' I said. 'Remember back when you moved in with me? That talk we had up on the roof? You trusted me to take care of you back then. Trust me now.'

'That was—' Anne said, then stopped. I'd seen Anne's

words – she'd been about to say 'that was before last year'. After a pause she went on. 'I can't stop thinking about it.' Her shoulders were hunched and she was looking down at the floor. 'All the ways they might catch me. I had nightmares about this place for so long. When I was here I dreamed every night about getting away. Then when I did, I kept being afraid that some day I'd be caught again. You don't understand – you don't know what Sagash did to me. What it was like. Getting away was the only thing I wanted. And now, it's . . . the one thing I did and it's all for nothing.'

'You aren't the same person you were,' I said quietly. 'And you aren't on your own any more.'

'I'm so tired of being afraid.' Anne sounded dull and weary and utterly wretched. 'I wish I didn't . . .'

'There's nothing wrong with being afraid of people who want to hurt you. I'd be more worried if you weren't.'

'Easy for you to say. You and Vari and Luna are never scared of anything.'

I laughed out loud at that. Anne looked up in surprise. 'What?'

'Anne, I'm scared of more things than I can count. If I ever sat down and tried to make a list, I'd be there all week.'

'But you don't . . .'

'I'm eight years older than you; I've had time to get used to it. Look, you remember when we first met? You were twenty then, right? When I was that age, I was *much* more screwed up mentally than you were. I'd just gotten away from Richard and I was terrified out of my wits that he'd come after me. I couldn't hold any kind of job or relationship, I treated everyone like they were out to get me and I slept with a weapon under my pillow. But it gets better. It takes time and you have to work at it, but it does.'

Anne was silent. 'Have you ever talked about it?' I asked.

Anne shook her head.

'Vari? Luna?'

'Vari knows bits. Little bits. Luna . . . she asked but . . .'

'Why did Sagash bring you here?'

Anne was silent for a little while, long enough that I started to think she wasn't going to answer. 'He found out about us because of Miss Chandler,' she said at last. 'She was his . . . student, I think. We didn't know. We just thought she was on her own: we'd never heard anything about Dark mages back then. I was payment. That was the way Sagash explained it. He wanted an apprentice, and I was the price.'

'And you lived here for nine months?'

Anne nodded, not meeting my eyes.

'What was it like?'

'It was horrible,' Anne said softly. 'The only other people were Sagash and his guests. Not all were Dark mages, but they were just as bad. I'd . . . I'd look at them when they came in and wonder what kind *this* one was, and whether Sagash would give me to them or not. I never had any say, not about anything. What I wore, what I did, where I went . . . He controlled everything. The only choices I had were the ones he gave me; he was changing me into something and I couldn't stop it. I just watched and I kept losing myself, one bit at a time . . . I tried to run away but it never helped: there wasn't any food and eventually I'd have to come back or starve. After the second time Sagash put a collar on me so he could hurt me and track me, and I couldn't even run away any more. I had to come back each time, for training . . .' Anne fell silent again.

'What kind of training?' I said quietly.

'I can't tell you,' Anne whispered. 'I can't, I don't . . .' Her shoulders shook and she started to cry. 'I didn't want to; he made me. It wasn't me. It wasn't me . . .'

I held Anne closer and she kept crying quietly, tears mixing with sniffs, one hand tight on the mesh of my armour at my chest. I didn't ask her any more questions. Maybe she could have answered and maybe not, but pushing her to do it felt too heartless. Eventually she fell silent. She was huddled up against me, the coat still wrapped around her, and listening to her breathing I realised she'd fallen asleep. From a glance into the futures, I could tell this slumber was a deeper one; she wasn't going to be waking up so easily this time.

*Well, now what?*

Anne was pressed up against me, which pretty much ruled out any more path-walking. We still needed to get out, but it wasn't immediately obvious how. Trying to retrace our steps to the main gate would just lead us into a battle with a squad of constructs, which would draw in Sagash's apprentices. I'd sucker-punched Darren once – I didn't think it would be so easy to do it twice.

The best approach would be to find some other way out, but for that I'd need Anne's help, and she was obviously exhausted. From the signs of it, she'd been using a combination of terror and her own life magic to keep herself in a state of hyper-vigilance for three days straight, and she wouldn't be able to think clearly until she'd had a chance to rest. For that matter, I was having trouble thinking clearly too. I hadn't had much sleep since this whole thing had started, and it had been a long day.

I rested my head back against the stone and gazed up at the beams of moonlight slanting through the windows. The creak of the sails, the whisper of wind and the distant waves blended together into a soothing, gentle sound. Anne slept next to me, still and warm. I found my eyes drifting closed, and chided myself, looking ahead to check the futures in which I sat here and stayed awake. It didn't look as though anything was going to disturb us – in all the futures I could make out, we'd be left alone until sunrise. Still, even if I'd checked, there was always the chance of something changing, no matter how small. I let my eyes close, feeling the presence of my armour around me, watchful.

I shouldn't go to sleep, but it felt good to rest my eyes. Just for a little while . . .

## 8

I drifted through dreams, old memories rising to the surface and sinking into the depths. A door opened and I stepped through.

As I did everything changed, becoming focused and clear. I was standing in a hallway made out of some kind of black stone. Soft lights glowed from holders, reflecting off the walls. The walls, floor and ceiling were all made of the same substance – it was somewhere between stone and glass, with a mirrored finish which cast back the light with perfect clarity. I brushed my fingers across it and found it cool and smooth to the touch. Turning, I saw an open doorway behind me.

I didn't recognise this place but there didn't seem to be any immediate danger, and I was curious. I walked down the corridor.

The corridor opened up into a large curved room. A long dining table of dark wood sat in the centre; bowls made out of a vivid green glass were spaced along its length. A little further away was a sofa and a set of chairs, all the same distinctive shade of green, contrasting oddly with the black-glass walls. Lights hung from the ceiling, but the room was dominated by the row of massive arch windows along the left wall. They had no glass or panes, and the view I glimpsed was so bizarre that I walked up and leant on one of the window-sills so that I could gaze out.

The windows led out onto a railed balcony made of the same strange black glass, and beyond was an impossible landscape stretching away to infinity. Giant trees rose beside mirrored lakes, stretching up into a clear blue sky. The trees were the size of tower blocks, and only the perspective gave a clue to how vast they were. The biggest looked as though it could have cast St Paul's Cathedral in its shadow, and tiny wooden buildings and round platforms peeked from its twisting branches. Further away, I could see rolling hills, distant grasslands and sunlit mountains on the horizon. All of the landscape teemed with life: birds flew; grass and trees and flowers crowded the hills. It was a lush, verdant land . . . until you looked down. A few hundred feet away, at ground level, the grass and trees were cut off abruptly, as though with a knife. A black wall formed a perfectly curved arc around my current location, stretching to the left and the right until it was hidden by the edges of the window. The difference was razor-edged and startling – outside the walls, flowers bloomed in grassy meadows, while inside everything was sculpted from the same black glass, without so much as a blade of grass to break up the unnatural smoothness. The outside was natural, wild and alive; the inside artificial, ordered and dead.

I was in Elsewhere, of that I was sure, but not any part of it I'd ever seen. Looking down at the ground and judging the angle, I had to be in some kind of tower. The arc of the walls made me think that they might go all the way around, forming a circle with the tower at the centre. There was something odd about the light: the lakes and the giant trees in the distance were all bathed in sunlight, as was the landscape to either side, but the place I was in now was dimly lit, the black glass reflecting only the light of an overcast day. Something about the layout made me think of the castle in the shadow realm, with the keep at its centre.

I stared down at the black-glass walls. They had to be thirty feet high, and I couldn't see any gates or ways to climb to the top. They didn't look designed to keep people out. It was more as though . . .

A voice spoke from behind me. 'They're to keep things in.'

I jumped, twisting in mid-air, coming down in a fighting stance. A blade of blue-white energy ignited at my hand and I held it pointing down at the floor.

The girl who'd spoken was Anne . . . or something that looked like her. She had Anne's face and eyes and slender height, but the rest of her was different. Instead of falling to shoulder-length, her hair stretched down her back, and in place of Anne's soft-coloured clothing she wore a floor-length dress of vivid scarlet which shone in the darkened room. She held something in her hands, though at this distance I couldn't see what. 'You were wondering about the walls.' She had Anne's voice, but it was stronger, more confident. 'They're to make sure what's in here stays in.'

I stared at Anne, or whoever it was. 'What are you doing here?'

'That's a little rude.' She walked towards the table, coming into the light from the windows. As she did, I saw that she was holding a long knife, tapping the blade against the palm of her hand. She placed it on the table with a *clack*, then nodded towards my right hand. 'You don't need that.'

I was still holding the energy blade. Elsewhere is fluid; creating a sword of magical energy is as easy as thinking.

You can make any tool or weapon you can think of, lighter than a feather and stronger than steel, with all kinds of amazing properties which could never exist in the real world . . . and they're all completely useless. I opened my hand and let the blade vanish. 'There you go,' the girl said. 'Relax. I'm not going to hurt you.'

I looked at her for a moment. 'You're not Anne,' I said at last.

'No shit, Sherlock. Did you think my hair grew twelve inches overnight?'

'The sarcasm is kind of a giveaway too.' I studied the girl. 'Whose Elsewhere is this? Anne's or yours?'

'That's a hard one to answer. Do you know how Anne can go without sleep?'

'I know it has to do with adjusting her biochemistry, but no.'

'Human bodies have safety cut-offs designed to force them to operate at lower capacity if they're short of resources like food or sleep. Anne can override those cut-offs and keep going when normal people can't – enough to kill herself if she's not careful. She's been doing that for three days straight, and that's why she's in a deep sleep right now. Too deep to touch Elsewhere.'

'And this is relevant because . . . ?'

'The cat's away, so the mice can play.'

I studied not-Anne. She *did* look like Anne, at least physically. But the way she moved and spoke . . . it was like a different person in the same body. 'Does that make you the cat or the mouse?'

'Let's just say I'm a side of Anne that doesn't get out much. Figures the one chance we'd get to talk would be now, but better late than never.'

'How long has Anne been using Elsewhere?'

'She started during her time with Sagash.' Not-Anne walked towards the windows, approaching me at an angle, shoes clicking on the black glass. 'An escape, really. He controlled everything in the real world so she built herself a refuge.' She came to a stop by one of the windows, looking out over the endless view. 'It's not just a backdrop. It's all detailed, every bit. It's quite beautiful, you know.'

Something in not-Anne's voice made me glance up with a frown. She was staring out at the distant forests, and there was a strange expression in her eyes – not hostile, but not happy, either. 'Have you been there?'

'I used to.' She stared out for a second longer, then shook her head and turned towards me. 'Has Vari told you about what Anne's home life was like back when they were both in school?'

'No. Wait, so Anne knew about Elsewhere last year? When I was using it with Deleo? She didn't—'

'In case you haven't noticed, Anne doesn't talk about herself much.'

I looked around the tower room of black glass and at the girl in front of me, eyebrows raised. 'No kidding. She didn't tell Vari?'

'No. Now shut up a second and listen. Anne spent a lot of her time as a kid having to take care of everyone else. Cooking, cleaning, nursing them when they were sick, that kind of stuff. She's always been good at noticing things – she'd see when people needed help, and when her magic developed it was the same thing but stronger. She could look at everyone and see how healthy they were; whether they were hurt; what their bodies needed. And she could fix it, or try to. But here's the thing – Anne doesn't actually *want* to do that all the time. Oh, don't get me wrong: she likes helping people and she wants to get married and have kids someday, not that there's much chance of *that* ever happening, but she doesn't want to be nurturing and mothering every single person she meets for the rest of her life. Things like that clinic? She doesn't do it because she wants to, she does it because she feels like she has to. Because she can heal people, so if she just leaves them alone, it's her fault, right? But it's a bottomless pit. Doesn't matter how many you treat, there's always another one. And you know what really gets annoying? Half the time they're not even all that grateful. The better you do your job, the more you fix people's problems, the more they take it for granted. They think it's just the way things are supposed to be.' Not-Anne stared at me. 'Do you know what it feels like to always take care of everyone and get treated like crap for it? It gets to you. Especially when you've got those gossip circles whispering behind your back.'

I looked back at not-Anne. 'So what do you want to do about it?'

'Hmph.' Not-Anne looked back out the window. 'It's not like I get the choice. She's too dutiful.' She paused. 'Or she used to be.'

'Before *what*? Before Sagash? Anne keeps dancing around it but she won't tell me. It's obviously really damn important but she can't make herself talk about it. You're here because you want me to understand, right?'

'Anne doesn't talk about it,' not-Anne said, 'because she really, *really* doesn't want anyone to know what happened in those nine months.'

'I was a Dark apprentice! Does she really think it's going

to be something I've never heard before?' I narrowed my eyes at not-Anne. 'She's not just afraid, is she? She's ashamed of something.'

'Yeah.'

'Ashamed of what? What did Sagash do to her? Did he . . . ?'

Not-Anne looked at me curiously, tilting her head. 'Did he what? Wait, are you asking if Sagash sexually abused her or something?'

I hesitated.

'Oh, for God's sake.' Not-Anne rolled her eyes in disgust. 'Use your brain. Anne is a *life mage*, she can paralyse anyone who touches her. Do you seriously think we need to worry about getting raped?'

'It's not something I like to talk about, all right?'

'Yeah, well, Sagash doesn't care,' not-Anne said. 'He's about as asexual as it gets and those bits of him withered years ago. I don't think he's got any physical desires *left*. He's not human enough.'

'So what *does* he care about?'

'Power and longevity. He wants to live here for ever and be king of his little world. Trouble is, you need subjects to be a king. Another twenty years and he'll probably go all-the-way crazy and disappear into here with his shadows and never come out, but for now he's still sane enough to get people to do what he says. And if they don't do what he says, he makes them.'

'And that was what he did to Anne?'

'That was what he did to Anne. He wanted an apprentice-assassin. Someone who'd go out of the shadow realm, bring him whoever or whatever he wanted for his experiments and kill anyone who pissed him off. He started training

Anne, and when she said no he hurt her till she said yes. Death magic has lots of spells for affecting living bodies and Sagash knows exactly how far he can go before they get lethal. No chance of the subject dying. Though they might want to. What he wanted Anne to do wasn't so bad to begin with. Spell practice, education – used her as a maid too, when he had guests around. He didn't need to; it was just to show her off: "Look how powerful I am. I've got a life mage waiting the table." She was still a slave, but it could have been worse.

'So then it got worse. After Anne had picked up the basics, he started putting her through combat training. He'd match her up against other Dark apprentices, have them duel until one couldn't fight any more. Anne tried surrendering – didn't work. The apprentice tore her apart and she got a torture session with Sagash for embarrassing him. After that, she fought. She wasn't much good, but she was powerful. You know how life magic works – it only takes a touch.

'But there was a problem. See, Anne was dangerous in a duel, but Sagash didn't want a duellist. He wanted an *assassin*, someone who'd kill for him, and Anne wouldn't kill. He threatened her, but that was Anne's line in the sand. She'd given up as much as she was going to and she said no. So obviously he tortured her, but she'd been learning from those fights and she'd figured out how to mute her pain receptors. Sagash could kill her but he couldn't hurt her. She told Sagash that she'd rather die than become someone like that.'

Not-Anne stopped talking. She looked out at the distant forests, and an unpleasant memory came to my mind. That night when I'd met Anne outside her flat . . . She hadn't said it in those words, but that had been the subtext, hadn't it? Given the choice of taking my help or living in danger, she'd picked danger. Better to die than become someone like Sagash . . . *or me?*

I shook my head hard, trying to forget that last thought. 'What happened?'

'Anne made a mistake,' not-Anne said simply. 'She thought Sagash needed her alive. But the way he saw it, he didn't need her at all. He was going to live for ever. Sure, he'd invested time in her, but he could always get another. He only wanted her for his Chosen, and if she wasn't willing to kill she wasn't any use to him. So he called her bluff. He put her up against a Dark mercenary in the arena. A kid, really, one of those child soldiers. Sagash must have fed him some story or other, promised him a reward, because he didn't talk, he just went for Anne and tried to kill her. Anne tried to disable him, but Sagash had given the kid a set of wards. Not against lethal attacks, just non-lethal ones. That was when Anne realised that Sagash meant it. She'd said she'd rather die – well, that was the choice he was giving her. Either she fought back and killed the guy, or she was going to die right there. No more life, no more growing up, no chance for a happily ever after somewhere down the line.'

'What did she do?' I asked quietly, even though I knew the answer.

'You know, most people never really think about how magic works.' Not-Anne leant back against the window's edge, elbows propped against the sill, watching me casually. 'Your magic's a reflection of your personality, right? Well, that goes both ways. If your magic's good at something, that says something about what kind of person you are. Life magic's really good at healing. And it's really good at killing.' She tilted her head. 'Do you know just how *tired* you can get of taking care of everyone all the time?'

I didn't answer. 'Anne got hold of that kid and ripped the life right out of him,' not-Anne said calmly. 'Took a few tries, but she didn't give up. And looking down at his body afterwards . . . In a way, that was where I was born.'

I stared at not-Anne as she leant against the window, the light from outside falling across the scarlet dress. Despite everything she'd been saying, she looked relaxed. I didn't know what to say.

'So, that night she stayed up thinking about killing herself,' not-Anne said. Her voice was so normal it was disturbing. 'Obviously she didn't. I mean, staying alive was why she'd done it in the first place, it'd kind of defeat the point, right? Things settled down; she recovered a bit, convinced herself she'd never do it again. Then Sagash brought in another kid. Same story, different guy. Second time was easier. Third was easier than the second, fourth was easier than the third. After a while Sagash stopped bringing them in. Either he was running out or he figured Anne had learnt her lesson.'

'How many?' I asked quietly.

Not-Anne shrugged. 'Enough.'

I looked at her in silence.

'Anyway, eventually Vari showed up and they broke out. Hurt Sagash but didn't kill him, more's the pity, and they got back to London and lived happily ever after . . . except they didn't. Anne couldn't accept what she'd done – couldn't accept *me*. Oh, she'd been fine with it when she *needed* me, but once she was safe, well, she didn't want me around any more, did she? So she tried to pretend the whole thing never happened. She avoided fighting and duelling, anything that could raise the wrong kind of questions, and put on the pacifist act instead. After all, the only ones who'd been there had been Sagash and the guys she'd been fighting, and since all except Sagash were *dead*, well, there wasn't anyone to argue, was there? Except me. So she shut me away.' Not-Anne gestured around her at the black-glass walls. 'In here. Where she can forget about me and all the ugly little secrets that don't belong in her perfect world. But she can't get rid of me – I'm part of her and she still needs me. When things get really dangerous she'll bring me out, long enough to keep her alive. She just won't admit it.'

I remembered the one time I'd seen Anne use her abilities to kill. I hadn't understood what I'd seen in her eyes, not then. 'Okay,' I said. 'You brought me here to tell me all this. Why? What do you want?'

'Why do you think?'

'Because you want to be in charge?'

Not-Anne rolled her eyes again. 'Jesus, you're paranoid. Okay, fine, *maybe* I'd appreciate it if she'd treat me a little better. But there's kind of a more pressing issue, don't you think?'

'You mean getting out of this castle.'

'Ding-ding, we have a winner! I might have been born here, but I'm not keen on staying for the rest of my life, which isn't going to be very long at this rate. I'm part of Anne, remember. She dies, I die. Plus no matter how much of a bitch she can be, I don't actually hate her *that* much. I want her out of here, and that means she needs to sort out her issues fast, probably within the next twenty-four hours, because somehow I don't think the Sagash Psycho

Club is going to wait around while she takes her time about it. She needs to stop fighting me or she's not going to make it out.'

I looked at not-Anne with raised eyebrows. 'And you think I'm going to be able to do this in twenty-four hours when literally every other person she's ever met hasn't been able to do it in five years.'

'Yeah, well, you're not my first choice either, but it's not like we're exactly swimming in options. Pity you didn't make a move on her last night – would probably have made her open up a bit. You could have spun her the "this might be our last night alive" line.'

I gave not-Anne an irritated look. 'That would have been manipulative, sleazy and extremely stupid given that we're in a *castle of people trying to kill us.*'

'Oh, don't be such a prude. She knows you think she looks hot after last year.'

'She's eight years younger than me.'

'So? Emotionally she's probably more mature than you are. Though that's not saying much.'

I sighed. 'You're a lot less nice than the real Anne, you know that?'

'Yeah, well, next time you're talking to her remember she *thinks* all this stuff; she just doesn't say it. Point is, ever since escaping to London she's been trying to play the good girl and it isn't working. That's why the Light mages don't like her – they can see she's hiding something. So we've got this stupid situation where she's too dangerous for the Light mages and not dangerous enough for the Dark ones. She needs to stop pretending.'

'Look, I'm not a psychoanalyst. Shouldn't you get an actual professional?'

'Right, after you wake up you can go shopping around the castle and find one, maybe have her sit down on a couch for a chat. *Oh wait.*' Not-Anne glared at me. '*We do not have time.* You want to drag Anne to a shrink, do it later. Right now you need to do whatever it takes to make her fight her way out of here.'

'Anne *does* know how to fight. I've seen—'

'No, you haven't. Against Vitus, maybe, and that was only because I was driving. The rest of the time she holds back. If she'd been serious, she'd have killed both those apprentices in her bedroom and we wouldn't be in this mess.'

'And then she would have been breaking the Concord.'

'Fuck the Concord. Every Dark mage in the country breaks it; why shouldn't she?' I started to answer and not-Anne waved her hand. 'Fine, whatever. I don't care about long-term solutions, all right? Get Anne out of here and you can do whatever the hell you want.'

'That bit we're agreed on.' I studied not-Anne. 'Does Variam know about you?'

'He's got his suspicions.' Not-Anne glanced out the window. 'Let's wrap this up.'

'One more thing,' I said. 'Don't take this the wrong way, but I'm getting the impression your priorities are a bit different from Anne's. Are you sure you want to get away from this castle as badly as she does?'

'Oh, please. Sagash has got the right idea about some things, I'll give you that, but we're just furniture to him. Anne and I might not always agree, but one thing we know is that we're not going to be a slave again. You think I want to be his tool until he uses me up? I want to be the one that everyone else is afraid of, who makes the decisions about who lives or dies and makes everyone shut up when she walks in the room. I don't want to be Chosen; I want to be queen.'

I looked back at not-Anne for a long moment, feeling a chill. I'd heard that speech before, or something very like it. 'It might be better for you and for Anne,' I said quietly, 'if you don't get what you want.'

Not-Anne shrugged. 'Not like I'll ever get the chance.' She pushed herself off the window's edge. 'Time's up.'

'Why? What's going to happen?'

'You ask too many questions, you know that?' Not-Anne walked away, deeper into the shadows of the tower. Only her voice echoed around me as she faded from sight. 'Just keep her alive. There's more hanging on it than you know.'

I started to answer, but she was gone. The room I was in was empty, and as I looked around I saw that the room was darker, the light fading. I started back towards the place I'd entered from; the lights above me began to dim and go out one by one, and I broke into a jog. I was alone in the tower, the glass corridors silent but for the sound of my feet. The door I'd entered by was at the end of the corridor, clearly visible in the shadows. I pulled it open, and as I did the last lights went out and I was left in darkness. I stepped through and back into my dreams, the doorway disappearing behind me as everything began to fragment and become fuzzy. Sleep came.

I woke up slowly. I didn't feel rested, but my neck and back were stiff and aching and I was too uncomfortable to go back to sleep. As I realised where I was, I remembered that I *shouldn't* be going back to sleep. In a moment I was fully awake and scanning for danger.

I was propped up against the wall, alone. Anne was gone; with her magic-enhanced physiology she'd recovered from the exertions of three days in the time it had taken me to recover from one. Looking into the futures in which I went down the stairs, I saw that she was in the room below. There were no signs of battle or danger.

Now that I was awake, I was uncomfortably aware of just how big a risk I'd taken falling asleep like that. Still, it had paid off, and both of us were rested — we'd need it for the day ahead. I pulled myself to my feet, wincing at the pain in my muscles. Sleeping in armour is really not comfortable.

The window on the north side of the room looked down onto the grass and the pool of water. From the grey-blue sky I knew that the sun had risen, but the bulk of the castle was blocking its rays and no direct sunlight was touching the grassy enclave. White birds — doves, maybe — were gathered at the rushes by the edge of the pool, dipping their heads to sip fresh water. It was a peaceful scene and I stood in the shadow of the window's edge, watching idly while I scouted through the futures ahead.

A stir of movement from the north side of the courtyard caught my eye; there was something in the shadow of a crumbling archway. Just enough reflected light came through for me to make out a small long-bodied animal, about the size and shape of a cat but with a pointed face and a thick bushy tail. Red fox. This shadow realm really must be old if it had its own predators.

The fox crept closer, revealing a red coat with splashes of white and black on its underside. A low pile of rubble hid it from the birds by the pool. It came to the edge of the rubble and froze, head down, eyes locked onto the birds in a stalking posture. I watched with interest, taking care not to move and draw attention; I've always liked animals, especially predators. The fox was quite still, focused on the birds, and it looked hungry. The doves didn't seem to have noticed it yet, but there wasn't any more cover. As soon as it took another couple of steps it'd be seen.

The fox held still and I kept a casual eye on it, my attention still taken up with scouting us a way out. It didn't look as though anyone was searching for us just yet, but I was still worried about the possibility of some kind of magical detection. The shroud over the place looked as though it would block most standard tracer spells, but my divination still worked, which meant other techniques might too. The shroud also wouldn't rule out more mundane methods of searching, such as just sending out scouts. I already knew those shadows could fly – if I were Sagash's apprentices, I'd be using them for aerial recon. They probably didn't have enough of them to cover the entire castle, but . . .

The fox crouched to spring, and I looked at it curiously. It was still the best part of forty feet from the birds—

The fox leapt; vanished. There was a scuffle and explosion of wings and the doves were airborne, flapping frantically up and away. I'd been about to turn; now I looked down in surprise. *What just happened?*

The fox was by the pool, its weight on one of the doves and its jaws locked tight. The bird was flapping feebly, trying to get away; the fox sank its teeth into the neck and twisted. There was a *crack* and the dove went still. The fox hoisted the bird up, looking quickly around, then trotted back towards where it had come, head tilted high so that the dove's wings trailed on the grass. It covered the distance back to the archway and disappeared into the darkness. The surviving doves were still in the air, circling; the whole thing had taken less than twenty seconds. Nothing was left except a scattering of feathers by the pool.

Footsteps sounded from below and Anne appeared in the stairwell, looking past me out through the window. 'Did you see that?' I said.

'The bird?' Anne asked. She was still wearing my great-coat. 'I felt it die but . . .'

'Not the bird, the fox. Did you see it move?' I'd seen the fox jump, a short bound of a foot or two, then all of a sudden it had been coming down on the bird.

Anne frowned. 'No. I think it's the same one that was here two days ago. It was on the other side of a wall, but when I got closer it just disappeared.'

'Holy crap,' I said. 'Blink fox.'

'What's a blink fox?'

'Magic-bred species – some twentieth-century mages made them as spy familiars. They look like a red fox, but they've got human-level intelligence and they can do short-range teleports.'

'You mean it was looking for us?'

I shook my head. 'No, it was hunting. If it was under a mage's control it wouldn't be that hungry . . . hmm.'

'Hmm, what?'

'I heard those two apprentices saying something about trying to catch a fox. Maybe we could strike a deal with it.'

Anne looked at me with raised eyebrows. 'Seriously?'

'It's been hiding out in this castle, probably longer than you. It'd know a lot about the place.'

'It probably belongs to those apprentices,' Anne said. 'Can't we just get out of here?'

'I guess.' I was reluctant – when I run into a new type of magical creature, my first instinct is to make friends with it, an old habit from my days as Richard's apprentice where the magical creatures tended to be better company than the humans. But Anne was right: we were on a clock. 'You said something yesterday about another way out?'

'There is, but . . . I'm not sure how useful it's going to be.'

I made a go-ahead gesture and Anne crouched next to me. She drew one finger across the flagstones of the floor, tracing lines. 'These are the edges of the castle.' She seemed to have recovered from last night, at least physically – her movements were quick and her voice soft and clear again. 'The outer walls are the lines of the stone; the bridge is here. Front gate.' Her finger drew back and tapped a marking a quarter of the way across. 'Sagash's keep.' She drew her finger back further, placing it on a spot in what would be the north-centre of the castle, mirroring the keep's position. 'This is the other exit.'

I studied the map. If Anne was getting the distances right, we weren't far away at all.

I should probably take a second here to explain some details about gate magic, because if you're not familiar with it, it's probably not obvious just how bad a position we were in here. Gate magic shapes portals between locations, creating a similarity between points in space so that you can step from one to the other. It can be used to travel from place to place within our world, to go from place to place within a shadow realm or (with more difficulty) to go from our world to a shadow realm or vice versa.

Gate magic can be blocked though, and the wards over this shadow realm were designed to do exactly that. Within the central keep, they would block any use of gate magic or teleportation at all. Outside the keep, the wards wouldn't stop you gating around the castle, but they *would* prevent you from using gate magic to get out of the shadow realm unless you were at one specific point (the front gate) and holding the key. It's a fairly standard security set-up – it makes it easy for the residents to travel around but hard for anyone else to enter or leave.

Unfortunately, neither Anne or I could use gate magic. We could use gate stones, but gate stones will only take you to one place, which would only be any use if we had gate stones keyed specifically to places in the castle, which we didn't. The same did *not* apply to Sagash's apprentices – it was more or less a guarantee that between them they'd have gate magic, gate stones or (more likely) both.

What all this meant was that as long as Anne and I were in this castle, Sagash and his apprentices had a huge home ground advantage. The only thing stopping them from gating to our position right now was that they didn't know where we were. As soon as that changed, they could just jump right on top of us and we'd have a hell of a time getting away from them. And even if they *couldn't* find us, they could just set up camp at the front gate with a bunch of shadows and wait for us to show up. Where else were we going to go?

But if there was a back door, that opened up some options. 'It's definitely an exit?'

'Back then it was. It might have changed.'

'Have you been there since?'

Anne shook her head. 'I couldn't have used it. It needs a key.'

'The same as the one for the front gate, or a different one?'

'Sagash never let me get close enough to see.'

'Probably a different one,' I muttered. Worth checking, though. 'What about surveillance? Is there any way for Sagash to pick us up while we're here?'

'He uses the shadows, mostly,' Anne said. 'He's got enough that he can turn the sky black with them, but most of the time he keeps them down in the tombs. He just relies on the fixed sensors instead.'

I looked up sharply. 'Fixed sensors?'

'At the front gate. They log everything that comes in or passes through.'

'So they would have seen us both come through?' I frowned. 'Why hasn't Sagash done anything?'

Anne shrugged helplessly.

'There's something strange going on. If Sagash was acting against us, the whole castle should have been mobilised by now.' I looked up at Anne. 'I don't think Sagash was the one behind the attack on you. I think it was just Darren and Sam, and now they're trying to keep it secret from everyone else.'

'But why?' Anne looked dismayed. 'I've never even met those two!'

It was my turn to shrug. From their conversation, it had sounded as though Darren and Sam had been afraid of Sagash finding out what they'd been doing, but if Sagash really did have that sensor net, wouldn't he have found out already? None of the explanations quite fit – there was some missing piece I hadn't figured out. 'I'm going to take a look at that back entrance,' I said. 'I need you to stay still and quiet for a bit.'

I found a place to sit with my back resting against the wall, while Anne sat cross-legged opposite me and watched quietly. As soon as I was settled, I closed my eyes, looking into the future in which I went downstairs and started going east. It didn't take long before I found the building Anne was describing, tall and rectangular and surrounded by high walls and colonnades. It looked as though it was—

The vision fragmented as the actions in Anne's immediate futures expanded to disrupt the point earlier in the chain at which I left. I frowned, routed around the disturbance and patiently traced my way back to the same building. A search of the ground floor discovered a circle made out of some greenish material which would show up to my magesight. Looked like a transport pattern. I looked to see what would happen if I used a gate stone within the circle . . . nothing. If I used the key focus as well? Also nothing. I wanted to try some command words, but the distance was hampering my ability to search. Maybe—

The vision fragmented again. 'Could you please stop doing that?' I said with my eyes closed.

'Doing what?' Anne asked.

'Talking to me.'

'I'm not.'

'You're thinking about starting a conversation, and each time you do it changes the futures.'

'I can't even *think* about talking to you?'

'You can think as much as you like so long as there's no possibility of you actually doing it.'

Anne didn't answer. The back gate didn't look good – maybe not hopeless, but I couldn't confirm that without getting closer. I switched directions, looking through the futures in which I headed towards the castle's main gate.

My future self worked his way south, following the mental map I'd worked out last night, around the keep. No sign of shadows or patrols. The future was starting to thin out, becoming delicate; hard to steer. A little closer and—

—again it broke apart.

'*Anne.*'

'I'm trying!'

'I know it seems like I'm just sitting here,' I said, 'but this isn't as easy as it looks and it'd really help if you could stop distracting me.'

Anne didn't say what she was thinking. I tried yet again to trace out the route to the south . . . The same thing happened.

Maybe I was going about this the wrong way. We needed a way out of here, but escaping this castle wasn't something I could solve alone. I was going to need Anne's help, and that wasn't going to happen as long as we kept putting off this conversation. 'All right,' I said. 'Go ahead and ask.'

'Ask what?'

'What you've been thinking about asking me since I got up.'

Anne was silent. I waited, counting off the seconds, watching the futures fork and twist, shifting with Anne's thoughts. 'Last night,' she said at last. 'Was that you?'

I just looked at her.

Anne let out a long breath and leant her head back against the wall. 'How much of it do you remember?' I asked.

'Bits and pieces. Like something you hear as you're falling asleep. It's hard to remember which parts are real and . . . She told you about the last time, didn't she? What I . . . when I was here.'

I nodded.

Anne closed her eyes. 'I wish she hadn't.'

'She . . .' I paused, mentally trying out different pronouns. 'That person I was talking to. Do I call her "she" or "you"?'

'I don't know,' Anne said with a sigh. 'Maybe that's the problem.'

'Why didn't you tell anyone about all this?' I asked. 'I know you've got your issues with me, but what about Luna? Or Vari?'

'I don't want them to see that side of me,' Anne said. 'I didn't want you to see it either.'

'Are you that ashamed of what you did?'

'Yes.'

'It doesn't really sound as though you had much choice.'

'I did have a choice. I could have *lost*. I thought about it, each time. But I didn't. I'd use my magic to . . . kill them, and afterwards I'd cry and I'd hate myself and I'd promise it was the last time, and then I'd do it again anyway.' Anne looked up at me with haunted eyes. 'Most people, when they hurt each other, they don't really understand what they're doing. When I look at someone I see *everything* – every layer of their body: skin and muscle and bone. You have to, before you can heal them. When you use that to *hurt* them, it's . . . vile. You're destroying something beautiful. You drain the life out from a body and you can *see* it: watch the blood vessels shrivel and the tissue wither. It's like their body trusts you, opens itself up and you betray it. And you know the worst part? It gets easier each time. You still know how horrible it is; you just . . . feel it less.'

'That's why you wouldn't duel, isn't it? Back when I first met you.'

'Sagash told me once that in the end you don't feel

anything at all,' Anne said quietly. 'You can still see what you're doing to someone's body; you just . . . don't care. I've . . . I've wondered how many more it'll take. Before I become like him.'

'I don't think it's just about the numbers. I mean, if something was going to push you over the edge, I don't think it'd be that.'

Anne gave a half-laugh, half-sob. 'Oh, great! So something *else* is going to turn me into a monster instead?'

*Oops.* Okay, so I probably wasn't the most tactful person to be having this conversation. But as the other Anne had pointed out, there wasn't exactly anyone else. 'I think you're setting much-too-high standards for yourself.'

'*Not* murdering anyone isn't a high standard.'

'I'm not talking about what you did back when you were Sagash's prisoner. That was just you being put in an impossible situation, and trust me, I know all about those. I was talking about what you've been doing afterwards. You took lives then, so now you're trying to avoid any kind of violence and only use your magic for healing. And maybe if you were one of the Light mages and you lived in that kind of protected world, then you could get away with doing that. But you're not, and you can't.'

Anne was silent. 'Second thing,' I said. 'I think you're too focused on yourself.'

Anne looked up with a frown. 'What?'

'This stuff you're beating yourself up over? You're only thinking about what *you* did, what *you're* responsible for. Everything you've told me about what happened back then, you've only talked about the choices you made. But that's not how the world works. Everyone makes choices and they all have a part in what happens. The way I see it, in terms of responsibility for those deaths, the order goes: number one, Sagash, for setting up the fights; number two, those kids you were fighting, for agreeing to whatever Sagash promised them; number three, the Council, for letting Dark mages like Sagash get away with this crap and not helping Variam when he went to them; and number four, you, for not being able to figure out some miracle way to fix it all. Taking all the blame isn't just wrong, it's self-centred. The world's bigger than just you.'

'Is that how you justify it?' Anne said quietly. 'What you did?'

I thought about it for a few seconds, then looked at her. 'Honestly? Yeah. I think after a certain point, if someone comes after you and won't back down, then it's on them.'

Anne was silent. 'Maybe you're right,' she said at last. 'But . . . it doesn't change anything. They're still dead, and I'm still that much closer to being like that.'

'Are you really that afraid you'll end up like the Dark mages?'

'Isn't that what always happens? Anyone who lives in our world, grows up as a mage – they only ever get worse. You meet apprentices, and they're mixed. Kind, cruel, everything in between. But the older they get . . . look at them. Sagash, Vitus, Morden.' Anne looked at me. 'I thought you were different. You'd been with a Dark mage, like me. But you were kind; you helped us. I thought . . . I thought if you could make yourself better, then I could too.'

I winced a little at that. She'd chosen a pretty bad role model. 'Anne, I'm not a hero. I'm just a survivor, that's all. If I ever seemed like I was trying to set myself up as more than that, that was my own mistake.'

'I know,' Anne said, sounding tired. 'I was building you up into something you weren't. It's just . . . It feels like the longer you live as a mage, the more you turn into what you used to hate.' She looked down at the stone. 'Maybe that's how it works in our world. The only heroes are the ones who die young.'

I gave Anne a disturbed look. 'That's a pretty depressing philosophy to live by.'

'Is it?' Anne didn't meet my eyes. 'I can't tell any more.'

I looked at Anne a second longer, then shook my head. 'All right, it's time we got moving. Whatever the answer, we're not going to find it sitting around here. Oh, and just so we're clear, I am *not* on board with you dying in this castle just so you don't turn into something worse. I like you alive and as you are, and nothing you've told me over the last day has changed my mind on that. Okay?'

Anne looked up in surprise. After a moment she smiled. It was a little half-hearted, but it was something. 'Good,' I said, and offered her my hand. 'Let's get going.'

There were two ways out of the windmill – the bottom and the top. At the highest level, a ladder led up to the roof where a wooden bridge led away from the sails back onto the castle battlements. Anne and I did a quick check for flying shadows, then headed back down. 'Are you going to be okay barefoot?' I asked.

'I can heal any cuts faster than I get them,' Anne said. She was still wearing my coat, bare legs showing as she moved. 'Do you want to try the back gate or the front?'

'Back. If there's a password I might be able to hack it if I get a good look.'

'If you can't?'

'Then we look for a backup plan,' I said. We left the windmill and began crossing the grass towards the entrance into the next courtyard. A few scattered feathers by the pool marked where the blink fox had made its kill. 'If worst comes to worst we can go to ground and hope Luna and Vari and Arachne work out some way to get in touch, but that's not . . .' I stopped walking.

Anne came to a halt and looked at me. 'What is it?'

'I'm not sure.' I frowned, looking ahead. I'd scanned the futures from the top of the windmill only a few minutes ago and everything had looked clear, but for some reason something was catching at my attention: some sort of encounter. It looked as though it was in the *immediate* future, but that didn't make sense – I would have seen that coming. 'Hold on.'

Anne tilted her head, puzzled. I looked into the futures in which we waited where we were. There *was* someone coming. *What the hell?* I couldn't see any immediate combat, but there was no way I should have missed something that blatant. It wasn't the castle – the shrouds didn't block divination magic. I couldn't have been *that* careless . . . could I? 'We've got company,' I said. 'Back to the windmill, quick!'

Anne's eyes went wide. We hurried back to the windmill and up the steps to the doorway, where I turned. That was better – now we had some cover. 'Who is it?' Anne asked.

'Working on it.' I still couldn't see any combat but that wasn't much reassurance – just because the encounter didn't start with violence didn't mean it wouldn't end that way, and we didn't have any friends in this place that I knew of. I focused on a single future, narrowing it down to get a clearer vision. It was a man, coming closer. Not Sagash.

Not his apprentices. That was strange – why was I standing like that? It was as though I were scared of something. It was a little tricky to focus on the image, but not too hard. There. It was—

Wait, that couldn't be right.

*Oh, Jesus.*

Anne looked at me sharply. 'Alex? Are you okay?'

I stood frozen, staring into space. All I could do was look at the futures over and over again, as if doing it would make them change.

'*Alex*,' Anne said, looking worried. She touched a hand to my shoulder. 'Your heart rate just jumped. What's wrong?'

My heart was hammering in my chest. I wasn't imagining any of it. It was all real. *Oh shit, oh shit, oh shit . . .* I felt my hands starting to shake and turned on Anne. 'Run. Now!'

Anne looked at me, puzzled. 'What?'

'Get out of here.' I spoke as fast as I could, the words tumbling out of my mouth. 'Someone's coming. You can't be here when he arrives. Get up to the top of the windmill; you can get away that way. Go!'

'Who's coming?'

'There's no time! Get out of here!'

'Then . . . why aren't you running as well?'

I was too paralysed to come up with an answer. Anne looked at me, then when I didn't reply she shook her head. 'I'm staying.'

'*No!*'

'If it's a person coming, I can defend myself better than you can.'

'I'm not asking!' Terror was making it hard for me to

think clearly. I pointed up towards the ceiling. 'Do as I say and get out of here, *now*!'

'You're not my master, and I don't think you're thinking straight. Besides . . .' – something flickered in Anne's eyes – 'I'm tired of things happening to other people because of me. Whoever's coming, it can't be Sagash or his apprentices or you'd have said. Who is it?'

I stared at Anne, then slumped a little. 'You win,' I said quietly. 'Make sure you don't regret it.'

Doubt showed in Anne's eyes, and she looked at me with a frown. I think it wasn't until then that she got a glimpse of just how afraid I really was. I turned towards the grassy space and we waited in silence.

I spend a lot of time running from things. It works, up to a point. Most of the time when you're in danger, the one who's threatening you isn't after *you*, not personally. They just want something you have, or you're in the way for some reason. Get away from them and stay away long enough, and things will change.

But sometimes what the other person wants isn't a thing, or a piece of information, or some other short-term goal. Sometimes what they want is *you*. And when that happens, then all running does is put things off. It'll delay them, but if they want you badly enough then eventually they'll catch up again. Sooner or later you'll have to face them – the most you can do is choose the time and the place.

Anne and I waited in the doorway, looking out across the pond towards the castle walls. To our left, the sails of the windmill kept turning, the rhythmic creaking sound echoing through stone and wood. The sun still hadn't yet reached a high enough point in the sky to look down onto our little enclave, and the grass and water were left in shadow. There was a doorway in the castle wall, and from the courtyard beyond I heard footsteps. At my side I felt Anne turn her head, looking through the wall towards something only she could see.

The footsteps grew louder and I felt light-headed, grey spots sparkling before my eyes. Old words came back to my mind, Tobruk's voice speaking to me from another time, vicious and cruel. *He's going to find you and he's going to hurt you and you're going to die. Make sure you stay alive till then, Alex. I want to see your face.* I'd never really believed he was telling the truth.

The man who stepped out onto the grass was maybe forty or fifty, though few trying to guess his age would have bothered. Everything about him was ordinary: brown hair, brown eyes, average height, average build. Most people would have glanced over him without a second thought. I couldn't have told you what he was wearing; just the sight of him was enough to freeze my blood. He stood in the shadow of the castle wall, looking straight towards me, and I held my breath.

'Alex,' Richard said. 'It's been a long time.'

## 9

I first met Richard in my last year of school, only a few days before my eighteenth birthday. Within a month I'd left school, left home and moved into Richard's mansion, the last apprentice of four. Richard is very good at being persuasive.

We studied magic in Richard's mansion, and were sent on missions together, but the lessons that really stuck in my memory weren't to do with magic or fieldwork, but ways of thinking. I'd always been clever, but for most of my life I'd never really *used* it for anything, at least nothing practical. I'd thought of intelligence as an academic thing, not something you used in the real world. Richard showed me differently. Seeing patterns and predicting them, analysing people's behaviour, looking multiple steps ahead . . . always thinking, always planning, never standing still. The other three threw themselves into their magic, and in raw power they left me further behind every day, but the biggest thing I learnt from Richard was that the mind can be a more powerful weapon than any spell. There were a hundred little tricks I learnt from watching him, and I remembered them all. It didn't take me long to decide that I was better than Richard was. I was still a teenager, and like most teenagers I was sure I was smarter than my teachers. Richard might be good at planning, but I was a *diviner*.

A year after I moved into Richard's mansion he sent us on a mission to Arizona, hunting down two kids our age, a girl and a boy. What happened to them both was ugly, and I started having second thoughts. After taking longer than I should have, I decided I was going to break the girl, Catherine, out from where Richard was keeping her prisoner. It never occurred to me that I could fail. I knew the mansion inside out, I knew the security systems and I could predict where everyone was going to be. I had it all planned out.

It didn't work.

I had a lot of time afterwards to think about what I'd done wrong. Looking back on things and picking up all the little details I'd missed, I realised that Richard had not only known what I'd been planning, he'd known pretty much *everything* that I'd been doing while I'd been at the mansion, all the little minor disobediences which I'd thought I'd been so clever in hiding. He'd let it slide, not because he hadn't known, but because I hadn't stepped far enough over the line.

Pain is an effective teacher. I learnt my lesson, and when I finally escaped the mansion, I did it at a time when Richard was too busy with his major plans to come after me himself. Instead he'd sent Tobruk. Tobruk was crueller and more sadistic than Richard, but for all his power he wasn't dangerous in the same way. I tricked Tobruk and lured him into a trap, and he paid for it with his life. And then I kept running and hiding, waiting for Richard to come after me himself, and I knew that if he did then that would be the end, because while I could outsmart Tobruk I could never outsmart Richard. It took me a long time to realise that Richard wasn't coming, and an even longer time to make myself believe it. I'd almost managed to convince myself that I'd never see him again.

Until now.

The castle was quiet. In the distance I could hear a bird calling, but here by the windmill the only sound was the rustle of the wind and the creak of the sails. I stood in the windmill's doorway, half a step in front of Anne, the two of us staring down at the man on the grass. The moment stretched out.

'I'm glad to see you're together,' Richard said. His voice was deep and powerful. The first few times I met Richard, that voice of his had always felt oddly jarring – you'd ignore him until he spoke, then all of a sudden he'd dominate the room. Once you got to know him better, you didn't need the voice to remind you. 'Why don't you introduce me to your companion?'

'I . . .' Speaking was difficult; my voice sounded cracked and uneven. I took a breath and tried again. 'This is Richard Drakh. My . . . teacher.'

I didn't turn to look at Anne, but I felt her tense as she made the connection. 'And you must be Anne Walker,' Richard said to her with a nod. He came to a halt and looked back to me with raised eyebrows, obviously waiting for me to speak.

I didn't. My mind had gone blank and I couldn't think of anything to say.

'No questions, Alex?' Richard said. He looked interested.

'How did you get here?' Anne said from over my shoulder. She was staring at Richard. 'Did Sagash let you in?'

'A reasonable conclusion, but no. Sagash is occupied with his own research these days, and he tends not to react well to distractions.'

'Then . . . how did you get in? The shadow realm's gate is locked.'

'Yes, it is.'

I swallowed and Richard turned his attention to me. I had to take a breath before I could trust my voice to be steady enough. 'Why are you here?'

'Now *that* is a more interesting question,' Richard said. 'What do you think the answer is?'

'I think you're here for me,' I said quietly.

Richard gave me a quizzical look. 'Strictly true, I suppose, but why?'

'Because I turned against you,' I said. It was difficult to say out loud, but I wanted this out in the open. 'That's it, isn't it? I betrayed you, so you gave me to Tobruk. Then when I got away, you sent him after me. Now you're here to finish what Tobruk started.'

Silence. The wind blew across the grass. Richard studied me for a long moment; I held my breath, and I could feel Anne doing the same. If Richard chose to make a fight of it, I had no illusions that I'd survive. The most I could hope for would be that Anne might get away.

Then suddenly Richard smiled. 'Alex. Not everything is about you.'

I stared at Richard. Whatever I'd been expecting, it hadn't been that. 'Did you really think I was here for revenge?' Richard asked. 'What would I be taking revenge for?'

'I . . .' I didn't know what to say. This wasn't how I'd thought the conversation would go. 'Catherine.'

'Catherine was a necessary component in my plans, and unfortunately she was not replaceable. You tried to remove her, and so I was forced to keep you confined. I wasn't going to kill you, Alex. I simply removed you from the situation until you could no longer interfere.'

I stared at Richard. 'As for Tobruk,' Richard continued, 'I did not send him after you. In fact, I specifically ordered him *not* to pursue you, an order Tobruk chose to disregard. If he had survived, I would have been quite as upset with him as I was with you.' Richard tilted his head. 'Does that answer your question? Let me put it another way. What significant harm have you ever done me that I would hold a grudge for?'

I didn't know what to say. I'd been keyed up, ready for Richard to attack. Except . . . I'd never really thought about why. I'd been so caught up in how I felt towards Richard that I'd never thought about how *he* might feel towards *me*. I'd tried to rescue Catherine, and I'd failed. I'd tried to stop what was happening in Richard's mansion, and I'd failed at that too. The four of us had ended up fighting and fleeing and dying until only one was left to take on the mantle of Richard's Chosen . . . just as he'd wanted.

Richard was right – I *had* only been thinking about myself. I'd hated Richard, but why should Richard hate me? He'd *won*. When you crush your opponents that completely, you don't carry a grudge against them afterwards.

'You're playing with us,' Anne said abruptly.

I looked at her in surprise. Anne was standing to her full height, looking across at Richard. 'Is this a threat? You found us, so unless we do what you want then you'll tell them where we are?'

Richard looked back at her calmly. 'What would you do if it was?'

I felt Anne tense. 'No,' I said sharply. 'Don't.'

Anne hesitated, looking between us, and the moment

was gone. 'I did not come here to assist Sagash or his apprentices,' Richard said. 'Your conflicts with them are no concern of mine.' He raised his eyebrows. 'Unless you'd like to change that.'

'Then how did you find us?' Anne said slowly. 'How did you know we were here?'

Richard glanced at me. 'Alex?'

My thoughts were starting to work again. My mind still felt slow and clumsy but I forced myself to think. 'He's not working with Sagash,' I said, half to Anne, half to myself. Richard didn't lie — that was one of the things which made him so dangerous. He might leave things out but if he said something directly, then you knew he was telling the truth. Either that or he was just good enough never to get caught. 'He found out some other way.' Richard had said that he was here for me, or partly so. Who had known I was looking for Anne? My friends, Sonder, Caldera . . . and the mages I'd spoken to at the Tiger's Palace. Ordith, Meredith . . . Morden. Arachne had linked Morden's name to Richard, and he'd said . . .

'Morden,' I said. I felt Anne look towards me and I turned my head just far enough that I could see her without taking my eyes off Richard. 'I saw him the day before I came. He told me to forget about you, that he'd find you and take care of it.' I looked back at Richard. 'He told you and you tracked us here . . .'

Richard gave me a single nod, the same gesture he'd always used when one of us had got something right. I felt a moment's satisfaction, followed by a chill. Was I trying to *show off* for Richard? That was insane. Within minutes of seeing him I was falling back into my old habits, apprentice to master.

That actually scared me more than seeing him did.

'You're here for me,' Anne said, and there was a new note to her voice, tense.

'More accurately, for both of you,' Richard said. 'I'd like to offer you a position in my organisation.'

There was a dead silence. 'You've got to be kidding,' I said. My mouth was dry.

'Not in the least,' Richard said calmly. 'As I expect you're aware, I've been quite busy since my return, and I'm somewhat understaffed. It's so difficult to find competent diviners. Life mages as well. You'd be working under me or my associates, primarily on political or investigative assignments. Similar to your freelance work for the Council, though I can promise considerably more support and benefits.'

I felt a chill at the word 'investigative'. *Talisid.* But Anne was already answering, and her voice was flat. 'I've had a Dark master already.'

'I am aware,' Richard said. 'However, I am not Sagash. I am only interested in willing servants.'

'Maybe you're not Sagash,' Anne said. 'But I've heard what happened to your last set of apprentices.'

'Ah,' Richard said. 'I suspect we have a misunderstanding. The Council may have assigned you to their apprentice programme, but quite frankly I think that reflects their own prejudices. I'd be happy to arrange instruction, but I believe treating you as an apprentice would undervalue your abilities. The position I was offering you was that of a mage.'

Anne stopped at that. 'And if we say no?' I said.

'You mean, what will I do?' Richard said. 'Nothing.'

'Then leave,' I said. It came out harsher than I'd wanted it to sound. 'The answer's no.'

'If that's your decision,' Richard said. 'Although there is more to my offer.'

'There's nothing you can offer that would make me work for you again.' I managed to keep my voice under control, but just barely. I'd been ready for a fight, but even the suggestion that I'd willingly go back to him . . .

'In which case you can say no once again, and that'll be the end of the matter. I do, however, strongly recommend that you hear me out. You may find it changes your opinions.'

I opened my mouth and felt Anne touch my side. It was only a brush of her fingers, but I got the message. With an effort I stayed quiet.

'Excellent,' Richard said. He didn't look at all bothered that I'd said no. 'There are two additional points to my offer I would like to make. First, as a member of my organisation, you would both fall under my protection. I imagine both of you have your share of enemies. I think you will find they would be far less willing to provoke me.'

'Yeah,' I said. 'Except that we'd pick up all of *your* enemies too. No thanks.'

'And secondly, I would be willing to assist you with your more immediate problems.'

*Here it comes.*

'You appear to be unwilling guests in this shadow realm,' Richard said. 'I can address that problem. In addition,' – he glanced at Anne – 'I can ensure nothing similar happens in the future.'

Anne reacted slightly. 'You escaped from Sagash once,' Richard said. 'And in doing so, you proved both your ability and strength of will. However, as you can see, Sagash's power vastly dwarfs yours. You and Variam both have to be aware that should Sagash ever devote his full resources towards recapturing you, you would have very little chance of escape. So far he has not, but at any point that could change. Do you really want to live the rest of your life with that hanging over you? I have some leverage with Sagash, and, unlike the Light Council, I can negotiate with him on equal terms. If you join me, I can guarantee as a condition of your employment that neither Sagash nor his apprentices will come after you ever again.'

I couldn't help myself; I turned to look at Anne. She hesitated, her eyes flickering from me back to Richard, and I knew she was torn. It was one of the things Richard had always been so good at: finding what someone most wanted and offering it to them.

Richard was still speaking. 'And then, of course, there's your current situation. You and Alex are in very immediate danger. I entered this shadow realm, and I can bring you out the same way – quickly and safely. If you decline my offer, I will not harm you, but I will not help you either. You will be left to resolve this problem alone.'

Anne still hesitated, and I held my breath. I wanted to urge her not to do it but I knew I couldn't. Staying here could mean our death. I was willing to risk that rather than go with Richard, but I couldn't make that decision for Anne. If she said yes . . .

The futures shifted . . . and steadied. 'You're right,' Anne said, and her voice was clear. 'We did escape from Sagash once.' She looked at Richard. 'We can do it again.'

I let out a long breath. 'As I understand, it took you some time,' Richard said.

'Except this time it's not Sagash,' Anne said. 'You said

it yourself. Sagash hasn't come after me. It's just his apprentices, and I can beat them. We'll find a way.'

'His apprentices, yes. They are, however, not alone.'

'Give it up,' I said. I felt confident now. Richard had taken his best shot, and it had failed. I didn't know why Richard was limiting himself like this, but as long as he was going to rely on persuasion we had the advantage. 'You wanted an answer; she gave you one.'

'There are, however, some facts neither of you are as yet aware of,' Richard said. 'You may have succeeded in evading the notice of your pursuers, but this has been because so far they have primarily focused on guarding the exits. As of today, they have progressed to searching for you more directly.'

'So they're looking for us. That's not news.'

'Don't place too much faith in this shadow realm's shroud,' Richard said. 'Anne may have stayed hidden so far, but she will not remain so for ever. If you stay here, Sagash's apprentices will find you. Very soon.'

'We'll take our chances.'

'Alex?' Richard said. 'When I said "very soon," I didn't mean "later today".'

I started to answer and paused. Richard was waiting, his hands clasped behind his back, and it was easy to look ahead. I could see movement, a lot like—

*Oh shit.*

There was movement at the edge of my vision. I looked up at where the castle battlements were silhouetted against the skyline and saw a black shape. One of Sagash's shadow constructs. A moment later, a second appeared.

Down at ground level, more shadows were emerging from archways: three, four, seven. They moved with a strange loping gait, white eyes glowing from within fuzzy darkness, quicker than something of that size should be. They took up positions on the grass, surrounding the windmill. Three moved to encircle Richard, arms hanging loose as they stared at him with empty eyes.

The shadows kept coming, moving out onto the grass, and now people were walking out with them: Darren, black clothes and dark skin blending into the shadows beside him. His eyes narrowed at me before switching back to Richard. The lightning mage, Sam, was close behind him, spreading out to cover Darren's flank. Finally there was the Korean girl, Ji-yeong. She broke away from the other two at the first opportunity, hands hanging near the hilts of her swords.

Sagash's apprentices came to a halt. The three of them formed a rough group, Darren and Sam close, Ji-yeong a little further away. The shadows were scattered around, and I did a quick count. There were twelve: ten on the ground; two on the battlements. I could feel Anne's tension from behind me. Richard stood between us and the apprentices, head turned to watch Darren and Sam. Between them and the shadows, he was close to being surrounded. The three groups – Anne and me, Sagash's apprentices and Richard – formed a triangle, almost perfectly equilateral. There was a silence, and I held my breath.

'Who the fuck are you?' Darren said, looking at Richard.

'Darren, wasn't it?' Richard said. 'I'll be with you in a moment.'

Ji-yeong spoke from the other side, looking at the lightning mage, Sam. 'Didn't you say there were two of them?'

'Not now, all right?' Sam said.

'Only two used the gates: Anne and Verus,' Ji-yeong

said. 'That was what you said, right? Because I'm counting three.'

'I said *not now*.'

'Children,' Richard said, with a note of authority which made all three apprentices turn to look. 'The three of us are having a conversation. I'll deal with your queries later.'

Sagash's apprentices stared at him. Sam seemed about to speak, but Darren cut him off. 'You know where you are?'

Richard sighed. 'I understand you have your obligations but—'

'You know where you are?' Darren said again. 'You're in our shadow realm. You have one good reason we shouldn't beat the shit out of you right now?'

'I'd prefer you didn't,' Richard said. 'I have a prior relationship with Sagash.'

'Oh, you're *friends* with *Sagash*. Funny how everyone's his friend as soon as we catch them.'

'You misunderstand,' Richard said, and his voice was calm. 'My relationship with Sagash is a professional one. As a matter of courtesy, I would prefer not to kill his apprentice in his own shadow realm.'

Darren stared. 'Who *are* you?' Sam asked.

'My name is Richard Drakh,' Richard said.

Sam stared at him, then spoke to Darren without looking at him. 'Darren? Back off.'

'Why—?'

There was an edge to Sam's voice. '*Back the fuck off.*'

Richard looked at Ji-yeong. 'And you?'

Ji-yeong studied Richard for a second, then pointed at Darren and Sam. 'I'm not with them.'

'Good. Sam, was it? You have someone you should be

reporting this to. I think it'll save time if I deal with her directly.'

Sam stared at Richard, then lifted something from a pocket and spoke quietly. I'd been watching, seeing the futures shift between standing and talking and quickly terminated flashes of violence, but now I strained to look ahead. *Who's he talking to?* Sam finished whatever he was saying and straightened up. No one was talking, and for a second I had a clear look through the futures. There was one more person coming, and it was—

I felt my heart sink with a kind of weary disbelief. *Oh, come on. Not now. This isn't fair.*

Footsteps echoed from the next courtyard over, and only a few seconds later a woman appeared in the archway, gold hair bright in the darkness. It had been a year and a half since I'd seen her, and she looked quite different from how I remembered. Gone were the cream-coloured suits and the high heels; instead she wore a simple grey-and-brown outfit designed more for practicality than for fashion. The confidence was still there though, and her sculpted features were as distinctive as ever. Before she'd looked like an aristocrat; now she looked like an aristocrat-turned-guerrilla. She came to a stop behind Darren and Sam, watching Richard.

'Mage Drakh,' Crystal said.

'Mage Crystal,' Richard replied.

'I'm sorry to interrupt,' Crystal said, 'but I have some business with those two.' She ignored us both completely.

'I'm afraid you'll have to wait your turn.'

'I think I've waited long enough,' Crystal said. Her voice was clear and there was something to it that gave me a chill. She didn't look at Anne.

'My interest pre-dates yours.'

'I know Verus was your apprentice,' Crystal said. 'I could be persuaded to leave him alone.'

'Crystal,' Richard said. 'I appreciate your efforts to come to a compromise. But please do not attempt to be heavy-handed. You do not have the power to even effectively *pretend* to threaten me. Anything you receive from me will be on my terms.'

Crystal was silent. She didn't move, but I saw the futures flicker. Just for a second I saw a flash of combat, there and gone before I could catch any details. 'Now,' Richard said. 'I have no intention of involving myself in your affairs with Sagash. Once I've finished with Verus and with Anne, I will be leaving.'

'Alone?' Crystal asked.

Richard raised his eyebrows. 'That depends on them.' And he turned back to us.

All of a sudden, everyone was looking at us – Richard and Crystal, Darren, Sam and Ji-yeong, the scattered shadows with their soulless white eyes – and I felt an ugly, sick feeling in my stomach. This was bad, very bad. Right now, Richard was the only thing holding Crystal and the apprentices back. The instant he left they were going to attack, and we were going to lose. Even against just Sagash's apprentices and their constructs, our odds would be bad. With Crystal as well . . .

'This is it?' Anne said quietly, and I knew she'd figured it out as well. 'This is the deal? If we don't join you, you leave us to them?'

'I did not bring you to this shadow realm,' Richard said. 'Nor am I the cause of your problems with Sagash. I can help, but there is a price.'

'If you want to help us, then *help*!'

Richard shook his head. 'No handouts, Anne. If you want my protection, you have to earn it.'

Crystal and the apprentices were still watching, silent and hungry. *Is there anything we can do with that?* 'You know,' I said, 'it's going to be really hard for us to accept your offer if that lot kill us.'

'True.'

'So how about we do this a different way? You get rid of them, and we'll talk terms.'

'I don't think so,' Richard said. He sounded amused.

'There might be something—'

'Alex,' Richard said. 'I'm glad you haven't lost your ability to think on your feet. But remember who taught you those tricks.'

*Crap.* Okay, so much for that plan. 'You know, for someone who's trying a recruitment pitch, you aren't selling this very well.'

'Then let's bring this to a close,' Richard said. 'The offer stands. Your service for . . . two years, shall we say? That seems a reasonable span. If you agree, you'll receive appropriate compensation and benefits. I'm not ungenerous. If you refuse . . .' He shrugged. 'I won't harm you, but I will not save you either. I do suggest you consider the consequences carefully before answering. I expect you could probably find your way out, Alex, one way or another.' He shifted his gaze to Anne. 'You, on the other hand . . . for all your power, I doubt you'd leave this castle again. Nor would your remaining days be pleasant.'

Anne didn't speak. Crystal didn't either. She was watching Anne with a flat, unblinking look.

'Well, then,' Richard said when we didn't answer. 'I do

have other commitments. I'll give you five minutes to make your decision, then I'll take my leave. Crystal, we should talk.' He walked to where Crystal was standing, weaving between the shadows without seeming to pay them any particular attention. Darren and Sam turned to stare as he passed, then looked back at us. Crystal stood her ground and Richard came to a stop beside her.

Anne and I were left alone with what felt like an entire army watching us. 'Um,' Anne said. Her voice was under control, but only just, and she didn't take her eyes away from the figures menacing us. 'Alex? Don't take this the wrong way, but please tell me you have some ideas.'

'I was about to ask you that.'

'Oh.'

My eyes scanned the area, looking for weak points. 'We could wait for Richard to leave, then make a break for it,' I said. The bulk of the shadows were on the grass, between us and the apprentices and the ground-level exits. Up on the battlements, two more shadows stood on a path cut into the castle walls, thirty or forty feet from the ground. The path joined to the windmill via the bridge and disappeared at the other end through an open doorway into a round-topped tower. 'Up and out through the roof, over the bridge, past those shadows to the door in the corner. If we can make it through into that tower, we can break line of sight long enough to get some distance on them. Try and lose them in the castle.'

Anne didn't look up. 'Do you think that'll work?'

I was silent for a second. 'No.'

'I can't fight that many shadows,' Anne said. 'I can't even fight one.'

'I know,' I said. Near the castle wall, Richard and Crystal were talking quietly. With my mage's sight I could pick out some sort of field around them, probably an eavesdrop ward. Darren was still watching us, and so was Ji-yeong. Two minutes gone.

Anne took a breath. 'What would Richard do if we said yes?'

'*No*,' I said. 'Don't even think about it.'

'I don't want to! But what *else* are we going to do?'

'Anything!'

'Even if he's a Dark mage . . . I'm more afraid of Sagash than I am of Richard.'

'If you knew him you wouldn't be,' I said. The old dread was back, gnawing at me. Richard was speaking quietly to Crystal. I was terrified that he'd feel my gaze, that he'd look up and meet my eyes and . . . what? I didn't know. All I know was that the thought of going back to him was worse than anything I could imagine.

'Then what are we supposed to do?'

'I don't *know*.'

Anne hesitated. 'What if we . . . left?' Her voice was lower still; she didn't look towards Richard and Crystal. 'Pretended to go with him. Then once we were out of this castle, we could—'

'That would be worse,' I said. I'd thought of that already . . . for about two seconds. 'Richard doesn't lie, not so you can tell. But if you make a deal with him and break it . . . I did it once. Just once.'

Anne turned to me, and a startled look crept into her eyes. 'You're scared of him.'

'More than anything in the world.'

'Why?' There was frustration in Anne's voice now. 'I

told you what happened to me when I was caught here. If we stay . . . What could be worse than *that*?'

'I don't— Look—' I felt clumsy; weak. Every instinct I had was screaming against going with Richard, but I couldn't find the words. 'You don't know what it was like. What Richard can do. This is what he does. He finds what you want the most, offers it on a plate. And the price is *you*. You say yes, he owns you.'

'I know it'll be bad,' Anne said quietly. 'I lived with Sagash and with Jagadev. I'm still here.'

'You'll be alive. You just won't be the same.' I looked at Anne. 'You're a good person. I believe that, even if you don't. But if you go with him . . . you won't be. Not by the end.'

Anne looked back at me, and this time she didn't answer. Seconds ticked away. I could feel Darren and Sam's eyes on us, wolves eyeing their prey. We had maybe a minute left.

'All right,' Anne said. 'You choose.'

'You mean—'

'For both of us.' Anne didn't take her eyes away. 'You're right. I don't know what Richard's like, but you do. You gave me some advice, the night before I came here, and I didn't listen.' Anne took a breath. 'So this time I will. You're better at working out the odds than I am. If we want to get out of this, what should we do?'

'I don't know *any* way of getting out of this!' My voice was harsh. 'Our odds suck both ways!'

Anne looked at me steadily. 'Then tell me which one sucks *less*.'

I hesitated.

If I'd been alone, I'd have said no in an instant. I figured my chances of breaking away from Crystal and the apprentices were okay. Not great, but okay. Not the sort of gamble I like, but when the alternative was going back to Richard, it wasn't even a choice. Compared to that, risking death sounded just fine.

But it wasn't just my death I'd be risking. Taking your life into your own hands is one thing. Taking someone *else's* life . . .

I looked down at Anne. She was looking back at me, slim and quiet and trusting, and my imagination showed me a vivid picture of everything Crystal would do if she caught her. When Vitus had tried to use Anne for his ritual, he'd cut her throat. Crystal hadn't had as much time to practise. She'd be slower, more experimental. It wouldn't be either merciful or quick.

If I said no, and the worst happened . . . I'd been responsible for those deaths last year and it had been as much as I could bear. If Anne ended up dead as well, I wasn't sure I'd be able to live with myself afterwards.

What would happen if I told Richard yes?

Then Crystal and the apprentices wouldn't matter any more. We'd follow Richard out of here, let him gate us away to . . . what? I didn't know and I was afraid to find out, but I'd survived time after time by making use of those more powerful than me. Was this really any different?

*Yes.* I couldn't manipulate Richard, but he could manipulate me. If I went back, I'd be his tool again. I'd spent more than ten years trying to escape Richard's shadow. The thought of going back was a horror.

But if I said no, I might be sacrificing us both.

The silence stretched out, seeming to sharpen, waiting. The birds outside had fallen silent and the only noise was the rustle of the wind. Richard was finishing up his talk with Crystal, their voices inaudible behind the ward, while a dozen pairs of eyes watched us. I felt as though I were balanced on a razor's edge. The choice was a horrible one. Go back to the one person in the world I most feared and hated, or risk my life and Anne's to a fate I couldn't see any way to avoid.

Richard turned away from Crystal and walked back towards us, stopping at the edge of the pond. Distantly, a corner of my mind noticed that a couple of white feathers were still floating on the water's surface. It had been no more than an hour since I'd seen the fox. How had things gone so wrong so fast? 'Well, then,' Richard said. 'Have you made your decision?'

Anne didn't answer. I hesitated, teetering on the brink. Before me, I could see the two paths opening up. I didn't know what to do.

Then in that moment of stillness, a memory came back to me, a vision of something which had happened a long time ago. A stone chapel beneath the surface of the earth, two apprentices before an altar, one awake and the other dying. Richard walking a slow circle around them, his voice hypnotic, seductive. The apprentice had listened, been given everything she'd wanted . . . and it had been the worst choice she'd ever made.

I didn't know which decision was worse. All I knew was that I wasn't going to make the same mistake that Rachel had.

I met Richard's eyes. Somehow I managed to keep my voice steady. 'The answer's no.'

Richard looked back at me, head tilted slightly. My muscles were tense, locked. 'Well,' Richard said. 'I wish you the best of luck.' He gave us both a nod. 'Until next time.' He turned and walked away.

Leaving us alone with Crystal and her army.

The temperature seemed to drop as Richard disappeared into one of the archways. Violence loomed in the futures ahead, growing closer and closer, and I took in the stances of the three apprentices. Darren was staring at me as though trying to bore his eyes through my skull. He obviously hadn't forgotten our last meeting; he'd go for me at the first opportunity. Ji-yeong was standing back, swords still in their sheaths. Up close she would be the most dangerous, but she also seemed the least committed to the fight. Sam was watching Anne, and I knew that, unlike Darren, his focus would be on her rather than me. But it was Crystal I was most afraid of, standing on the grass and looking after Richard, apparently ignoring us. She was the most powerful of the four by far, and she was a mind mage. Her defensive magic was weak, and Anne and I would have been able to take her easily if she'd been alone, but as long as she could stay behind the shadows and the apprentices, she could just keep hitting us with mental attacks over and over again and we wouldn't be able to do a thing to fight back.

In the courtyard beyond, Richard's footsteps faded from earshot. I knew we had only seconds. 'You don't want to be working for Crystal,' I told the apprentices. 'If she—'

Crystal spoke over me. 'Take them both.'

And all hell broke loose.

Darren and Sam fired at the same time. Darren's spell was death magic, negative and kinetic energy woven together into a bolt of darkness, while Sam's was a blue-white flash of lightning, there and gone in an instant, travelling flat across the earth in a path real lightning could never follow.

I'd already started my jump back, catching Anne by the arm and pulling her with me. The black-and-white bolts split the air where we'd been a second ago and the *crack* of the discharge hammered my ears, stone dust filling the room.

By backing off we'd broken their line of sight; we had about five seconds before they made it to the door. Anne was already running for the stairs, cat-quick, as I pulled a pair of golden discs from one pocket. Two flicks of my wrist sent them bouncing to either side of the doorway, then I was running after Anne, taking the steps two at a time. Two steps, four, six, eight, and I heard running footsteps from behind. Without turning, I called out the command word for the discs.

Magic flared behind me, a wall of force coming into existence to block the entrance to the windmill. An instant later Darren slammed into it, the thud muffled through the barrier. I didn't look back to see how much damage I'd done. *Up.*

Ground floor, first floor, second. My heart was racing, feet hammering the stone. Crystal could sense us through the walls; she'd know what we were doing now and it would all come down to who was faster. Anne held back at the ladder, letting me take the lead, and I scrambled up, wooden rungs under my hands turning brighter in the light until I came out onto the roof of the windmill, wind buffeting my clothes and hair.

There was a shadow there, wings unfurled, and it reached for me. They'd sent it to block us in, but just an instant too late. I ducked under the arm, slammed the point of my dispelling focus into its torso and felt the spell discharge into the construct's body. The shadowy figure shuddered and came apart, disintegrating into black smoke as it fell towards the grass below. I felt Anne's presence behind me as I darted across the bridge, towards the wall and our way out, taking in the situation at a glance.

One more shadow on the wall ahead, three more in the air, wings flapping as they headed towards us. Darren was down by the door trying to smash his way through the forcewall; I couldn't see Crystal or Ji-yeong but Sam was up on the wall ahead and to the left, blocking the tower door that was our way out, lining up a shot. I didn't know how he'd got up to our level so fast, but it was too late to change the plan. I charged.

Darren and Sam saw the movement and reacted, but if there's one thing divination magic is good for, it's dodging attacks. I saw the bolts coming, skimmed past the futures in which I was hit to pick one of the handful where I wasn't. Electricity and death magic cut the air with a *crack*, hitting the spot where I would have been if I hadn't broken stride, and then I was over the bridge and onto the wall and facing the shadow. Constructs are strong, tireless – and predictable. I let its first grab fall short, closed under the second, caught the shadow's arm, my fingers sliding over the weird alien texture, spongy and dry and smelling of dust-bones-ash, then I was twisting it around to block a third deathbolt from Darren below. The shadow jerked as the kinetic energy ripped through it and I kicked its body off the wall, smoke trailing from the hole in its torso as it went tumbling down. And then I was alone on the ramparts with Sam, solid wall to my right and a sheer drop to my left to the grass below.

Sam stood his ground. It was the first time I'd gotten a good look at the lightning apprentice, and as I closed the distance I had what felt like a long moment to study him: slim and quick-looking, blond hair combed back, blue eyes nervous but not afraid enough to run. He threw another lightning bolt and I had to throw myself into a roll this time as the blue-white energy flashed out from his hands, electricity stinging my shoulder and leg as I came back up. My hand was going to the hilt of my knife but a spread of futures flashed before my eyes, electricity leaping down the metal blade and into my skin, and I changed motions mid-draw. The shock shield came up around Sam at the last instant, crackling white, but it was my armoured forearm that slammed into him and the spell-mesh absorbed the discharge. Sam went staggering back, teetering on the edge of the drop, and I moved in to finish him.

And everything went wrong.

A mental blow hit me. I'd been bracing myself for an attack from Crystal ever since we came up into view, but this wasn't the domination attempt I'd been anticipating; it was a blast of pure psychic force. I had an instant's warning, then the attack was hammering into my mental defences, raking my thoughts. I felt Sam readying another attack and twisted right on instinct, but this time he didn't send lightning, he turned *into* lightning, and with a crack and a smell of ozone he was gone from in front of me, leaving only a purple after-image. Another deathbolt from Darren went hissing past and I could hear the wingbeats of shadows, only seconds away. All of a sudden we'd lost our momentum.

Behind me, Anne was duelling Sam. He'd re-formed on

the wall next to her, and she managed to catch him before he could get out of reach. Green light flickered and Sam staggered, but it had been a stun spell, not meant to kill. I felt the surge of another mental attack, and this time it wasn't aimed at me. Anne reeled and Sam braced against the wall, levelled a hand at her while she was still disorientated and hit her in the chest with a lightning bolt from five feet away, blasting her right off the wall and into space. I froze for a second, shock and terror jumping through me as her wide eyes met mine, then she was falling, thirty-five feet straight down to the ground below, hitting the grass with a *thump*.

*Shit!* I started to turn back but the shadows were landing on the wall now, one ahead and one behind, and I had to duck away. Dispel focus wasn't recharged. Below, Anne was struggling to rise; Crystal was striding across the grass towards her and she hit her with something else, making Anne's head jerk back. Three shadows landed around Anne and began punching downwards, their movements mechanical, steady. Anne disappeared in a sea of rising and falling blows.

With a snarl I got my knife into the first shadow and ripped it open from stomach to chest. Black smoke billowed out but it only bashed me backwards, nearly sending me into the claws of the second. Crystal was hitting Anne again, Darren was circling for a clear shot and I knew with a sudden ugly sickening feeling that we'd lost. Three more shadows were flapping closer, blocking my route to Sam, who was charging a spell behind them. The only route left was the doorway behind me at the end of the battlements, and in a few more seconds that too would be blocked.

I turned and ran, dodging past the last shadow to sprint out of sight into the darkness.

I fled through the castle, and the apprentices followed.

I've spent a fair amount of time in combats over the years, and most of that time has been spent running away. It's an underrated combat strategy with some very definite advantages. It does admittedly carry the risk of being shot in the back, but generally speaking most people can't aim and run at the same time, which means that once they decide to chase you, attacks mostly come out of the equation and it becomes a contest of speed and information, which suits me just fine. It can actually get kind of fun after a while, as long as you're faster than the other guy. All the excitement of a fight; none of the worry about having your internal organs carved out.

But leaving someone behind *while* you run away is horrible. I haven't had to do it often – one of the few bright sides of not having many friends – but I hate it. Every step you take is a reminder that you're getting that much further from the person behind you. Logically, I knew that running was the only real option and that Anne had been lost as soon as she'd fallen from that wall – if I'd stayed behind there was no way I'd have been able to get her out, and they'd have got me too. But knowing all that didn't make me feel any less of a coward, and it didn't stop the creeping mixture of fear and anger and shame. All I could do was jam a lid on it to shut it out, and focus on staying alive.

I ran north-east, deeper into the castle. From glances through the futures, I knew that both Darren and Ji-yeong were after me, with Sam a little behind. Crystal wasn't coming, and I knew why – she'd already got what she wanted. In a straight fight, without the advantage of surprise, I could take out maybe one of the apprentices, two if I was very lucky. Three wasn't even worth thinking about. I needed to string them out.

My feet pounded on flagstones, dust flying up from the ancient courtyards, flitting from shadow to light. The castle seemed to watch me as I ran, silent and indifferent, just one more actor on an endless stage. The futures shifted, and I knew one of the elemental mages was gating ahead to try to cut me off. Darren – no, Sam. I switched course, angling south-east. By the time Sam's gate completed and he stepped out onto the tower he'd been meaning to ambush me from, I was far out of sight. He tried another gate, and I turned north-east again, and this time he didn't manage to pick up the trail. The futures in which I met Sam thinned and faded.

Three or four shadows were still in the air above. They flew slower than I could run, but they didn't have to worry about walls and I was having trouble shaking them. From their movements it looked as though they'd been ordered to follow me. There was a cross-shaped building to my right and I changed direction to run inside.

The interior was cool and dark, with a trace of dampness in the air. Giant machines of wood and rusting metal stood silent in the gloom. I knew the constructs would be hovering above, waiting for me to come into view, and I leant against the wall, breathing hard. My chest and limbs were burning as I scanned ahead. Four exits on this floor – no, five. All led out into the open. Darren and Ji-yeong would be here in about three minutes, tracking the hovering shadows to the building below. I needed something that would give me cover – *there*. Two sets of stairs leading down into the darkness. On the left path the futures grew cluttered and tangled, but on the other my future self kept going. I turned right.

The stairs led down into a vast cavern of sandy-coloured rock. Water filled the level below, forming a vast natural reservoir, waterwheels and cisterns groaning and creaking in the gloom. From up ahead, I could see daylight shining from two wide openings. I jogged along the edge of the reservoir and came out into dazzling sunlight.

I'd arrived on the eastern cliffs, on the edge of the castle's bedrock. No sheer drop this time; narrow walkways and bridges were layered down towards the ocean, flat levels like a giant's staircase. Below and to the north, pathways wound their way to cave mouths, black dots against the brown-and-yellow rock, and I started running down towards them.

I was most of the way there when I sensed the shadows returning, and I had just enough time to get under cover before the black dots reappeared far above. They circled, ranging left and right as I stayed hidden. They couldn't see me as long as I stayed here, but the overhang I was using stretched only a little way and as soon as I turned down onto the next flight of steps I'd be in view again. Minutes ticked by. The shadows overhead wheeled and turned. I was covered in sweat; my heart was thumping and heat was pouring off the stone. The air was fresh and smelt of salt, the cries of gulls echoing from far below. Looking ahead, I couldn't see any way of moving without drawing the shadows' attention – all I could do was wait and hope they guessed wrong about which way I'd gone.

Slowly, the shadows' pattern changed. Now only two

were staying out over the cliff; the others were moving back west. I looked into the futures of what would happen if I went out . . . good news and bad. The good news was that I'd managed to split them up again. Only one of the apprentices was coming down the path towards me.

The bad news was that it was the one out of the three I least wanted to pick a fight with.

The staircases and bridges built into the cliff face blocked any direct line of sight, but the shadows could see me from the air. If I made a break for it I could probably get away – at least in the short term – but I'd probably draw the attention of one of the others and that was a risk I wasn't willing to take. I stayed where I was, using my magic to scout out the ground on which I'd be fighting.

The ledge I was standing on was a long shelf of yellow bricks, about three-quarters of the way down the cliff, the stones old and chipped but stable. I was hiding behind a row of eight square pillars which supported the next level up of the cliff architecture, while behind me a wooden footbridge crossed a gap to another platform and the stairs down. The stairs led down to another path which twisted and doubled back underneath; the drop to the level below was forty feet straight down and sheer, as was becoming irritatingly common in this place. It wouldn't have killed them to put in a few railings. The main expanse from the pillars to the ledge was thirty feet wide, giving room to move as long as you didn't get too close to the edge . . . I touched the life ring in my pocket. If I went over, I'd have maybe a second to break that before I hit the stone.

Just as with Anne, I could tell the moment I came within lifesight range. The futures of contact paused, shifting, then the shadows changed direction, flapping down to land between the bridge and me, blocking my way forward.

I abandoned my cover, walking out into the middle of the open ledge. Sunlight washed over me, the heat already beginning to dry the sweat on the exposed skin at my hands and face. The only sound was the whine of the wind and the crash of the waves on the rocks below. Behind, the two shadows were fuzzy black patches in the sunlight, white eyes expressionless. Glancing through the futures, I knew they'd been ordered to block me in. They wouldn't attack – yet.

A figure appeared from the way I'd come, moving at an unhurried walk. The swords at her belt swung slightly as she descended the stairs. Once she was forty feet away, she stopped and the two of us watched each other.

## 10

Yun Ji-yeong was tall for a girl, though still shorter than Anne or me. She wore a white sleeveless top and grey leggings, the twin short-swords hanging off her belt. Her right hand rested on one of the hilts, and her fingers tapped it as she watched me with a considering sort of look. Now that I got a proper look at her she seemed young, twenty at the oldest. Despite the fact that she'd been chasing me for a good half-hour, she wasn't breathing hard. The sea breeze blew across both of us, tugging at my armour and rippling her hair.

I spoke first. 'So I don't think we've been introduced.'

'You're the one who's been making trouble for Darren and Sam.' Ji-yeong tilted her head, studying me. 'You don't look like much.'

'I suppose I don't.' I was aware of the two shadows at my back but didn't show it. 'Yun Ji-yeong, right?'

'That's right. Not running?'

'I'm pretty sure you're faster than I am.'

Ji-yeong smiled. 'That's why it's fun.'

'For you, maybe.' Scanning the futures, I couldn't sense any immediate aggression. 'Mind if I ask you something?'

'Like what?'

'I've been kind of getting the feeling that you're the odd one out in your trio.'

Ji-yeong frowned slightly. 'Sorry?'

'Darren's friends with Sam,' I said. 'Sam's friends with

Darren. I don't think Sam and Darren are friends with
you.'

'They've always been like that.'

'So I'm curious. Why are you helping them?'

'I knew you'd gone down here,' Ji-yeong said. 'I've had
a lot of time to explore this castle. Darren figured you'd
gone south.' Ji-yeong shrugged again. 'I haven't told him
yet.'

I noticed the 'yet'. 'Why, was there something you
wanted to ask?'

'Why does Crystal want that girl?'

'Do you know what Crystal did before she came here?'

Ji-yeong didn't take the bait, but from her body language
I was pretty sure the answer was no. *Interesting*. 'Crystal used
to be a Light mage, researching life extension,' I said. 'She's
got a ritual that she thinks will give her immortality. She
tried to get Anne once, and ever since she's been hiding.
She's been here, what, two months?'

'Three months.'

I nodded. 'She can't set foot in Britain, not safely. So
she sent Darren and Sam to do her work for her.'

Ji-yeong tapped her sword hilts thoughtfully. 'You know,
I'm a bit surprised you don't know all this,' I said. 'Crystal
was big news for a while. Don't you get out much?'

'No,' Ji-yeong said, slight irritation showing on her
face. 'Sagash hardly ever lets me go out. It's really
annoying.'

'You didn't get invited to the party?'

'Sagash made me stay and guard the castle.'

'You don't have a flat in London or something?'

'Sagash won't get me one.'

'Seems a bit stingy.'

'I know, right? We're his apprentices, but he's too cheap to spend any money on us. It's not as though he's poor.'

'Darren and Sam seem to have their own places.'

'Oh, they're not theirs. That flat of Darren's belongs to his sister. And Sam lives with his parents.'

'What about you – your family back in Korea?'

'Yeah.'

'Do you stay in touch?'

'I call once a week or so. We do video calls on Skype.'

'I guess you can't really get an internet connection here.'

'No, I have to gate out to London. It's a pain; it'd be nice to do it from my room in the keep.'

'Shadow realms are a bit inconvenient that way.'

'I know.'

There was a pause. We looked at each other across the stone.

'So are you going to come along quietly?' Ji-yeong asked.

'I think I'd rather not.'

'I could kill you and drag your body back,' Ji-yeong said brightly.

'That seems like a lot of work. I'm kind of heavy.'

'Oh, two of these shadows can carry a body easily as long as they don't fly.'

'Okay, leaving aside just how disturbing it is that you know that particular detail, who exactly would you be taking me back to? Crystal or Sagash?'

'Sagash,' Ji-yeong said. 'It's one of our jobs. We're supposed to stop anyone getting in here without Sagash's permission.'

'Darren and Sam managed to screw that one up pretty badly.'

'Yup,' Ji-yeong said with a smile. 'Telling Sagash is going to be fun!'

'So that's your plan?' I said. 'You take me back to Sagash, tell him what happened, get Crystal and Darren and Sam into trouble and come out looking good?'

'Pretty much,' Ji-yeong agreed. 'You coming?'

'How about we do this a different way? The way I see it, Crystal, Darren and Sam don't like any of us very much right now. And it doesn't sound as though you like them that much either.'

'Not really. I only went along with them because I didn't have anything to do. When Sagash is busy with his research, it gets *really* boring. You and that girl are the most fun we've had for months.'

'So why don't we work together?' I said. 'The only reason I'm here is to find Anne. And you don't care if she gets out of here, right?'

'Not really,' Ji-yeong said. 'But I don't care if she *doesn't* get out of here, either. And if I go back to Sagash on my own, he's not going to listen because it'll just be my word against theirs. But if I bring *you* back then he can question you for proof, and I get the credit.'

'Slight problem with that plan,' I said. 'I don't really think I want to cooperate.'

'That doesn't matter,' Ji-yeong said. 'I watched you fight Sam. You haven't got anything that can hurt me.'

'You could still—'

'Nope,' Ji-yeong said. Steel rang as she unsheathed her two swords, sunlight glittering off metal. 'Done talking. Time for me to kick your arse.'

I sighed. 'Well, can't blame me for trying.'

'Don't worry,' Ji-yeong said. 'I'll make sure to keep you

alive for afterwards.' She spun the swords from a forward to a reverse grip and back again, then advanced. I backed towards the pillars as she drew closer.

Ji-yeong was slim and fit. She wasn't obviously muscular but I could see the life magic woven through her body, reinforcing and strengthening. I know life magic can be used for enhancement, but I've never seen it used much – Anne can do it, but only the basics. For Ji-yeong, enhancement seemed to be her speciality. The spells were densely woven, complex and hard to read, but they looked like direct boosts to her physical abilities. Not only was she fitter than me, she was probably stronger and faster too.

But no matter how strong or fast, she was still an apprentice. If Ji-yeong was better than Anne with that kind of life magic, she had to be worse with others. Her two swords were less than two feet long, on the borderline between sword and knife. I was fairly sure they were focuses of some kind, but the fact that she'd drawn them suggested that she couldn't paralyse or kill with a touch the way Anne could.

Ji-yeong caught up with me when I was still a few feet from the pillars. I stopped retreating and stood side-on, my hands low. Ji-yeong made an experimental cut at my wrist and I twitched it away; she tried twice more for face and arm and each time I swayed just out of range. The next thrust was a feint: she stepped through and spun low, whirling through a full circle to slash with the other sword at ankle height. I jumped back, retreating into the cover of the pillars.

Ji-yeong came up gracefully. 'Not even going to try?'

'I think I might be a little overmatched,' I said dryly.

'Boring,' Ji-yeong said, making a face. 'Thought you were going to make this fun.'

My divination was my only warning. The right sword missed my face by about three inches, and I leapt back as the other cut the air where my arm had been. Before I had the chance to catch my balance Ji-yeong was on me again, moving at full speed this time. She *was* stronger than me, and frighteningly quick. Her swords were a blur of metal.

But while Ji-yeong was fast, she wasn't that good, something I'd already suspected from her choice of weapons. Wielding two swords at once looks good in the movies but doesn't work too well in practice – it isn't really possible to strike effectively with both sides of your body at once, and the human brain isn't wired to operate both hands simultaneously and independently. There are a few niche cases where it can work, but most of the time you're better off learning to use one weapon well instead of weighing yourself down with two. Ji-yeong didn't look like she'd spent much time learning to use her swords at all. Her attacks were showy and inefficient, much of her speed wasted on unnecessary motion.

I backed away, ducking and slipping the attacks as Ji-yeong pressed me. Her movements were a blur, but I could see her strikes coming and they hit nothing but air. Surprise showed on her face, then concentration. I kept giving ground, dodging between the pillars to interfere with her swings. The more I watched the way she moved, the more sure I became that she didn't have much experience against skilled opponents.

On the other hand, if you have enough unfair advantages, you don't *need* experience. I could dodge Ji-yeong's attacks, but none of my magic items could hurt her. My stun focus wouldn't touch her reinforced body, and the dispel would be an annoyance at best. Glitterdust could blind her, but with her lifesight she didn't need eyes to know where I was.

Well, if magic wasn't going to work, I'd have to do this the regular way.

I still hadn't made any attacks of my own. With no threats to make her careful, Ji-yeong was getting more aggressive, taking less trouble to guard herself. A shock went up my arm as one of her swords grazed me, my armour taking the blow. I stepped back around one of the pillars, my right hand going to the sheath at my belt, turning sideways so my body hid the movement. Ji-yeong followed, slightly off-balance from the angle.

This time as she stepped in so did I. Her arm hit my shoulder and I caught it; Ji-yeong was just starting to pull back as my right hand came up in a flash of steel. The knife cut deep, severing tendons, and her hand spasmed open, sword clattering to the stone as she broke away.

Ji-yeong caught her balance and we stared at each other. Blood welled from the ugly wound at her wrist, running down her now useless fingers and dripping to the bricks. Without taking my eyes off her I stepped to the side and bent to pick up her discarded sword, then flicked the blood from my knife and returned it to its sheath.

As I did, I noticed the blood had stopped dripping from Ji-yeong's fingers. Green light glowed about her wrist; the gash narrowed and closed, skin and vein and tendon re-knitting. In only a few seconds her arm was whole again. She flexed her fingers experimentally, then shook off the blood and switched her remaining sword back to her right hand.

*I hate fighting life mages.*

'Nice trick,' Ji-yeong said flatly.

I lunged. Ji-yeong's sword parried mine with a clang,

slashing back at me as I leant away from the riposte. She was fighting at full strength now, and from her stance it was clear she'd finally started taking me seriously.

Our swords clashed again and again, footsteps stuttering on the stone. The sea breeze whirled around us, carrying away the smell of blood and sweat. Now that our weapons were matched, my longer reach let me slash Ji-yeong across the forearm and knee. Blood welled up, but the gashes in her skin healed almost as fast as I could inflict them. I moved in . . . and this time Ji-yeong came in to meet me, sword thrusting low. My precognition showed me a brief agonising vision of the sword ramming through my armour and into my stomach, and I threw myself desperately to one side, aborting my attack. The blow clipped me, spinning me off balance, and I hit the ground hard, rolling and coming back to my feet before Ji-yeong could follow up.

'You're good,' Ji-yeong said. She wasn't even out of breath. 'You did beat Darren, didn't you?'

*This isn't working.* Ji-yeong could heal herself; I couldn't. None of her attacks had gotten through my armour, yet I was more hurt than she was.

But even life magic has limits. If I could hurt Ji-yeong badly enough, I could take her out of the fight: force her to shut her body down to heal. A sword or knife wasn't going to cut it. I needed really excessive force.

Ji-yeong attacked again, slashing and stabbing. I gave ground, nicking her once or twice, but this time she didn't even slow down. The fight had moved away from the pillars and Ji-yeong used her speed to put herself between them and me, forcing me towards the cliff. I let Ji-yeong drive me back towards the edge.

Five steps to the edge, four. My arms ached from the strikes, and sweat dripped into my eyes. Three steps, two steps and I held my ground, aware of the sheer drop behind me. Ji-yeong didn't let up, striking again and again, trying to push me back over the edge. Her blade slipped past my guard and I had to block with my forearm, the impact sending a shock up the bone.

My next parry was at an awkward angle, and with a ring of metal the sword spun from my hand. I jumped left as the sword clanged to the stone, only a foot or two from the edge. Ji-yeong moved to block my path to the sword as I circled around.

Now Ji-yeong was the one with her back to the drop. The classic move at this point would be to kick her off and send her falling to the stone below, but that was clearly exactly what she was expecting and she was holding herself low and braced, making herself a difficult target. Staying low, Ji-yeong edged towards where the sword lay, one inch at a time. Her foot came up against the blade with a click, but she didn't take her eyes off me. I didn't move. Ji-yeong crouched down, reaching for the sword with her left hand. Her fingers closed around the hilt.

I charged, left hand slipping into my pocket. Ji-yeong straightened in a flash, coming side-on to make herself a difficult target, but I didn't slow down. If someone knows you're coming and has time to brace themselves, then pushing or kicking them off a ledge is really hard.

*Tackling* them off, though . . . that's easy. As long as you don't mind coming along for the ride.

I slammed into Ji-yeong at full speed. Her sword flashed up and pain flared along my face, but I was heavier than her and my momentum carried us both over the edge.

When you fall your first reaction is to grab something and Ji-yeong's arms went reflexively for me, but her fingers were locked around her swords and the blades scraped off my armour. We fell apart, accelerating, and with my left hand I snapped the item I'd drawn from my pocket.

Life rings look like small hoops of metal and glass, woven in a twisted circle. As the ring broke the spell within it activated, expanding to engulf me in a bubble of air magic. The spell lightened my body, steadying my motion, and suddenly I wasn't accelerating any more, just sinking at a steady rate of ten feet per second. I started carrying life rings after an incident a couple of years ago involving a burning building: when you have to make a quick exit from somewhere high up, it's useful to be able to fall like a feather.

Ji-yeong didn't have a life ring. She fell like a rock.

A human body hitting a hard surface makes a very distinctive sound: a kind of *snap-thud*. The impact drives the breath from the lungs so there's no shout or cry. I landed a few seconds later, touching down gently; the life ring's magic lingered a moment longer, then dissolved into the air. One of Ji-yeong's swords had bounced towards the wall. I picked it up, testing the edge to make sure it hadn't been dulled or chipped, then walked over.

Ji-yeong had fallen forty feet onto flat stone: crippling if not fatal for a normal human. Life mages are tougher, but even so they've got their limits. Ji-yeong was lying flat, legs twisted in a way that suggested multiple broken bones, struggling to breathe. In my mage's sight trails of green energy twined frantically around her body and limbs; I couldn't make out the details but I knew what they were doing. I leant over and placed the point of the sword under Ji-yeong's chin.

Ji-yeong's eyes came open, hazy with pain. 'I know you can regenerate from that,' I told her. 'Try anything and I'll drive this sword through your jaw and into your brain. Clear?'

Ji-yeong had to try a few times before she managed to speak. 'Okay,' she said in a raspy voice. She had to keep her head still to stop the point of the blade from breaking the skin.

I straightened up, moving the sword away. 'Where's Anne?'

'Windmill,' Ji-yeong said with difficulty. 'Crystal.'

'That was where she was *then*. What about now?'

'Don't know . . . Crystal . . . moving her. Sam's shadows.'

'Through a gateway?'

'Doesn't have gate stones . . . Foot.'

'To where?'

'Keep.'

That had been more than half an hour ago. Even on foot, Crystal would be back at the keep by now. 'How much does Sagash know?'

'He doesn't.'

I dipped the sword towards her. 'Don't lie to me.'

'I'm not!'

'You're telling me none of this showed up on the sensors?'

'Crystal messed with them.' Ji-yeong's words were clearer now; she'd already begun to recover. 'I looked. There wasn't any proof, that was why . . .'

*Why you wanted to take me back instead. Yeah, you might not want to remind me of that little detail.* 'Where's Sagash?'

'His lab. He went in after he got back from the party.'

'What's he working on?'

'I don't know. Doesn't tell us about research. Stays in there for days. Doesn't tell us why.'

Ji-yeong was watching me closely, holding very still. I couldn't sense any deception, and from the futures it looked as though she was going to cooperate, at least for now. Blood was dripping from my chin; that last slash had scored along my cheek. I brushed it off, leaving a messy red streak along my hand. 'Crystal found us. How?'

'A focus. Time magic. She didn't—'

'Where in the keep is she taking Anne?'

'I don't know—'

'Bullshit. Maybe Crystal didn't trust you with her plans, but you're smart and bored and you just told me you had nothing better to do than figure out what they were up to. Give me your best guess.'

Ji-yeong hesitated. I twitched the sword again. 'All right,' she said. 'Wait. The sub-basement.'

'Where?'

'The north-east corner. There's a backup – Sagash used it for experiments before he moved up to the second floor. It's got the most defences.'

'What kind?'

'Shadows. Fixed attack wards. And barriers, and locks.'

*And Crystal and Darren and Sam behind them.* I felt a sinking feeling. I couldn't get through that.

I looked down at Ji-yeong. I don't know what she saw in my face, but it made her flinch. Her cuts had all stopped bleeding and she was breathing smoothly again, but she couldn't move, not yet. 'Who else is in the keep?'

'I don't know about anyone else. I swear.'

'Are we going to have any more trouble?'

Ji-yeong hesitated. 'No?' she said at last. She sounded

as though she was hoping very hard that was the right answer.

I looked down at Ji-yeong a second longer, then turned and ran, heading towards the stairs up and the long winding path that would take me back up to the castle.

I kept running until I found an empty building, then hid in the shadows and path-walked, sending my future self racing back the way I'd come.

Nothing. The windmill was empty. I couldn't find any trace of Crystal or Anne, and Darren and Sam were gone as well. The skies above the castle were clear. Everything I could find confirmed what Ji-yeong had already told me: they were back in the keep.

Fear and worry nagged at me but I pushed them back, trying to focus. Crystal had Anne. What was she going to do with her?

She'd want to use her in her ritual, the same one that Vitus Aubuchon had been midway through when we'd stopped him the last time. I didn't know what details Crystal might have added or changed, but I was absolutely sure that it would end with Anne's death.

How fast would Crystal do it?

I had the ugly suspicion that it would be soon. So far, Crystal had kept this whole scheme a secret from Sagash. Doing all this right under Sagash's nose in his own shadow realm could not have been easy. No matter how good Crystal was at double-dealing, she'd want to finish this quickly, before Sagash caught her out.

And that meant I didn't have long. Hours, maybe.

What was I going to do?

I paced, walking back and forth in the shadows. My

bruises from the fight still ached, and pain pulsed from the shallow gash along my face. I could fight my way into the keep; try to break Anne out. It was the classic heroic thing to do, and it was pretty much guaranteed to fail. If I was strong enough to take them all on by myself, Anne wouldn't have been captured in the first place.

I could sneak in. Bypass the shadows, find Anne . . . except that finding Anne would also mean finding Crystal. All that would achieve would be to start a fight in the heart of Sagash's fortress. And again, inevitably, I'd lose.

I made a sound of frustration, putting a hand to my forehead. No matter how I weighed the odds, I couldn't see how I could win this. On one side was me, and maybe Anne if I could find her. On the other side was Crystal, Sagash, Sagash's apprentices, Sagash's constructs and God only knew what else. This was his place of power, where he was strongest.

I could try to call in help from the Council. This was exactly the proof that Sonder had been looking for and if I could get the message out that Crystal was here then the Keepers would force their way into this castle if they had to burn down the whole shadow realm to do it. But to get a message out, *and* convince the Keepers I was telling the truth, *and* have them get in here . . . even if I could do it, it would take too long. By the time the Keepers arrived Crystal would be gone, and Anne would be dead. If I wanted to help her I'd have to do it myself.

But how?

Maybe I was looking at this the wrong way. I couldn't beat Sagash and Crystal with brute force, but that's not what I'm good at anyway. What did I have going for me?

Knowledge. I knew that Crystal had been behind all this

from the beginning. She must have been watching Anne, using her pawns to operate at a distance, staying hidden away in Sagash's shadow realm where she was safe. The last time Crystal had done this, she'd abducted targets from the Light apprentice programme and she'd drawn the Council's anger. She'd learnt from her mistakes; this time she'd waited until Anne was out of the programme and alone.

But she hadn't done it with Sagash's help. If Sagash had bent his full power towards capturing Anne, he could have done it faster and better. Crystal would have known that, yet she'd kept it secret from him.

She wouldn't have done that without a reason . . . and I had a suspicion of what that reason might be. The technique Crystal and Vitus Aubuchon had worked out had never been designed for sharing. Crystal might have some sort of research agreement with Sagash, but she wanted to keep the rewards to herself.

Sagash probably wouldn't be too happy about that.

Maybe I didn't need to break Anne out. Maybe I just needed to break in.

I walked out of the shadows to the doorway where the sunlight painted a yellow-gold box on the stone, then knelt on the floor and started going through my pockets. I could probably find an entry to the keep with just my divination given time, but time was something I didn't have – I needed to get in, and fast. What did I have that would help?

I was still carrying Ji-yeong's short-sword. It looked like a low-power dispelling focus, probably designed to cut through energy shields like Darren's and Sam's. It hadn't been much use against my armour, but it should work fairly well against the shadows. I set it to one side.

My dispelling and stun focuses I set aside without a second glance. Glitterdust, ditto. Two forcewalls, two condensers, a healing salve . . . I should patch up that slash; the bleeding would be annoying. I unscrewed the jar and smeared the paste along my cheek where Ji-yeong's blade had cut me; it stung and itched. I closed the jar and went back to searching.

Combat knife, microlight, picks, my phone, Darren's phone. I went to the pocket with my other one-shots. Signaller. Flash flare. Three gate stones. Pouch filled with . . . dispersion dust? Why do I even carry this stuff? Trail pouch. Probes. Alabaster cat — how did that get there? That's right, I'd stuck it in my pocket while talking to Luna a few days ago. Designed to summon cats, but it worked on dogs . . .

. . . would it work on other canines too?

I stared down at the little alabaster figurine, looking into the future to see what would happen if I used it. Minutes stretched out. Nothing . . . *There!* A flash of excitement went through me and I focused on the figurine, channelling my magic through it.

Calling an intelligent creature is harder than calling an animal. A summoning focus doesn't have the power to compel; the most it can do is send an invitation. I kept the flow of magic to a thread, a gentle suggestion, and waited.

Five minutes passed, ten. I stayed sitting on the stone floor. After a while, I closed my eyes.

The flicker of space magic came from my left, then to the right. A pause, then it came again, alternating between directions. The switches were irregular, unpredictable. I knew I was being watched and didn't move, letting my observer get a good look. At last I spoke. 'I'd like to make a deal.'

No answer. I opened my eyes to see the blink fox half hidden behind one of the pieces of machinery. Hidden in the shadows, its reddish coat looked grey, and its pointed muzzle was tilted down to the stone. Amber eyes reflected the daylight back at me, sharp and watchful.

I moved around to face it, keeping my motions slow and careful. The fox tracked my movements, unblinking. 'I know you can understand me,' I said. 'I'm guessing you're wondering if this is some sort of trap and I'm here to catch you. I'm not. I'm a mage from the outside world, from London . . . Come to think of it, you might not you know where London is. Never mind. Point is, I'm trying to get out of here, along with my friend, and I could use some help.'

The fox didn't respond. 'I'm guessing you aren't especially thrilled to be here,' I said. 'Sagash's apprentices want to catch you . . . or re-catch you? Whichever, I'm sure there's a reason you're not hanging out with them. And I doubt this castle is all that nice a place to live. It's kind of lonely and I imagine you get a bit sick of pigeons. If I get back outside I could take you with me. Once you got through to the other side of the portal, you could blink off and go wherever you liked. Not like anyone could catch you, once you had space to run.'

No answer. 'So?' I said. 'Interested?'

The fox looked at me.

'Is that a yes or a no? Help me out here.'

Silence.

'Okay, I know you can't talk, but could you give me some kind of feedback? Bark once for yes, twice for no, that kind of thing?'

The fox gave me a look.

'Fine, no barking. All right, let's try this another way . . .

I'm guessing you're at least a *little* interested in getting out of this shadow realm. If you're not, then just walk off.'

The fox turned its head towards the shadows, paused a moment, then turned back to me again.

'I'll take that as a yes. Will you help me out?'

No response.

'What's the problem – you don't think you're getting offered enough? Well, while we're here there's not much I can give you but . . . I could give you a place to stay, if that's what you're looking for. Might even be able to help you find some others like you. You're not the only blink fox out there.'

Again the fox didn't move, not obviously, but something about its posture looked a little more alert. 'So what do you say?' I asked.

There was a pause, then the fox trotted forward, emerging from the shadows and into the light. It moved with the trotting, dog-like/cat-like gait of city foxes, agile and quick. Now that I could see it clearly I was surprised at how big it was. Orange-red fur covered its back and sides, becoming dusty towards the haunches; the ears, legs and tail were black with reddish patches, and splashes of white covered its throat, under-muzzle and tail-tip. I wasn't sure, but I thought I could make out a few traces of blood in the white fur of its throat. It sat, tail curled around its feet, and watched me.

'So, I'm Alex Verus,' I said. 'Want to shake paws?'

The fox gave me a look.

'Just offering. Okay. I need to get into the central keep.'

The fox gave a sharp exhale-sneeze and gave its head a quick shake.

'I know it's not exactly a safe plan. I'm kind of short on options.'

The fox looked in the direction of the front gate.

'Wouldn't work; there's a squad of shadows guarding it. Besides, I'm not just looking out for myself. I need to get my friend out too.'

Head tilt.

'She's a human mage, female. You saw her a couple of days ago. She's Sagash's enemy as well.'

Tail flick, another look towards the gates.

'No, I'm not leaving her behind. I promised I'd help get you out, remember? Same goes for her. I don't leave people behind if I can help it.'

The fox tilted its head, seemed to be thinking about it, then twitched its ears.

'So like I said, I need to get into the keep. Can you get me in?'

The fox seemed to consider for a moment, then blinked.

'Is that a yes?'

Blink.

'One for yes, two for no, right?'

Blink blink.

'Wait, what?'

The fox let its tongue pant out. It looked like it was grinning.

'A blink fox who's a troll. Great.' I stood up, wincing a little at the stiffness in my muscles. The fox watched but didn't jump back. 'You ready to go?'

I set out south-west towards the keep. The fox trotted behind at a distance.

I spent most of the trip thinking about Richard.

It had been more than ten years since I'd seen Richard in the flesh, but it felt like less. Last year I'd made a couple of ill-advised trips to Elsewhere, viewing the past through Rachel's eyes. It had been there that I'd learnt why Richard had vanished all those years ago – he'd used a blood sacrifice to open a gateway to another world. Leaving Rachel in charge of his estate, he'd disappeared . . . until now.

Why had he come back? I didn't even know enough to make an educated guess. I'd never really understood Richard – what he wanted, what kind of person he was, what his ambitions were. The ease with which he'd been able to find the two of us had shaken me. If he'd wanted us dead or captured, he could have done it without lifting a finger.

But he hadn't. He'd offered us a chance to join him, and walked away. Why?

No matter how I thought about it, the only answer that made any sense was that he'd meant it. He really *had* been offering us the opportunity to join his team. And when we'd said no, he'd let us go . . . leaving the door open for the future.

His last words had been *next time.* Richard could be a lot of things, but one thing I'd never known him to be was inefficient. If he did something, it was for a reason. And that meant that he thought next time I might say yes.

The thought of that was so terrifying that I almost didn't want to get out of the castle. Crystal was dangerous, Sagash was deadly, but both of them put together didn't scare me even half as much as Richard did. Crystal was a known quantity – she was a plotter and I wasn't going to underestimate her – but I'd beaten her once before. And while Sagash might be pretty terrifying in his inhuman way, he didn't have much reason to notice me. Richard did.

And then there was the lurking fear underneath that

Richard's offer had been our only way out. That by saying no, I'd guaranteed that neither of us would get out alive. The plan I had in mind was *very* dicey. If it didn't work, then my choice to turn Richard down might end up being the biggest mistake I'd ever made . . . and one of the last.

*Well, at least if I get killed doing this I won't have to deal with Richard afterwards. That's a plus.*

I'd make a really bad suicide counsellor.

I shook it off and kept walking. One way or another, this would be over soon.

## 11

Sagash's keep looked even more intimidating up close. Black walls stretched up to the sky, battlements topped the towers and small arrow-slit windows peeked out over nearby courtyards. The main entrance was a small inset door. Looking at the keep from here, the out-of-place feeling was stronger. The rest of the castle might be ancient, but it was cohesive. The keep didn't fit: it felt darker, colder. Two shadows stood guard outside.

A quiet whine made me turn aside from where I was crouching, overlooking the front gate. The fox looked towards the gate, looked back at me, and blinked twice. 'I'm not even thinking about it,' I said. 'Even if I got past the shadows, they'd see me coming.'

The fox trotted a few steps away, then looked back at me again. 'That way? Okay . . .'

The fox led me down some steps, around the corner of a building, through a ground-floor window into a room filled with wooden crates and to a dark stairwell leading down. It trotted down two steps and then looked back, amber eyes shining out of the blackness. I followed it down.

The steps led down into tunnels. It looked as if it had once been some sort of sewer, but the tunnels were bone dry and covered in dust. The fox led me left and right and left, winding back and forth, and before long I'd lost all sense of direction. The tunnels were pitch-black and I used my torch to navigate, freeing up my divination magic to try and map out the maze. The fox led the way, slipping through narrow passages, pausing at intersections for me to catch up. Twice I had to squeeze through gaps which were roomy for a fox but only *just* big enough for a human, the second of which had been caused by a very unstable-looking rockfall. I held my breath the whole way through.

At last the fox led me to a solid wooden door, dark brown in the glow from my torch. I tried the handle: it didn't open and I inspected the keyhole. 'Looks like it's locked . . .' I glanced down at the fox. 'Not that you care. Is it bolted or barred?'

The fox seemed to think about this for a second, then winked out in a flicker of space magic. A few seconds later it reappeared, then blinked twice.

'All right.' I set to work with my picks. Lock-picking isn't a speciality of mine, but I keep my hand in. The lock was stiff but its design was old and simple, and after a few minutes there was a scraping sound and a click.

The door opened into an ancient storeroom. It didn't look very different from the tunnels, but I knew I was getting close. A ladder led upwards, and I could feel the presence of a gate ward above.

I closed the door without re-locking it. This time the fox didn't move ahead, staying by the door. 'I know,' I said. 'You don't want to go into the gate ward.'

Blink.

I couldn't blame the blink fox. If my only defence was teleportation, I wouldn't want to go into an area that blocked that either. 'I'm going up,' I said. 'You should find a place with a view of the exits and sit and watch for a while. I haven't forgotten my promise. If you see me come out, link up with me and we'll try to make it out from there. If you don't . . .' I trailed off, wondering how to finish that sentence.

The fox tilted its head, watching me, then there was a flicker of space magic and it was gone, leaving me alone in the room. I started climbing.

The ladder came up into another storeroom. The door wasn't locked this time, and I came out onto a ground-floor corridor.

I could tell the instant I stepped into the keep. The walls here were smooth instead of rough, dim sunlight filtering through the narrow windows onto black stone instead of the yellowish bricks of the rest of the castle. The air was cold, and I found myself shivering. I could feel magical auras overlapping around me, but I didn't stop to analyse; it was only a matter of time until Crystal or the other apprentices picked me up. Speed was my best defence now, and I moved quickly down the corridor, scanning ahead. At the end was a staircase, leading up and down. I wasn't sure, but I thought I could hear a very faint murmur of sound from below. The sub-basement Ji-yeong had told me about; Anne would be down there. I went up.

Sagash's laboratories on the first floor were very easy to find, marked by a cluster of wards and protective spells. The door was solid metal and wouldn't have looked out of place on a missile silo. I studied the adjacent panel on the wall, then touched a finger to a small recessed sphere and channelled a thread of magic through it. I stood back and waited.

Twenty seconds passed, forty. I forced myself to stand still and look relaxed. I knew I was being watched but didn't let myself glance up. At last there was a click from the panel.

'Mage Sagash?' I said. 'My name's Verus. If it's convenient, I'd like to have a word.'

The silence dragged out: fifteen seconds, thirty. Then there was a muffled thump and a grinding sound and the metal door swung open, moving very slowly before stopping with a clang. I stepped inside.

The room within was shaped like a wide cylinder. The door I'd entered by led onto a balcony that ran around the upper level, looking down onto a bare circular floor on which a ring was marked. At the opposite side of the balcony, another open door led deeper into the keep. A set of metal stairs curled down from the balcony to the lower level.

It didn't look like a laboratory. It looked like an arena. Why Sagash kept an arena between his personal lab and the rest of the keep was a question I wasn't sure I wanted to know the answer to.

Sagash himself was standing in the open doorway leading through to the labs, and the past few days hadn't improved his appearance. He was dressed in black, the clothes dusty and ragged, as though they'd been worn for a very long time, and he stood very straight with his hands clasped behind his back as he watched me. He didn't speak.

'Sagash,' I said. 'Thank you for seeing me. I understand you're quite busy.'

'Explain why you are here,' Sagash rasped. His voice was just as unnerving as I remembered.

'Well, I did try to set up an appointment, but you're a hard person to reach.'

'Do not play games. If your master has sent you here for some purpose, reveal it.'

*Ding.* I didn't let anything show on my face, but I felt a little surge of excitement. Maybe I could pull this off after all.

Light mages think all Dark mages live in a state of violent anarchy. They're half right . . . but only half. Dark mages might compete with each other and they might prey on each other, but they're not completely stupid. If they always fought on sight they'd have wiped themselves out long ago, and what's developed over the years to regulate that is a kind of code of conduct. The catch is, the code only applies if they consider you a Dark mage in the first place. When I'm with the Light mages, the fact that I'm Richard's ex-apprentice is an albatross around my neck, but when I'm with Dark mages then in a strange way it makes me part of the club. Dark apprentices like Darren and Ji-yeong fight first and talk later. Mages like Sagash and Morden talk first, *then* decide whether to fight. Dark negotiations are a razor's edge, civility side by side with the potential for sudden violence. Light mages have trouble with that, even when they know intellectually how it's supposed to work – there's just something about it that they're never quite comfortable with. Maybe you have to grow up with it.

The funny thing was that really, all the work I'd done to get the blink fox's help and sneak in had just been to make a first impression. My plan centred on talking to Sagash – in theory I could have just walked up to the front gate and rung the doorbell. Of course, that would have meant getting past his apprentices and Crystal. Showing up like this was a statement: I was telling him that his shadows hadn't been able to keep me out, and his apprentices hadn't either. It was a provocation, but still less dangerous than to let him feel as though I was weak enough to be brushed aside. I needed to treat with him as an equal.

'So I don't know if you remember, but we've met before,' I said. 'It was—'

'In the Tiger's Palace.' Sagash didn't bring up the changes I'd made to my appearance. Fashion clearly wasn't one of his interests.

'Oh good. So I don't need to go over that again.'

'You approached me for information on Anne Walker,' Sagash rasped. 'If you have disturbed me to repeat the same question I will be unhappy.'

'Actually, what I had in mind was the opposite. I have some information I'd like to trade.'

'Explain.'

'Basically it has to do with the project you're working on. There's a plot against you that I've found out about. In exchange, I'd like you to help me out with what I asked you about before.'

'What plot?' Sagash rasped. He didn't move, but I knew I had his attention. When you're dealing with paranoids, a conspiracy is an easy sell.

'So have we got a deal?'

'You are trying my patience.'

'I'm not asking you to do anything that'll require any expenditure of time or resources on your part,' I said. 'Or that'll require siding with any factions. You won't even have to leave this shadow realm. All I'm asking is that after you've heard what I have to say, if you agree that what I've just said is fair, you'll help me out.'

Sagash stared at me. I waited, hiding my tension. I didn't know how much time I had, and with the conversation with Sagash occupying all the visible futures I couldn't look far enough ahead to see. I listened for the sound of movement in the corridor behind.

'Your terms are provisionally accepted,' Sagash rasped. 'Convince me I should keep them.'

*First step done.* 'Well, then,' I said. 'I'm afraid you've been led down a dead end. The research you've been working on isn't going to be any use for extending your lifespan, or anything else for that matter.'

'Your reasons for this conclusion?'

'Let me take a guess,' I said. 'You've been extra busy lately. In fact, I'd guess that the only spare time you've taken has been to visit that party. I'm also going to guess that the reason the research has been taking so much time has been because of Crystal. Either some extra details she just recently told you about, or something she suggested you do.'

'You are well informed,' Sagash rasped. 'Please explain how you came to know of Crystal's presence.'

'Oh, I wasn't looking for her. Though the Council are . . . which I assume is why you haven't been advertising it. I'm guessing the idea is that no one's supposed to draw attention to her being here? Having a bunch of Council Keepers banging on the front door would be a bit of a disruption.'

'It appears disruption is inevitable. Once again, explain how you came to know of this.'

Sagash hadn't closed the door behind me, and from down the corridor I was starting to hear snatches of voices. Both Crystal and Darren could sense me through walls; they'd probably started hunting me down within seconds of my entering the keep. *Let's see if I can time this just right.* 'Because someone in your castle decided to kidnap Anne Walker and bring her here, all while keeping it a secret from you so that you'd be left to deal with the consequences afterwards.'

'Who?'

I paused a few seconds, listening to the approaching footsteps. *Three . . . two . . .* 'Her,' I said, and pointed towards the doorway just as Crystal appeared.

I had to give Crystal credit. The shielding around Sagash's lab had hidden me from her mindsight, but as she saw me she didn't even blink. Darren and Sam piled through after her and I stayed calm, watching with folded arms. Darren and Sam saw me and tensed, Darren's expression darkening as black light gathered at his hands.

'Hold.' Sagash's rasping voice cut across the room.

Darren's spell winked out instantly. Sam looked cautiously between Sagash and me. 'Master,' he said. 'Is there a problem?'

'An excellent question,' Sagash rasped. 'I was under the impression that you were keeping my castle free of outsiders.'

'Sorry, they've been busy,' I chipped in. 'They're the reason Anne was in this castle in the first place, and they've been spending the last few days trying to catch her without you noticing.'

An identical pair of *oh, shit* expressions crossed Darren's and Sam's faces. They'd obviously been expecting me to blast my way into the keep and attack – they hadn't been expecting me to go to their master, and it was clear which they thought was worse. I saw a new set of futures branch off, Crystal backing off towards the door, and I opened my mouth to call her out.

Sagash beat me to it. Two shadows appeared in the doorway, blocking the exit, and the futures of Crystal retreating winked out. 'Mage Crystal?' Sagash rasped. He hadn't given any order that I'd seen, but the two shadows had their eyes fixed on the mind mage. 'If you're not too busy, perhaps you could clarify.'

Crystal paused, and for a fraction of a second I saw a branching spread of futures of sudden violence, Crystal trying to fight her way out through the shadows, Darren and Sam switching suddenly from attacking to helping—

—and gone. 'That mage's name is Verus,' Crystal stated. 'One of the agents the Council sent after me to terminate my research. He's a diviner, and highly dangerous. We should kill him immediately.'

'That *would* keep me from telling Sagash what you've been up to, yes,' I said dryly. 'Assuming you could pull it off. Did you interrupt your ritual on Anne to run up here, or did I make it before you had the chance to start?'

'He's lying,' Crystal said calmly to Sagash. She didn't look at me or acknowledge my presence. 'I've dealt with this man before and he is a highly accomplished manipulator. Trust him or let him live and you'll be destroyed as Vitus was.'

'I hope you haven't been using her as your social secretary,' I told Sagash.

'You need to—'

'Enough,' Sagash rasped.

Crystal and I fell silent. Darren and Sam were standing between us, hesitating. They might have taken the lead in the fight at the windmill, but here they were both very obviously out of their league.

Sagash pointed a skeletal finger at me. 'You claimed my apprentices are the reason this girl is currently within my castle.'

'Darren and Sam kidnapped Anne Walker four days ago,' I said. 'Though really, they were just doing what they were told. The one who wanted Anne was Crystal, and she used mind manipulation to manoeuvre Darren and Sam into doing what she told them and thinking it was their own idea.'

Sagash looked at Darren and Sam.

Darren hesitated. 'Uh . . .'

'That's not exactly . . .' Sam began.

*Huh*, I thought. *Guess that last part was actually true.* I didn't have any proof that Crystal had used her magic to manipulate the two of them – I'd just thrown it in because there was absolutely no way Crystal could prove she *hadn't* done it.

'Perhaps I should make my questions simpler,' Sagash rasped. 'Is Anne Walker currently within my castle? Yes or no will suffice.'

'Uh . . .' Sam said. 'Yes.'

'Where?' Sagash said.

'In the holding cells.'

'Why?'

'Uh . . . do you mean why did we put her there, or why she's in the castle . . . ?'

Sagash looked at him. 'Right,' Sam said hurriedly. 'So, well, Crystal said that you needed this girl for your project, so we had to bring her in alive. Then, uh, we had to catch her again. Which we did.' Sam looked from Crystal to Sagash. 'Right?'

Sagash stared back at Sam for a moment, then turned to Crystal.

'I've been concerned for some time about our progress,' Crystal said, just as though Sagash had asked the question.

She sounded much calmer than she had any right to be.
'The replication issues have been making me suspect that
we need a particular type of live subject. The girl in question has some traits which make her particularly suitable.
Since it wasn't practical for me to go myself, I asked Darren
and Sam for their help.'

Sagash watched Crystal expressionlessly. 'And you saw
fit not to tell me this because . . . ?'

'I wasn't sure whether this girl would give us the information we needed, and I wanted to have solid results before
I presented anything to you. With hindsight, that was a
mistake. I should have kept you informed about the details.
However, from what I just saw during my observations
before I was called away, it's paid off. I'm confident that
with her as a subject we should be able to extract everything we need.'

'She's . . .' I began, then tailed off. *What was I going to say?*

'Verus doesn't have anything to offer,' Crystal said when
I didn't continue. She didn't look at me. 'He wants the
girl and knows he doesn't have the power to take her
himself, so he's trying to talk you into handing her over.
The fastest way to resolve this is to remove him.'

It felt as though there was something I should be saying,
but I couldn't think what it might be. 'Verus?' Sagash
asked.

Sagash was looking at me, and Darren and Sam too.
There wasn't any immediate threat of violence – yet – but
I was very much aware that my life was on the line here.
Still I hesitated; trying to think of an answer felt like
swimming through fog. I'd had some argument I wanted
to make, just a second ago.

'Your silence is not compelling,' Sagash rasped.

I still couldn't think of what to say. I'd felt like this before, but the memory was hard to place. *It was when* . . .

And suddenly something clicked. I spoke with an effort, not letting myself think about it. 'Be easier to answer if Crystal would stop screwing with my head.'

The fog vanished from my thoughts with a snap, and all of a sudden I could think clearly again. Sagash had turned to look at Crystal, and I knew he was studying her with his magesight. Mind magic is hard to detect but not impossible, especially if you're looking for it, and as long as he was focused on her, Crystal couldn't risk anything. 'That's better,' I said, keeping my voice calm as my thoughts raced. I needed to pull the subject away from me, attack where Crystal was vulnerable. 'So, I'd like to make two points. First, while there's nothing preventing you from attacking me, I'm not actually your immediate problem. The Council are going to be coming, and while it's Crystal they really want, they'd be happy to make space for accomplices. Secondly, you might notice that Crystal hasn't given any kind of plausible answer for why she's been keeping all this secret from you. If she'd been planning to share, she would have brought you in from the start. Hiding it from you took major effort on her part, and she wouldn't have done that just because of the chance that it wouldn't work. She did it because she knew you wouldn't have agreed to the plan – and you *definitely* wouldn't have agreed to her making use of what was yours.' I nodded towards Darren and Sam.

'He's stalling for time—' Crystal began.

'Enough,' Sagash rasped. Crystal fell silent immediately, and I followed her lead. Darren and Sam kept their mouths shut too, probably grateful that Sagash's attention wasn't on them. Sagash stared between the two of us, tapping one skeletal finger. The seconds stretched out; I held still, on edge. It was all going to come down to which way Sagash decided to jump, and the futures were blurred and flickering. He hadn't made his choice yet. If he decided to side with Crystal . . .

The futures wavered and settled into a branch. 'You present me with a dilemma,' Sagash stated. 'You, Verus, have violated my territory and drawn the attention of the Council.' He didn't ask what had happened to Ji-yeong. A caring master, Sagash was not. 'Your motives are quite transparent, and as Crystal points out, your bargaining position is poor. You want the girl, yet have little to offer in exchange.'

'Apart from the information I've just given you.'

'A valid point,' Sagash rasped. 'It is clear I have allowed myself to become overly distracted. Had I been supervising my domain more closely, this would have been arrested earlier.' His gaze came to rest on Crystal. 'As you may recall, our original agreement stipulated that you would avoid such actions as this. The fact that you have made use of my apprentices for your personal reasons – and drawn the attention of the Council as a result – does not please me.'

'We don't yet have any evidence that the Council knows,' Crystal replied. 'If they knew for sure then they wouldn't have sent Verus; they'd have sent a squad of Keepers. The fact that he's here on his own means that they don't know yet. The only way they'll find out is if he reports back.'

'Or if Sagash just hands you over to the Keepers himself,' I said to Crystal. 'What was the reward up to again?'

Crystal didn't answer. 'It seems we are at something of

an impasse,' Sagash rasped. 'Both of you wish me to side with you against the other. However, neither of you can present a convincing motivation for my support.'

'All we need to do is—' Crystal began.

'You have made your preferences clear,' Sagash rasped.

Again Crystal fell silent. I knew Sagash had made up his mind, and I didn't have any more high cards left to play. I could try to use my connection to Richard, but it would be no more than a bluff. Sagash looked towards Darren and Sam. 'So far you have both singularly failed in what has been expected of you. Let us see if you can remedy this. You have heard the petitions. What would you say is the most appropriate method of resolving this dispute?'

Darren and Sam looked at Sagash, then each other. I was expecting Sam to answer, but it was Darren who spoke first. 'Uh,' he said. 'Trial by combat?'

'An excellent suggestion,' Sagash rasped.

*'Suggestion' my arse. He knew what he was meant to say.* Already I was calculating my chances. Duels aren't my speciality, but they're not Crystal's either. She'd got the best of me at the windmill, but I'd been too busy running to hit back. The last time we'd gone one-on-one, I'd beaten her. Not perfect odds, but . . .

Crystal's thoughts must have been running along the same lines. 'Wait,' she said. 'This makes no sense. There's no reason to use a method like—'

'Don't fancy your chances?' I said.

Sagash raised his eyebrows towards Crystal. 'You have some objection?'

'The decision is yours, obviously,' Crystal said, changing track without the slightest pause, 'but it should be your *decision*, not the outcome of some uncertain combat. Why trust the result to something so unreliable? Whether Verus or I can prevail in a duel has nothing to do with which course of action is the most profitable.'

'Your point would be valid,' Sagash rasped. 'However, I fear you are under a misapprehension. You will indeed be fighting a trial by combat. Just not against Verus.'

I stared at Sagash. *Who does he——?*

And then I got it. 'Wait,' I said sharply, taking a step forward.

Before my foot had touched the ground, Darren, Sam and Sagash had turned on me. Darren and Sam both had a hand raised, watching. Sagash didn't move, but from the doorway and from the darkness of the room below shadows moved, shifting their positions, white eyes locking onto me. I froze.

'Were you attempting to give me an order?' Sagash asked.

'You don't need to do this,' I said quickly. 'We can——'

'Thank you, Verus,' Sagash rasped. 'I will take your suggestion under advisement. At present I am considering you a neutral party. I suggest you take no action to alter your position.'

*You evil-minded bastard*, I thought furiously. I knew what was going to happen, and there was nothing I could do to stop it. Crystal was frowning slightly. A moment later I heard a metallic creaking noise as a door on the lower level swung open.

Sagash had to have some way of controlling the shadows without verbal commands. He didn't seem to have any trouble commanding multiple shadows at once either, given that he'd done all this while still threatening me. A part of my mind noted that and filed it away, while most of my attention was drawn to the scene below. Two shadows loped in, followed by four more, and between the middle pair, being marched between them with their claws gripping her arms, was Anne.

Anne looked . . . bad. Dried blood was crusted at her wrists and spattered across her shorts and the pink T-shirt, which had picked up some more holes since I'd last seen her. The coat I'd given her was gone, which seemed like an unnecessary indignity on Crystal's part, though I guess given what else they'd been about to do to her, something as small as that wouldn't really have been a big concern. But she was alive, and she wasn't moving as though she were hurt. Her gaze flicked to me as she came in and stayed there for a second before being dragged away to the dark figure of Sagash at the other end of the room.

Crystal was standing on the balcony directly above Anne, but I saw her go still as she finally figured it out. 'Anne,' Sagash rasped. 'Welcome back.'

Anne was silent.

'This makes no sense—' Crystal began.

'You have difficulty following my reasoning?' Sagash rasped. 'Then let me explain. You chose to hide Anne's presence from me. Verus's explanation for this lapse of judgement on your part is that you were attempting to consume her and depart. It strikes me that the simplest way for you to prove your good faith in the matter is for you to eliminate her yourself.'

'We need her for our research. If she's dead we—'

'—can find another,' Sagash finished. 'Her continuing presence while we work here would be a . . . temptation, wouldn't you say? I believe this shadow realm will function more efficiently with only one of you.'

Crystal was still. 'Very well,' she said at last, her voice colourless.

'Besides,' Sagash rasped. 'I am, after all, a researcher.' His eyes came down to rest on Anne. 'Let us see how your skills have developed. Are you aware of why you are here?'

Anne glanced down at the duelling circle on the floor, then up at Sagash. Her voice was quiet in the echoing room. 'I know what you want from me.'

'Excellent,' Sagash said. 'In which case I see no reason to delay.'

'Mage Sagash,' I said. I kept my voice polite, even though politeness was the last thing I was feeling. 'Would it be possible for me to speak with her before the duel?'

'For what reason?'

'Because depending on the possible outcomes, it may be pretty damn difficult for me to speak with her *after*.'

Sagash gave me a considering look. 'You have five minutes.'

I headed for the stairs down.

# 12

By the time I'd reached floor level, the shadows had brought Anne to the far side of the duelling ring. They released her but held their position around her, white eyes staring. I didn't look around, but as I walked towards her I scanned the area. There were three doors, though only the one through which Anne had been brought was still open, and eight shadows with more above. I briefly calculated the odds of us successfully making a break for it under the noses of Sagash, Crystal, Darren and Sam and decided they were close enough to zero to make no difference.

Anne looked worse up close. The blood crusting her wrists was covering two ugly-looking wounds between hand and forearm which looked like they'd pierced through and through. Her skin was paler than it should be, and she'd picked up some new bruises on her face and legs. But her eyes were steady, and she was looking at me with some expression I couldn't place.

'Are you okay?' I said quietly once I was within earshot.

'Why did you come back?' Anne said.

'Nice to see you too. You got the gist?'

'I've done this before.'

'Good. Okay, not good, but—'

'I'm supposed to kill Crystal,' Anne said, her voice flat.

'That'd be the better out of the two alternatives, yeah. You up to it?'

Anne looked at me without speaking for a second. 'Why did you come back?'

'Where else was I going to go? You're welcome, by the way.'

'You're *welcome*?'

'Okay, maybe I'm missing something here, but I was under the impression Crystal was—'

'About to kill me.'

'Okay . . . then how exactly is this any worse? Work with me here. We don't have much time!'

'Time . . .' Anne passed a hand over her face. 'You don't understand what you've done.'

'Then *tell* me!'

Anne closed her eyes briefly, then opened them again. 'I told you back at the windmill,' she said. 'This was what I was afraid of. Not Crystal. This.'

'You've got a chance here,' I said. 'Okay, it's not a great chance, but it's something. If you can beat Crystal, then Sagash might let you go.'

Anne gave a sort of half-laugh, despairing. 'He's never going to let me go.'

'How are you so sure?'

'Because he's *Sagash*.' Anne shook her head. 'You don't understand. With Crystal it would have been quick. Now . . . You haven't made it better. Just slower.'

I stared at Anne, re-evaluating. I didn't like the idea, but I had to admit it was possible. 'Okay,' I said. 'So, new plan. Don't kill Crystal. Just take her down, hurt her a little but leave her able to get up again and—'

'Alex,' Anne said, and all of a sudden she looked very tired. 'Just stop.'

'And do what? Give up?'

Anne looked past me towards the floor, and when she raised her eyes again there was something distant and alien in them. 'Do you know how many people I killed in this circle?'

'No, and right now I don't care.'

'I do.'

'We do not exactly have very much choice here!'

'There's always a choice,' Anne said quietly.

'To do what? Stand there and get killed?' Anne didn't answer and my heart sank. 'No! Anne, I'm out of tricks here. I haven't got anything more up my sleeve. I'm counting on you.'

'To do what?' Anne's voice was weary. 'Be her again?'

'If that's what it takes to stay alive? Yes.'

'I'm tired of making that choice.'

'The other is worse!'

'Is it?' Anne asked. 'Isn't that how you become a Dark mage in the first place? They don't come from nowhere. Darren and Sam didn't. All you have to do is choose yourself over everyone else. You tell yourself it's just one thing . . . and then after that there's another and another. Until you're not sure how much of you is . . .' Anne shook her head. 'I'm tired. Of all the death, and justifying it to myself. Getting more like them. If I die here . . . it stops.' She was silent for a moment. 'Maybe I deserve this.'

I stared at Anne, frustration mixing with fury. I'd never felt more distant from her than I did now. Guilt I could understand. But just giving up, *letting* someone destroy you . . . I wasn't getting through and we were running out of time. I looked around to see that Sagash was out of sight, up on the balcony above, his shadows still watching. Crystal had descended and was standing at the other end of the duelling ring; Darren and Sam watched cautiously from a distance.

*This isn't working.* Anne wasn't listening to me. I needed to get through to that other Anne, the one I'd seen in Elsewhere. Hadn't she said that she came out in times like this? Why wasn't Anne acting like that now?

*Because that side is weaker.* She'd admitted it, or as good as. Anne could keep her bottled up. And if she decided not to fight, then that other side would die with her. Maybe I could persuade her—

*No.* I was doing this the wrong way. That other Anne wasn't a creature of reason; she was instinct and emotion. I needed something more primal. 'Is that how you think this is going to be?' I said. 'You die here as some sort of martyr?'

'It's not like—'

'Yes, it is. You think you're going out as a hero. You know what you're going to be remembered as? A coward. Crystal'll take her time finishing you off while Darren and Sam and the rest laugh at you. You're a joke to them. The little girl who everyone can push around.'

'Why are you being like this? I thought you'd understand!'

'Understand what? That you're trying to commit a really twisted version of suicide-by-cop? That doesn't make you a good person, it makes you mentally ill. Oh, and by the way, what makes you think they're going to kill you? Crystal still needs a research subject, remember? If she beats you she can probably beg a favour from Sagash to keep you around. Of course, they wouldn't need all of you. An experiment doesn't need arms or legs. I saw someone like that in a Dark mage's lab once. The mage kept him around as a curiosity. At least, I think it was a him. After you cut enough bits off it gets kind of hard to tell. No eyes either, or tongue. Could still scream, though. They could probably keep you alive for a good fifty or sixty years. Does that sound like fun? Nice way to spend your time?'

Anne was staring at me. There was disbelief there, and horror – and a seed of anger too. *Good.* 'But sure,' I said. 'If you think that's worth doing, then go for it. Not that it'll just be you. Once you're gone, you think Crystal and Sagash are going to have much motivation to keep me around? Oh, and let's not forget Variam! If you don't get back to London, you think he'll just sit around and wait? He'll find a way to come after us, and Luna as well. And the same thing'll happen to them. I'll be dead, your friends will be dead and you'll be in a screaming tortured existence for the rest of your life, all because you decided not to fight back – but hey, you'll have the moral satisfaction of not having killed anyone. Anyone else, that is. I'm sure that'll make it all worthwhile.'

Anne's face had gone white. 'Well,' I said. 'I guess if I'm not going to be seeing Vari and Luna again, then at least I won't have to explain to them that this was your fault.' I turned away and paused. 'Or then again, maybe Sagash'll keep *them* around as well. Do the same thing to them that he did to you.'

I walked away. I didn't look back at the expression on Anne's face – I knew what I'd see if I did. I climbed the stairs back up to the upper level, tension and anger mixing with self-loathing.

Most of what I'd just said to Anne had probably been a lie. The last time Anne had been the target of a ritual like this, they hadn't been aiming to torture her, just to kill her, and I had no idea of what was going to happen to me afterwards or what Luna and Vari might be doing. But I'd known that Anne hadn't been in any kind of state to sit down and think that out rationally. She was despairing and vulnerable and I'd hit her where she was weakest, breaking her resolve so that she would do what I wanted.

*I really am Richard's apprentice.*

A feminine voice spoke inside my head. *Don't flatter yourself.*

I started slightly, looking around. Sagash was still at the far end of the balcony, apparently indifferent. Darren and Sam were down at ground level. Anne hadn't moved . . . and neither had Crystal. She was looking away from me, arms folded. But it was her voice I'd heard.

*You know*, I said silently, *it's not polite to listen in on private conversations.*

*Did you think diviners were the only ones who could eavesdrop?* Crystal replied. The whole sentence was delivered in an instant, faster than speech but without any loss of meaning. Strangely enough, Crystal's voice actually sounded *more* distinctive this way: it was cool and precise, matching her perfectly. *And once again, don't flatter yourself. I've met your master. He wouldn't have let himself fall into so vulnerable a position.*

*I could say the same for you*, I said. *How long have you been working on this plan, by the way? I'd love to know just how many months of your work I managed to screw up.*

*More than you know.* Crystal's voice was cold. *Normally I don't allow myself the luxury of revenge. But let me give you one piece of advice. Don't be here when I step out of the circle.*

*Confident, aren't you? If you couldn't beat me, what makes you think you have a chance against Anne?*

*If I'd really wanted you dead, you wouldn't be here. A mistake I won't repeat. Last chance, Verus.*

*I'll make you a counter-offer,* I replied. *You and me and Anne all team up and get out of here. You have to know by now that Sagash isn't going to let you keep Anne alive.*

*Really,* Crystal said. *You expect me to betray Sagash to help the two of you escape?*

*The three of us, not the two of us, and yes.*

*Do explain why.*

*Because you've got a better chance against Sagash than you do in that duelling ring against Anne.*

*That would have been more convincing if you hadn't just been trying and failing to persuade her to fight at all.*

'Time.' Sagash's rasping voice cut across the room, and I nearly flinched. 'Prepare yourselves.'

At the far end, the shadows closed in on Anne, forcing her towards the circle. Darren made one half-hearted step towards Crystal as if to do the same. She gave him a single level look which stopped him dead, then walked to the circle's edge.

*Well?* I asked, scanning ahead to see what would happen if I stood where I was. *What do you say?*

*Verus, if you actually believed she could beat me, you wouldn't be bargaining now. All you have are empty threats.*

Sagash was about to say something about terms. After that, the future forked and became blurry, but I could just make out a shifting blur of combat. It looked as though . . . *huh.* I looked away after only an instant, hiding what I'd just seen behind other thoughts so Crystal couldn't catch it.

'Stand ready,' Sagash rasped.

Crystal stepped over the edge of the ring, her eyes on

her opponent. A moment later, Anne did the same. Her head was tilted down, her hair hiding her eyes so that I couldn't see her expression, and she was holding very still. I wished for Crystal's telepathy so that I could know what Anne was thinking. But since I couldn't . . . *Do you know what your problem is, Crystal?*

*You're going to lecture me on* my *problems? Really?*

*Lack of empathy*, I thought. *You can read people's thoughts, but you don't recognise them as belonging to real people. You don't pay attention to their motivations or what they care about; you just use brute force to make them do what you want.*

*So you're capable of seeing the obvious*, Crystal replied. *Congratulations. You're correct: I don't care what you want, or what she wants, or Sagash, or his apprentices. You, all of you . . . you* irritate *me. You have no idea how tedious it is to hear your thoughts go round and round obsessing about your petty little problems. All I wanted was to complete the ritual and never have to see any of you again. Instead you've managed to make it all pointless. If you'd just waited a few more hours, I would have been able to put this girl to use. Now I'm going to have to kill her to no benefit at all. And then I'm going to leave, and then I'm going to start all over again to find another suitable specimen, going through as many adepts and apprentices as it takes. You're so concerned about the lives of apprentices? Far more are going to lose their lives as a result of what you've done today, all because you had to interfere. You can think on that as you watch her die.* Crystal's voice cut off abruptly.

So much for negotiations.

'The duel is to the death,' Sagash rasped. He'd taken a step forward and was standing on the edge of the balcony, looking down like some necromantic version of a Roman emperor at the games. 'The victor will retain their life, and my favour. Do you understand these conditions?'

'Yes,' Crystal replied. She hadn't taken her eyes off Anne.

Anne stayed silent and still.

'The duel will begin on three,' Sagash rasped. 'Are you prepared?'

Crystal gave a short nod. Anne didn't.

'One,' Sagash rasped.

The room was silent. Below, at floor level, Sam and Darren watched from behind Crystal. Sam looked nervous, his pale face tense. Darren was watching avidly. Death mages have a reputation for loving combat, the deadlier the better. Scattered around were the shadows, their white eyes a silent audience.

'Two.'

Silence. Both Crystal and Anne were still; they'd each chosen what they were about to do. From somewhere deeper in Sagash's laboratory I could hear a very faint ticking sound, echoing into the arena. There was nothing more I could do. I'd played all my cards; now I'd see whether it had been for better or for worse. I held my breath.

Sagash opened his mouth to say 'three', and Crystal struck.

I've seen a lot of duels, but most have been the non-lethal kind favoured by the Light Council. A Light azimuth duel usually takes the best part of five minutes, counting breaks. Death duels are much faster.

I'd been expecting Crystal to try and dominate Anne, but the spell she hit her with was a blast of pure mental force. I felt the backwash from all the way up on the balcony, and it was stronger than the attack she'd used at the windmill – a lot stronger. My mental defences are better than most, but all of a sudden I wasn't so sure that rematch would have been a good idea. If I'd been the one to step into that circle, I might not have come out again.

But I wasn't the one in that circle, Anne was. And Anne . . .

It's strange, the ways you see people. I'd known that life mages can act as assassins but I'd never thought of Anne that way. It wasn't how she'd first come across, and first impressions are hard to shift – no matter how many times people had told me Anne was dangerous, she hadn't *felt* dangerous, at least not to me. Even when she'd flat-out told me what she'd done, I'd never really been able to connect the words with the image I had of her. Shy, gentle, slightly awkward; a healer, not a fighter.

Anne came off her starting position like a sprinter, heading straight for Crystal. She didn't move like a duellist but like a runner, eyes locked on her target. Crystal's spell hit before Anne had taken her second step and Anne stumbled briefly but kept going. It wasn't that the attack was weak; it was that she didn't care. The only thing she was paying attention to was closing the distance.

Crystal took a step back, eyes going wide in alarm. Her hand came up and I felt the surge of another spell, then Anne was slamming into Crystal, rocking them back. There was a blur of movement, magic and green light, and all of a sudden Crystal was falling. She hit the floor with Anne above her, Anne's hand coming down to rest on Crystal's body, over her heart.

Crystal looked up, obviously dazed. Her eyes focused on Anne and she froze. Anne was crouched over Crystal, her right hand resting with fingers spread over Crystal's chest, between her breasts and a little to the left. Green light glowed at Anne's fingers; it was a soft colour, the shade of new leaves in spring, but I knew what the spell did and from the expression in Crystal's eyes she did too.

Time stretched out. After the brief flurry of activity the chamber was silent again. Anne was motionless, the spell hanging ready at her hand. The only movement I could see was the rapid rise and fall of Crystal's chest, and she was holding very still. I looked into the futures and saw them fork. In one, Anne stood up and let the spell drop. In the other . . .

Then that second future winked out. Anne stood up, letting the spell vanish from her fingers. She looked up at Sagash. 'No,' she said, her voice carrying clearly in the silence. Her posture and stance had changed: she was the Anne I knew again. 'I'm not going to be like you.'

I held my breath.

Sagash looked down at her from his perch on the balcony. The two of them locked eyes. 'Disappointing,' Sagash said at last, his rasping voice echoing.

Anne didn't reply and again the silence stretched out. 'Well,' I said brightly. 'Good match; glad I was here to see it. The two of us really should leave and let you get back to work.' *Anne, please don't say anything to piss him off; please don't say anything to piss him off . . .*

Anne stayed quiet. Sagash regarded her for a moment, then spoke in his rasping voice. 'I think not.'

*Oh shit.*

'You said that the winner would have your favour . . .' I started to say. Even before the words were out of my mouth I knew it wasn't going to help.

'And their life,' Sagash rasped. 'The conditions for victory, however, were the death of the other party.' He looked down at Anne and Crystal. 'It appears we have two losers, not one.'

There was a rustle of movement from around the chamber, barely audible, as the shadows shifted their position. 'You wanted to see how Anne's skills had developed,' I said. 'You've got your data, right?' *Scan the futures . . . no, there was no way talking was going to work, not now. I aimed my thoughts at Crystal.* Hey, Crystal! Wake up!

'Indeed.'

'There's nothing stopping you from letting Anne go. It's not as if she came here because she wanted to.' *Hey! I'm talking to you, you psychotic bitch. I know you can hear me; you eavesdrop on everyone else—*

Crystal's voice spoke into my head. She sounded shaken but lucid. *I heard you the first time.*

'Do not play games with me,' Sagash rasped. 'You are obviously well aware of what Anne did the last time she visited my realm. Until now, I did not consider her a high enough priority to be worth pursuing. If she simply presents herself, however . . . No. I believe Anne will be remaining.'

*Last chance,* I thought towards Crystal. *Do you want to get out or not?* 'As a matter of fact, I don't know the details,' I said. 'What did Anne do to offend you so badly?'

*If you're making the same offer—* Crystal began.

*Yes, and before you ask, I know I was your enemy five minutes ago. You're cold-blooded enough to switch sides that fast, you know it and I know it, so let's not waste time. Yes or no?*

'Anne remains my legal apprentice,' Sagash rasped. 'As her master, I both expect and require—'

Sagash kept talking, but I wasn't paying attention. I looked at him, pretending to listen, all of my thoughts focused on Crystal. *I don't think you're in much of a position to promise anything*, Crystal replied.

*I'm in a better position than you. Sagash is going to kick me out, but you and Anne are about to become permanent residents. You want to get out of here; I want Anne out of here. For the next five minutes we've got a common enemy – you wait and it's going to be just you on your own. Either you make a break for it, or you stay and take your chances with Sagash. Pick!*

An instant's pause. *Very well*, Crystal said. She'd recovered and her voice was steady again. *I presume you have some sort of plan.*

*Depends what I've got to work with. Now, I know you've prepared some sort of escape route where you abandon everyone else and keep yourself alive, because that's what you do. I'm going to guess it involves those two idiot apprentices?*

*I can control them briefly.*

*Good. I'll distract Sagash. Talk to Anne, get her onside.*

Silence. I suddenly realised that Sagash had finished speaking – what had he just said? 'I can understand why you would have reason to be upset,' – blatant lie, but whatever – 'but revenge seems a rather unprofitable way to resolve this.'

'Revenge is irrelevant.'

Out of the corner of my eye, I saw Anne start slightly, look down at Crystal, then back up. 'Maybe some sort of compensation—'

'No,' Sagash rasped. 'She is a liability. I see now that I was in error to have taken her in. A mistake I will now correct.'

'There is one other thing you might want to consider,' I said. *Crystal, we're running out of time. Get on with it!* 'My old master has expressed an . . . interest in Anne.'

'Your master does not rule here.'

'But you could—'

'Enough,' Sagash rasped, his voice final. 'I am willing to allow you safe passage, Verus. That can be revoked.'

*There appears to be a problem*, Crystal said calmly into my head.

*Fix it!*

*Anne refuses to believe me when I tell her this is your idea. Apparently she doesn't trust me.* Crystal's voice was ironic. *I can't imagine why.*

'I see,' I said, and bowed my head slightly to Sagash. 'Very well.' I turned away and looked down at Anne. 'Anne? Do as she says.'

Anne's eyes widened slightly. *Do it*, I thought.

Four of the shadows started to move towards Anne, acting on Sagash's unspoken orders. An instant later Darren started to walk in the same direction. Sam gave him a puzzled look.

Anne's head came up sharply; she'd caught something in his body language. Sagash gave Darren a dismissive look. 'Stay.'

Crystal's voice spoke into my head. *Three seconds.*

I shifted slightly, slipping one hand into a pocket at an angle Sagash couldn't see. Darren was still heading towards Anne and so were the shadows. Sagash started to say something to Crystal, saw that Darren hadn't stopped and looked at him in annoyance. 'You are not—'

*Now*, Crystal voiced.

Everything happened at once.

The first two shadows reached Anne, claws extending. As they did, Darren blasted them with two bolts of death magic, one after the other at point-blank range. The spells were constructions of kinetic energy, giant wide-finned darts designed to tear through constructs, and they did just that. The shadows disintegrated, the magical effect which animated them failing. Sagash's eyes went wide in sudden fury and his hand came up, darkness gathering just as I threw a condenser right at him.

Sagash saw my throw and switched focus instantly. Death mages like Sagash are combat specialists, and virtually every spell they can cast is designed to either protect them or kill someone else. They're very good at what they do, and I had absolutely no chance against Sagash in any kind of fight. Nothing I had would so much as scratch him.

But Sagash didn't know that.

Sagash's first spell was a shield, a translucent bubble of black energy coming up around him. The condenser hit it and shattered, mist flooding out to cover him and a forty-foot sphere of the balcony in fog. Sagash's second spell was a defensive one too and so was the third, protective effects wrapping around his body and immunising him from anything that the fog might be carrying. And by the time he'd figured out that the fog wasn't actually dangerous, I'd vaulted the railing and dropped to the floor below.

The shadows which had been going for Anne were crumpled heaps, dissolving into smoke. Sam was on his knees, clutching at his head, and Crystal's eyes were locked onto him as she hurried towards the exit. Darren was moving ahead of the two women and covering them, his movements stiff and mechanical. All the other shadows, a dozen or more, stood silent and still; Sagash hadn't yet given them new orders.

I ran for the exit. Darren reached it first and halted with

a jerk. A spell flickered at his hand, wavering between the shadows and Crystal. 'Anne,' Crystal said; she didn't take her eyes away from Sam and her voice was tight with strain. 'Get rid of him.'

Anne hesitated, and I felt a surge of death magic from behind. I just had time to dive left before the spell exploded between us.

The few times I've been hit with high-level battle magic I've never felt it. You usually don't even know whether you've been hurt until afterwards; the amount of destructive power is so far out of human scale that your nervous system doesn't know how to handle it. Your perception of time distorts, leaving blank spots in your memory. With hindsight, my best guess is that it was an area attack, some sort of blast or vortex.

The next thing I remember is scrambling to my feet. I felt as though I was further to the left than I should have been, but the doorway in front was open. Anne was up and moving and the two of us ran for the exit; I caught a glimpse of a body to one side and then we were into the corridor and out of Sagash's line of sight.

It wasn't until the second corner that I realised someone was behind me. I turned, still dazed, fumbling for the sword at my belt—

—and Crystal gave me an irritated look as she brushed past. Dust and dirt caked her left side and there was a bloody scrape on her cheek, but she didn't look seriously hurt. *Keep moving*, she said. We were out in one of the corridors – I hadn't had a chance to map it but Anne was leading the way.

As we reached a corner a keening, whining sound went through me, so high-pitched it was on the edge of hearing.

I could feel a trace of magic in it, but couldn't tell what it was. 'What was that?'

'Shadow call,' Anne said, at the same time that Crystal said, 'A command to the constructs.'

'The gate—' Anne began.

'No.' I shook my head and pointed to an arrow-slit window in the corridor. 'Look.'

Anne looked as though she'd rather be running, but Crystal moved to my side. The window gave a narrow view out of the south side of the castle towards the main gates and the bridge. For a moment, all I could see was the skyline over the buildings, then I saw a dot against the clouds, rising up from the edge of the castle. Then another. Then . . .

That didn't look like dots. It looked like a cloud. 'Anne?' I said, not looking at her. 'How many of these shadows does Sagash have exactly?'

Anne let out a breath. 'That would be . . . all of them.'

'They'll surround the keep and form a perimeter,' Crystal said. 'I hope you weren't planning to use the front door.'

'Incoming,' I said. The shadows from the duelling hall were moving. 'That way.'

We hurried down a turning and to the right. In the futures spread out ahead of me, I could see the shadows moving through the corridors of the keep, their straight-line paths becoming a blur of combat when they intersected ours. I looked at Anne. 'I can get us out through the tunnels if we can make it to the ground floor.'

'The main stairwell is trapped,' Crystal said.

'There's a back staircase that way,' Anne said.

I glanced through the futures. No shadows; it looked

clear . . . Wait, someone was there. *Huh.* I gave a sudden wolfish smile. 'That'll work.'

A side door took us into a narrow stairwell. I got halfway down, paused for two seconds, holding my hand up for Crystal and Anne to wait behind me, then walked down onto the landing and turned. At the bottom of the stairs, just turning in from the main corridor, was Ji-yeong. She was on her feet, battered and limping, one sword sheathed and the other scabbard empty. She was just about to start up the stairs when she saw me.

I looked down at Ji-yeong.

'Oh, no.' Ji-yeong put up both hands and stepped away. 'I am not doing this again.' She backed out of the doorway, turned and ran.

Crystal gave me a look with eyebrows raised. 'I see you've displayed your usual talent for making friends.'

'What happened with her?' Anne asked.

I started down the stairs. 'Not now, all right?'

The shadows kept searching, but there weren't quite enough yet to cover the whole keep and we made it down to the basement. I yanked the door shut behind us and we were in the tunnels.

'How did you find this place?' Anne asked, looking around.

'I got lucky,' I said, conscious of Crystal's eyes on me. I looked at her. 'Sagash is using the shadows to seal up the keep, right? How long do we have before he figures out we're not there?'

'Five to ten minutes.'

'He'll have sent another group to the front gate,' Anne said.

'I assume your way out involves the back door,' I told Crystal.

'Fortunately, yes,' Crystal said. 'I suggest we go a little further from the keep's wards before gating.'

'You know, Ji-yeong thought you didn't have any gate stones for the keep.'

'Ji-yeong is an apprentice.'

I led the way through the tunnels, the white flicker of my torch marking our path. Crystal followed and Anne dropped back, keeping Crystal between us. I was sure Crystal didn't miss the subtext, but she didn't say anything. Crystal wasn't the only thing on my mind – I'd told the blink fox to find a place with a view of the exits and wait. Right now, the keep exits would be swarming with shadows. An obedient person would sit and watch. But someone who was used to thinking for themselves would see the shadows, decide that no one was getting out that way and go looking for the one route that they knew *did* work . . .

We'd reached one of the choke points, where I'd had to squeeze past the remains of a rockfall on the way in. Something in the futures drew my attention and as I tilted the torch beam down I saw a flash of amber eyes. 'We should be far enough,' I told Crystal. 'Put the portal there.' I pointed to the middle of the corridor. 'I'll check for where we'll be coming out. Anne, you're on lookout.'

I saw Anne's eyes drift behind me. To her eyes, I knew the blink fox would be a beacon of life in the darkness. 'Just watch for Sagash and his apprentices,' I said, putting a little emphasis on the words. 'I'll handle everything else.'

Anne gave me a look, then nodded. Crystal had been taking a small item from a hidden pocket. If she'd noticed

Anne's instant of hesitation, she didn't show it. 'Is our destination safe?'

'Well, I guess that depends on where you keyed that stone, doesn't it?'

'If this gate is going to open into a pack of shadows, it would be helpful to know in advance.'

'I won't be able to tell until closer to the time,' I said. Which was actually true. 'Trust me, if your spell's about to get us killed, I'll make sure you don't finish.'

Crystal raised her eyebrows, then turned and began focusing on the gate stone. Behind my back I held up a palm towards the blink fox, then one finger, then made a beckoning motion before taking my hand away. I knew it was smart enough to understand speech; I hoped it was smart enough to understand sign language. I didn't turn around to look, but I sensed the fox draw back slightly.

Crystal's gate spell was under way; there was no visible light but I could see the portal beginning to form. Her spellcasting was precise, controlled . . . better than mine, in fact, at least when it came to gates, which was mildly irritating. I let that annoyance occupy the front of my mind, using it as a shield to mask what I was really thinking.

I hadn't forgotten that Anne and I were standing within arm's reach of someone who not only had tried to kill us both multiple times, but who would do it again with roughly the same level of concern that most people give to clipping their nails. Crystal was standing only a few feet away with her back turned. My hand was only inches from the hilt of Ji-yeong's short-sword. Very distantly, at a level of my mind that I did *not* allow myself to focus on,

I was aware of how easy it would be to take a step forward, yank her head back as I brought up the sword—

I forced the thought away. Not yet.

The gate was forming and I focused. As the future in which the gate materialised became closer, I checked what would happen if I stayed put, went through it, moved left and right. 'Clear,' I said just before Crystal finished and the oval portal appeared in the corridor, filling the dark tunnel with sunlight.

Crystal moved to the gate, looking to either side. Through it I could see the walls of a stone room, sunlight painting the floor. Crystal began to step through and I followed instantly, beckoning behind my back as I did. I felt a flicker of space magic, almost lost in the more powerful signal of the gate, as something blinked through the portal and out of sight.

We came down into a windowed room with dust motes floating in the air, a double circle of dark green stone set into the floor. 'You don't need to follow quite so closely,' Crystal said over her shoulder as Anne stepped through behind us.

'Just making sure.' It was the next gate I was worried about. I couldn't let Crystal use it first; in fact, I didn't want her to be the one opening the gate at all. Too easy for her to let it close while I was halfway through. 'Anne? This the place?'

Anne nodded. As Crystal let the gate close behind us, Anne moved to the window and looked out, shading her eyes. 'Alex?'

I already knew what I was going to see, but even so, viewing it with my own eyes gave me a chill. There was a swarm of black dots in the sky. I tried to imagine how long we'd last if that many shadows landed on us, and quickly stopped imagining. 'Crystal? Does Sagash know that *you* know about this place?'

'I imagine we'll find out within the next few minutes.'

'Guys?' Anne said, 'I don't want to rush, but about fifty of those shadows just started heading this way.'

Crystal walked back to where we were standing and held out a fluted rod. She'd drawn it out without my noticing. 'I hope you brought a gate stone to an outside location.'

I looked back at her for a second, then shook it off, took the rod and went through my pockets for my gate stones. My shop, the safe house, the park . . . I didn't want Crystal near anywhere I lived. I held the rod and the stone to Anne. 'Here.'

'Keep it touching the end of the rod,' Crystal said. 'The encoding will do the rest.' She seemed quite unconcerned. *What are you up to?*

Anne moved to the green circle and started focusing on the gate stone, keeping the rod touched to it. You don't realise how much of a hassle it is to try and get around wards until you finally use the right key. Green light welled up around her hands and I could already see the gate starting to form; Anne knew this castle *very* well and the gate stone was doing the rest. Looking ahead, I knew that the shadows were on their way, but they wouldn't make it in time. For the first time, I started to let myself believe that we might actually make it out.

I couldn't see the fox, but without turning to look I knew it had moved around to behind us, hiding in the doorway. It would be able to teleport straight through. A green-ringed oval was forming in front of Anne, the portal becoming opaque, and I moved forward casually, placing myself in front of Crystal. Crystal didn't seem to notice.

The gate flickered . . . and opened. Leafy branches and green grass showed through the portal, a cool breeze blowing through. It wasn't so very different from the greener areas of the castle, but it meant everything to me, and the sight of the world outside the shadow realm was a rush. I jumped through, coming down on grass, and into the beams of sunlight that came down through the leaves above. The hum of traffic sounded through the trees, and I could hear distant voices from outside the park. We were in London again, and I felt light-headed with relief. Just for an instant, my guard wasn't up.

And against someone who can read your thoughts, an instant's too long.

Pain exploded inside my head and my vision greyed out. It felt like being hit with a horrendous headache, distilled and concentrated into a couple of seconds. Nausea and dizziness flooded over me and I stumbled.

As my eyesight came back, I found myself looking back at the portal. Crystal had stepped through and was just turning to look back into the shadow realm. She was coming around to focus on Anne, and at some distant level I knew that she was going to hit Anne before Anne could follow her through. Crystal couldn't beat Anne in a fair fight, but she didn't need to: she just had to break Anne's concentration on the spell. I fumbled for a weapon, but I was still dazed and my reactions weren't fast enough.

There was a flicker of space magic and a red-brown shape latched onto Crystal's arm. Crystal screamed, jerked away. The blink fox hung on, eyes glinting, teeth sunk into Crystal's forearm as she frantically tried to shake it off before sending another mindblast into the fox from two feet away.

The fox dropped, hitting the grass with a thud. Crystal looked up angrily, blood on her arm . . .

. . . and found herself facing Anne.

In the couple of seconds Crystal had been distracted, Anne had made it through. The gate flickered and faded behind her as she dropped concentration on the spell, letting the gate stone and focus fall to the grass.

Anne looked at Crystal and slightly flexed the fingers of one hand.

Crystal turned and ran. She bolted through the leaves and under the low-hanging branches and was gone, racing footsteps fading into the distance. Anne watched her go, then turned to me. 'I'm all right,' I said, pulling myself up and stumbling a little.

'I know,' Anne said, reaching out to place a hand wreathed in green light against my chest. Energy flowed through me and my head cleared, the pain vanishing. 'Are we safe?'

I looked into the future and saw . . . nothing. No combat, no danger. Crystal wasn't coming back. 'We're safe.'

'It's finished?'

'It's finished.'

Anne nodded, then her legs seemed to give way and she slumped to the ground, kneeling on the grass, head down. I started to reach out, then stopped myself and pulled out my phone, speed-dialling a number. It rang twice before picking up. 'Caldera,' a suspicious voice said in my ear. 'Who is this?'

'It's Verus,' I said. 'I'm at the park we use for gating in Camden and so's Crystal. I last saw her sixty seconds ago heading north.'

'*Crystal?* Are you sure?'

'Just pass it on to whoever's job this is,' I said wearily. The adrenalin rush was wearing off and I felt utterly exhausted. 'I'm going home.'

'Wait! How did——?'

I hung up and switched my phone off. To one side, the blink fox had pulled itself upright and was looking at me. 'Thanks,' I told it simply.

The fox blinked at me, then tilted its head up and sniffed the air, nostrils flaring to catch the spring breeze and the scents of grass and flowers. It came to its feet in a flowing motion and trotted away without a backward glance.

I watched the fox disappear into the undergrowth, then shook my head and held my hand down to Anne. 'Let's go.'

Anne looked up at me and for an instant I could have sworn she looked surprised. Then she put a hand into mine and let me pull her up. She looked around and took a deep breath, then started walking. I fell into step beside her and we headed home.

## 13

And that was that. Mostly.

The Keepers didn't catch Crystal, which wasn't exactly a surprise given that she'd probably been out of the country again before I'd finished that phone call. They settled for interrogating us instead. I gave them an edited version of the story which I don't think made them very happy, especially the 'working with Crystal to escape' part. I claimed that it had been under duress and I'd had no other choice, and, given that Sagash wasn't exactly going to come down to the station to give a statement contradicting me, there wasn't much the Keepers could do to prove otherwise. All the same, I got the definite impression from most of the Keepers I spoke to that they didn't think saving Anne in exchange for Crystal had been a good trade. I disagreed, but since no one seemed to care very much what I thought, I kept my opinions to myself.

The Keepers had a try at interrogating Sagash too. I didn't get to watch, which was a shame since by all accounts it was fairly entertaining. After a brief but eventful exchange of views, Sagash sealed off his shadow realm, leaving the Keepers twiddling their thumbs outside. A full assault on the shadow realm might have been possible, but without Crystal there no one on the Council had the motivation to push it through. Instead the Keepers ended up trying to enforce some weird kind of inter-dimensional siege, which isn't really very effective when the residents of the place you're besieging can gate to any place on Earth. On the positive side, it did give Sagash a reason not to come to London after me, which from my point of view was just as well.

Ironically enough, the one who came out of the whole thing looking the best was Sonder. He'd been the one in charge (on paper at least), and right from the start he'd gone on record insisting that Crystal had been behind Anne's disappearance, even when no one else believed him. Caldera probably could have poked some holes in that story, but she kept quiet and Sonder got the credit.

For my part, I had to put up with a certain degree of grilling, but it was nothing I hadn't done before. It also helped that with Caldera and Variam I had a couple of Keepers on my side for a change. Compared to the shadow realm, it was actually kind of relaxing.

I got out of the Keeper station in Westminster the day after getting back to London. It was late afternoon and the street was filled with noise, the road busy with cars and buses. Someone was waiting for me on the street, and as I started down the steps I shook my head. 'Why does it not surprise me that you knew where I was?'

'You did send a message,' Talisid pointed out. He looked the same as ever, blending neatly into the Westminster crowds. I started walking north and Talisid fell into step beside me. 'I'm glad to see you're in good shape.'

'I'm going to take a wild guess and assume you got the story from the Keepers.'

'The story you and Anne told them, yes.'

'Yeah, well, I told them the truth, just not all the details.' I paused, not looking at him. 'We met Richard.'

Talisid didn't break stride. We kept walking along the pavement, adjusting our course to avoid the pedestrians coming the other way. 'I see,' Talisid said.

'You don't sound surprised.'

'I had my suspicions.'

'Yeah, I know. You were right.'

'I appreciate the information,' Talisid said. 'Does this mean you've come to a decision on my offer?'

'I'm glad you brought that up,' I said. I'd had a lot of time to think in between the rounds of interviews by the Keepers. 'You know, the more I thought about what you were offering, the more it seemed a little weird. Don't get me wrong, I could do the job. But so could a lot of other people.'

'Fewer than you might think.'

I shrugged. 'Either way, I couldn't shake the feeling that you were putting in just a little more effort than I was worth. So I started thinking about what might be so special about me. And the biggest thing that stood out? My link to Richard.'

Talisid didn't answer. 'You said you wanted me to work as an investigator,' I said. 'You didn't say what I'd be investigating.' I stopped, looking at Talisid, forcing him to turn and face me. 'Richard found us in the shadow realm. He offered me my old job back. I think you've known for a while that this might happen. You didn't want an investigator. You wanted a double agent. Someone close to Richard and reporting back to you. You wanted to recruit me before Richard did.'

The pedestrian traffic streamed past as Talisid hesitated, people giving us irritated looks. I knew he was deciding what to tell me. 'The truth, please,' I said quietly.

Talisid sighed slightly. 'Part of my job involves planning

for future possibilities. The possibilities are not always pleasant.'

'Really.'

'Our models estimated a low to moderate chance that Richard would attempt to recruit you within two years of his hypothetical return,' Talisid said. 'The probability was assessed as being too low to justify the security risk of sharing the information.' He paused. 'I requested that you be told regardless. I was overruled.'

'And that was my role in your *model*,' I said. 'Spying for the Council. Just out of curiosity, what life expectancy did your analysts give me if I said yes?'

'Believe me when I say that I understand exactly how dangerous Richard is,' Talisid said. 'But for that very reason it's critical that we learn more about his plans. I know how much we would be asking, and I'd be authorised to offer a great deal in exchange.' He paused. 'You would probably be doing more to work against Richard's goals than any other mage in the world.'

I was silent.

'Forgive me for asking,' Talisid said. 'But when Richard asked you to join him, what was your answer?'

'I gave him the same answer I'm going to give you right now.' I leant close to Talisid. He didn't flinch, and I spoke very clearly. 'I am not going back to Richard. Not ever.'

Talisid studied me for a long moment before replying. 'He may not give you the choice.'

I walked away, disappearing into the crowd. Talisid didn't follow.

That evening found me alone in my flat.

After meeting Talisid, I'd been to visit Arachne. I told her everything that had happened, both in the shadow realm and after. We talked for a long while, and by the time we'd finished and I'd left to make my way home, the sun had set. I was tired, but I was too wired to sleep. I sat at my desk and stared out the window, my thoughts going round in circles.

I'd been at it for an hour before something made me look up. I turned around on my chair to see a blink fox sitting in the middle of my living room floor, its tail curled around its legs.

I stared at it. 'How did you get in here?'

The blink fox just looked at me. 'I have gate wards specifically to *stop* people sneaking in like this,' I said. 'And I didn't give you my address.'

The blink fox yawned, came smoothly to its feet and disappeared out the door. I got up and followed to see it sitting in my kitchen. It looked at me, then at the fridge, then back at me.

'You've got to be kidding.'

The fox blinked twice.

'Okay, I know I promised I'd help you out, but this is ridiculous. You do *not* need my help to feed yourself.'

The fox looked at the fridge again, flicking its tail from side to side. I'd just opened my mouth to say something else when I heard the bell ring downstairs. 'Now what?' I muttered, and turned to the door before pointing at the fox. 'You stay here.'

The fox tilted its head.

I opened the shop door. 'Hi.'

'Hey,' Anne said. She looked better, if a little tired. It actually felt a little weird to see her in normal clothes again.

'The Keepers let you out?'

'A few hours ago. Vari picked me up.'

'Oh. Cool.'

There was an awkward silence. Anne stood on the doorstep. Outside on the street, a car buzzed by.

'Do you want to come in?'

'Sure.' Anne stepped inside and glanced up. 'Did you know you've got a fox in your kitchen?'

I sighed. 'I don't suppose that lifesight is any good for figuring out what blink foxes eat?'

'. . . and they didn't ask much else,' Anne said fifteen minutes later. We were sitting in the living room; the muffled crunch of eating came from the kitchen. 'They didn't seem to care about anything except Crystal.'

'Did they give you any trouble?'

'Not compared to last time.'

'That's not saying much.'

'It's not, is it?' Anne said. 'I think my standards are getting low.'

'Did you come here from the station?'

'Vari picked me up. We . . . had a lot to talk about.'

The crunching sounds from the kitchen stopped. A moment later the blink fox trotted into the living room, jumped up onto the sofa, turned around several times before settling down in a tight curl, nose to tail, yawned loudly, then laid its head down and appeared to go to sleep.

'What's it doing here?' Anne asked curiously.

'I have no idea,' I said in annoyance. 'I thought this thing was trying to get *away* from mages. I figured as soon as I gave it a way out, it'd disappear into London and we'd never see it again. I wasn't expecting it to walk into my bloody living room.'

Anne smiled slightly. 'Maybe it trusts you.'

'Don't know why.' I looked at the fox; it seemed to have gone to sleep. I couldn't figure out why it would let its guard down like that. If my experience of mages had been limited to ones like Sagash and his apprentices, I wouldn't have been that keen to find more of them. But everyone has their own story . . .

I stole a glance at Anne. She was sitting quietly on the other end of the sofa, dressed in her street clothes, looking out the window at the Camden night lights. Yet only yesterday I'd seen her walk into a duelling circle, bloodied and half dressed and surrounded by enemies, and destroy Crystal in five seconds flat. No matter how vivid the memory, it was hard to match it with what I was seeing now. It really did feel as though she were a different person.

'Do you mind if I ask you a favour?' Anne asked.

'Sure. What is it?'

'Vari and I went back and had a look at my flat in Honor Oak,' Anne said. 'It's not damaged or anything, but . . . well, after what happened, I think I need somewhere a bit safer. So I was wondering . . .'

'Wondering?'

'Whether you could help me set up some defences,' Anne said. 'Like you've got here. Gate wards and things, so people can't just teleport into my bedroom. Sonder's letting me stay over for now but . . . sooner or later I'd like to have my own place. Somewhere safe.'

I looked at Anne for a second, then nodded. 'I think that's a good idea.'

There was a pause. Anne hadn't brought up the subject of what I'd told her before that duel, and it was making me feel awkward. If she was upset, she wasn't showing it.

*Well, maybe you should stop guessing and ask.* 'I'm sorry about yesterday,' I said. 'About what I said at the arena. I didn't mean to . . .' To hurt her? That had been *exactly* what I'd been trying to do. Okay, so telling the truth might not be the most diplomatic option . . .

Anne looked down at the blink fox. It was snoozing, its chest rising and falling very slightly. 'If you hadn't told me that, I'd probably be dead.'

I didn't answer.

'Vari was telling me about what happened while I was gone,' Anne said, looking up at me. 'Did you know that he and Luna were looking for a way to gate into Sagash's shadow realm?'

'I heard,' I said. I still wasn't sure how I felt about the fact that one of the things I'd told Anne in that arena had actually been true. If Vari and Luna had been able to pull it off, they might have saved us both . . . and they might have died pointless deaths.

'I told Vari he shouldn't have been trying to go after me,' Anne said, partly echoing my thoughts. 'He said he didn't care: he'd have done it anyway. It made me . . .' Anne trailed off and started again. 'I know I haven't been the easiest person to be friends with lately. I knew I was in danger but . . . I never really put it together that I was putting all of you in danger too.'

'You ought to be thanking Luna,' I said. 'She was the one who pushed me into going back to your flat.'

'I will. But . . . you didn't give up on me, even when I wanted you to.' Anne looked at me. 'I won't forget that.'

'Yeah, well, don't make a habit of it, okay? I really don't want to go jumping into any *more* shadow realms after you.'

Anne smiled slightly. 'No, I think I got the message this time.'

We sat quietly for a little while. The fox opened one eye briefly, then stretched out on its side and went back to sleep. 'That other version of you that I met in Elsewhere,' I said. 'Do you talk to her?'

Anne shook her head.

'Maybe you should try.'

'What do you mean?'

'I think . . .' I hesitated, trying to figure out how to say it. 'I think you've been so afraid of that side of yourself that you've gone too far the other way. You've been pushing yourself to be good and peaceful all the time, and you don't have any kind of safety valve. I know I might not be the best role model but . . . speaking from experience, accepting your dark side works a lot better than trying to shut it away.'

'Even after seeing her?' Anne said quietly.

'I'm not saying I'd like to have her around for dinner. But I don't think it'd be a bad thing if you let yourself act a *little* bit more like that.' I shrugged. 'Besides, if she can't reach you, you can't reach her. If you always keep her shut away, then how's she ever going to get better?'

Anne looked surprised, then thoughtful. Talking to Anne felt more comfortable now. Somehow I'd never really noticed how much she'd been keeping back until she started doing less of it.

'Have you heard anything more about Richard?' Anne asked.

I shook my head.

'What are you going to do?'

'I don't know,' I said. I got up and walked to the window

to stare out into the night, then sighed slightly. 'But I know what I need to *be* doing.'

Anne waited, listening. The living room was silent but for the whisper of night-time traffic. 'Back when I first met you, my life was . . . I want to say easier, but that's wrong. Simpler, maybe? It wasn't *safe*, but all the dangerous stuff was temporary. I always knew that if I could just last it out, then things would go back to normal. And when that was done I spent most days running my shop. I had time.'

'And now you don't,' Anne said.

'You remember the last thing that Richard said? "Until next time." He doesn't give up.' I turned to look at Anne. 'He'll be back. I don't know how, or when. But there's a clock now. A month, six months, two years – I don't know how long, but I can feel it ticking. And when it runs out, if I don't have what I need . . .' I shook my head. 'Most of the last ten years, I've been drifting. I can't do that, not any more. I need to be ready.'

'Not just you,' Anne said. 'We.'

'You know how powerful Richard is,' I said. 'He'll have allies.'

'So do you,' Anne said. 'Luna, Vari, Arachne. Me. And the mages you know from the Council, like Sonder and Talisid. You're not Richard's apprentice any more. You've got friends.'

I looked back at Anne, then smiled slightly. 'I guess that's a good start.'

I stayed standing by the window. After a moment Anne rose, moving next to me. We stood side by side, looking out into the darkness of the Camden night.

# extras

# about the author

**Benedict Jacka** became a writer almost by accident, when at nineteen he sat in his school library and started a story in the back of an exercise book. Since then he has studied philosophy at Cambridge, lived in China and worked as everything from civil servant to bouncer to teacher before returning to London to take up law.

Find out more about Benedict Jacka and other Orbit authors by registering for the free monthly newsletter at www.orbitbooks.net

**if you enjoyed**
HIDDEN

look out for

# THE OVERSIGHT

by

**Charlie Fletcher**

# Chapter 1

# The House on Wellclose Square

If only she wouldn't struggle so, the damned girl.

If only she wouldn't scream then he wouldn't have had to bind her mouth.

If only she would be quiet and calm and biddable, he would never have had to put her in a sack.

And if only he had not had to put her in a sack, she could have walked and he would not have had to put her over his shoulder and carry her to the Jew.

Bill Ketch was not a brute. Life may have knocked out a few teeth and broken his nose more than once, but it had not yet turned him into an animal: he was man enough to feel bad about what he was doing, and he did not like the way that the girl moaned so loud and wriggled on his shoulder, drawing attention to herself.

Hitting her didn't stop anything. She may have screamed a lot, but she had flint in her eye, something hard and unbreakable, and it was that tough core that had unnerved him and decided him on selling her to the Jew.

That's what the voice in his head told him, the quiet, sly voice that nevertheless was conveniently able to drown out whatever his conscience might try to say.

The street was empty and the fog from the Thames damped the gas lamps into blurs of dull light as he walked past the Seaman's Hostel and turned into Wellclose Square. The flare of a match caught his eye as a big man with a red beard lit a pipe amongst a group standing around a cart stacked with candle-boxes outside the Danish Church. Thankfully they didn't seem to notice him as he slunk speedily along the opposite side of the road, heading for the dark house at the bottom of the square beyond the looming bulk of the sugar refinery, outside which another horse and carriage stood unattended.

He was pleased the square was so quiet at this time of night. The last thing he wanted to do was to have to explain why he was carrying such strange cargo, or where he was heading.

The shaggy travelling man in The Three Cripples had given him directions, and so he ducked in the front gates, avoiding the main door as he edged round the corner and down a flight of slippery stone steps leading to a side-entrance. The dark slit between two houses was lit by a lonely gas globe which fought hard to be seen in murk that was much thicker at this lower end of the square, closer to the Thames.

There were two doors. The outer one, made of iron bars like a prison gate, was open, and held back against the brick wall. The dark oak inner door was closed and studded with a grid of raised nailheads that made it look as if it had been hammered shut for good measure. There was a handle marked 'Pull' next to it. He did so, but heard no answering jangle of a bell from inside. He tugged again. Once more silence greeted him. He was about to yank it a third time when there was the sound of metal sliding against metal and a narrow judas hole opened in the door. Two unblinking eyes looked at him from behind a metal grille, but other than them he could see nothing apart from a dim glow from within.

The owner of the eyes said nothing. The only sound was a moaning from the sack on Ketch's shoulder.

The eyes moved from Ketch's face to the sack, and back. There was a sound of someone sniffing, as if the doorman was smelling him.

Ketch cleared his throat.

'This the Jew's house?'

The eyes continued to say nothing, summing him up in a most uncomfortable way.

'Well,' swallowed Ketch. 'I've got a girl for him. A screaming girl, like what as I been told he favours.'

The accompanying smile was intended to ingratiate, but in reality only exposed the stumpy ruins of his teeth.

The eyes added this to the very precise total they were evidently calculating, and then abruptly stepped back and slammed the slit shut. The girl flinched at the noise and Ketch cuffed her, not too hard and not with any real intent to hurt, just on a reflex.

He stared at the blank door. Even though it was now eyeless, it still felt like it was looking back at him. Judging. He was confused. Had he been rejected? Was he being sent away? Had he walked all the way here carrying the girl – who was not getting any lighter – all for nothing? He felt a familiar anger build in his gut, as if all the cheap gin and sour beer it held were beginning to boil, sending heat flushing across his face. His fist bunched and he stepped forward to pound on the studded wood.

He swung angrily, but at the very moment he did so it opened and he staggered inward, following the arc of his blow across the threshold, nearly dumping the girl on the floor in front of him.

'Why——?!' he blurted.

And then stopped short.

He had stumbled into a space the size and shape of a sentry box, with no obvious way forward. He was about to step uneasily back out into the fog, when the wall to his right swung open.

He took a pace into a larger room lined in wooden tongue-and-groove panelling with a table and chairs and a dim oil lamp. The ceiling was also wood, as was the floor. Despite this it didn't smell of wood, or the oil in the lamp. It smelled of wet clay. All in all, and maybe because of the loamy smell, it had a distinctly coffin-like atmosphere. He shivered.

'Go on in,' said a calm voice behind him.

'Nah,' he swallowed. 'Nah, you know what? I think I've made a mistake——'

The hot churn in his guts had gone ice-cold, and he felt the goosebumps rise on his skin: he was suddenly convinced that this was a room he must not enter, because if he did, he might never leave.

He turned fast, banging the girl on the doorpost, her yip of pain lost in the crash as the door slammed shut, barring his escape route with the sound of heavy bolts slamming home.

He pushed against the wood, and then kicked at it. It didn't move. He stood there breathing heavily, then slid the girl from his shoulder and laid her on the floor, holding her in place with a firm hand.

'Stay still or you shall have a kick, my girl,' he hissed.

He turned and froze.

There was a man sitting against the back wall of the room, a big man, almost a giant, in the type of caped greatcoat that a coachman might wear. It had an unnaturally high collar, and above it he wore a travel-stained tricorn hat of a style that had not been seen much on London's streets for a generation, not since the early 1800s. The hat jutted over the collar and cast a shadow so deep that Ketch could see nothing of the face beneath. He stared at the man. The man didn't move an inch.

'Hoi,' said Ketch, by way of introduction.

The giant remained motionless. Indeed as Ketch stepped towards him he realised that the head was angled slightly away, as if the man wasn't looking at him at all.

'Hoi!' repeated Ketch.

The figure stayed still. Ketch licked his lips and ventured forward another step. Peering under the hat he saw the man was brown-skinned.

'Oi, blackie, I'm a-talking to you,' said Ketch, hiding the fact that the giant's stillness and apparent obliviousness to his presence was unnerving him by putting on his best bar-room swagger.

The man might as well be a statue for the amount he moved. In fact—

Ketch reached forward and tipped back the hat, slowly at first.

It wasn't a man at all. It was a mannequin made from clay. He ran his thumb down the side of the face and looked at the brown smear it left on it. Damp clay, unfired and not yet quite set. It was a well made, almost handsome face with high cheekbones and an impressively hooked nose, but the eyes beneath the prominent forehead were empty holes.

'Well, I'll be damned . . .' he whispered, stepping back.

'Yes,' said a woman's voice behind him, cold and quiet as a cut-throat razor slicing through silk. 'Oh yes. I rather expect you will.'

# Chapter 2

## A Woman in Black and the Man in Midnight

She stood at the other end of the room, a shadow made flesh in a long tight-bodiced dress buttoned to the neck and wrists. Her arms were folded and black leather gloves covered her hands. The dress had a dull sheen like oiled silk, and she was so straight-backed and slender – and yet also so finely muscled – that she looked in some ways like a rather dangerous umbrella leaning against the wood panelling.

The only relief from the blackness was her face, two gold rings she wore on top of the gloves and her white hair, startlingly out of kilter with her otherwise youthful appearance, which she wore pulled back in a tight pigtail that curled over her shoulder like an albino snake.

She hadn't been there when Ketch entered the room, and she couldn't have entered by the door which had been on the edge of his vision throughout, but that wasn't what most disturbed him: what really unsettled him was her eyes, or rather the fact he couldn't see them, hidden as they were behind the two small circular lenses of smoked glass that made up her spectacles.

'Who—?' began Ketch.

She held up a finger. Somehow that was enough to stop him talking.

'What do you want?'

Ketch gulped, tasting his own fear like rising bile at the back of his throat.

'I want to speak to the Jew.'

'Why?'

He saw she carried a ring of keys at her belt like a jailer. Despite the fact she looked too young for the job he decided that she must be the Jew's housekeeper. He used this thought as a stick to steady himself on: he'd just been unnerved by her sudden appearance, that was all. There must be a hidden door behind her. Easy enough to hide its edges in the tongue and groove. He wasn't going to be bullied by a housekeeper. Not when he had business with her master.

'I got something for him.'

'What?'

'A screaming girl.'

She looked at the long sack lying on the floor.

'You have a *girl* in this sack?'

Somehow the way she asked this carried a lot of threat.

'I want to speak to the Jew,' repeated Ketch.

The woman turned her head to one side and rapped on the wooden wall behind her. She spoke into a small circular brass grille.

'Mr Sharp? A moment of your time, please.'

The dark lenses turned to look at him again. The silence was unbearable. He had to fill it.

'Man in The Three Cripples said as how the Jew would pay for screaming girls.'

The gold ring caught the lamplight as the black gloves flexed open and then clenched tight again, as if she were containing something.

'So you've come to sell a girl?'

'At the right price.'

Her smile was tight and showed no teeth. Her voice remained icily polite.

'There are those who would say *any* price is the wrong one. The good Mr Wilberforce's bill abolished slavery nearly forty years ago, did it not?'

Ketch had set out on a simple errand: he had something to sell and had heard of a likely buyer. True, he'd felt a little like a Resurrection Man skulking through the fog with a girl on his shoulder, but she was no corpse and he was no bodysnatcher. And now this woman was asking questions that were confusing that simple thing. When life was straightforward, Bill Ketch sailed through it on smooth waters. When it became complicated he became confused, and when he became confused anger blew in like a storm, and when he became angry fists and boots flew until the world was stomped flat and simple again.

'I don't know nothing about a Wilberforce. I want to speak to the Jew,' he grunted.

'And why do you think the Jew wants a girl? By which I mean: what do you think the Jew wants to do with her?' she asked, the words as taut and measured as her smile.

'What he does is none of my business.'

He shrugged and hid his own bunched fists deep in the pockets of his coat.

Her words cracked sharply across the table like a whiplash.

'But what you think you are doing by selling this girl is mine. Answer the question!'

This abrupt change of tone stung him and made him bang the table and lurch towards her, face like a thundercloud.

'No man tells Bill Ketch what to do, and sure as hell's hinges no damn woman does neither! I want to see the bloody Jew and by God—'

The wall next to her seemed to blur open and shut and a man burst through, slicing across the room so fast that he outpaced Ketch's eyes, leaving a smear of midnight blue and flashing steel as he came straight over the table in a swirl of coat-tails that ended in a sudden and dangerous pricking sensation against his Adam's apple.

The eyes that had added him up through the judas hole now stared into him across a gap bridged by eighteen inches of razor-sharp steel. The long blade was held at exactly the right pressure to stop him doing anything life-threatening, like moving. Indeed, just swallowing would seem to be an act of suicide.

'By any god, you shall not take one step further forward, Mr . . .'

The eyes swept over his face, searching, reading it.

'Mr Ketch is it? Mr William Ketch . . . ?'

He leaned in and Ketch, frozen, watched his nostrils flare as he appeared to smell him. The midnight blue that the man was dressed in seemed to absorb even more light than the woman's black dress. He wore a knee-length riding coat cut tight to his body, beneath which was a double-breasted leather waistcoat of exactly the same hue, as were the shirt and tightly knotted silk stock he wore around his neck. The only break in the colour of his clothing was the brown of his soft leather riding boots.

His hair was also of the darkest brown, as were his thick and well-shaped eyebrows, and his eyes, when Ketch met them, were startlingly . . . unexpected.

Looking into them Ketch felt, for a moment, giddy and excited. The eyes were not just one brown, not even some of the browns: they were *all* the browns. It was as if he was looking into a swirl of autumn leaves tumbling happily in the golden sunlight of a blazing Indian summer.

One look into the tawny glamour in those eyes and Ketch forgot the blade at his throat.

One look into those eyes and the anger was gone and all was simple again.

One look into those eyes and Bill Ketch was confusingly and irrevocably in something as close to love as to make no difference.

The man must have seen this because the blade did something fast and complicated and disappeared beneath the skirts of his coat as he reached forward, gripped Ketch by both shoulders and pulled him close, sniffing him again and then raising an eyebrow in surprise, before pushing him back and smiling at him like an old friend.

'He is everything he appears to be, and no more,' he said over his shoulder.

The woman stepped forward.

'You are sure?'

'I thought I smelled something on the air as he knocked, but it didn't come in with him. I may have been mistaken. The river is full of stink at high tide.'

'So you are sure?' she repeated.

'As sure as I am that you will never tire of asking me that particular question,' said the man.

'"Measure twice, cut once" is a habit that has served me well enough since I was old enough to think,' she said flatly, 'and it has kept this house safe for much longer than that.'

'Are you the Jew?' said Ketch. His voice squeaked a little as he spoke, so happy was he feeling, bathed in the warmth of the handsome young man's open smile.

'I do not have that honour,' he replied.

The woman appeared at the man's shoulder.

'Well?' she said.

The chill returned to Ketch's heart as she spoke.

'He is as harmless as he appears to be, I assure you,' repeated the man.

She took off her glasses and folded them in one hand. Her eyes were grey-green and cold as a midwinter wave. Her words, when they came, were no warmer.

'I am Sara Falk. I am the Jew.'

As Ketch tried to realign the realities of his world, she put a hand on the man's shoulder and pointed him at the long bundle on the floor.

'Now, Mr Sharp: there is a young woman in that sack. If you would be so kind.'

The man flickered to the bundle on the floor, again seeming to move between time instead of through it. The blade reappeared in his hand, flashed up and down the sacking, and then he was helping the girl to her feet and simultaneously sniffing at her head.

'Mr Sharp?' said Sara Falk.

'As I said, I smelled something out there,' he said. 'I thought it was him. It isn't, nor is it her.'

'Well, good,' she said, the twitch of a smile ghosting round the corner of her mouth. 'Maybe it was your imagination.'

'It pleases you to make sport of me, my dear Miss Falk, but I venture to point out that since we are charged with anticipating the inconceivable, my "imagination" is just as effective a defensive tool as your double-checking,' he replied, looking at the girl closely. 'And since our numbers are so perilously dwindled these days, you will excuse me if I do duty as both belt and braces in these matters.'

The young woman was slender and trembling, in a grubby pinafore dress with no shoes and long reddish hair that hung down wavy and unwashed, obscuring a clear look at her face. At first glance, however, it was clear she was not a child, and he judged her age between sixteen and twenty years old. She flinched when he reached to push the hair back to get a better look at her and make a more accurate assessment, and he stopped and spoke quietly.

'No, no, my dear, just look at me. Look at me and you'll see you have nothing to fear.'

After a moment her head came up and eyes as big as saucers peered a question into his. As soon as they did the trembling calmed and she allowed him to push the hair back and reveal what had been done to her mouth to stop the screaming.

He exhaled through his teeth in an angry hiss and then gently turned her towards Sara Falk. She stared at the rectangle of black hessian that was pasted across the girl's face from below her nose down to her chin.

'What is this?' said Mr Sharp, voice tight, still keeping the girl steady with his eyes.

'It's just a pitch-plaster, some sacking and tar and pitch, like a sticky poultice, such as they use up the Bedlam Hospital to quiet the lunatics . . .' explained Ketch, his voice quavering lest Mr Sharp's gaze when it turned to add him up again was full of something other than the golden warmth he was already missing. 'Why, the girlie don't mind a—'

'Look at her hands,' said Sara Falk.

The girl's hands were tightly wrapped in strips of grubby material, like small cloth-bound boxing gloves.

'Nah, that she does herself, she done that and not me,'

said Ketch hurriedly. 'I takes 'em off cos she's no bloody use with hands wrapped into stumps like that, but she wraps whatever she can find round 'em the moment you turn your back. Why even if there's nothing in the rooms she'll rip up her own clothes to do it. It's all she does: touches things and then screams at what ain't there and tangles rags round her hands like a winding cloth so she doesn't have to touch anything at all . . .'

Sara Falk exchanged a look with Mr Sharp.

'Touches things? Then screams?' he said. 'Old stones, walls . . . those kind of things?'

Ketch nodded enthusiastically. 'Walls and houses and things in the street. Sets 'er off something 'orrible it does—'

'Enough,' said Mr Sharp, his eyes on Sara Falk who was stroking the scared girl's hair. Their eyes met once more.

'So she's a Glint then,' he said quietly.

She nodded, for a moment unable to speak.

'She's not right in the head is what she is,' said Ketch. 'And—'

'Is she your daughter?' said Sara Falk, clearing something from her throat.

'No. Not blood kin. She's . . . my ward, as it were. But I can't afford to feed her no more, so it's you or the poorhouse, and the poorhouse don't pay, see . . . ?'

The spark of commerce had reignited in his eyes.

'Don't worry about that blessed plaster, lady. Why, a hot flannel held on for a couple of minutes loosens it off, and you can peel it away without too much palaver.'

The man and the woman stared at him.

'The redness fades after a couple of days,' he insisted. 'We tried a gag, see, but she loosens them or gnaws through. She's spirited—'

'What is her name?' said Sara Falk.

'Lucy. Lucy Harker. She's just—'

'Mr Sharp,' she said, cutting him off by turning away to kneel by the girl.

'What do you want to do with him?' said the man in midnight.

'What I *want* to do to a man who'd sell a young woman without a care as to what the buyer might want to do with or to her is undoubtedly illegal,' said Sara Falk almost under her breath.

'It would be justice though,' he replied equally softly.

'Yes,' she said. 'But we, as I have said many times, are an office of the Law and the Lore, not of Justice, Mr Sharp. And Law and Lore say to make the punishment fit the crime. Do what must be done.'

Lucy Harker looked at her, still mute behind the gag.

Mr Sharp left them and turned his smile on Ketch, who relaxed and grinned expectantly back at him.

'Well,' said Mr Sharp. 'It seems we must pay you, Mr Ketch.'

The thought of money coming was enticing and jangly enough to drown out the question that had been trying to get Ketch's attention for some time now, namely how this good-looking young man knew his name. He watched greedily as he reached into his coat and pulled out a small leather bag.

'Now,' said Mr Sharp. 'Gold, I think. Hold out your hands.'

Ketch did so as if sleepwalking, and though at first his eyes tricked him into the thought that Mr Sharp was counting tarnished copper pennies into his hand, after a moment he realised they were indeed the shiniest gold pieces he had ever seen, and he relaxed enough to stop looking at them and instead to study more of Mr Sharp. His dark hair was cropped short on the back and sides, but was long on top, curling into a cowlick that tumbled over his forehead in an agreeably untidy way. A single deep blue stone dangled from one ear in a gold setting, winking in the lamplight as he finished his tally.

'. . . twenty-eight, twenty-nine, thirty. That's enough, I think, and if not it is at least . . . traditional.'

And with that the purse disappeared and the friendly arm went round Ketch's shoulder, and before he could quite catch up with himself the two of them were out in the fog, walking out of Wellclose Square into the tangle of dark streets beyond.

Ketch's heart was soaring and he felt happier than he had ever been in his life, though whether it was because of the unexpectedly large number of gold – gold! – coins in his pockets, or because of his newfound friend, he could not tell.